PHANTOM JIGSAW

LEVITY BROWN

This novel is entirely a work of fiction.

The names, characters and incidents portrayed are the work of the author's imagination. Any resemblance to actual persons, living or dead, is purely coincidental.

Phantom Jigsaw

ISBN: 978-1-9192577-4-7

Copyright © Levity Brown 2010

The rights of Levity Brown to be identified as the author of this work have been asserted in accordance with sections 77 and 78 of the Copyright Design and Patents Act of 1988.

All rights reserved. No part of this book may be reproduced in any form or by any electronic or mechanical means, including information storage and retrieval systems, without permission in writing from the author, except by reviewers, who may quote brief passages.

Editorial support and publication assistance from Creative Words Ltd
www.creativewords.cc

www.levitybrown.co.uk

BUMPY LANDING

When the Boeing 747 finally came right down the beaches of the West Coast of England, skimming the palm trees with its humped back, Jason Black was in a moment of quiet agony. He had awoken from a sleep which left him bewildered; a sleep that had grown as a spell of dreamy confusions, part cracked, part gravelled with faults, but each opening out on that secret world he knew intuitively as home.

Wiping his face from forehead to chin, he remembered belting himself into a window seat and closing his eyes to summon the sights of his native land, to wonder what wretched memories would surface. As it so happened, it was not wretched memories that ploughed into his dreams but something entirely beyond his understanding.

'Did you have a nice sleep?'

Only now had he noticed an old lady sitting beside him, knitting a multi-coloured length of plain and purl. From her fast-working needles, it fell over her skirted knees and onward much further than he could see.

So, out of curiosity, he asked, 'What are you knitting?'

'A scarf,' she answered, aiding understanding no further.

'It would appear a very long scarf.'

'Well, dear, that's because there are many memories. When you get to my age, you tend to have a lot of them.' Placing her needles aside, she reached down and brought up a wicked section knitted in red and struck a worn and bent finger to the stitches. 'Here was an occasion when two unwelcome visitors showed up on my doorstep; a most unpleasant encounter if ever there was one. I so dislike people who think they can come for tea and biscuits, hoping to leave with the family silver. Never mind, I soon gave them short change.'

'When did you start it?'

'At a very good memory, soon followed by a bad one.' She sighed heavily. Her hands were quiet now, and her face had grown deathly white. 'Ah, well,' she said. 'Without good and bad memories, we never grow wise.'

'I suppose not.' But after a moment's reflection, he tempered his opinion. 'Why not observe other people's mistakes to avoid making them yourself. That way, you have far more good memories than bad ones.'

She harrumphed and took up her knitting again. 'Sometimes, dear, good people have to get on with their lives rather than find time to watch other people making mistakes.'

'Ah.'

'Ah, indeed.'

That might have been the end to their conversation. From Jason's advantage, he was content to linger on the woman in his dream while the jumbo jet made its approach to Heathrow airport.

'More to satisfy my personal curiosity,' the old lady said. 'Would you care to tell me what you were dreaming? You muttered something about a jigsaw puzzle.'

'My brother,' he replied, taking his eyes away from the sky, 'manufactures jigsaw puzzles, and in that respect, I suppose it was natural to dream about one. Some things are a bit sketchy, as most dreams are, but I distinctly felt the urgency to complete a blank puzzle which wasn't blank, if that makes any sense.' He shrugged it away. 'However, there was this girl who was very good at fitting the nubs into the voids. In the language of jigsaws, it's the fitting of nubs into the voids that gives the sought-after lock. I distinctly had this feeling of apprehension —sinister, even— yet challenging; challenging to what degree, I have no idea. The one thing that really sticks in my mind is the girl...like the puzzle, she too seemed real and no doubt I met her at some stage. Since I travel a lot, she may have been a stewardess or a waitress, someone who caught my eye.'

'Perhaps your subconscious is seeking a good woman.'

Jason blinked. 'Show me a good woman and I can show you the dust from Mars.'

'Oh my, we do have a little tickle in that throat. Did you catch a bad cold?'

'More like influenza.'

'Bad experiences are equally important to bring a man to his senses, ready to gauge the next woman in a clearer light. This girl, what was she like?'

'Erm, let me think a minute.' A few things he would keep to himself. 'She was comical really and very pretty, almost perfect.'

'None of us is perfect, dear. Not even my husband when he was alive. I gain the impression you're not looking forward to going home.'

'Seven years is a long time.' He admitted as though he had disappeared like a falling sun. 'I left Norfolk to take up a position in Boston. Yes, there were problems, mainly about Strident Cutter and how the old man ran it. We never saw eye to eye. He thought I was too immature to run a business. I thought he was too drunk to run one. In his day, men were conscripted at sixteen, so that never held water.'

'How right you are, dear...so many poor souls died; never came home after the war. Such a sad state of affairs. Those left standing never counted as wounded; living together, as they did, for months on end, cheek by jowl, with minimal privacy. The Home Guard had an easier time of it, but not in London. They soon had their flash of excitement when Germany dropped its doodlebugs.'

'Do you live in London?'

'I am visiting my daughter and grandchild, a lovely girl with her head full of nonsense. No doubt she will grow out of it. And if all goes well, I shall return to knit in those happy memories and retire in warmer climes. And where are you heading?'

'Little Smeet, not far from Norwich.'

Leaning beyond him to catch a glimpse at the weather on rooftops, and smelling of perfumed witchery, she said, 'Such a pity we cannot bring the sun from Boston to London.' And then she uttered, 'goodness,' at the plane's sudden descent. 'Do you mind if I hold on to you?'

Wondering if he would ever escape the drawbacks of old age, he fed her hand through the crook of his arm, and there she remained like a muted spirit until the plane's wheels touched ground. Then her hand slipped away and, wordlessly, she rolled up her knitting, stowing it neatly inside her tapestry bag. At some point shortly after the customary pattern of alighting and a few chosen words of farewell, they parted company.

Moving on in the general direction of the luggage pickup, Jason Black was a man on a mission, tall, strong, his eyes near-dark and sharp, the slightly skewed nose and trace scars suggesting a life almost lost. There was no conventional dress, no indication of status. The boots were well-worn, so too his leather jacket, and the Homburg was his friend to the enemy of his wheat-coloured hair. He grabbed his well-travelled suitcase from the carousel and picked his way through the wave of human traffic, put a cigarette in his mouth but never lit it. The times he had tried to give up smoking, hopeless measures undertaken by a desperate man. From passport control, he spotted his name chalked on a board held high by a driver with a cap pulled down to his ears. They exchanged a few words and proceeded outside, where raindrops tapped on the brim of his hat like irritable fingers. When he looked up, they fell on his face. This was a pause worth savouring, because for him, the world would soon be complicated again.

In the motor, he sank heavily into the back seat and passed the time away talking about Little Smeet to the driver, why it lived by the easy laws of hedgerows and farmers, and why it was a funnel for winds and a channel for the floods. He always believed it was like an island, possessed of curious survivals and one of them being Strident Cutter.

Three hours later, the motor swung into a tree-lined gravel driveway leading to the formidable Manor of the Black generation. The property was swallowed in a haze of dark mist, and partly came alive as the headlights tracked the high-pitched roof and tall sash windows with concrete sills.

After he paid the driver and watched the rear lights disappear from view, his twin emerged in the semi-gloom. Tony was the same height, though not as broad, the hair much darker and obedient. Apart from the minor facial deviations, the unmistakable likeness was there, sometimes bathed in the contradiction which seemed never to have been resolved. They briefly raked over each other, gaining fresh layers of change, then went inside. For Jason, he felt his exhaustion rising.

'Do you mind if I go straight to my room?'

'Squirt, I want you to know, I'm really glad you came. How long can you stay?'

'Until we get your problem sorted.'

And that seemed to put a smile on Tony's face.

In silent comment, they climbed the extravagant staircase. Ahead, white light impatiently squeezed under Susan's door, and Jason wondered if she was awake, thinking about him. His brother's wife had become a moot point, so intense it sometimes croaked a loud song in his guts, but it was such a twisted and crippled memory, and it brought no angels or explanations.

At his own door, Jason leaned on the handle and fell into his old room. The attachment to the dream was not so fragile. He admonished the worst by applying layers of the best, pushing forward the notion of a sensual woman with emerald green eyes lusting after his body, truly exaggerated, but the thrill of it coursed through his veins. Now he wondered if every beat in his heart separated him from eternity.

To a new dawn and the sound of a closed door, Jason woke to a lighter room that had remained untouched in seven years. He slipped out of bed with a yawn, shook into his old dressing gown and went into the bathroom. In the mirror, he saw a face that was not his face. There was a rash moment in time when he considered private surgery, had the mindset of a changed man, yet it was a cry to God which went unanswered, and considered there was advantage to looking like this, to separate his identity from a twin who was blessed with obedient hair and good looks. He set about having a shave, scraping against twenty-four-hour growth whilst wanting to find something visibly changed, but there was nothing. He had simply accepted this was him, the blemishes exaggerated on haunted ground, the return to the familiar.

Idly, he then descended the stairs, unaccustomed to the sudden coolness, the sound of his bare feet on wood. Jason had forgotten the extreme generosity and opulence of his ancestral home, which had areas of hot and cold, dark holes and its districts of terror and blessed sanctuary. His growing years were for the most part spent in the kitchen, warm and low, whose fuss of furniture seemed never the same after his mother had died. Here, he switched on the kettle and stared beyond the closed patio doors into a feast of manicured lawns and ostentatious shrubbery. A distant bird of prey buffeted by the strong winds flew high, and the trees moved with a dry roaring that seemed a natural utterance on the landscape. What season fermented in that dream, he wondered. Was it winter that came to the boil in her arms?

'Never slept that well.' Tony emerged in a Bond Street suit, his face composed of worry. 'What do you think we should do, Squirt?'

But it was the dream more than the business that had Jason stumped. 'I had this crazy dream on the plane. Everything was going to pot and…'

'Everything is going to pot. Tea or coffee?'

'Either will do. We had to find some pieces of a…'

'Do you still smoke?'

The brows met. 'Tony, are you interested in this dream or not?'

'Is it going to conjure up an answer to my problem?'

Rather than respond to this, Jason changed his expression to one of the most intense interest; the concept came in a headlong rush. 'How hard would it be to piece together a blank jigsaw puzzle?'

'Look, Squirt, you need pictures unless it's a blue sky you're thinking about. It's money I need, not a cut back on inks.'

'I left my cheque book at home.'

'I'll pay you back.'

'It's still in Boston.' The iron frost of destitution had finally clamped down on his twin, no longer to be thawed by another orgy of borrowing. 'I understood last year when the old man died, Sam Claggart was prepared to buy you out.'

'Bloody Claggart,' Tony said it bitterly, pouring hot water into two cups. 'Only the world leader in jigsaw puzzles and tight as a gnat's bum. He's still interested but won't budge on the price.'

'What did he offer?'

'All the debts cleared, the workers stay on. Susan and I get to keep a position in the firm as damn cutters and shoved into one of the cottages.' Tony swung round to make his view heard. 'But the assets have been undervalued. I mean, the land and buildings are worth more than the debts. You'd think he would cough up a little more to give me some cash. Do you still take sugar in your coffee?'

Jason shook his head. 'Have you had an independent valuation?'

'Yes, and he refuses to accept it. His solicitor went on and on about the condition of the cottages, how the factory is falling apart, but there's nothing that bad, nothing that a bit of mending wouldn't sort out...the machinery is still good....never had any trouble apart from replacing a few cogs.'

'And Susan, what does she have to say?'

'Christ, we've had more rows than hot dinners. She's dead against Claggart's offer, and in a way, I agree, but we are really in a sticky situation. The business is on the brink of bankruptcy.'

The door flew open, and trouble walked in with an attitude. 'Just look at this,' Susan scowled, fanning her polished red nails. 'I caught it on that damn filing cabinet. Oh well, I suppose I shall have to re-do them.' She looked at Tony, ready to obliterate his senses, then her gaze briefly snagged on Jason, critical as usual. 'Why don't you get a crew cut?'

'Why don't you let yours grow?'

'I like mine short.'

'Quite.'

Believing his point had been made, he turned to reignite his conversation with Tony, but Susan said, 'Tell me, Jason. Have you found yourself a girlfriend yet?' He squared his shoulders. 'Come now, don't be shy. There must be someone who loves you.'

A light flickered from his dream, the type of woman he would like to have languishing in his arms. He tried to clear his mind, to make sense of the absurd. Separate events, a single goal, he thought. 'Susan, are you making us breakfast, or does a man stand hungry in this house?'

'I'm not your servant. Ask your brainless brother.'

'I can't cook,' Tony said. 'That's your job.'

And then the argument started. Susan bemoaned Tony's handling of the situation, the burdens of failure in his capacity to run a business and the occasional jibe about his secretary, claiming she was as dozy as a limp celery stick. To this, Tony gave Susan short shrift by a degree of reproach. Their words hung in the air like dirty laundry. Jason tried to ignore it, moving around the kitchen with a mug of sugared coffee, checking the dresser drawers and poking his head into the pantry. But every now and then, he glanced back at his twin, staggered by the difficulties Tony had to surmount and the little interest he possessed in Susan. Finally, Susan walked out, slamming the kitchen door.

'I'm going to get dressed.' Jason let the words hang for a moment, aware how miserable his brother felt. Now, a sudden glow of loyalty was rekindled as he privately exulted in the concept of a new future for Tony.

In his bedroom, Jason grabbed a clean shirt from the suitcase, and in the briefest of pauses, he was entering that dream again. His make-believe woman with no name, the soft gleam of black hair tied in a plait, her body like silk, playing her part in the rock and thrust of sexual pleasure. By far, the certainties of business were easier to negotiate than the uncertainties of a dream.

Outside, the only clouds were pale and icy thin, and the chill swept through his bones as he crossed the road and turned left into the high street, which was like Norfolk as a whole, slow and secure in the belief progress would take a long while to stamp its mark. He stopped off for a paper, stood outside the newsagent's to read the front page news, where the three-day week still lingered on in people's minds. Then he heard a banging noise of wood against wood and looked up.

It was thin Mary Waters coming from one of the cottages. Her husband, Misery, so named because he had the charm of an undertaker and the humour of a corpse, had worked at the factory as a cutter for as long as he could remember. She spirited across the road to welcome him back, enough to let him know how much he had been missed. In these unchanging landmarks, he wondered if he could make a life here again, but of course, there would always be Susan.

Retracing his steps, he strode past the Manor that was the secondary edifice to dominate this village and carried on toward the adjacent land, watching the common trait of mist cradling a huge corrugated structure sitting ugly by the river. It would appear nothing had changed for Strident Cutter. Tony had been given the opportunity to improve this building, but instead, he followed the same pattern as his father and his father before him. The clackety-clack of old die-cutters pounded across the estuary, and he wondered if by any leap of imagination there might be some improvement inside. There was none.

The noise was deafening, and the factory was cold. Familiar faces wrapped up in caps and bobbled hats sent a look of recognition as he processed the aisles, then a hand clamped firm upon his arm, forestalling his journey to the office.

'Look here, boy,' Misery shouted above the din, confused about a leaky cutter. 'Thass oil but where it comes from has got me stumped. Hev yew got any idea?'

Jason went down on his heels and looked underneath a mass of iron workings. 'If it had been leaking, there would be traces around the bolts, so it must be coming from somewhere else. What does Tony have to say?' His words had been absorbed by the noise, watched as Misery sent his hand to his ear, so he motioned to an area without shouting and repeated, 'What does Tony have to say?'

'Carry on as usual. He don't care just as long as them cutters are going. How did it go in America?'

'Good. I travelled a fair bit. I was in Antarctica last year.'

'Tony mentioned yew wus collecting snow.'

'I only collect it when I need to build a snowman.'

Misery was silent, not even a smile to testify he was alive.

Jason turned and walked away, could see his twin through the half-glass office partition, feet up on a desk, enjoying the warmth of a heater and angered when he shot through the door. 'Is it any wonder you're in deep shit? Where is Susan?'

'Search me.'

Without hesitation, he yanked Tony out of the executive chair and sat down, anxious to get a handle on the business debts. He spent a long while buried in paperwork, finding irregularities and unnecessary expenditure. Frustrated with the ill-prepared accounts, illogical labelling and the order books half full, he came to the point of considering Claggart's offer. Would his brother thank him for that?

'Take his offer.'

'Huh? Is that the best you can come up with?'

'Take his offer. He promises to keep on the workers, including you and Susan.'

'Can you see Susan in a pair of overalls? I don't think so.'

Jason lit his fourth cigarette, the smoke whirling above his head and unfolding as it had before. 'Claggart has the outlets. He has the means to invest; you don't. You're borrowed up to the hilt on the cottages, the house is mortgaged to the tune of ninety-eight percent and the only saving grace seems to be this building, though what Claggart sees in it is beyond me.'

'You've forgotten the asset in this land. We just need to get over the hump.' Tony wrestled with his red braces; every thought required effort, and he was about to give Jason ammunition to bring up the past. 'What about lending me some money? I'll pay you back.'

'I gave you thirty grand two years ago! And what did you do with it? Swapped the Jag for a new one and took damn holidays on the French Riviera. Take his offer.'

'We come out with nothing.'

'But it keeps you out of the bankruptcy courts and gives you a place to live.'

'That would mean they would own the cottages and Manor.'

'What did I tell you when I gave you that money? I told you to take them out of the business and use them as independent collateral, but no, you had the bright idea to keep them with the same bank that eats people like you for breakfast.'

Tony offered another excuse. 'It's bloody Dad's fault. He wouldn't do it.'

'He should have bought expertise; someone who knew how to handle it.'

'I can handle it.'

'It seems like it, doesn't it?' Jason stood, slid his hands in his trouser pockets and gave Tony a level stare. 'Take his offer, and if what I have in mind works, then you might stand a chance. Do you remember what I told you this morning about a blank puzzle?'

'Are you mental or what? People want a picture.'

'And one will come when the pieces interlock.'

'What?' Tony shook his head. 'This is 1974, not science fiction.'

'I can do this, Tony.'

'Then why didn't you do it before?'

The irony, of course, was that Jason would have swapped his job in America for Strident Cutter in the blink of an eye if it had held the remotest possibility of doing the work he loved. 'Okay, this might sound strange, but I fell asleep on the plane and had this really weird dream about us piecing together a blank jigsaw puzzle. As soon as the pieces interlocked, writing appeared, though I cannot remember what it said. There was this girl helping us to fit the pieces, and for some unknown reason, I had her pegged as my girlfriend.'

'It was probably Susan scrambling your mind like she scrambles mine.'

'She was nothing like Susan. How bad is it between you two?' Jason saw the brown eyes turn away for a split second, but it was enough. 'Are you sleeping with your secretary?'

'Can't help it, Squirt. Claire sees to my needs.'

'I see you still lack scruples. And Susan? How much does she know?'

'Yeah, alright, she has her suspicions, but I'm not that daft. Both of us want a divorce, but she's tied to this business as much as me.'

'Explain?'

'Dad added a codicil to his Will after Susan and I got married. I never knew about it until he popped off last year. He gave her fifty percent of the business. Don't ask me why. Perhaps he was trying to punish me, who knows, but she certainly knew.' Tony slumped on the edge of the desk like a defeated man. 'I knew the moment I placed that sodding ring on her finger, it was a bad idea. Hey, I thought; so what if she's money-hungry? I can supply the goods, and Dad said it was a good move. But she changed overnight, treated me like the damn plague.'

'Then we have a problem.'

'Look, if you can pull this off, why do I need to sell the business?'

'Let me tell you where I am, Tony. I am not in the business of keeping your lazy wife in luxury. Get rid of her. We can use the factory's resources to see how it pans out. By allowing Claggart to step in and make good on your losses, it keeps everyone on and forces her hand. It will also give me time to develop the concept.'

'But she'll never agree to the buyout, not unless she comes out with some money.'

'Then we have to make sure she has nowhere to go.'

'Ah, so in effect, I would be better off in the long run.' Tony was seeing his way back in. 'I could probably buy back the business.'

'You would be a stupid man to do that. Your best bet is to do a deal with one of your other rivals.'

'I want this business. It's been in our family for three generations.'

Jason puffed out his cheeks. It was like an old record being played again and again. 'You're not capable of running Strident Cutter. You have never taken advantage of your markets; have failed to invest in new machinery; and your product lines live in the dark ages. I never understood why you felt the need to keep with the old man. You had a good education. You could have gone into teaching. You loved history, especially military history.' He stepped toward the glass partition, anxious to get the moral implications into his brother's head. 'Look at them, Tony. Take a long, hard look. They have given their all and relied on you to look after them. And this is how you repay them.'

'I pay them a decent wage.'

'You pay them peanuts.' Jason swung his head round. 'Take his offer, work for a change. Help yourself by helping me to get you on your feet and keep them employed.'

'So what do you get out of all this?'

'I came here because you're my brother, so start acting like one.'

'And meanwhile?'

'We engage in subterfuge; absolute secrecy. By the looks of it, as soon as you agree to the deal, you will have to move into one of the cottages.' Jason began to track the office, wondering where he could set up his equipment. 'When we move out of the Manor, I can stay at the Pig and Whistle, get one of the large rooms backing onto the yard. However, before we can go ahead, I must contact the Patent Office in London to see if the concept has been registered. If not, I shall put in a provisional.' He bent over the desk and began writing. 'There are things to be done.'

Tony looked over his shoulder. 'Like what?'

'You will make an inventory of the stock. Keep back some inks, we shall need them, and ring round to see where I can pick up these chemicals and equipment.' He held out his hand. 'Give me your car keys?'

Tony sent a wan smile and passed them over with the reality finally dawning that Strident Cutter was in the last of its days under the ownership of a Black.

About an hour later, Susan arrived at the factory. There was a hysterical tinge to her voice after Tony explained his intentions. 'So how much do we get out of this?' she asked, and he replied, 'a roof over our heads.' It seemed the arguments between Tony and Susan belonged forever, and that the miracle of their survival was made commonplace by the durability of Strident Cutter to stay afloat.

The day crept away, two brothers, each pursuing the same objective but in different quarters. While Jason was in London going through the paper formalities, Tony was in the store room up to his neck in dust, searching for inks he never knew existed. It was Tony's agony and Jason's pleasure.

By nightfall, Jason turned into the drive and immediately set about looking for Tony. Since he was not at the Manor, he picked his way to Strident Cutter, which quietly confirmed the absence of workers, and in contrast to the morning, images of the past felt very daunting.

Tony had a weighted and worried look on his face when Jason stepped into the store room and said, 'Nothing has been filed, so I made a preliminary registration.'

Tony's eyes lit up, then closed in on themselves. 'I'm out of condition,' he claimed and slumped on a half-empty carton, denting and sagging, grumbling around his thighs. 'Susan hit the roof, but what's new?'

'You look like a coal man. Have you seen your face?'

'Have you seen your hair?' Tony brought out a packet of cigarettes and offered one to Jason, but he refused. 'Christ, I need a hot bath and a whisky. If Claire wasn't ill, I would ask her to give me a back scrub.'

'You do realise what this means, or have you changed your mind?'

'No, it's great news, really great. It's Susan, she does my head in.' Clenching the lit cigarette between his teeth, Tony stretched over to grab a grubby puzzle box. 'By the way, I found an old try-out. I thought we could do a practice run...see how hard it can be to get going on a blank puzzle.'

'Good thinking. Any news on my equipment?'

'Gilmore in Birmingham has the chemicals. Around the corner from him, there's a company that sells your type of equipment. I gave them a ring and they confirmed they have what you want. Shall we go tomorrow?'

'I shall go first thing. You stay here and keep an eye on Susan.'

'Come on, Squirt. Don't leave me here with a sodding vampire.'

'Then buy some garlic.'

RIDDLE OF MOLLY TURNER

Jason returned from Birmingham three days later. All the wheeling and dealing put his dream fairly and squarely at the back of his mind. Never once did he consider failure and regarded the dream was a desperate attempt to telegraph details from the subconscious to the conscious about a new invention. The woman with green eyes was placed in forgotten isolation.

He parked in the drive next to Susan's silver Mercedes, stepped out of the Jag and walked up to the Manor with the key ring twirling about his index finger. Then all of a sudden Susan was upon him.

'You,' she said poking him in the chest 'should go back! I never agreed to the deal with Claggart.'

'The bank foreclosing or Claggart's offer? Personally, I would choose the latter.'

'Oh don't give me that air of superiority, Jason Black. I know you inside out.' She walked on, her voice climbing in discord. 'I got rid of you once and I can do it again.'

It raised such frightful images he did not respond, was tempted to reach the more cynical conclusion this was her perfect way to blackmail.

Moving inside the house, buoyed up with the enormity of the prize at stake he began to hear music. It came to him in fragments of strings and errant horn sequences echoing off the long and high walls leading to the kitchen.

With his back to the room, Tony had his hands in his trouser pockets swaying to a contented rhythm at the closed patio doors.

'What have you got to be so happy about?' Jason asked, tossing his hat on the table.

His brother swung round with a start and turned off the radio. 'Squirt, you need a drink,' he said excitedly and reached for the port bottle resting on a wooden draining board, smelt the stopper and poured deep red liquid into two crystal glasses. 'Have I got news for you? Henshaw got in touch with

Claggart's solicitors and told them we're on for the deal. I made it clear they have to act fast before I change my mind. They're sending someone down from Australia to negotiate the valuation. Then I told Henshaw, Susan might make it difficult.' Handing a glass to Jason he said, 'Guess what? There was a clause in the deeds dating back from Granddad's day. Only a Black has the last say. Even if Susan owned ninety percent of the business, as a direct descendent I have the authority to sell any part of the assets on this land, even the corrugated structure.'

'A strange thing to do.'

'Hey, no stranger to what's in here.' Tony placed his drink aside, whooshed opened a cupboard drawer and brought out a small cardboard box, frayed at the edges, torn on the corners. 'Now take a look inside.'

Jason shuffled the lid from its tatty base and traced two fingers across loose pieces of a jigsaw puzzle. Of a single fact he had become certain, all were blank. 'Yup, okay, so it's the try-out.'

If it was mystery and wonderment he required, Tony was certainly providing it. He lifted the latch to the pantry door and half disappeared inside, re-emerging seconds later with a large plastic tray. 'I put some together,' he said placing it on the table.

Jason's expression was unchanging.

Molly Turner, not yet a woman

endured the pain of a cutter.

Black, said he, it is neither my fault

nor even my matter.

Death ensued, a contract made,

bore witness by the physician.

The past lay deep in grief and pain,

waiting for revision.

'Now the important thing to remember,' Tony went on eagerly, 'is that they came from the same box.'

If Jason had to understand what Tony was implying then truly this seemed a remarkable puzzle. 'Did the words come by the use of heat?'

'Look, Squirt, last night I opened the box here in the kitchen while Susan was taking a bath and by the time she came down, I'd only fitted about thirty pieces. I almost gave up on the bloody thing but she pointed to some black bits. We then got into another argument because I accused her of writing on it. Anyway, she walked off in a huff and I carried on. So I got to thinking, it must have been Granddad's invention. In that head of yours you must have buried the memory and it came out in your dream.'

'So you hold no credence to what apparently seems to be a form of complaint in our history books?'

Tony stood in contemplation for a moment. 'Not really. Anyway, if it's true it's all in the past.' He sat down at the table, full of enthusiasm looking at the puzzle. 'So what do you think?'

'Hard to tell,' Jason replied in the process of handling a piece. 'It might be invisible ink though usually it needs heat to bring the element to the forefront and then it fades. Where did you find the box?'

'In the store room, you remember. It was among other Misery's try-outs. As I was dumping them, I thought, why not keep one back to see how hard it could be to connect a blank puzzle. Dad must have known about this.'

Jason shook his head. 'So why not use it to advantage Strident Cutter?' He popped two pieces of bread in the toaster and folded his arms leaning against the worktop, trying to make sense of the secrecy. 'This type of chemistry was unheard of in Grandfather's day, and if so, why a riddle of our history, why not a picture. No, I am not convinced. I do not trust Susan.'

'What? You think she invented this?'

'Tony, do you have a problem with your brain cells? Susan couldn't invent an overcoat. I am suggesting she has the wherewithal to deceive. She needs to create grandeur and pyramids of gold among dissention. Was she still in the house when you completed the verse?'

'Yes, but-'

'There you have it.' Jason was not ready to accept the impossible. 'Did the old man ever speak about a Molly Turner?'

'I never heard the name before. Besides, Dad was drunk half the time. It might have been his gammy leg. It did give him jip, certainly in the winter though it never stopped him from screwing nanny. I can remember a time when I saw him wiping his eyes, genuinely missing Mum.'

Jason met his brows, placing his burnt toast on the kitchen table. But not everything conspired against him, not when he tasted Mrs Tooley's home-made jam. 'How can you remember, we were three years old when Mother died.'

'Okay, so maybe he cried years later. As soon as you left, he got worse, spent most of his time shuffling his feet around, which was good because it gave us the opportunity to do what we liked in the firm.'

'And most certainly you did.'

'I didn't want you to go. I wanted you and me in the business.'

'With Susan in my face.'

'Oh come on, Squirt. Sarcasm is too petty an emotion for you.'

'Do not credit me with too much nobility. I may be many things, but not a saint. You were my brother last, a Judas first.'

'I had no choice. She was pregnant.'

Jason looked down at his half finished toast with lost appetite. Wiping his mouth with a handkerchief, he realised it was time for the sordid details to surface, to clear the seven year air that had set them apart. 'It was my child, not yours. If you need to lay blame, lay it at my feet. I felt disinclined to marry a whore and considered she was yours for the taking.'

Tony waited a beat and glanced at the jigsaw. There might have been a glint of revenge in his eye or brotherly malevolence. Even so, his rage erupted. He banged his fist on the table. The action caught the lip of the tray and sent it somersaulting in the air. It seemed to float there a while then made a crash landing on the tiled floor, pieces of the puzzle strewn everywhere.

Jason half expected this sort of reaction and comprehended, always did. 'What is done cannot be undone. Consider it fortunate she had a miscarriage.'

Even armed with this piece of advice, Jason knew Tony still felt aggrieved. 'The bitch told me it was mine! What a stupid prick I was. Okay, so I shouldn't have gone behind your back but she was offering it to me on a plate. So you let me be the frickin' patsy? Buggered off, leaving me to deal with a vampire sucking my blood for seven years? Why the hell didn't you say something, anything, even a hint?'

Taking a piece of the puzzle out of the jam pot, Jason held it up. 'Like this, I was in a sticky situation. The old man wanted me to stay but I disagreed to the way he ran Strident Cutter. Remember the argument, here in this kitchen, how he threatened to cut off my allowance?'

'Was Susan pregnant by then?'

'So she said. As you know, I had two years remaining to complete my studies. The Boston Institution expressed an interest in my paper. I went to see Susan after the row with the old man and told her I was going to take up their offer, that we should get married and settle in America.' He shrugged. 'You know how arguments begin and end, the middle more revealing. So that night I just packed my bags and left.'

'You never said you were serious. Hell, marriage, what a bummer. It wasn't as if you were all over her at the time. I know it doesn't excuse my behaviour but tell me honestly, were you really cut up about it?'

Anxious to steer the conversation away from the past, Jason pushed back his chair and got to his feet in one springy movement. 'Come on, help me to unload.'

'Where do you want to set up?'

'My bedroom would be a good place.'

Galvanised into action, the next hour they were animated, clearing up the floor, going in and out of the house, up and down stairs with boxes, planting them in Jason's bedroom. It still had the musty smell of damp brocade curtains and the dark stains of polished silver between filigree pattern work surrounding frames and mirrors. Without a fire crackling in the grate, the room would look and feel cold on such days but of course there was wonderful Mrs Tooley to keep the home fires burning.

The thought of it made Jason smile. 'So Tools is still around?'

Tony tore open a box. 'She's really looking forward to seeing you. Virtually every day she asked about you. Sometimes she drove me round the bend, but hey, I told her it's not my fault your job sent you round the world. I told her you had to sod off to collect some equipment. She comes in at mid-day, has her own key and if you see her sneaking a tipple don't say anything. Where do you want this?'

'Place it on my desk and bring the puzzle up here.'

Jason's thoughts about this spun into the question of how the puzzle was able to sustain its print. Notwithstanding the possibility of Susan's scheming intervention, it seemed, even without further examination it had the hallmarks of a scientific breakthrough. Yet still he stirred with unreasoning coincidences of a dream about a blank jigsaw puzzle to the one he was about to test.

Tony walked in and put the puzzle beside the microscope. Jason foraged about and took a marked piece. He held it under the lens, adjusted accordingly. Moments later, he squared his shoulders and came to an obvious conclusion. 'Susan is the culprit.'

'Not sure about that.'

'Why?'

'Because I saw the words appear. I tried to tell you but you were set on it being her.'

Jason bit down on his bottom lip. Then that negates Susan, he thought. He could feel himself slipping into unknown territory. 'Patterns are hard to detect in jigsaws until one has a sufficiency of pieces. There are two aspects of this, one being the qualitative properties of the elements, and the other the emerging quantitative measure.'

'Huh? Run that by me again?'

'The facts are that I had a dream, which apparently is in the process of manifesting itself into reality. Are we to assume the third player in this game has yet to appear? If so, what shall we learn?'

'So you did dream about Susan.'

Jason rapped his knuckles on Tony's head. 'Wake up! Did I not say earlier, she was nothing like Susan? Did you keep Grandfather's old records?'

Shrouded in secrecy, a distant sound broke through their conversation. Like cold twin stars, linked but divided, they shared the same mode and habits. Both stood frozen until Tony clicked his fingers and said, 'It's probably that guy.'

'What guy?'

Tony took advantage of the situation and rapped his knuckles on Jason's head, imitating his brother's deeper voice. 'Wake up! Did I not say earlier, Claggart was sending a man to negotiate the valuation?' He smiled, backing off toward the door. 'I got Tools to make up a room next to Susan's. She was praying he might be a snorer to keep her awake.'

From the day he brought her to the Manor, Jason knew Mrs Tooley had taken an instant dislike to Susan. No doubt it was an exceptionally trying situation to be in, so powerless, so little in control, and yet so accountable to Susan.

Jason held back, locking his bedroom door then carried on downstairs. When he walked into the drawing room he was hit by an invisible lump hammer. From head to toe she was an elegance of manner, stripped of artificial flavouring. Her black plait was coiled to the nape of her neck, and her eyes shone emerald green that virtually matched the simplicity of a trouser suit. She was so far removed from the likes of Susan that he wondered how she became secretively beautiful and alone.

'Merluza Claggart.' She held out a hand to Jason. 'But please, call me Luze.'

'Why are you here?' he asked, his wits half lost. He saw in her expression that he troubled her, that perhaps a woman doing a man's job was incomprehensible to him, like the astronomical distances between two planets.

'Do women have to be disposal pleasures rather than tread a meaningful life?' Luze made her next cast at Tony. 'Do you wish me to find alternative accommodation?'

'No!' Jason said quickly and held a finger toward her. 'Do not move. I shall be back.' Motioning to Tony, they walked briskly across the silent, spongy carpet and into the library whereupon Jason said sharply, 'She's mine.'

'What? Did I miss something?'

'She is the girl in my dream, the missing link in my life.'

'Sorry, Squirt, but I thought she was the missing link in the puzzle.'

'Tony!' Jason irritated, was anxious to lay down the rules. 'Keep your mind focused on the business and off Luze.'

'Hey!' Tony bit back. 'It's you who needs to keep your mind off Luze! She's Claggart's daughter or did you just forget that? Mess with her and you mess up our plans. She should stay at the Pig and Whistle.'

'No. The whole of her stays here...' Jason's voice trailed off dubiously, and he wondered what the parts of that whole might be. 'Make up Mother's room overlooking the river,' he went on, sure of his ground. 'And make up a fire.'

Leaving the library behind, Tony muttered a resentful word, committed to obey while Jason followed his dream. Love impulse required no sense.

'Would you like a cup of tea?' Jason asked and carried on through the interconnecting doors. If she answered, he never heard. He switched on the kettle and put two spoonfuls of coffee in the teapot, self conscious and conscious of her aura. 'To be truthful, we were surprised to discover you were Claggart's daughter.'

'People who begin a sentence *to be truthful* very rarely are. I thought you were making tea.'

'Err...I was making coffee.'

'I see, so the coffee pot is for tea.'

'Teapot or coffee pot, I see no difference.' And he grinned, feeling like a prize idiot. He looked at her thoughtfully. Whatever did she really make of all this? When she laughed his world lit up like a huge firework. And he thought of what else he could say. Remember me, we made love by the fireside and can we make love again. But no, in the chaos of his mind he found order. 'It can be unappealing for the woman to be the fountain of wisdom.'

'I'm not here to be appealing, Mr. Black. I am here to check things out before my Father commits himself.'

'Call me nuts but do I seem familiar to you?'

Her eyelids fell to her shoes. It was almost ten seconds before she looked up and said, 'I can understand why you are called Nuts. I do hope we get through this as painless as possible. Are you here to assist your brother in the negotiations?'

'Did your father believe his daughter would soften the blow?'

Luze seemed to stare momentarily into her own internal distance which suggested a hint of concealed pain. 'There was very little time to get organised due to your brother's urgency and since my Father's right hand man was busy, I came in his place.'

Beginning to see the lapping coincidences, Jason smiled intuitively. He had established the dream and the puzzle was aided by unknown forces, had blindly considered that whatever challenges they held he would surmount them without difficulty for here was Luze, his mystery woman, his prize at the end of an ill-fated rainbow.

The conversation was now merely an interval for positioning. He was studying her as openly and intently as she studied him, but as grit in the eye could vex a giant, so too the handsome Tony could discomfort Jason.

'Have you told her about Susan?' Tony asked.

'Why should I tell her about Susan?'

'Because it's like you said. She's going to create pyramids of gold.' Tony sent an apologetic smile to Luze. 'My wife soon to be ex believes she owns fifty percent of the business. I have the legal right to sell the assets but as far as the depreciable assets go, she has the right to refuse any offer or valuation you place on them.'

'Our offer will be based on the land and buildings, the silk screen printer and one cutter. If Susan wishes to take the rest, then we have no problem with that. However, I would like to remind you my Father has given his word to keep the workers employed. But he cannot keep the workers employed if he takes over an empty factory. In that event, a percentage will be deducted unless, of course, you can find alternative equipment to tide him over.'

'Why one cutter,' Tony asked. 'Why not base the valuation on four?'

'Gentlemen, I don't wish to be rude.' Luze stifled a yawn handing her empty cup to Tony. 'Can we discuss things tomorrow?'

'I'll show you to your room.' Jason felt he had got off to a rocky start, it being difficult to adjust to this extraordinary situation. He looked round and saw her overnight case in the drawing room so he walked through the interconnecting doors and picked it up.

'Thank you, Nuts.' Luze sent a genial smile at Tony. 'Goodnight, Tony.'

'Goodnight, Luze.'

At the bottom rung of the stairs, she asked Jason, 'What time do you normally get up?'

'I suggest you have a lay-in, get a good night's sleep.'

'There's no need. I slept on my Father's plane. It was the drive from Heathrow that was tiring. The chauffer was lost. I venture to say it seemed as though we would never find Little Smeet. It's so cut-off from everything yet from what I glimpsed it looks very nice.'

'It is nice in an extraordinary way.' He opened the door and stood there. 'Would you like me to bring you a cup of tea in the morning?'

'No thank you,' she replied taking her case then stepped into pink-flocked wallpaper and a four-poster bed, dropping her reserve. 'Oh!' she exclaimed, 'this room is loverly, just loverly.'

'It was my Mother's room. It faces east and more often than not you can see the sun rise over the river. Copernicus nudged us to a beautiful but nevertheless minor planet in orbit around the sun. Since then, the sun has been elbowed out to an insignificant location in an insignificant galaxy in an insignificant cluster in what may prove to be an insignificant universe.'

Her eyes flickered. 'Not worth mentioning then. Where is the bathroom?'

'Next door to your right or you can use the one next to my room.' The door slowly closed nicely on his face. His method of courtship was still in working progress.

Strolling downstairs like a walk in the park, he reminded himself of Shelley's words. '*He gave man speech, and speech created thought, which is a measure of the universe.*' Now he believed Luze was his composite singularity where he would act as her fusion.

'Why did she call you Nuts?'

'Because I acted the imbecile.' Jason advanced to the drink's cabinet. 'Do you want a brandy?'

'Make it a single. So I take it you're Nuts from now on.'

He passed a glass to Tony then fell into a leather armchair, wondering whether the intensity of his desire had somehow brought into being the very thing he sought. 'Her father has his own private jet, she has no Australian accent as such, no wedding ring on her finger, no sense of self and is unknowledgeable about the cosmos but she is perfect.' At that moment he was in her fiery bed, somewhere between his tortured patience and exhausted nerves. 'Where is Susan?'

'Search me. Last time I saw her is when we argued about the puzzle. She's going to flip her lid when she sees Luze.'

'Not if you make it clear your interests lie elsewhere.'

'Ah, you make a good point. It might go in our favour, a woman thing.'

'So you think they might discuss Tampax?'

'Look, it's no good getting tetchy, Squirt. Ever since you came on the scene, I don't know whether I'm coming or going. My assets are about to be sold off for peanuts. There's a puzzle upstairs doing its own thing, a strange woman sleeping in Mum's bed, and somewhere in between, I might survive Susan and live beyond poverty.'

Jason got to his feet. 'Do you require another drink?'

'No thanks. So how are we going to play this?'

'In the morning, you go to the factory and leave me to handle Luze.'

'In which case, you need to check her chemical symbol.'

Jason let that slip by. 'See if you can find a Molly Turner in the records.'

'Do you think Luze had the same dream?'

And why not. 'One cannot dismiss this possibility.' Falling back into the armchair, he felt himself pinched of energy. 'If she did have the same dream, she certainly never gave any indication to that effect. I find the whole thing quite bizarre. How can one have a dream that plays itself out to reality? Surely, such a feat goes beyond the realms of what we know. Or are we to assume the dream is reality and reality is the dream.'

'It's too much for my head. I'm going to bed.' Tony placed his empty glass on the mantelpiece. 'Who knows, we might wake up and find Luze is a bloke.'

Jason leaned forward and studied his boots in a romantic break of the past, the travels they shared and the time he purchased them. Then quickly his thoughts reverted to his mother, painful thoughts for the most part. There had been happier times, when she was alive and although he could barely remember them, he knew he was happy. It was his father who had deprived him of contentment through a monotony of disasters in which drink, gambling and lust played more or less equal parts.

Another drink later, Jason made tracks for his room a little light-headed. Before turning the key in his lock, he hesitated with modest ambitions. Should he squeeze her door open and see if she was waiting for him? But he was not meant to peep and pry and be the butt of good natured jokes. The tug of yearning subsided and he slipped into his bedroom thinking about her name, Merluza, a Spanish name for the colour of green. He lay on the bed like a taunted man, his face aglow looking up at the ceiling. Slowly his eyes closed, drifting into the realms of fantasy.

The next day descended in patterns of drizzle and mist where Jason woke to an almost slapdash love fully clothed, spread eagled on the bed. He shot up and looked at his watch. It said 11:40 am. Sudden death! Plans made last night just flew out the window.

He stepped into a bath, which although it nearly scalded him, was somehow comforting. Here his thoughts travelled to the future, ridiculous notions about making a life with Luze and then all those widdle worries rushed in, like her falling for a mad chemist with hair stuck up like the arched back of a hedgehog.

Much later and more at ease, he pulled on a jumper and a pair of worn jeans, and without so much as a hiss or a boil from the kettle he grabbed his jacket and hat, bumping into Mrs Tooley who was shaking her raincoat by the umbrella stand.

'My, haven't yew grown, boy. It must be all those hamburgers. You've been sorely missed, did yew know that? Well, of course yew must. What's the matter, boy? Cat got your tongue?'

He smiled and things sung constant. 'How have you been, Mrs Tooley?'

'Mrs Tooley indeed,' she harrumphed marching towards the drinks cabinet. 'Has these past seven years made yew absent minded?'

To him, she had not aged, still short and slightly dumpy, her face at times the radiance of a saint, at others the blank watchfulness of an insect. 'So, Tools, how have things been?'

'I can't complain. I won't say I'm sorry to hear about your father. After yew left, he wus virtually confined to this house. Mind yew, I paid no attention even though he still found it necessary to pinch my bum. Did Tony tell yew about Franny Whistle? Her dad finally passed on. Now she runs the pub with that stupid boyfriend of hers. No one ever sees him since he got that television to play with.'

Twirling the hat in his hands, he said, 'Tony has been rather busy.'

'Well of course he's been busy finding ways to spend your money.' She drank her sherry in one go, puffed out her cheeks and poured another. 'The vicar still complains about the bell tower and Smelly broke his leg last week. He wus run over by Mrs Stockton's boy. He got himself a mini, races up and down the high street showing off. And what about yew? Are yew happy?'

'I missed your pies.'

She swallowed the second glass of sherry in the same manner then marched up to him. 'Oh, I did miss yew, Jason. I wus glad you left to make a good life. Tony told me about your medal and shaking hands with the president. That must have been a proud moment in your life.'

'It was a little unnerving.'

In her eyes was a glow of happiness. Wiping her tears with the back of her hand, she reasserted her authority. 'I do upstairs first then work down so don't think yew can change my ways.'

'I made my own bed.'

'Not like your brother and not like that cow Susan. He thinks women should be strapped to the oven and she thinks she's the Queen of England.'

'I was just on my way to the factory. The new guest arrived. I put her in the room overlooking the gardens.'

'Her, yew say? Thass going to be interesting.'

Certainly there were things that had remained the same about Mrs Tooley.

This time Jason took the route by the river. He walked down the garden path from the kitchen patio doors and met the water's edge, turned left into the adjacent land and worked his way up behind Strident Cutter.

Inside the packing hall, a nervous something throbbed in his stomach when he saw Luze emerging with her hair tied back against a light green fluffy jumper. Her full lips parted in a half-radiant smile, waving a clipboard in her hand.

'I overslept,' he said.

'You're entitled to do that. I have seen no sign of Susan.'

'Is Tony here?'

'He's in his office looking glam in his red braces. I do believe he thinks he's James Bond.' She turned her gaze on a box full of papers, held by a young worker. She said thank you to him and placed the clipboard on top then took the box from him, which in turn was taken out of her hands by Jason. 'Thank you, Nuts.'

'Do you want this in the office?'

'Yes,' she said walking on. 'They're for Tony. Have you seen Claire?'

'No, what's she like?'

'I have no idea. Tony tends to think he has a secretary with big boobies.' Luze stopped in mid-stride and stared thoughtfully into space. 'Who would disappoint aliens looking for intelligent life around here?'

'Luze, I must apologise for my behaviour last night. It was totally out of character.'

'I know this is hard but the workers will be treated well.'

They went through the factory where the noise deafened the workers and where those worker's faces appeared more desperate and cold. Jason wondered if Luze had told them why she was here. 'Have they been told?' he stupidly asked because she never heard.

Tony looked up from his chair when the two walked in. 'Hey, Squirt, you missed a terrific breakfast this morning. Luze makes a great scrambled egg.'

Jason placed the box on his desk. 'Why did you let her cook breakfast?'

'Honestly, it was no trouble,' she said cheerily. 'I shall leave you two alone.'

Tony got to his feet and delved into the box, pulling out a ledger. 'The world is changing, Squirt. The damn unions are to blame, well not entirely but they have encouraged women to think they can do a man's job. Take Luze, she told me I should learn how to cook. Said I needed to be independent, even mentioned I should try ironing my shirts.'

'I iron my shirts and cook.'

'More fool you. Why do you think women were born?'

Jason shook his head in partial disbelief, realizing his brother harboured deep chauvinistic qualities. 'You wouldn't last five minutes with American women.'

'Forget America, they shoot their presidents. Mind you the Labour Government has made a cock-up of things.'

'Perhaps we should have a woman Prime Minister.'

'It'll never happen. She would arrive in the House of Commons with her shopping basket.' Tony began to turn over a few pages and discovered an invoice. 'Ah, what have we here?'

Jason walked round to take a look.

Tony continued, 'I found a mention of a Mrs Elizabeth Turner being paid wages. Her name carries on through a few years but there is no record of wages for a Molly Turner. But this is interesting because here it mentions a fee paid to our Grandfather, Doctor Robert Graves on 30th October 1942 for services rendered to Mrs Turner. It looks like Granddad Black picked up the tab.'

Something popped into Jason head. It seemed so irrelevant but talking about dates just made him say, 'the old man died last year on the same date. What else did you find?'

'Not much else. Basically, it looks as though he paid wages during the Second World War to few employees yet he must have had more than fifty working here, which suggests he employed children, probably because the men got conscripted. Though he could have employed passing labour and paid them cash.'

'Unless we can trace this Elizabeth Turner, we will not know for certain it was her child.'

Tony sat back, locking his hands behind his head. 'Are you going to speak to Luze, or shall I?'

'She will regard me mad.'

'She calls you Nuts so you're half way there. Ask her outright if she shared your dream. See if we can find out what's happening.'

Jason could never have imagined such a contrast, both in surrounds and position. A week ago he was among his contemporaries without a care in the world, laughing in the heat of the day. Now he was cutting through cooler climes, befuddled over a mysterious jigsaw puzzle and a woman called Luze. Touring the divisions of the factory, stopping on occasions to speak to the workers who complained radically about the cold, Jason looked ahead as the die-cutters continually thrashed down to make jigsaw puzzles, and noticed Luze on her heels, head bent, smearing something between her fingers. She got to her feet and cupped her hands to Misery's ear. Misery then pressed a button and the die cut closed down.

'Thass not right, boy,' Misery said when Jason got close. 'The leak has worsened. It don't sing sweet like the others.'

'Do you have an empty tobacco tin?' Jason asked.

Misery brought one out from the underside of the cutter. He tipped the tin and retrieved some keys, blew away bits of hand rolling tobacco and passed it to Jason who then scooped up a sample from the floor.

'Nuts, why is this factory so cold?'

'Tony never installed heating.'

'But it's warmer outside than in here. The workers are freezing.' She huffed into the ether. 'Look, I can see my breath.'

Jason motioned toward the packing room so they could talk without raising their voices. 'Luze,' he said when she halted with a shiver. 'Do you have an open mind?'

'I'd like to think so.'

Impelled to take off his jacket, he placed it around her shoulders. 'When I was on the plane, coming home to help Tony, I had this dream. You were in it and-'

'Try a new line and it might get my attention.' She yanked the brim of his hat over his eyes. 'There, much better. Now try again.'

Displeased, he just stood there. 'Let me know when you are ready to take me seriously.'

Defiantly, she removed his hat and wore it herself. 'Tell me truthfully,' she said almost blind, 'can you take me seriously?'

He laughed deep from his belly and considered there was probably no one more capable of bringing him out of his shell than Luze. 'I like you calling me Nuts.'

'It suits you,' she said, handing over his Homburg. 'I have never met anyone so bonkers. Do you improve with age?'

'Hang around and you might find out.' That never went down too well, so he added, 'I wear this to keep my hair in place.'

'Nothing will keep your hair in place unless you shave it off and look like a turnip. Far better to look like a lion than a turnip, wouldn't you say?'

He chuffed in how she viewed him and pulled his jacket further round her shoulders. 'This lion was on the plane and had a really weird dream.'

'Weird?'

'The nuts and bolts were such that you were helping us to complete a blank jigsaw puzzle. I woke up and your face was clearly imprinted. I paid no heed to the dream until Tony found a try-out box, you know the sort I mean.'

'Not really. Can you explain?'

'In the old days when these types of cutters were used, sometimes the thin strips of metal that clamped down on the cardboard sheets would misalign. So what you would do is recalibrate the cutter and send a couple of blank sheets through in order to save on the inks.'

'Pappy has a big cutter.'

'Pappy?'

'My Father,' she confirmed. 'Please, tell me more.'

'Well Tony took the box home thinking it would be fun to piece together a blank jigsaw puzzle and suddenly words appeared.' He paused to let that sink in. 'Last night, before you arrived, I examined the puzzle and it was no hoax. The writing somehow appeared and I cannot explain it. I then re-evaluated the variables and considered if my dream is to be played out, the likely scenario would be for you to come on the scene. At that point you knocked on our door.' In this breathing space, she did respond. Her hands were clasped together, resting against her mouth so it begged the question, did she believe him? 'I am telling the truth, Luze. I can show you the puzzle. Unfortunately, the first pieces Tony put together slipped off the tray and broke up but we can piece them together again.'

'What did the words say?'

'It was a riddle about a young girl called Molly Turner enduring the pain of a cutter. Have you heard the name?'

She shook her head. 'Are you certain it was me in your dream?'

'Absolutely certain, a good reason why I acted the idiot last night, but I could hardly tell you at the time, could I?'

'Why me?'

'I wish I knew. But for certain you are here instead of this other bloke your father sent down. And at this point in time, that is all I am certain about.'

'What was I doing in your dream?'

'Helping us to fit the pieces.'

'Just fit the pieces, nothing else?'

He felt himself flushing and cleared his throat but heard his voice go an octave higher. 'There were moments when we socialised.'

'Socialised, as in having a party?'

'Luze, it was just a dream.'

'But it would appear more than a dream.'

At that moment, Tony emerged. 'I think it's the ghost of Molly Turner.'

'If you believe in ghosts,' Jason said, 'then you believe in goblins, witches, vampires and werewolves. There is not one recorded sighting.'

'That's not true,' Luze quickly broke in. 'Some people have encountered ghosts. You know poor souls refusing to leave their earthly bounds.'

'Where is the proof of this unseen world thought up by a group of demented idiots?'

'Nuts, our inability to count, weigh, sort or photograph some things doesn't mean that those things are non existent.' She folded her arms. 'Okay, Nutty Professor, what's your opinion?'

'Sense of reason, cause and consequence when my rational mind has already worked out this is some form of chemical reaction. Yes, I agree reality is not always quantifiable but given time it can be quantified. If I am to be convinced on anything, I could believe in extra terrestrials because to consider we are the only life in this cosmos is like burying your head in the sand.'

'So you think the puzzle is an alien?' Tony asked.

Jason and Luze laughed.

'Hey, you won't think it funny if it turns out to be true. I suggest we all go home and show Luze the puzzle. After dinner, we can go to the Pig and Whistle. What do you say, Luze? Fancy a drink at our local?'

'Sounds good to me. Misery told me your grandfather, Edward Black, established the business in the early part of this century. I'm surprised for such an astute move he never invested in a new factory.' She stared at their blank faces and continued to chip away at principles. 'It's not as if he never made any money. I understand he built the workers cottages and the Manor.'

'We never had a chance to talk to Granddad,' Tony said. 'He died before we were born but Dad said he took over an ailing business and money was tight.'

'That is not strictly true,' Jason corrected, walking on. 'Edward Black set up after he saw an opening for jigsaws in this country. Jigsaws really took off in America during the depression. And remember, there was no television in those days. Even now, many households do not own a television.' Now Jason was intent on impressing Luze with his knowledge of jigsaws. 'John Spilsbury, a much admired eighteenth century London engraver and mapmaker who, in 1766, had mounted one of his maps on a sheet of hardwood and cut around the borders of the countries using a fine-bladed marquetry saw. It was labour intensive, an expensive product enjoyed by a relatively niche market of upper-class families. Over a century later, with the introduction of the treadle saw, what had previously been known as dissections, not a word with particular enjoyable connotations came to be known as jigsaw puzzles. Then a sudden leap of engineering, cardboard being die-cut, a process whereby thin strips of metal with sharpened edges are twisted into intricate patterns making the whole process much faster and cheaper to produce, like the cutters we have here.'

'And I suppose your grandfather saw a golden age beyond the horizon, an enduring success producing a range of jigsaw puzzles reflecting the need for sentimental scenes, a good entertainment for a small price. What made him set up in Little Smeet? Did he come from these parts?'

To which Jason or Tony was unable to answer.

Sentimentality played little part in Edward Black's nature but he felt a flush of triumph as he looked out upon the glistening waters for the hundredth time and again found nothing he disliked about Little Smeet.

Here, he rated the simplicity of minds, people with large callused hands criss-crossed with the scars and scratches of hard work and thought, what better than to take advantage. There was no better arrangement for Edward. The land upon which he stood was the product of a bet, and there a corrugated structure sat ugly by the river waiting for a very cheap labour force that was abundant in this farming community. A moral compass was not an option because he had grandeur in mind.

Edward was an industrialist without principle, resplendent in his silk waistcoat while his bead-black eyes flickered to watch the noisy cutters beat to his tempo. From profits gained he built a fine detached three-storey Manor to accommodate his extravagant lifestyle then constructed workers cottages to keep the wages even lower. The death of his wife and the announcement of World War II made little impact. On the contrary, he gained. Men that worked the machinery were conscripted to make way for a far cheaper labour force, easily manipulated. The complaints by dirty-skirted aprons and the ravages of war could wait for the urgent batches to meet the demand of London retailers.

Indeed, nothing was beyond his reach until 30th October 1942. What was about to happen would alter the course of his destiny, and that of others around him. It would create a series of events to touch upon his grandchildren and ultimately launch something so extraordinary that it answers to a hugely important question; when does a soul mean to die?

RIDDLE OF TOM TURNER

'Tony, it won't work if you intend to fry eggs in that pan.' Luze tapped his hand with a spatula. 'You should grill the bacon.'

'Why do I have to cook when you're here?'

'I am the guest, remember? And if you intend to move into one of the cottages without Susan then you must learn to fend for yourself.' She sent her eyes at Jason. 'Your brother is a nincompoop.'

Jason tugged thoughtfully at his earlobe, his expression almost serene. Luze had made the kitchen come alive, elbowed Tony without spite, stirred the atmosphere with her deranged sense of fun and sometimes opened wide her eyes, shaking her head at each new revelation about Tony, and never took offence to his bigoted view.

Tony shoved a plate under Jason's nose. 'What do you think?'

'Call that breakfast.'

'I call it shit. Are we possessed by some damn demon or what?'

Jason picked up the tempo by taking the plate from Tony and dumping the contents in the bin. 'The way I see it, we have an advanced puzzle.' Retrieving an egg from the fridge, he said, 'I admit, it has me vexed but what we should do is add more pieces to the puzzle.' He threw the egg in the air, caught it from behind and cracked it on the rim of the frying pan. No two guesses why Luze picked up an egg, her face full of bewilderment. 'You need to practice on a couple of balls,' he said and watched her smile widen. 'Have dinner with me tonight?'

Luze opened her mouth to speak but Tony broke in, 'Shall we take her to St George's?'

None of this had been without its anxieties. Jason had undertaken hopeless measures to get Luze alone, but unfortunately Tony was constantly latched to their sides, probably hoping never to set eyes on Susan again.

'I suggest,' Luze offered, waving the spatula like a baton. 'I stay here and add more pieces to the puzzle. Last night we only tackled the pieces that showed the riddle of Molly Turner.'

'And I shall call upon Father Michael. Tony, you go to the factory and see what else you can dig up.'

'Where is your wife?' Luze asked Tony.

'She went berserk the other day and stormed off. Hey, nothing unusual about that but generally she creeps back within hours. Luze, now we've reached an agreement on the valuation, how long do you intend to stay?'

'I should have made tracks. I will ring Jeremy Hubbard later tonight and let him know the details so he can tell Pappy.'

'Why not speak to your father direct?' Jason asked.

'I wanted to come here with Jeremy and take the opportunity to visit the Norfolk Broads but Pappy said I would be a distraction. His word is usually final, but as you see, it worked out quite differently.'

'Is your father's plane at Heathrow?'

'Probably not...it's probably on its way to Portugal to pick up my brother, who also works in the firm. Pappy very rarely leaves his desk, and when he does it's usually for a fishing trip.'

They ate contentedly, talking with their mouths half-full. All the information up to this point was processed again and again until Jason, abruptly, left the table with the yearning ambition to hold Luze. But this was out of the question.

He seized his hat and jacket from the coat stand, stepped into rain that crushed down upon his Homburg and shoulders and forged ahead, on the opposite side of the road to the Catholic Church, a former sanctuary for his troubled years. He had known Father Michael for most of his life, a tall, thin man with light sprung glasses sitting on a long and large nose, blissfully born with a sense of humour. Sprinting towards the vestibule, he could smell the beginnings of breakfast. The priest had maintained his habit.

'Hello, Michael,' Jason said, removing his hat.

'Jason!' exclaimed Father Michael at the altar. He offered both hands, shaking Jason's with gusto. 'Let's see Mrs Tooley so she can lay another plate for breakfast.'

'I have already eaten, thank you.' He fell into step. 'Since when has Tools worked here?'

'Poor Mrs Farrow passed away six months ago but she had a good life.'

Their conversation was functional, brief discussions about how something was to be arranged or a passing enquiry about a state of health and how mass was said in English instead of Latin. Eventually they came circumspectly to the point.

'Your face tells a picture of concern, Jason.'

'Michael, do you give credence to supernatural forces?'

'That's like asking me if I believe in miracles. We are not so apart in our beliefs. In your line of work there is always a positive to cancel a negative. This is no different from the Almighty to the devil himself, although I have a feeling Lucifer is gaining ground. My church is not as full as I would like. This force, by what manner does it come?'

'In the form of a jigsaw puzzle,' Jason replied digging into his pocket. 'The pieces Tony put together were blank and then a riddle appeared.' He looked down at the verse earlier scrawled on paper. 'Molly Turner, not yet a woman endured the pain of a cutter. Black said he it is neither my fault nor even my matter. Death ensued, a contract made, bore witness by the physician. The past lay deep in grief and pain, waiting for revision.' He looked up. 'The latter line concerns me. Waiting for revision? I wonder if it means we have to pay a price in order to put right what Grandfather did.'

'I know the tale to some extent. Her grave lies in the cemetery.' Father Michael clasped his hands and placed them in his lap, his face a mask of resignation. 'No-one has ever visited that grave, Jason. No, dear, dear me, no-one ever does. Every year the church receives an anonymous donation in return for flowers placed on her grave at the anniversary of her death. Of course, I was not presiding over this parish at the time but my predecessor spoke of the unfortunate occurrence.'

'So what happened?'

'Would you first care to tell me how you came by this puzzle?'

Jason enlightened Father Michael then concluded, 'Luze came here to negotiate the valuation with Tony. Now that this has cropped up, she will stay longer to help before going back.'

'Are you sad the business is being sold?'

'In a small way, yes. In other ways, no. Tony is not capable of running the business and I worried about the workers and their future.'

'Yes,' Father Michael agreed. 'Your brother is not exactly geared for business. Perhaps his head is more in the clouds than on terra firma.'

'Tell me about Molly?'

'From what I understood, she was far too young to be working those cutters, a beautiful, happy child. She had very long hair. Unfortunately, her bun became loose and her hair was caught in the machinery. If she had just kept still and allowed the cutter to do its own thing she would have been saved but she tried to unravel her hair and,' he shrugged, 'her death was instantaneous.'

'It's wat went before thass should never hev happened.'

'Have you been eaves dropping again, Mrs Tooley?'

She plonked a sizzling plate in front of him. 'Jason has a right to know the truth.'

'Then tell me, Tools. I want to know.'

She drew up a chair, helping herself to a rasher of bacon off Father Michael's plate. 'My Mum knew Elizabeth Turner,' she said tearing off the fatty rind. 'She wus a captain's wife renting that place the other side of Smelly's farm. Not as fine as yours mind yew but she wus a woman of some bearing. Her husband wus a Captain in the Royal Navy and before he wus called to duty he met up with your grandfather, Edward, who waged a bet. So sure wus his ground, Captain Turner offered the very same lands your business, house and all the cottages stand upon today.'

'And what did Edward offer?'

'The very same house Captain Turner and his wife rented. Your grandfather never had need of it, spent his time in London but Norfolk always drew him to his roots. Each placed their bets on the table by a flick of a card. Captain Turner claimed your grandfather cheated. Anyways, Captain Turner took his loss with great animosity.'

'What happened to Elizabeth?' Jason asked.

'Ah, well, yew see, there's a thing. The land belonged to her and when she found out she tried to bargain with your grandfather but he would hev none of it. Then a few years later, Captain Turner went down with his ship and she couldn't afford the rent, so your grandfather offered her a cottage and work at his factory. And that suited him fine.'

'How do you know all this?'

'My Mum, God bless her soul, used to clean house for your grandfather, besides everyone knows how Molly died and it weren't her hair.'

Jason sat back, folding his arms. 'I would like to know too.'

She grinned firmly, nodding slightly. This was a story to be seasoned, crammed with superfluities.

And it began on an important date, 30th October 1942 after twelve years of limitless success for Edward Black.

The lighting was dim, the smell of grease rife and the clackety-clack of machinery pounded across the flatlands and estuary, darkened by the late hour that offered a foreboding presence. Edward had toured the divisions of his little empire, the isles between the die-cutters, the store room full of inks and cardboard, had witness the slackness of weary women and children, and had threatened non-payment for any who disrupted his target. It was the hypnotic throb of greed drumming to his tempo until his mood swung, restless with the pang of annoyance when he heard the high pitched scream of a woman's voice that sounded so acute it made him shudder to think. He knew not where it came, except, as he turned, he saw a small crowd of dirty-skirted aprons descending upon one of the die-cutters. As he drew closer, the soles of his polished leather shoes smeared the warm blood trailing on the rutted concrete from a twelve year old girl. Her name was Molly Turner, not yet a woman, held unconscious in the lap of her distraught mother hunkered to the floor.

Sickened by the open wounds showing sinews and bones, her arm ragged, bloodied and limp, the gravity of the situation became clear almost immediately. It was madness. Cries of dissent were strong, animosity rife. Edward had to work fast to quell dissension and conflict. With a heave, he launched poor Molly into his arms, bade her mother to follow while commanding the workforce back to work with a growl in his voice. His thoughts travelled to different matters as he steadied his pace through the exit point, blood and mother trailing behind out to the open and into his Bristol sedan. He was grateful the journey was short. Gone were the aspects of his structure which had earned it the sobriquet of Strident Cutter. He sped past the collection of high street shops and found himself on the wealthy doorstep of a friend, a celebrated physician who greeted the circumstance with horror.

The physician, Robert Graves had imagined the thin strips of metal with sharpened edges clamping on flesh, making the cuts ragged but swift, calculating almost instantaneously this fair headed child had lost a considerable amount of blood, doubtful her life could be saved let alone her arm.

The encroaching atmosphere in the surgery was touching minds, affecting reason. 'I will make amends,' said Edward to secure Elizabeth's silence but she replied, 'you seek to protect your name, Edward Black not for the welfare of my daughter.'

Alas, poor Molly never survived. Graves stood rigid and awkward, ill-prepared to respond while Elizabeth felt lost in a world of terrible sorrow, embracing lifeless Molly in her arms. She had known the worst of Edward Black by previous, devious means and now she was nursing a far greater pain. No spite-filled words could bring back her daughter. The atonement and settlement was unfolding. Elizabeth realised what Edward was up to and did not make it that easy, making him alternate offers with oblique accusations. In front of the silent physician, who bore witness to the deal, Edward agreed to tutor her son, aged fourteen at the time, into the business. A lifespan was being mapped for Tom Turner.

Mrs Tooley poured hot water into the teapot. Of course she had more to say, Jason could see that but he noticed it was not just him listening intently but also Father Michael.

'Tom Turner did well for his age,' Mrs Tooley continued. 'Within a short time he became skilled and got over his nightmares. Oh, he did love his sister, and he proved himself equal in the eyes of your grandfather. But here's a funny thing. Two years after the death of poor Molly, your grandfather received a telegram to tell him his youngest son died serving for King and Country. After that, Elizabeth showed some sympathy and things changed. Your grandfather got very close to the Turners. He understood the sting of losing a child. He wus a little like yew, Jason. He would always keep his emotions bottled up but he struggled to hold back his tears when he received that telegram. Then in 1945, just before Christmas his other son returned from the war and that wus your dad. Oh, he wus a handsome man. All the ladies loved him. He wanted to take advantage of his brother's death and saw his future running Strident Cutter. I remember my Mum saying Charles wus sitting by a log fire in that front room, still in his uniform drinking brandy saying not a word, just content to sit there opposite Edward smoking his cigar. Then suddenly your grandfather told him Tom Turner should share in the business, continue to manage and all that.'

She paused for breath and raised her brows. 'Well, yew can imagine the horror on your dad's face. He jumped up like a jack rabbit and said, look here, are you suggesting a young whipper-snapper be taken into the business? Your grandfather wus ever so upset. He tried to tell him how Tom knew the business, would be a good asset, went on to explain he had nothing to lose, said if his brother wus alive it would still be fifty-fifty. No, your dad weren't too happy about that. They wus nose to nose in a terrible row, especially when your grandfather announced he wus making a new Will. He said it wus fair considering what lay in the past. Your grandfather openly admitted the bet wus not won fair and square. He asked your dad not to take the same path as him and demanded that his wishes be honoured. My Mum said it wus a terrible Christmas. Your dad wus stomping around like a bear with a sore head but your grandfather wouldn't give in and blow me down, he popped his clogs before things could be sealed. Some say your dad had something to do with it.'

Father Michael sprang to life. 'Mrs Tooley! There is no shred of evidence to suggest Charles Black murdered his own father. You cannot go around casting aspersions based on gossip.'

She stiffened. 'Many a true word spoken in gossip.'

'It's many a true word spoken in jest,' he corrected.

'What's there to laugh about?' Ignoring Father Michael's stern authority, she turned to Jason with zeal. 'Ever asked yewself why your dad married the doctor's daughter the same year your grandfather died...and quickly.' She got to her feet. 'Your mother, Katherine, God Bless her soul, I heard wus not exactly the best catch in the world what with her being ten years older than your dad.'

The men watched her squirrel back to the kitchen and it was Father Michael who said, 'Do not pay too much attention to Mrs Tooley. She has a good heart but spends much of her time gossiping.'

'Would Elizabeth agree with your thoughts, I think not. Is it any wonder such animosity delivers evil into this world? The question we face is how to undo what has been done.'

'And what has been done, Jason? You cannot change the past. Let us try to get things in perspective. Do you know for certain this puzzle is out to cause malevolence or out to offer the truth?'

Jason held his breath then exhaled as though he hardly knew the answer himself. 'So far nothing untoward has happened but I just have this bad feeling something will. I remember waking from the dream as though it was sinister yet it clouded over quickly when I recalled Luze. I know there are more pieces to be connected and I suspect the next riddle may just be about Tom Turner, who knows. Yesterday, it was so very cold in the factory, in fact unbearably cold. It never felt natural. Maybe it's my imagination but I hesitate to wonder about the last line on the riddle....waiting for revision. How can I undo what has been done, Michael?'

'I have no personal experience of apparitions, if indeed they are but I do believe there are tormented souls refusing to leave their earthly bounds. As doctrine to a faith that performs exorcism, I may be tempted to write to Father Levin. But from what I gather it would appear there is more to this puzzle. Perhaps to reveal the truth is part of your destiny. Pray to God and ask him to forgive the sins of your ancestor and seek for his guidance.'

'I need more than prayers, Michael. I need to find a remedy to cure the ill.'

It was a matter of necessity. Jason was prepared to embrace not just his destiny but that of his brother against the unfathomable jigsaw puzzle. But he could not escape the feeling of trepidation, the imaginings that things will get far worse before they get better.

The rain had abated. In its place, the clouds grew lighter and the wind played spitefully about his legs while he crossed the road toward the Manor. When he entered the house, he took off his jacket and hat, placed them on the coat stand and called out for Luze. No response, so he raced the stairs, taking the treads two by two, falling into an empty room. The fire was lit but she was not there and it worried him. He went to his desk and looked down at five little piles of jigsaw pieces just like his dream. She had logically separated all the different sizes and set them apart. Then his eyes wandered to the puzzle on the tray, the latest pieces fitted, what she had achieved to date and it proved to be as he suspected.

But when it came, he cried and tried,

it was to make amend.

Half his worth upon his death,

the message he doeth send.

In spite of that his son returned

to thwart a true decision.

The past lay deep in grief and pain,

waiting for revision.

Believing dangerous days were to follow, he reached for his worn out suitcase on top of the wardrobe, brought it down on the bed and flipped up the lid. Before him, lay the answer to his irrational thinking. He withdrew a shiny steel gun from its leather holster and flicked the chamber. It twizzled at speed. Then, while he was filling the chamber with bullets Luze walked in and gasped.

'Why do you have a gun?'

'Luze, I'm afraid for you.'

She pinched his cheek. 'It's different for men, they only have to worry about one penis, and women have to worry about everyone else's.'

He chuckled. 'Do you ever take things seriously?'

'Mammy says I'm like a little girl skipping in the wind. But she forgets I am a grown woman with a sense of humour.' She pushed the suitcase aside and lay back on the bed, propped up by her elbows with legs dangling over the side. 'Did you know it takes seventeen muscles to smile and thirty-four to scowl? So why do we double our efforts to be unhappy?'

'That is a very interesting analogy.' He sat beside her, placed his hands behind his head and also lay back. 'We have to scowl in order to tighten our muscle formation. If not, our laughing muscles would create more wrinkles.'

'Does everything have to be analysed in scientific terms?'

'I live with discipline every day.'

She turned on her side to face him, reaching out to touch his past. 'How did you get those scars?'

Despite his awkwardness, he smiled. 'It happened a long time ago.' Then he glanced up and took a quick inventory of the ornate ceiling rose. Could he tell her his thoughts, he wondered, could he place his heart in her hands as easily as she was now placing her head on his shoulder? 'Luze,' he said in an almost whisper. 'Will you have dinner with me tonight?'

'How would that be possible when so much is going on?'

'Surely we can find some time together.' Then it occurred. 'Where did you go?'

'I popped to the factory. It was freezing and the workers walked out. You know that cutter? Well, it started up all by itself.'

So it has begun. 'Did anything else happen?'

'Well, one cannot be certain if it was mass hysteria or what but Tony claimed he had seen the ghost of Molly Turner. He was ever so funny, running around like a headless chicken and hiding in the store room. Misery led a revolt and the men walked out. I left Tony to cover up the cutter. He was not a happy man.'

'I suppose this doesn't bode well for the factory, does it, Luze. Your father is not going to take on a menacing phantom, if in fact it is a phantom.'

'Nuts, it doesn't matter,' she said sitting up. 'My Father wants to pull that factory down. I shouldn't be telling you this but he sees a new factory on this land.'

'So why bother with any equipment. The workers will be out on their ear.'

'No, because while they work in the old factory, he will be building a new one then he will install a new cutter, state of the art. It can outrun the four of your old die cuts.'

'So he's going to pull this house down?'

'Please, don't say anything to Tony,' she pleaded. 'I think he has a fondness for this drafty old place.'

In a way, so did he. 'What about the cottages?'

'Oh, he will upgrade them. He's a good business man, Nuts. He wants to keep the workers on and pay them a decent wage, and they will have their own pension schemes.'

'Perhaps this is why you were part of my dream. Perhaps you are the answer to make the revision, to give something back to this community.'

'Do you think so?' As she platted her hair with extreme dexterity, Jason looked on in wonderment. 'How do I look?' She asked.

He held her gaze and it all welled up within him. 'You look beautiful.' He had never paid such a compliment to a woman but it was a mere statement of fact.

'So what exactly do you do?'

'I am a chemist by trade,' he replied sitting up. 'But I also branch into physics, the two really go hand in hand so I sort of cross the bridges and explore.'

'After the deal, are you going back to Boston? I know you love it here. I've seen how you are with these people and how you worry about them. Why did you leave?' She paused for his answer. There was none. 'You don't like talking about your past, do you?'

'I say chaps,' Tony strode in, his eyes went to the gun which had slipped to the floor. He picked it up, saying to Jason, 'this is bloody fantastic. Where did you get it?'

'Most men in America carry guns to defend themselves.'

Tony closed one eye and sent his sight skimming along the line of the barrel as though he was aiming up a target. Suddenly it went off! A bullet flew through a single pane, glass cracked, bits clinked and chinked to the floor and they all peered down to focus on a lifeless blackbird, its feathers cruelly stark and spread on the gravel driveway.

Jason snatched the gun. 'You cannot run a business, you cannot iron, you cannot cook and most certainly you cannot handle a gun. What are you good at?'

'Obviously not bloody much. I just killed one of my relatives. Did Luze tell you what happened at the factory?'

'Yes.' And then Jason went on to explain the story told by Mrs Tooley earlier that day.

By which time, the question of taking Luze out for a meal had been abandoned, replaced by Mrs Tooley's pie. They then settled in the drawing room with all its past trappings, and profound works of art that appeared priceless to the untutored eye.

Tony passed over a mug to Jason, sat down on the sofa and crossed his legs. 'The bastard poisoned Granddad and Robert Graves knew. The ultimate cover up, a doctor able to sign the death certificate, no questions asked, no inquest. He must have been pretty desperate to palm off his daughter. I thought Mum looked quiet pretty in the photographs.'

'It would appear there was considerable truth in the gossip,' Jason said. 'The first riddle confirms the waiting for revision and when it was about to come, the old man interfered. It makes you wonder what else there is to know.'

Luze padded into the drawing room with a plate of biscuits sending her eyes in different directions. 'Tony, where did you put my coffee?'

'I left it on the draining board.'

'Tony!' She frustrated and turned on her heels.

Keeping his voice low, he asked Jason, 'did you have some pussy?'

'What is wrong with you? We are in the middle of a crisis and all you have on your mind is sex.'

'And you don't?'

Alone he would agree.

'He must have known.' Luze reappeared with her coffee and Jason thought thank God for that. 'Your mother must fit in this somewhere. Can you be sure she had pneumonia? Perhaps she was bumped off too.'

Jason picked up a photograph. Her hair was the same straw colour as his and he wondered if she too suffered with an unruly crown, wondered how much she understood and wondered again if she asked any questions about her husband's behaviour. 'I have vague memories of Mother but we never had much to do with her parents, the Graves. In fact, I cannot remember them at all.'

'So what do we know so far?' Luze needed to summarise and settled by the hearth with her knees curled up to her chin. 'Edward Black swindles Captain Turner out of his wife's land. She, Elizabeth, lands up with her two children in one of the cottages and working in the factory. Then, obviously, through bad working practices, her daughter Molly dies and Edward takes her son under his wing.' She looked up to Jason who was leaning against the mantelpiece. 'Your father came home from the war in 1945, just before Christmas, which gave very little time for him to acquaint himself with Katherine before he popped off your grandfather in the early part of 1946.'

'And your point?' Jason asked.

'You have to exclude your mother as co-conspirator. A woman needs far more than a few weeks to be cajoled as an accessory for murder. I think your father was desperate to get rid of your grandfather as soon as he realised his Will was going to be changed. He had to stop him quickly but he needed an ally, a doctor able to sign the death certificate so he made a play for the doctor's daughter, Katherine. He offered her marriage then her father was confronted with a dilemma. Suddenly, there is Edward Black, dead but what of? Robert Graves had his suspicions but if he speaks of his suspicions his daughter's happiness is in jeopardy and, who knows, in those days fathers wanted their daughters off their hands. After all, she was ten years older than your father, virtually left on the shelf. Thus far, Robert Graves signs the death certificate, hitherto Charles marries Katherine and then you two are born. What Elizabeth and her son felt is anyone's guess. They must have viewed your father a greater monster than Edward, wouldn't you say?'

'I go along with that,' Jason agreed. 'So these other pieces, what else is there to learn? How worse can it get?' Just then the clock struck nine and his mind was on that anvil of creation. He looked down at Luze. 'Would you like to go to Norwich?'

She shook her head. 'I think we should go to the Pig and Whistle. We must show unity and concern.'

It was not the answer he expected but all things considered, she was right. He left his cup of coffee on the mantelpiece and grabbed his hat and leather jacket off the coat stand in the hall. Luze had borrowed one of Tony's jumpers and it swamped her. A pang of jealousy swept through him. It was an emotion he had never felt before and like the chemist he was he started to analyse the composition of endorphins.

Closing the front door behind them, Jason walked on and suddenly felt fingers threading through his. He looked to the side of him and smiled down at Luze. She appeared just as eager to make that attachment and the emotion of jealousy was immediately supplanted by the emotion of longing. *Luze*, he said her name softly just to be certain, just to be sure it was her hand he was clutching and not a dream. He wanted to tell her how he felt. He wanted to say he owned the world with her beside him but he was frightened, scarcely believing he was heading towards a part of his dream that could possibly come true.

The village was wrapped up in a mask of night with its own smells and sounds. They walked to the end of the drive with the Catholic Church clearly outlined ahead, then turned left, crossed the road and headed towards the Pig and Whistle while the wind was gathering speed, slapping their faces and making an effort to be heard.

Here, where it was like walking into a miasma of smoke from puffing pipes and lit cigarettes, Jason was the first to notice a different atmosphere from last night. Voices were in whispers, groupings were tight and faces looked up, inquisitively, as though expecting some answers. He turned to Franny Whistle, a red-head busty and blowzy lady with freckles burning on her cheeks, born to run a pub, never short in coming forward with her thoughts.

'What's going on in that factory of yours?'

'Nothing.'

'That's a funny nothing.'

'Hey,' Tony said, digging deep in his pockets. 'We're on the case.'

'And wat case is that?' Misery voiced out, emerging from a dimly lit corner with an empty pint mug in his hand. 'I hear the temperature is colder in your past than in your factory. Thass a possessed cutter.' He paused to a room backing him up. 'Are we to be kept in the dark as to wat really happened to Molly Turner?'

'And what do you know of Molly Turner?' Jason asked.

'We hear there's more than meets the eye.'

Arr, more than meets the eye.

'We're not going in until that factory gets back to normal.'

Arr, not until it gets back to normal.

Tony angered at the dissent. 'I see loyalty is fast becoming a thing of the past!'

Argument followed. The currents of dissent were strong, personal enmities, alliances and interests emerging or fragmenting.

'Stop!' Jason yelled with all his lung power. Instantly, the snug went silent. Everyone froze in a tableau of gaping mouths. It had served its purpose, had quelled disunity. 'Drinks are on me.' Everyone scrambled to the bar. He kept his expression inscrutable, but lowered one eyelid at Luze in a furtive wink.

She blew him a kiss and said, 'Once we have completed the puzzle, we shall look back on this and smile.'

'Ah, hum, we have a slight problem, chaps. There are some pieces missing.' Tony stared at their suppressed mouths. 'I counted 351. Now logically, it should be a 400 piece jigsaw so that means 49 pieces are missing.'

'Why didn't you mention this before?' Luze asked.

'I forgot, okay? I just forgot.'

'We need those pieces.' Jason said. 'They must be somewhere in the factory. The boxes you discarded. Where did you put them?'

'In the rubbish bin.'

'Then that is your starting point. Luze, what would you like to drink?'

'Not for me, thank you.'

Jason looked at her for a long moment and worried about her position. He sat down on a stool and leaned his hands on his knees, rubbing his palms gently up and down the worn jeans. 'Luze, you need to go home. I can see we have placed you in a ticklish situation.'

'I should telephone my Father.'

'And what will you say?' Tony worried.

'I can hardly tell him the truth. He would never believe me. But I have to stay because I might be here to make the amendment. Nuts, you stay here with Tony. Keep him company.'

'Luze,' Tony asked before she left. 'When you speak to your father, is there any chance in putting a good word for me?'

'And what do you wish me to say? That your resume reads like a graveyard and it's still in working progress?'

She brushed past Tony and for the first time, Jason noticed the shadows beneath her eyes, the fatigue and weariness in her face. He recognised in her expression the fear and uncertainty that walked hand in hand with loyalty. 'You know damn well the predicament we placed Luze in. And you have the temerity to ask her for favours.'

'Hey, smack my hand, why don't you! She's the one who went over her father's head and came here. It's not my fault that pieces are missing.'

'I suggest the factory remains closed.'

'I can't close the factory! If I don't fulfil those orders, the men won't get paid.'

'I shall cover any shortfall.'

'That's damn decent of you, Squirt. I'll pay you back.'

'I am concerned about Luze being left on her own. With Tools she is safe but if Susan turns up, there's no telling what will happen. You stay here and inform the men. A little public relations exercise wouldn't go amiss.'

Without an upward glance, Jason stepped out of the Pig and Whistle. Headlights bucked and swayed as it picked its way down the lane. The mini caught up and sent a wash of gutter puddles over his boots. Ten squidgy minutes later, he breathed a sigh of relief. Susan's car was not in the drive. Impelled by impatience, he rushed the front step of the Manor and strode into the hall. The lights were off, apart from the one on the landing. Heading upstairs, a kaleidoscope of possibilities exploded behind his eyes. He had journeyed the dream now he wanted to journey the reality, the impossible made possible. In his mind a single thought.

He rapped a knuckle gently on her door. 'Luze, we need to talk.'

'What about?'

'I would prefer to see you rather than wood.'

She opened the door. Barefoot, she was so much smaller than he and that seemed only to increase his terrible hunger.

'Did you speak to your father?'

'I chickened out.' She went to the fireplace warming her hands. 'I just couldn't do it, Nuts. It would mean I would lie to Pappy and I didn't want to lie and I didn't know what else to do.'

'I promise we shall get this sorted.'

'Oh I do hope so. Pappy has been angling to get a foothold in England for ages. He was so keyed up to get this one.'

'Why?'

'Because it's a bargain.' She looked away. 'I'm not very good at negotiations, am I? I suppose you will be haggling over the price.'

'The price is a done deal, no going back.' He placed his finger under her chin and gently pulled her face towards him. 'Did you know there is symmetry between us?'

'Symmetry?'

'An object is symmetrical if an action carried out on it leaves it apparently unchanged. In other words, if you close your eyes for a moment, then when you open them again you are unable to say whether I have carried out an action or not. Shall we test the theory?'

Luze regarded him for a moment then closed her eyes. He lightly touched upon her lips like a floating snow flake on a dessert floor and still this was not enough.

'Luze, where we stand is where my dream embraced symmetry in your arms. Is it possible to test that theory too?'

'I have to be honest with you, Nuts. I am spoken for.'

'Spoken for, as in married, spoken for?'

Luze shook her head and he breathed a sigh of relief. 'Jeremy Hubbard, my Father's right-hand man. Well, I am engaged to him, or rather Pappy agreed on my behalf to marry him.'

'Do you love him?'

'I have known him since childhood.'

'That does not answer my question.'

Events had brought them close, sexual union could bring them closer. His lips wandered on her face, to her neck, his hands to the small of her back pulling her into him.

'Luze,' he whispered, 'answer my question.'

'No,' she softly replied.

RIDDLE OF MARIA O'GRADY

Jason with his head in the clouds carefully opened the door to her room, sneakily spilled his near dark eyes each way along the corridor then tiptoed downstairs to the kitchen and confidently punched his fist in the air and voiced, YES!

After making coffee, he strolled into the drawing room with a grin plastered on his face. There he stayed until he heard creaks and sighs coming from upstairs, the flush of a toilet and slow footsteps descending. He went to the interconnecting doors, stood partly hidden in the shadows to swim in her movements, feeling like an ant in a jungle overwhelmed by its opulent clusters. She was moving among shining saucepans and breathless pot-plants whose cool green leaves scattered the ledges and caressed the caddies.

'You look lovely,' he said.

'Oh!' She startled, turned and he lived forever in that smile. 'Have you been up long?'

'I never slept,' knowing full well she had.

He worked his arms about her as she spoke with girlish smiles and giggles, her hair hung loose and something else he could not readily identify, sweetness that was hers alone.

'Hey!' Tony yelled, striding in, the consequence of having an indiscrete brother. 'I figured it out. If your father wants to keep on the workers and buy new machinery, he will want to install the latest cutter and that won't fit in the factory. You're going to pull this house down, aren't you? Did you know about this, Squirt?'

In the dumb silence that followed, Jason noticed his twin had not shaven for two days and that his hair was unkempt, his eyes showing the obvious signs of worry as they shifted from one to the other.

'I was not privy to details,' Jason finally admitted. 'But yes, I was made aware of this yesterday.'

'And where am I going to live when I buy back my business?'

'Nooo,' Luze said, working her hair into a plait. 'What makes you think you can do that?'

'Luze,' Jason intercepted quickly. 'I promised Tony to stay here and work something out for his future.'

'That's wonderful, Nuts. What sort of thing did you have in mind?'

'Err, I have yet to establish that.' A lie?

She held Tony's troubled brown eyes. 'You might as well know, Pappy has big plans and will never sell.'

'I want this business back,' he jibed.

'Well you can't have it back!'

'You don't know that for sure!'

'If you knew my Father, you wouldn't say that!'

'Enough!' Jason split them apart. 'You're acting like a pair of quarrelling siblings instead of mature business people. We have greater imperatives than worrying about assets. I'm going to skip breakfast and make more enquiries about the Turners. Tony, I want you to go to the factory and search in those bins. Luze, you stay here and try to finish off the puzzle. Do I make myself understood?'

They nodded in synchronization.

Jason walked off smiling. Regardless how they behaved, he realised these two had established a warm relationship of sorts but how deep it went confused him. Luze had made her mark so easily and quickly in the Manor as though she belonged forever, and Tony had taken advantage of her good nature. But now was not the time to analyse it further.

In the high street, sitting on the low wall outside the pharmacy, Jason saw a young man with a sketchpad, pencilling in an outline of the cottages opposite. He did not recognise the face but the face seemed to recognise him. 'Hello, Mr Black,' the voice called out and how Jason began to hate that name, his own name that held privilege in the ranks of notable chemists. He remembered the way people used to look up to the Blacks when he played pirates with his chums on the river. Did they ever view him with respect? Did they ever know about his ancestor's past? Of course they did, he thought. They looked up with fear not with reverence in their eyes.

So it was to some degree that Jason's first port of call should rest at Father Michael's feet, privy to past events. But this priest was unable to shed further light, had somehow managed to persuade Jason to kneel in contrition while anointing his forehead, not that he had an apology to make.

As Jason walked out of the church he smacked into Tony. 'What are you doing here?'

'Luze sent me to keep you company.'

'And?'

'Susan turned up looking pretty smug. Luze locked herself in your bedroom. The factory is like the arctic, bloody freezing. There were icicles on that cutter, Squirt.'

'Did you find the other boxes?'

'Ah, yes...good question, a very good question.'

Jason held his hand to his ear. 'I cannot hear the answer.'

'The thing is Misery put a match to them to create more room for the rest of the rubbish. I know you're a bit pissed off with my big mouth but why would one box, a box I might add, picked out from all the rest have some of its pieces in other boxes?'

'Mmm, you may have a point.' Satisfied with that, unsure what his next move should be. 'I wonder who pays for Molly's grave to be serviced each year.'

'Would it do any good to dig Molly up?' Tony joked. 'I mean if her body wasn't there then we'd know we have a walking zombie.' And snapping his fingers, he added, 'Perhaps that's it, a walking menace, come to haunt the Blacks.'

One had to make allowances. 'I question who made the puzzle in the first place and why.'

'Since it's not of this world it can be anyone's guess. So far, we have one suspect, Molly. What we don't know is whether Tom or his mother is still alive.'

Jason's eyes turned baleful, coming across his father's grave. 'Based on what Tools has related, if I were Elizabeth, I would find some way to seek revenge upon our family.' He walked on until he found Molly's headstone. 'Maybe you were on to something.' Then he squinted back, nodded and said, 'Odd the old man should die on the same date. Perhaps it's not a coincidence.'

'Do you think the pieces are hidden in Molly's coffin?'

'Other events happened after Molly died.'

'You think they might be in Dad's coffin.'

'I really worry about you, Tony. Am I to assume you were always like this or shall I put it down to Susan messing with your head?'

'Look, it was just a thought. Any idea is better than none.'

'I cannot remember a Tom Turner or Elizabeth Turner. Do you see their headstones here?'

'Yew wus little mites when he went to prison.' It was the lone voice of Mrs Tooley. Her tightly curled hair shone bright in the mid-day winter sun while she folded her apron in ritual. 'His mum left the village along with Maria O'Grady.'

'Who is Maria O'Grady?' Tony asked.

'She wus a pretty young thing...worked for Franny's parents behind the bar. I know it wus the same year your poor mum died. Franny would know more.' She sighed, staring at Molly's headstone. 'Never had much luck, the Turners...still, never mind. I'm off to yours.'

'Tools, keep an eye on Luze. Susan is there.'

'Don't yew worry, Jason,' she sniggered into her folded apron. 'I won't let any harm come to that little angel.'

Laughter was forced and nervous in the Pig and Whistle. Occupants looked into their mugs or at their own hands, wariness in their faces until Tony went over to speak to them.

'Two of your best, please, Fran.' Jason asked.

Franny avoided eye contact, pulling at the pumps behind rows of brass bells. He wondered what tale she could reveal to offer enlightenment, and would that enlightenment be pleasant? Franny Whistle was roughly the same as age as him but he never forgot how he laid at her nimble mercy at junior school. At a time when country schooling was little more than a cane-whacking interlude in which boys picked up facts like bruises and the girls scarcely counted at all, her modest ambition was to run after him. She would chase him through the playground with a tennis racket, angry he had stolen her balls.

'Anything else?' She voiced sharply.

'Sorry about last night, Fran. It was uncalled for.' But she remained quiet as he passed over the money. 'Is anything the matter?'

Franny leaned over the bar, dropping her voice to a harsh whisper. 'Come round the back and be discrete.' She took him past stacks of crated fruit juices and out to an open yard housing empty firkins. The seven foot high perimeter brick wall was frosted, a deposit of ice crystals. 'Woke up this morning and this is what confronted me, near had my fingers off. Don't you be telling anyone or my business will suffer. There's enough strange talk going on about your factory.'

Grimly, he poked a finger at the wall and pulled back with the bite of permafrost.

'And don't give me a lecture on winter,' she told him. 'This isn't natural.'

'What do you know about Maria O'Grady?'

'Has this got anything to do with your new lady friend?'

'Why do you say that?'

'Misery said the trouble started when she arrived.'

'Utter nonsense. Her father is going to take over Strident Cutter and everyone here, including you, will benefit. Now what do you know about Maria O'Grady?'

'She was a looker,' Franny obliged. 'So my Dad reckoned. She came on the scene just after the New Year in 1950 because that was the year Uncle Sid drowned in the river with his goat. She never stayed long, not after that fight with your father.'

'What fight?'

'How do you think he got that limp?'

'He said he was wounded on the Normandy Beaches.'

'Aww, what rubbish. You know full well your father was one for porkies. Spent most of his time based in Lincoln, dodging propellers. The whole village knows how he got that limp. April Fool's Day, right on the button, three months after Maria O'Grady turned up. Tom Turner was waiting for your father right outside this pub, foaming at the mouth like a wild dog. They were at each other's throats and Tom stuck him with a knife.' Her eyes went vacant. 'There was something fishy about that.'

'Fishy?'

'I remember Dad saying it took three of them to get Tom off your father. Apparently, Tom was angry for not having his own way with your grandfather's business. But my Mum said that fight was over something different. Everyone seemed to like Tom. He even bought me liquorice sticks.'

'What happened to Tom and his mother? Did you know Elizabeth?'

'He got shipped off to prison and died there. Elizabeth left with the O'Grady girl. No-one knew where they went, probably back to Ireland. That's where she was born, in Ireland, the O'Grady girl.'

'Fran, think carefully. Did my Father ever have a thing for Maria O'Grady?'

She burst into mocking amusement, nudging him in the ribs. 'All the men had a thing for the O'Grady girl, especially your father.' Then she hummed, running a finger around her chin. 'This is only gossip, so don't quote me. But some say around these parts the fight was about her.'

Jason closed his eyes as though he was trying to summon up the past, eager to envisage what might have happened where he stood. Could it be a terrible deed had taken place in the dark, late at night in this quiet back yard?

In the weeks that led up to April Fool's Day, 1950, Charles Black had felt the gossip of rebuttal, the humiliation and ridicule as Maria spurned him more than once. Life in the Manor sitting sweetly by the river became intolerable. He sulked, raged at his wife, angered at the whining of his three year old twins and neglected his duties at Strident Cutter, all for the want of Maria. Then, on that fateful night, nursing a sharp and sensitive pain, he watched her laughing and talking, and sending her smiles to others but not him. Whore, he thought, she does this purposefully, wants to tease me, to bring me to my knees. As he endlessly tracked her movements across the gnarled and knotted floor at the Pig and Whistle, he believed for one second she had beckoned him. No better timing than when she stepped outside to bring in the refills, bottles stored in the yard. The pub was noisy by then, locals gulping down pints and raising their voices to each other.

'Well, if it isn't my little pretty,' Charles said closing in, 'what have you saved for me?'

Maria backed away, against the wall and thought of Tom, of how he might avenge her. She had few weapons with which to resist. It lasted as long as it would take to heat up milk on a stove, a crude and rough moment where he was careful not to leave a mark that would otherwise offer a tell-tale sign.

'You would do well to say nothing of this,' he said doing up his fly. 'I hold weight in this village. It would be your word against mine.'

The parting was abrupt but the incident never went unnoticed. Tom walked in with his usual smile and right away Maria whispered hoarsely in his ear. His eyes narrowed to the man he despised. Then he strode outside to wait in a murderous zone, the night cool and misty yet bitterly frosty in his heart. The encounter was planned to the point of precision.

'Black!' Tom shouted, the clamour of an angry voice demanding justice.' You have the breeding of a bastard commoner!'

'She gave herself freely, opened up to a better man.'

The eyes of Tom Turner shone with vehemence and certainty as he swiftly came forward and flayed his enemy to the ground. From a skirmish it became a frenzied attack, savaging blows returned with the same force, defending, deflecting and seizing moments to cause bodily harm. Charles was advantage both in the art of combat and with what lay in the lining of his coat pocket. As he pulled out a knife, it seemed to be the choice of weapon where both knew the odds tipped in Charles's favour. But after an ill judged move, Charles stumbled and the blade went wide. Tom seized the moment and kicked it out of his hand, raced to retrieve it then buried the steel edge into his enemy's leg, rendering Charles crippled for an enduring battle.

In spite of that, three random shouts and interjection held Tom at bay, physically dragging him off a blood soaked Charles. They were attempting to make sense of the enveloping chaos. And Charles was quick to lay blame, to account for his actions, to vilify Maria and to openly scorn Tom Turner.

'She's a whore, trying to seduce me so I would part with my shares.'

'Lying seems to be the currency of your world, Black!'

Charles turned to John Whistle. 'Look at the knife, John. Is that not a cutter's knife. You know I have no need to work the cutters. He was plotting to get the business and when I returned from the war, he claimed I had no right to share in my father's estate. Often, he spoke how unfortunate I never died on the battlefield. My only mistake was to show leniency, keep him on as my father wished.'

Tom spoke. 'It was you who plotted and schemed to get rid of your father, seeking help from Robert Graves, your accomplice!'

This was a daring accusation. What chance for Tom now? He had sealed his fate, and nobody, not even the County Court thought to exhume Edward Black's body.

As Maria and Elizabeth mind-numbingly looked on to see Tom Turner dragged by his heels to serve time behind bars a plan was in the making. By all things human there was something far worse to offer into this world of pain, a cruel induction to make it entirely worthwhile.

Outside, with the day almost gone, the twins processed the pavement very slowly with despondency. There was no evidence to suggest Maria had been raped or if the fight was really about her but the indications were pointing that way.

'Fran was too young to remember what was said outside the pub that night but I am pretty certain the fight had something to do with Maria O'Grady.' Jason sighed without an upward glance. 'Mother died later that year. Perhaps she knew, perhaps it weakened her immune system and she just fell foul to pneumonia.'

'But where the hell was her father?' Tony angered. 'What was he doing? He was the doctor, for God's sake. Can we assume he packed up and left?'

'I would hazard a guess and say yes.'

'Do you have any doubt about Graves covering up Grandad's death?'

'None whatsoever...if we are to believe in the puzzle's sincerity and with the facts we know to date, I am convinced he was party to murder. When we go in be careful what you say in front of Susan.'

'Do you think she knows any of this?'

'Perhaps, perhaps not...most of the village seems to know. You never mentioned anything about the puzzle, did you?'

'No way, Squirt.'

Bracing themselves for a tense atmosphere, instead they heard laughter and smelt the evening meal of home cooking. They looked at each other in silent communication then walked into a kitchen which was swirling with smoke and light, under the supervision of Mrs Tooley.

'About time,' Mrs Tooley said with a steak and kidney pie in her oven-gloved hands. She slammed the oven door with her foot and laid the pie on a place mat. 'Now all yew hev to do is drain the peas and spuds,' she told Susan. 'Pour the gravy from the pan into the jug. Can yew do that?'

'Do I look that stupid?'

'Suit yerself. I'm off.'

There was a degree of courtesy as Jason took a chair and made sure he would sit next to Luze. Luze smiled and said nothing while Susan dished up. When it came to serving, she had no method, a dab on each plate in any old order, the peas rolled about and the crust on the pie sunk into the middle as the knife went in.

'Well,' Susan said sitting down. 'Isn't this cosy.'

'Where have you been?' Tony directed his question to Susan.

Susan ignored him and looked across the table. Her eyes flickered to Luze then to Jason who sat directly opposite. 'So, Jason, I understand you've been a busy boy.'

'Meaning?' He muffled.

'Come now,' she said, toying with her food. 'Let's not pussy foot around. Luze has laid her cards on the table and I agree. The business should be sold to Claggart.' Tony choked on a piece of meat and she slapped his back hard, sarcastically voicing, 'are you alright, my darling?'

Tony gasped for air, finally spilling out his words hoarsely. 'What changed your sodding mind?'

'Why do you always assume I work against your interests?'

'Now see here, Susan, let me give you a piece of advice.'

'My dear, don't give anything to a woman she cannot wear.'

Luze burst out laughing, waving her hand in front of her face. 'Sorry, but it was rather funny. I told Susan the cottages would be up-dated in time. They can make a nice home, even if they appear very small, especially against the spaciousness of this Manor.'

Jason stared at Susan who looked particularly chic in a tailored red dress, her eyes glistening to the ghost of her past. 'Are you telling us you're prepared to move into one of the cottages and work your butt off in the factory?'

'No,' she told him. 'I am confirming that whatever papers Tony needs me to sign, I shall not hinder or thwart the buy out. My incompetent husband can move into a worker's cottage and get his hands dirty. As for me, well, let's not be coy. We all know a divorce is imminent, so now is the time to go our separate ways.'

'What? Just like that?' Tony said, shifting in his seat.

'Have you changed your mind?' Susan asked.

And then the argument started.

Jason winced and turned to Luze, whose lips were parted as she hung on their every word with rapt attention. 'Do you like steak and kidney?' He asked.

Luze locked on to his eyes for a brief moment and nodded.

'Her gravy can be a little lumpy,' he tried again then he heard his name, and was reluctantly drawn towards Susan. 'You know my feelings. Make your own way in life.'

'Luze, did I tell you how I met Jason?' At that point, Jason wished he could fall into a black hole. 'He was studying to become a chemist of sorts. There was a time when he asked me to marry him. Isn't that so, Jason?'

He swallowed hard and said nothing.

'Of course,' Susan went on, 'typically him, he ran away from his responsibilities.'

Jason had no more patience to pretend otherwise and threw down his knife and fork. 'Okay, Susan. If you want to play dirty, let's play dirty. Before you completely poison her mind, remind me what you were doing with my brother.'

'I say, Squirt, is all this necessary?'

'The truth should always come out in the open.' Luze said and the table went quiet. 'And no-one seems to know the truth except Mrs Tooley.'

'That cow is a meddling frump,' Susan hissed. 'She forgets her place in this household.'

'If you feel that way, why do you keep her on?' Luze asked.

Tony opened his mouth to speak but Susan shot back. 'We keep her on because my stupid husband thinks she's the answer to everything around here. If it had been left up to me, I would've got rid of her years ago.'

'It must be hard for you, Susan,' Luze said in placatory tones. 'I mean, it must be awful to live under such intolerable circumstance, whispers behind your back and...'

'What whispers?'

'How you feigned your pregnancy.'

The suggestion put the torch to Susan's temper. She shot to her feet and threw her serviette across at Luze. 'That cow is a liar! Tony, tell her. Tell her how I lost my baby.'

But Tony kept quiet, along with Jason, absorbing new information.

Luze held up a fork and pointed it toward Susan. 'You are a very deceitful woman. You played the oldest trick in the book. When you saw no prospect in Jason, you made a play for Tony.'

'Oh, listen to Miss Goody Two Shoes! What would your father say about Jason going between your legs?'

'That's enough!' Jason pushed back his chair. 'Return to your make-believe world and leave us in peace.'

Susan walked round and held a finger and thumb a centimetre apart, close to his face. 'You are that near to oblivion, Jason Black. She may be grateful just to be eclipsed by the long shadow of your accomplishments but mark my words. I will have the last laugh.'

When she walked off, the room fell silent and Jason never moved. He ran the images through his head over and over, each time altering some detail, all of them horrible. A hand clamped on his shoulder.

'Forget it, Squirt. She's mental.'

Jason looked back at Luze, her expression unchanging. 'What you said. Is it true?'

'The guilt was written all over her face.' Luze began to collect the plates. 'Mrs Tooley lightly skipped over the details but we both agreed the likelihood of Susan being pregnant was a million to one. All it needed was a little pushing in the right direction. No matter how long ago, any woman who had lost her baby would burst into tears or show terrible sadness. I never saw any of that, did you?'

Jason glowed. This was no ordinary little girl skipping in the wind. In his eyes she was beautiful, resourceful, and witty. Against Susan, there was no comparison and he felt deeply for his brother. A certain grandiosity and priggishness may have been fully fledged in Susan from the beginning but he knew Susan had conceit and a certain cunning counterbalanced by some very winnings ways.

'Are you going to tell me what you two have been up to?' Luze asked at the sink.

'Did you finish the puzzle, Luze?' Jason asked.

'Yes, and another riddle came up. It was not very nice. There was no name but it refers to Irish eyes.'

At that, Tony left the kitchen and Jason slipped up behind Luze. He nuzzled her neck, whispered in her ear, smelled and touched her skin. 'Please do not think ill of me.'

She turned with her hands held high, soap bubbles running down her arms. 'Nuts, it's not your fault. Tony is the one who caught a cold. Are you going to tell me what you've been up to?'

He kissed her quickly on the lips. 'Dry your hands and come up to my room. I need to see the riddle.'

Unsure where Susan had got to, Jason opened the front door to see if her Mercedes was still there. It was. He closed the door glumly and went upstairs thinking of his brother's misery.

'I was a stupid prick,' Jason said and pulled Tony's head towards him. 'At the very least, I could have had it out with you before leaving.'

'Seven frickin years I put up with her crap. You're right, I am frickin stupid.'

'No, never say that. Your problem is your penis. It should be between your legs not in your head. Now keep focused. I promise you a better future.' Jason glanced at the riddle. 'Well, well, it seems we were right.'

> *Alas this son did not desist*
>
> *when he sought a certain lust.*
>
> *Black, said he to Irish eyes,*
>
> *your words are lost in dust.*
>
> *Yet to the rescue came a man*
>
> *to fight on one condition.*
>
> *The past lay deep in grief and pain,*
>
> *waiting for revision.*

After reading the verse for a second time, Jason collapsed on the bed, placing his hands behind his head. 'Tony, why did we not hear about this before? Okay, I went off to Boston but still, we were twenty at the time, old enough to be told about what went on.'

Luze walked in with tea and biscuits and placed the tray by the hearth. 'I thought a nice cuppa would go down well.'

Jason propped himself up on his elbows. 'Luze, the girl in the riddle is Maria O'Grady. Franny at the Pig and Whistle filled in the blanks. Apparently, there was a fight outside the pub on April Fool's Day in 1950 between the old man and Tom Turner. Tom was Maria's sweetheart.'

'What happened to Tom?' Luze asked.

'He died in prison.'

'And what happened to Maria?'

'We think she left this village with Tom's mother,' Tony said. 'Also, Franny's back wall is covered in permafrost, just like the cutter. It came this morning.'

'Wow, it's like a horror movie. Let's hope we have seen the worst.'

Tony snorted. 'Fat chance of that happening.'

'Look on the bright side. We have Jason.' She fluttered her eye lids. 'And he has a gun.'

Jason grinned, sharing her enjoyment. 'And my aim is better than yours.'

'Now see here, Squirt. There's so much insult a man can take from his brother. I may be a prat at times but I'm not like Dad. He killed Granddad and raped a woman, not to mention he married Mum to keep her quiet.'

'So what do we do about the missing pieces?' Luze went to sit on the bed.

'The way I see it, we have a clue in a date.' Jason swung his legs round. 'Molly died on the 30th October, the same date as the old man. If the pieces are anywhere, it's possible to consider they are hidden somewhere in this house.'

'Why would the pieces be hidden?' Luze queried.

'I am still working on that. Tony, when the old man died, did you find anything in his private papers?'

Tony sat the other side of Luze. 'No pieces of a puzzle. If anything, I might be tempted to reach a cynical conclusion that Strident Cutter is not meant to be sold off. Perhaps Molly's ghost has always been here. Perhaps she wants to keep here and hates the idea of the factory being pulled down.'

'Nobody else saw a ghost,' said Luze. 'Was it male or female?'

'How should I know, I never looked up its skirt.'

'Ah, so it was a woman.'

'It could have been a kilt.'

'Does it matter?' Jason said. 'At this point in time, the cutter is frosted just like Franny's back wall. If we can complete the puzzle, it might end this madness. The way I see it, those missing pieces are not at random. The puzzle was designed to show four riddles, the far corner pieces left until last.'

'Left until last,' Luze muttered to herself. 'When I eat my food, I always leave the best till last.'

'I always leave the worst till last,' Tony said.

There was a long silence between three brass monkeys sitting in a row. It was a question of finding those pieces. Disregarding why they were lost or hidden, Jason felt time would work against them and came to a totally unjustifiable mental leap.

'We have to dig him up.'

'Eh?' Tony looked sideways. 'Say that again, Squirt?'

'You were the one to suggest the idea.'

'I never considered doing it. What's wrong in searching under the floorboards?'

'I have no compunction digging up a corpse,' Luze said. 'What do we have to lose?'

'Everything,' Tony balked. 'We shall get into serious trouble. Father Michael will excommunicate me.'

'Are you a Catholic?'

'That's not the point. I have my reputation to consider.'

'It's your reputation that's at risk,' Jason said. 'If this carries on, the whole damn village is going to drag up our past, slap it at our feet and refuse to enter that factory once they get the gist of supernatural forces.'

'But the factory is being pulled down,' Tony argued.

'And what about Franny's business?'

'You can be a right pain in the arse at times, Squirt. And why his coffin?'

'It wouldn't be in Molly's coffin because things happened after she died.' He glanced at his watch. 'It's ten-thirty. We shall leave at the bewitching hour. Luze is the look out. Tony and I will dig.'

'What's the bewitching hour?' Luze asked.

'When Susan is asleep,' they replied.

THE LYNCH PIECES

Hush! Keep your voices down!

Chappy, the local bobby, flushed from his walk settled on the dwarf wall outside the church. His torch lived around him, a kind of puddle of light that never kept still. Save for his yelping walkie-talkie, the cemetery was silent.

As the earth leapt up and fell back down in a hole growing more perilous by the minute, Jason whispered, 'Are you certain he was buried and not cremated?'

'Of course I'm certain.' Tony wheezed. 'Whew! I'm knackered.'

A head appeared over the hole. 'Come on you pommies. A Dingo can dig quicker than you. Are you certain he was buried and not cremated?'

Jason should have known Luze would tease him for this, should have guessed her deranged sense of fun stretched beyond normal limits. He shook his head with a thud of gratitude for a dream that delivered her into his arms and carried on digging.

Then all at once his spade hit wood. Another fallen earth, an eructation of sound, the lid burst inward and the twins went feet first into the grizzly sight of a half-decomposing body, that of Charles Black.

Tony grabbled and removed the splintered lid to forage inside an opulent interior while Jason held the torch, looking on with ambivalent eyes.

'Nothing here,' Tony kept mumbling as he worked his way down to the trouser pockets then he told Luze, 'here, hold this.'

With that she scornfully tapped the artificial limb on his head. 'You cannot pull him apart. It's sacrilegious.'

Jason puzzled. 'When did he have his leg off?'

'That's how he died, Squirt. He never came round from the op. The undertaker got a spare limb from the hospital to fill his trousers.'

It was farcical, certainly no sight for the faint-hearted. But in the hunt, there grew despondency, a feeling they were wasting their time. Jason hauled himself out of the hole, unimpressed with the progress made so far then took the rum bottle from Luze, noting her expression. The vision of a withered and contorted face was not something she expected to have feelings about but nonetheless it had sickened her, and all at once she threw up, the convulsions discharged down the hole, sending a mark of disgust.

'Tony, take Luze back and look after her. I can finish up here.'

In wordless gratitude, Luze turned away under the comfort of Tony's arm leaving Jason in the shadows of an eerie cemetery punctuated by the hoot of an owl. But he was glad of the solitude. It gave him room to manoeuvre on his thoughts and to wonder what they had done was designed as a comprehensive exercise to teach a lesson.

Upon the last shovel load, he pounded the ground with his feet, powerless to flatten the mound, so he disguised it with torn pieces of ivy then folded the tarpaulin, tucked it tight under his arm, picked up two spades and walked off, looking back once. Damn and blast! The limb was resting on the headstone. Picking that up too, fully laden he weaved the cemetery keen eyed, crossed the road and travelled the Manor's driveway among its shaded borders.

The front door flew open and a hand yanked him in. 'Give me that,' Tony said and together they padded silently to the kitchen. 'I checked on Susan. She's still out like a light. Luze is upstairs in your room.' Then he opened wide the patio doors and threw the tarpaulin and shovels on the lawn. 'I'll see to that later.'

'Is she alright?' Jason asked, placing the limb on the table.

Tony astonished. 'What possessed you to hang on to that?'

'The hole was already filled in before I spotted it.'

Picking the limb up with gusto, Tony swung it round where a projectile shot out of its cavity and across the floor upon which Jason stood. Retrieving it, Jason chuckled with delight merely to release the floodgates of his curiosity, realising that within this tightly rolled dirty brown paper bag, pieces of a jigsaw puzzle existed, demonstrating once again they were aided by unknown forces.

On the last count, Jason looked up. 'There are exactly 49 pieces.'

'How the hell did they get in Dad's leg?'

'One should ask, why hide the pieces in the first place.'

From the kitchen they proceeded upstairs and went into Jason's bedroom whereupon Jason showed Luze their discovery.

Naturally she asked, 'Where did you find them?'

'Tony shook a leg.'

Humour had its place, but what an adventure. There they were, fumbling, tickling, remonstrating and chiding, it became increasingly easier to complete the puzzle, one by one, nubs into voids, the journey's end to grow less protesting. Before a new dawn, before blackbirds pecked at the sills, and even before the milkman pushed open his door, the puzzle was complete. Though here lay a conundrum, for they had slogged and slaved, staring blankly at nothing.

'What do you make of it, Squirt?'

'Tony, have you ever called me Jason?'

'Don't think I have. Luze calls you Nuts, so what's the difference.'

But his name had little to do with situations of chance. Neither Tony nor a fresh commitment to title him correctly would alter his predicted course. 'Okay, what are we missing?'

Luze crept in with a pot of coffee. 'It's all quiet downstairs...no sign of Susan.' Placing the pot on the hearth, she sat crossed-legged by dying embers and began pouring. 'Has it ever occurred that perhaps there is no fourth riddle?'

Jason was similarly confused. 'If there is no fourth riddle then it suggests there is nothing else to learn, so why hide the last pieces?'

'Tony,' Luze said, passing over his cup. 'Perhaps you two were meant to acknowledge your ancestors' misdeeds. By finalizing the puzzle you have done exactly that.'

'But Luze, there has been no revision,' Jason argued.

'How can you alter the past? Edward tried to do the right thing. He lost a son to make him realise what Elizabeth went through. Your father was the real horror. He connived, murdered and raped. Where else would one put the lynch pieces? He's the real villain. Now you know this, and the puzzle is complete, would it not be safe to assume your quest has been completed.'

'She might be on to something, Squirt. We should check out the factory. You know, see if things are back to normal.'

Jason stared into the embers, reflecting a deep rooted feeling the supposed *quest* was too *easy* though what he considered *easy* might have been hard for Tony. 'I had the impression there should be a fourth riddle. It seems so illogical to have pieces hidden and then go to all that trouble to find them with nothing to show.'

'Nuts, I hate to put the damper on things but I must return home. Can we go to the factory and see what it's like then I can pack.'

'Luze, can I drive you to Heathrow?'

'It's a long way. Are you sure?'

'No problem.' He took the cup away from Tony's protesting lips and said, 'Let's go. Luze can stay here and keep warm.'

There was a strange silence when they walked through the entrance of Strident Cutter. No restless machinery with endless shifts, turning and cutting, rolling and printing, the hard crash and clatter that sang to the tune of Tony's mismanagement. They walked the aisle solemnly for it did no good to be hopeful, not when the factory felt so cold and ominous. Then Jason facilitated, threw back the cover where Tony bore passive witness, both caught in the moment of surprise, cheering to a frost-free cutter, their sounds of the coming day supplanted it.

And that seemed to be enough for they were now tired and exhausted, wearily strolling back to the Manor.

'It's a long drive,' Tony said and Jason felt he was foraging for details. 'Are you letting her go or what?'

'What is meant by what?'

'Squirt, don't get blinded. She's Claggart's daughter, remember? It's alright to get it out of your system but anything else is treading on shaky ground.'

Jason frowned. 'I want to share my life with Luze.'

'Waugh!' Tony held him back. 'How do you think she'll react when she finds out about your intentions?'

'I shall tell her the truth.'

'And you think she'll just accept it? *Oh, Nuts, I'm so happy for you and yes, Pappy will be over the moon to let you use his equipment.* I don't think so. You heard what she said. Her father will never sell this business. Unless you come up with the goods and shove it under his nose, I don't stand a chance. Such a puzzle will revolutionise the industry and he'll have no choice but to do the deal.'

'She will understand. I know she will.'

'Then why didn't you say when you had the chance?'

Jason remained quiet.

'Come on, Squirt, you know I'm talking sense. Sure, keep in touch but don't do anything stupid to mess up our plan. Remember your promise to me.'

Jason walked off. He had not bargained or calculated the view of difficulties he might have to surmount in order to keep Tony sweet. He ignored Susan switching on the kettle and made his way upstairs, popped into the bathroom and ran the taps, shaved while the bath filled then submerged himself in hot water, erasing the traces of sweat and grime. When he came up for air, Tony was relieving himself with casual primitive in the white china toilet bowl.

'Had a thought....why Luze? Where does she fit in? I mean, what was the point of including her in your dream?' Tony further exerted his interest for intrigue. 'You would have still encouraged me to sell to Claggart and, naturally, I would've followed the exact same path, cleared out the storeroom, found the puzzle, etcetera, etcetera....so what's the connection?'

Jason submerged again, rinsing the shampoo from his hair and thought further about it so when he emerged, he spat out water and said, 'I realise how you feel, Tony. However, maybe, just maybe I am meant to meet her father and work out a deal, develop the patent under his wing.'

'I can see where you're taking it but where does that leave Strident Cutter? He'll still want to pull this house down or do you think you can change his mind?'

To say Jason had lost interest in the mysteries of the paranormal would have little meaning but it was clear that his mental and professional mind was, at this point in time, on securing his future with Luze.

'Tony, I shall keep your best interests at heart but right now I would like to get dressed and spend what time I have left with Luze before she flies off to Australia.'

Tony was now in the process of shaving. 'Jason,' he said, the name noted, 'you can browse through my wardrobe and pick out a nice suit.'

'You can call me Squirt.'

Tony's wardrobe was awash with Bond Street suits and crisp shirts that hung in colour formation, a symbol of taste to which he cleaved during the long years of draining the business dry. Jason picked out a navy pin-stripe, pale yellow shirt, yellow tie and black shoes. This was as much as he seemed to need. After dressing, he combed his hair, and, as usual, gave up when it refused to lie down. Then he went to a sock drawer, pulled it right out and forage at the back, gaining access to his mother's jewellery box. He placed it on the chest of drawers and opened the lid.

'What are you doing?' Tony walked in.

'Where is Mother's diamond necklace?'

'Luze is rich enough to buy her own bloody necklace.' Tony tipped the contents out on the bed and made a search of his own. 'Hell, where are the earrings to match?'

'Susan!' Jason guessed.

'She doesn't know where I hide Mum's jewellery but Tools does.'

'Why would she steal Mother's jewellery?'

'Well, I haven't paid her for quite a while. Come to think about it, I can't remember the last time I did. Maybe she was strapped for cash but that necklace was worth a sodding fortune.' Then he watched Jason pick out a pearl and emerald ring, had immediately cottoned on and snatched it out of his hand. 'Have you lost your marbles? Proposing to Luze won't soften her father.'

'Give me that ring.'

Tony shook his head, returning the pieces into the jewellery box when a foot propelled him to the floor. A finger went to his nose.

'Do that again and I shall drown you in the river. Now give me that ring.'

There, it shone equally bright as her eyes, glistening with modest ambitions. Tucking it inside the suit jacket, Jason adjusted himself and went down stairs where he could not hope to prevail against Susan's rancour.

'Well aren't we the smarty pants. Going to a party, darling?'

His eyes went to Luze, making that excursion over her face and body. To him, she was like a shooting star, which proclaimed standards of culture Susan could never hope to attain. 'Shall we leave and get a bite to eat on the way?'

Turning to Susan, Luze said, 'Thank you for your hospitality.'

'The pleasure was all yours,' Susan replied, spiteful and sarcastic.

Outside, Jason placed her overnight case in the boot, walked round to the driver's side and shrugged out of his jacket, throwing it on the back seat of the Jag. 'I must apologise for Susan,' he said. 'I know Tony can be an idiot at times but not even he deserves that nasty piece of work.'

As he switched on the ignition her hand slipped onto his left leg and suddenly, he was aware of a benign feeling, yes of love, as though he were being overlooked by someone that cared for him very deeply. And even though he may not have been certain before, he was certain of it now. Luze was his destiny as surely as he was hers.

'Mrs Tooley thinks the world of you,' she said as he hit the road. 'It nearly broke her to pieces when Susan treated you badly, and your father was much the same.'

He laid his hand over hers, squeezing her fingers. 'Tell me about your father and this chap he wants you to marry.'

'We have had our moments. But Pappy trusts Jeremy implicitly and because he's older, he makes suitable husband material. The problem is he keeps patting me on the head like his pet Labrador.'

'What, your father?'

'No, Jeremy. Okay, so I went a little off the rails and yes, Pappy was anxious to steer me in the right direction. So we came to an understanding. I could choose my boyfriends on the proviso of him choosing them for me.' She laughed, was a romantic, and never wholly taken seriously. Yet within her, he knew she nourished a delicacy of taste, a brightness of spirit, which though continuously bludgeoned by her father's great shadow she remained uncrushed. 'Pappy speaks his mind and warms to honest men because arrogance is very rarely supplanted by decency.'

'Do you regard me as decent?'

'I knew right away you were my cup of tea.'

'Really,' he chuffed. Now he wondered if she saw him fresh with hopes that never clouded from the moment she met him. 'What was it about me apart from acting the fool?'

'Surely chemical reactions were bouncing between us when we met.'

'Since you had approximately one minute and thirty seconds in my company at a distance of four paces, the chemicals in my body would not have reached you in time to react with yours, so the probability of choosing my brother above me is eighty percent in his favour, taking in the variance of our looks.'

Luze blinked and remained quiet.

'Do you take after your father?'

'No, I take after Mammy. Once, she dressed up like a hoopoe bird and swooped in front of him when he put the key in the lock. He staggered back and fell down the steps, landed in hospital with a broken arm and asked the nurse to get him a bunch of flowers to make Mammy feel better.'

'Your family sounds wonderful. I suppose Tools told you how I got these scars.'

'You know she favours you more than Tony.'

'That's because Tony was the old man's favourite. I was the rebellious one.'

With a squeeze of his leg, she coaxed him to speak more of his past, to push those guarded boundaries that had kept him a little remote. Now he made a good first impression, merging effortlessly with his surrounds.

'As you know, my Mother died when we were three and although I can hardly distinguish one moment from the next under her wing, I missed her smells and arms. I never really got to grips about the old man until he came home one day drunk as a skunk. It was on our seventh birthday and the nanny he employed to look after us had made us two birthday cakes. She made mine in chocolate and for Tony, his was vanilla with icing on top. The old man made a fist and sent it into Tony's cake so I picked up mine and threw it in his face. That was my first taste of his temper.'

'You protect Tony a lot. Mrs Tooley mentioned how you helped him out financially. And I saw the look on your face when Susan almost admitted what she had done to you both. I think you feel things very deeply.'

'And you, Luze. I expect you have had your moments.'

'Moments?'

'Yes, experiences with men.'

'Like you have with women?'

'I did not mean to imply-'

'It matters not. I have had a host of men. Sometimes I found it hard to distinguish one from the other, you know, the usual falling in love bit where Pappy was there to beat the crap out of them.'

'So no, is the answer.'

'Nuts, how on earth could I have great experiences with a Father like mine? I am convinced he has eyes at the back of his head. It was only because of twisting Jeremy round my little finger did I manage to come here...though goodness knows what Jeremy has been put through. I promised him I would return almost immediately. Instead I let the jet fly off and stay to play my part in a mysterious puzzle. It's strange how thinks work out. Why was I in your dream, Nuts?'

'Perhaps to make you realise you would be marrying the wrong man.' He waited for some kind of response and when he glanced quickly to his side, he caught her stifling a yawn and wondered if she had caught his inference. 'Do you live with your parents?'

'No, I share a house with my brother in South Melbourne. Pappy has a brilliant house overlooking the bay. He once served in the Royal Navy that's why we all gather round the camp fires at weekends and pretend to raise the British Flag.'

'What made him start up in business?'

'Mammy said he was fed up with coming home on short leaves so he saw an opening in jigsaw puzzles. I remember when he came home for good. He picked me up in his arms and tickled me with his beard and said he was going to shave it off.' She stifled another yawn. 'It was lovely to get all inky between his feet.'

Exhibiting the signs of exhaustion, he watched her pull back into the seat with closed eyes, head facing his way. Now he went a step further and created a vision of himself and his future. The hero, inspiring, truthful, always honourable, his ambition could be focused. He would buy a beautiful house with all the frills and trimmings, keep her safe where their children would pad the rooms, sleepily seeking their beds until the nightfall brought its own sounds.

Parking at Heathrow, she woke automatically, stretched her arms in front of her while Jason retrieved her case from the boot of the Jag. It was dark, and the broken skies cloaked the incoming and outgoing, choking the air with sound. In ordinary circumstance there would be a candlelit dinner, the glow-warm dimness to execute a proposal but this was no ordinary circumstance.

So within the walls of Heathrow airport, Jason made do with a restaurant that worked fast and statutory, spent leisurely time enjoying her company, holding her hand across a poorly laid table and behaving as though he had entered a world of summertime.

Luze looked at her watch. 'Nuts, I think it's time I went into the Departure Lounge.'

He felt his collar tightening, considered he might be jumping the gun but such difficulties were easily surmounted when he looked at her face. Jumping to his feet, he walked round to her seat then she stood, which was unexpected. Apart from that little set back, he delved into his pocket, working his fingers inside then pulled out the ring. 'It belonged to my Mother.'

'I cannot possibly take it, Nuts.'

'Why?'

'Because it should remain in your family.'

'No, Luze it's from me to tide you over, no, not tide you over....what the hell am I saying.' He took a deep breath. 'Marry me.'

'Oh,' she feigned, swaying towards him. 'This is so sudden, it's making me hot.'

'How can it be sudden? We ate each other alive.'

'But, Nuts a few hours ago you were packaging me like a chemical laboratory. I thought you wanted to test the theory between your dream and reality.'

'And you let me. Why?'

'Because, I...I...well, because...err, because-'

'Because you know I am the one.' He fed the ring on her finger, grateful it fitted, sort of. 'Luze, the language of chemicals is as beautiful and as mysterious as you. I am dead without you, alive with you. Please be my composite singularity.' He lifted her chin. 'Can I be your fusion?'

'It's beautiful,' she croaked. 'I shall cherish it forever, and yes, please be my fusion, always.'

'Luze, I know I'm not really up to par in the romantic stakes but I have never been so sure about us. Dream or not, there will never be another woman for me.'

'Ditto, Jason.' She said his name. 'Even before I came here, I knew in my heart I would never marry Jerry. I have just been so silly letting Pappy run my life. I have never come close to anything like this. Who or what was behind that puzzle, I am truly, truly grateful.'

He placed his hands to each side of her face, wiped her moist eyes with his thumbs and kissed those lips that had kissed his skin, had cherished his body and had loved him without asking for anything in return. 'Luze, when you arrive home, telephone me. I want to meet your father, have a man to man talk. Will you be alright handling Jerry?'

She nodded. 'It's Pappy I find hard to handle.'

'Leave him to me.'

He kissed her again and reluctantly let her go where she occasionally looked back, smiling and waving until he could see no more of her. It would be a vision to take with him, always. Now there were only memories and a long drive home.

Before the clock struck midnight, Jason walked through the door, his head in the clouds and noticed the drawing room light still on. There he saw a miserable face locked in some kind of stupor. Tony was sitting in one of the leather wing-backed chairs by the hearth, a drink in his hand relaxed on his knee. His eyes veered to Jason but he said nothing, just waved him in.

'Has Susan been giving you the third degree again?' Jason strode over and stoked up the fire. 'You should be in bed getting a decent night's sleep, instead you're freezing your balls off getting pissed.'

Tony leaned over the arm of his seat and proffered a full glass of whisky. 'You'll need this.'

'Why?'

Again Tony leaned over the arm of his seat and proffered a photograph. 'It was taken outside the Pig and Whistle in the early part of 1950. The woman is Maria O'Grady next to a man called Tom Turner.'

At a glance, Jason had identified the similarity between Luze and Maria O'Grady but no similarity to Tom Turner and felt his own heart beats getting louder. His whisky hand shook, trembling with the thought Luze might be his half sister and lifted his eyes towards Tony who then handed a magazine picture published eleven years later. Their faces were taut and shining, squinting into the sunlight. The couple had been labelled as Mr and Mrs Sam Claggart, their arms around the shoulders of two children, Merluza and her brother, Adrian.

Jason remained motionless, content to prolong the agony, feeling a dying, disintegrating netherworld around him, thinking how sinister the circumstance. Moments later he gulped a good part of his whisky, anxious to hold the crying in his throat, sitting down slowly as if he were embracing the inevitable.

'I walked in the kitchen,' Tony said, anxious to convey his story. 'Tools had Susan round the neck, trying to strangle the bitch. It was bloody mayhem. I couldn't get her off Susan and when I did, Tools ducked under me and gave her one in the face. I have never seen Tools so angry or move so quickly. She was like slippery grease lightening, knocked Susan back two feet, giving her a nose job. Susan rushed out of the house screaming, yelling bloody murder. Next, Chappy turned up by which time Tools had drowned half a bottle of sherry. It transpired Tools found the photographs under Susan's mattress. Susan stole them from Dad and wheedled the truth out of him. He admitted Luze was his daughter and in return he gave Susan Mum's necklace and earrings to keep quiet. When she realised her days were numbered, that you were gong to put up a fight, she sold them to a broker, that's where she went, to London. Then the moment she saw Luze, worked out you two had a little thing going on, it was a huge bonus. She was going to tap you for money in exchange for keeping quiet.' Tony sat forward, his voice contrite. 'I am so fucking sorry, Squirt. I wish I could turn back the clock but I can't.'

Feeling a deep well of pain coming from the pit of his stomach, Jason was grasping for hope. Hope it was all a mistake, that somehow someone had mixed things up or that Susan doctored the photographs. 'But Luze said her father was in the Navy, came home on odd occasions. And how can she have a brother if Turner was in prison. It doesn't make sense.'

'Squirt, I wish I could find the answers but it's there, the proof is in front of you. It adds up, the puzzle, Luze coming here, the lot. It was never about revision, or a fourth riddle. It was about revenge by some damn demon with a rotten sense of humour. I know this sounds bonkers, but I think it was Dad all along.'

Jason finally fell to the impact of truth and wondered how it would ever be possible to let her go, live with it for years, unable to find a love comparable. Life and death, fate and chance, space and time; the answer was somewhere in those equations. At a deeper level, he wondered why the weed of crime bears bitter fruit. Wiping his eyes with the balls of his hand, he took in a shuddering breath and looked Tony squarely in the eye. He was ready to face what he had to face but did not want to face it alone.

'Tragic irony or poetic justice, the consequences of my actions are just too appalling to consider but for Turner to set out and destroy Luze seems to be a disproportionate response.'

'Look, Squirt, think about it logically. Hell, I've spent the last four hours with my brain wrapped around this. Luze wasn't supposed to come here, neither were you. Whoever was behind that puzzle had nothing to do with Tom Turner. Sure, Turner wants his mother's land back but he would never risk sending Luze before the deal was done. My bet is that she doesn't know who she really is. Probably Tom Turner and Maria O'Grady are the only ones who do, trying to cover up a bad past. It had to be Dad, that's what I reckon. He doesn't want Turner to have the business, knock this place down and all that.'

Jason nodded slowly as it came together. 'She speaks highly of her father and how he protects her interests. I cannot see how he would wish her any harm.'

'You have to get in touch with her, Squirt.'

'And what do I say? Do I fly half way across this globe and see Turner? Babble my head off about a phantom puzzle instigated by my Father, I think not. Luze has to face the truth, far better it comes from her parents than from me. Oh bollocks, she'll never want to see me again. How was it left with Chappy?'

'Susan wanted you arrested for shagging Luze but good old Tools soon put a damp squib on that accusation. She said Susan's credibility was hardly noteworthy and that Luze came over to break the news of her being our half-sister. Then Tools demanded Susan be arrested for blackmailing the old goat but since he's dead, Chappy said it would never stand up in court.'

'But why did the old man succumb to blackmail? It makes no sense. None of it is making sense.'

'Of course it makes sense,' Tony said. 'He never got remarried because he wanted Maria. He's been pining for her ever since she left. His tears were never for Mum. That's why he wanted you in the firm, to run Strident Cutter and make it grow so he could have Turner by the balls. He knew what Turner was doing. Waiting for the day he could make his move. But Dad had me, second rate arse twitcher and Susan knew how to handle him because she knew he was living for the one thing he could never have and that was Maria O'Grady.'

Jason tried to take his mind off her hard and crawled back into himself wondering if he could still have a life here. 'If Turner wants this business, then he will not let his daughter's indiscretion get in the way. In fact he will take steps to protect her and keep her from returning. But will he come here to run the business?' It took a while to consider his options, stay or leave, but the more he thought about it, the more it made sense. 'I think not, which may give us a window of opportunity to develop the concept. We could slip in at night to run trials using the factory. Turner need never know.'

'I want the business back, Squirt. And don't give me that same old rhetoric. Either he sells or the patent is sold to another competitor. That'll make his damn empire look sick. He should have told Luze. He should have done the decent thing then none of this would have happened.'

The Tony magic was already working, creating a sense of purpose, conveying confidence, and engendering closeness but Jason was not nearly ready to be dispatched from his nightmare.

SALE OF STRIDENT CUTTER

Gossip came on the dust and the wind, with whispers on lips. Within days, the whole of Little Smeet revelled in the chinks of two different tales; one spoken by the credible Mrs Tooley, the other by Susan's vitreous tongue.

Jason was not in a position to take note of any gossip since he continued to feed his body with whisky, a liquid remedy to make it all go away. From glass to glass in trackless movements, it licked down his throat and mapped his brain stuck fast in dreams. For the first time in his life he felt truly alone in a world whose behaviour he could neither predict nor fathom.

Mrs Tooley summed up the action to Tony as 'an unpleasant hiccup.' But she remained anxious and was not above showing it. 'Yew got to make him eat.' She stared beyond the interconnecting doors. 'Look at him, slouched in that chair holding a whisky bottle just like his father.'

'Hey, that's how men cope.'

'Yew should know better, encouraging him like that.'

'I never encouraged him. I was dead against it.'

'I wus talking about drink, not Luze. Bah, yew make me angry.' Tools stomped up to Jason and pulled back his head by the scruff of his hair. 'Yew must eat, my man or yew'll be rotting in that chair just like your father and I won't thank yew for that. Nor will Luze.'

Luze. He heard her name. 'What's up, Tooly Wooly?'

'Now listen, my man. Do yew think you're the only one suffering around here. How do yew think she's feeling? How do yew think her father feels?'

Jason's head was swimming with her rhetoric.

'Bah! He's not listening.' She proceeded to the kitchen and grabbed the cup Tony was holding, twizzled on her heels and quickly stomped back to the drawing room. 'Come on, my man,' she said pouring warm tea over his head. His only reaction was to wipe his stubbled face with an open hand so she continued to fill her voice with scorn. 'Yew stink like Smelly but he has an excuse. He lives with his cows. Yew live in that chair feeling sorry for yewself! Drink is not your answer.'

'It's my answer.'

'Yew hev other choices.'

His voice issued slow and painful. 'Choice is an illusion created between those with power and those with not. I have no power to undo what is done.'

Mrs Tooley smiled and looked back at Tony. 'He's still in there somewhere. Help me to get him to the table and run a bath for him.'

The village was clearly no pagan paradise, neither was Mrs Tooley conscious of showing tolerance. Minor offences cropped up throughout the years. Quiet incest, drink and rustic boredom were responsible for most. The village neither approved nor disapproved, but neither did it complain to a higher authority. Chappy was the local scene and his punishments were confined to the parish.

Jason felt himself plucked from the chair, coursing a giddy path to the kitchen. His body felt dank with the swamp of sweat, where his shirt now wrapped his goosy flesh. Plonked in a chair, he slouched unkempt looking down at a plate full of food and pushed it aside.

Mrs Tooley pushed it back. 'If yew don't eat, as God is my witness I shall keep hounding yew until yew share the same coffin as your father.'

Jason now thought of him merely as a number in a long line of equations that set about destroying his dreams with Luze. Stabbing at a piece of steak, he shoved it in his mouth just to be obliging. Amused as though he had somehow fooled Mrs Tooley, instead his taste buds grew in shades of hunger and he plundered the spoils of her cooking without pause.

Wiping his mouth with the back of his hand, he finally concluded, 'I have been an ass.'

'No harm done, leastways not to your liver. Tony is running a nice hot bath so hev a soak and a good sleep. Wake up in the morning nice and fresh and help in the factory.'

'What has happened in the factory?'

'Yew hev to show your face, put an end to the gossip.'

'What gossip?'

'Susan's gossip, what else.' She clasped her hands, resting them on the table. Her eyes were understanding, their gentleness at odds with the severity of her voice. 'There isn't a man or woman in these parts thass not got a skeleton in their cupboard but if yew keep here, hiding from them they're going to know something wus wrong. There's no shame in the Lord's eyes loving your sister because it weren't your fault. Everything yew two did wus out of innocence, true and well meant.'

'Where is Susan?'

'That bitch found herself a fancy man. I threw her clothes out of the window and locked her out. She won't be bothering us none. But she left with a wicked tongue and you've got to show your face, act as though yew treated Luze with respect or else you'll make me out a liar. Now hev your bath and listen to wat Tony has to tell yew.'

Upstairs, he wandered into *her* room, remembered how he looked on in speechless lust when she offered herself freely. It smelt of paradise, and her one dress hung over the bedstead, the light shade concertinaed on the floor and pink flocked wallpaper, the pattern bright and clear, and all the bits and pieces that had no particular place but belonged to her. Now they were gone. Only the wallpaper remained and somehow it never seemed the same, the pattern dull and unclear but once his mother's tribute. Similarly he could barely distinguish one misery from the other.

He walked on with despondency and went into the bathroom where Tony had his sleeve rolled up, his fingers swimming in hot water, the steam dispersing around him.

The acknowledgement was prompt.

'You look like shit.'

Jason turned. A mirror swung into sight and flung him an unwanted glimpse of his face, the expression that was not his face. He had been living by longing rather than business law, tore off his reeking clothes, and purged his body in hot water. 'Tools said you had something to tell me.'

'Two bits of news...first Luze telephoned and-'

'Why didn't you wake me?'

'You were drunk, not asleep.' He passed over the razor and Jason refused. 'Come on, Squirt, you need a shave or are you growing a beard?'

That sounded intriguing, another mask to hide his identity. 'What did she say?'

'Apparently her father went ballistic the moment she returned home, and she couldn't make it out. Then he calmed down, told her the truth, that he was Tom Turner trying to hide his shady past. Of course, Luze already knew about it because of the puzzle. Then the moment he told her she was our half sister, she flipped her lid. I asked her if she told him about you two but she said no. Bottom line, she had a younger brother because Turner escaped after his trial, took his mother and pregnant Maria to Australia.'

'Why was it kept from Luze?'

'Turner didn't want her to know in case it changed their relationship.'

'How is she?'

'Bearing up, a bit like you...she asked me to tell you that she will always be your composite singularity, whatever that means. Anyway, the gist of it is that Turner hasn't twigged about you two getting up to hanky panky. She's keeping it that way. She also said she had to take off the ring. I told her that you would want her to keep it, am I right?'

Jason nodded. 'So when is she 'phoning again?' He saw a jittery look on his brother's face. 'Well?'

'She doesn't want contact, Squirt. Look, she was down. Sometimes I could hardly register what she was saying between her sobs. Give her time, who knows, we can all meet up for a beer and laugh about it.'

Jason's spirits quailed and did not question it further.

'Henshaw Junior got in touch,' Tony continued in a lighter tone. 'Turner's solicitor is still anxious and wants to tie things up by January, which doesn't give either of them long to get things organised since Christmas is round the corner. I have to inform my customers that it's business with Claggart sometime in the New Year. I could do with a bit of help in the office. Are you up for it?'

'What is your secretary doing?'

'Ah, that's a sore point....she pissed off.'

Jason ducked under the water and thought about it. When he emerged, he said, 'I am convinced a secretary has only existed in your head.'

Tony smiled by the door. 'Luze said a similar thing.'

Jason lay back against the enamel and closed his eyes to think of that lost moment, a chance to hear her voice, a chance to share his pain and say the one thing he never said at the airport. I love you. Would it have mattered, he wondered. Would it have made a difference? He studied his hands, the hands that had touched her flesh, hands that had pulled her naked body close to his and hands that had passed over a ring the colour of her eyes. 'What have I done,' he whispered, and he knew the answer.

Unable to lie still another moment, he heaved himself from the bath with nothing but contempt for Tom Turner. It galled him to think that this man had said nothing, had let time slip by without a hint of her history. Was it treachery or by necessity? The question remained unanswered through the night and beyond.

Jason spent the following day at the factory. It was difficult to get his act together. Workers disposed themselves solemnly around his heels where he was unable to look them in the eye. He could sense their strangeness of tone, their examination with sly speculation. In the end his nerve broke and he just disappeared to walk the path along the river in dark windy weather trying to rid the humiliation from his thoughts.

Unlike other areas of Norfolk, villages near to the water, Little Smeet never developed thriving boat building and hiring industries. The wildlife was plentiful where the great crested grebe, mallard and teal was a common sight, and where the rare bittern was not often seen, but its strange booming call heard at night sent messages down his spine. Far from being censorious of its haunting sound, Jason was impressed by it. To him, the call was like a melody of a love penalised by blood. It ran through his veins as surely as it ran through hers. And he was powerless to do anything about it.

After Christmas, Jason surfaced with a new frame of mind, triggered by the stress of it all, inner conflicts created by his feelings for Luze, and later by the struggle to discipline his brother to get organised. He was now inclined to take a more pessimistic outlook on life and the only thing which appeased him the most was initiating the development of his puzzle. He still positioned himself properly, as well as astutely, and became the man who saw what Turner's intention was and did what he did because he had a better view of Strident Cutter.

Documents flew hither and thither by air, from Melbourne to Norfolk, from solicitor to solicitor. What a performance. The deadline surpassed January and touched upon the early part of February where the twins were called into Henshaw Junior's office smelling of leather and oak. John Henshaw Junior, the senior partner, was leaned forward taking control of the preliminary chitchat, a man who was glib and engaging with a mellow, almost professional baritone. At forty-five, he was the son of the firm and spent most of his time balancing the egos of some of the richest people in Norfolk.

Jason was reading a document, standing by the window in one of Tony's Bond Street suits. His looks had been starkly transformed by a thick cropped beard augmenting his dark eyes, both of which corresponded to his mood.

'John, there is no provision for secure tenancy.'

'Why would there be?' Henshaw replied. 'Workers only have secure tenancy while they do their job, and do it properly. Claggart would be very stupid to do otherwise.' He looked back at Tony. 'You do understand what this means?'

'Yeah, yeah, I understand. I move out of the Manor this week and into number 18 but it will be his responsibility to put in some decent heating and it needs a new kitchen.'

'Did you do that for your tenants?'

'I had no money.' Tony excused his deplorable attitude.

'I would consider myself fortunate you are not out on your ear.' Henshaw pushed back his chair and stood up, flaying out the survey map on his desk. 'I need you to confirm the boundaries.'

The land, with road and river frontage was a vast rectangle occupying a fair chunk in the village. As one stood with their back against the cemetery, looking across the road there was a large corrugated structure that sat deep with its own access. Adjacent, to the right, Edward Black had built the

Manor central on the land thus taking a good proportion for extravagant gardens. To the farthest right, twenty tide cottages, built in a uniform manner, ten facing ten with a narrow dirt track in between. Access to the track came directly off the high street, opposite the Pig and Whistle, and anyone with a mind for business could see the potential for this sprawling enterprise.

It was at this point Jason felt his brother's tension rising, the missed opportunities, his impending gloom of moving down a number of pegs for a number of months.

Henshaw brought out his pen, unscrewed the top and handed it over to Tony. 'Sign here, here, here and here.' He sidled up to Jason, modulating his voice. 'Great pity you left.'

Jason kept his vista fixed on the tumbling snow flakes, watching them fall like little constellations. 'There is still hope some good may come of it.'

'Perhaps this will show him a little humility, and some restitution for the past.'

Jason turned his head slowly round and looked closely at Henshaw. He saw that professional smile which gave nothing away. 'Amends for his incompetence or for our blood line?'

'Is there a difference?'

'There you go,' Tony said, tossing the pen to Henshaw. 'Cheap at half the price....John, what's my position with Susan?'

'She has a capacity for histrionics.'

'Tell me about them. Is she divorcing me or am I divorcing her?'

'To save costs, she has agreed to a two year separation so the divorce will go through on mutual grounds.'

'What about that bloke she shacked up with?'

'What about him?' Henshaw turned to Jason. 'Remember you have a week from today to get your brother organised.'

This seemed to be the end of the transaction and they moved on.

Debate still sounded when they arrived at the Manor which portrayed a picture postcard residence. Snow made everything pretty and glistening as though no blemishes existed at all. As soon as they trampled through the front door, they smelled Mrs Tooley's steak and kidney pie. She was upstairs, vacuuming and singing to her heart's content. Tony went straight to the drinks cabinet. 'I must be out of my mind. I signed my death warrant.'

'The bank would sell off the assets at rock bottom prices just to get rid of them. Thank your lucky stars I negotiated a six month contract for your employment with Turner. Tow the line and keep your head down.' Jason said it in such a way as to infer repercussions if he did otherwise.

'What guarantees do I have your puzzle will work?'

Jason went down on his heels to stoke up the fire. 'I still have to modify the ratio of potassium because of the viscosity and osmotic pressure.'

'What's that in straight language?'

'I have a fair way to go.'

'Are you coming to the meet?'

'What meet?'

Tony clicked his fingers and brought out a letter from his inside suit pocket. 'Sorry, Squirt. I forgot to tell you but the big man himself is coming down to talk to the workers, me being one of course.'

Squeezing his eyes into sparrow feet, Jason held Tony in contempt. 'What the hell is wrong with you! Why is Turner coming here? Why do you think that is, Tony?'

'Not with you, Squirt?'

'Turner is out to humiliate us. When is he coming?'

'Next Monday, first thing at eight. Hell, there was nothing I could do about it.'

'You could have informed me so arrangements could have been made to steer his course.'

'Like what?'

'We shall never know, shall we, since you live in cloud cuckoo land.'

Conversation was interrupted when Mrs Tooley walked in, taking off her apron and folding it in half. 'Father Michael said to remind yew lot about the church bazaar.'

'Tools, take a seat.' Tony went to the cabinet and poured out a sherry. 'I expect you've heard I have officially signed over Strident Cutter.'

'Hev I got the sack?'

'Jason is moving into the Pig and Whistle. I'm moving into number 18. Turner has given us a week to get out. Now, keep it to yourself but it's fairly certain this house is going to be knocked down. On my new wages, I won't be able to keep you on but Jason got Turner to consider a position for you, though what it is, we don't know. The thing is you don't have to take it up if you don't want to.'

She sat in nostalgia, a buckle of skin folded below each eye, wet and swollen thinking of her time, all those years with the Blacks. They were hardly the best payers, indeed they sometimes forgot but they never begrudged her a drink now and then. 'Not sure I would get along with him.'

'You were the only one to get along with Dad,' Tony reminded.

'Your dad wus easy to handle. If ever he pinched my bum I would smack him on his gammy leg. That soon put paid to his jaunts.' She looked around the room and sighed. 'My Mum liked working here, especially when yours wus alive, God bless her soul. She left my Mum these pearl earrings. I wear them all the time. Place isn't going to be the same. I had hoped now that Susan wus out of your life we could have a bit of peace and quiet.'

Jason dug into his pocket and brought out a wad of notes. 'Here is a little something for you, just to show our appreciation.'

'Oh, you're a good man, Jason. Not like this one who moans about my gravy.'

'I like your gravy,' Tony said. 'It's him that moans about it. Anyway, I might have a reversal of fortune and if that's the case I shall buy you something nice.'

She glanced to each side of her and to what she was sitting on. 'This will never get in one of those cottages. I could do with replacing my settee.'

Those gentle words wounded Jason, the last nail in his coffin, such finality and it was then he realised this was not just a home for Tony but his home too where parts of his mother's memory still remained.

'Your dear mum,' she continued, 'liked it here, always had her windows open. Should've been closed then she wouldn't hev caught pneumonia. Roit, best be off. My George will be wondering where I got to.'

Jason stepped forward. His influence was deep and far-reaching. 'Tony, get Tools another sherry. What about the windows, Tools?'

'It don't do to bring things up, Jason. Yew should know that. Let sleeping dogs lie and get on with your life.'

'Did the old man have anything to do with my Mother's death?'

'She never bargained for a man like your father, thass fer sure. My Mum said she wus in a poor state of health but she would open them windows just to annoy him. He'd come in moaning about the draft.'

'Did my Mother know Maria O'Grady?' Tony asked, refilling her glass.

She stared at her drink then swallowed it whole. 'I suppose it don't hurt none to say but my Mum had just come back from shopping, walked in the kitchen and saw them two together, roit in this very room, talking in whispers.'

'When was this?' Tony asked.

'Just after Tom Turner's trial.'

'What happened after that?' Jason asked.

'She left, Jason, what else? She wus all dressed up quite posh, so my Mum reckoned. Before, she never had a penny to rub together but there she wus in fine silks getting into a posh car with Elizabeth Turner. It wus said Robert Graves went to old man Henshaw with your dad before he married your mum. Graves wanted to protect his daughter's interests so he couldn't get his hands on her money.'

Tony was alerted. 'Did you say money?'

'Oh yes, she had money all roit. The Graves owned a lot in Norfolk. After your mum died, old man Henshaw came here and left your dad with a blank face. He thought he would hev it but it wus all gone.'

'Gone where?' Tony asked.

'Your guess is as good as mine.'

'Where did Grandfather Graves go?' Jason asked.

'There wus great animosity between the Graves and your father then some time later shortly after your mum's death Graves packed up his surgery and we've never seen hide nor hair of him since. He had a lot to say for himself at the trial but some folks say he wus scared of your dad......poor Tom never had a chance...anyways, don't yew be thinking anything foolish? And no more digging up coffins! Father Michael wus none too pleased about that. The past is past. Gone! There's been enough misery around here wat with yew and Luze being pulled apart like that. Turner wus liked in this village and he's going to make good in that factory. Tony's got his life back and yew must bury your pain, Jason. Go back to Boston and pick up your life there.' She passed over the glass. 'I hev to be going, thanks for the sherry. My George will be wanting his tea.'

Jason never said anything, because there was nothing to say.

'I believe Tools. Mum died of heartache. She found out what Dad did and she just didn't want to live any more.'

Of all the things that Tony had said, Jason thought this was the most poignant and it brought a single cohesion of understanding. 'I felt my world had collapsed when I lost Luze. Mother must have felt ten times worse. Not only did she feel betrayed by her own father but also by her husband, a rotten bastard. Give me the opportunity to have my time with him again and I would make his life far worse.'

'Do you think Henshaw knows the full story about Mum's money?'

Jason had this indiscernible feeling Henshaw was holding something back, something far more important, but he felt disinclined to extrapolate. 'If we dig up the past, we could be creating conditions that might threaten our long term survival. We need to keep Turner sweet.' Then he changed the conversation, keeping his mind focused and off Luze. 'Do you want to give your settees to Tools?'

Tony sent his eyes to the grand piano. 'Do you still play?'

'Yes, I have one in Boston.'

'How much money do you have?'

'None of your business.'

'That much?'

A week later, Jason noticed the effect of his brother's changing life style. Tony was no longer strutting and parading like a peacock but instead finding himself deep in the reality of life. A further victim had been claimed. Most of his furniture, too large by half, had been sent to the local auction house or given away by coercion. In contrast, the cottage was cold, damp and small, creating a depressing home for a man who once benefitted from other people's efforts.

And if Jason thought that was demeaning enough for his twin, he could see how Tony suffered sideway glances turning up at the factory in a pair of overalls first thing Monday morning. Although he declined to go to the meet, he changed his mind and set off early through the snow. It was a fundamental exercise to get the measure of Turner.

Workers arrived dead on eight and forestalled in carrying out their duties. All of them had congregated in one spot, virtually hugging each other in the cold, and waiting for direction while a man, dressed in a cashmere coat with salt and pepper hair, stood aloft on a trestle platform. His features were too distant for Jason to gauge but he measured his height and weight as powerful.

When Turner held up his hand, not a whisper could be heard, not a man shuffled, moved, coughed or created sound. 'You know my face but not the name. My name is Tom Turner. Those who knew me well let them speak my name for I shall not bow to any other. Unlike the Blacks who have been the masters of their own misfortunes, I shall take you forward into a new era where each shall prosper from their endeavours. There will be no division of duty or favouritism. Every man will learn each other's trade and every man will learn new trades. For here, where we stand on my mother's land, a revolutionary compass beckons.'

Jason imagined the purpose of Turner's graphic description was not for his private satisfaction or to remind himself what had happened. That might have been sufficient for many but what Turner craved was recognition. So after that short, sharp introduction, Jason watched Turner jump down from his platform and continue a slow and methodical circuit, weaving in and out of the workers as he spoke fluently about the success of Claggart, how it occupied the Eastern Seaboard and Europe. Turner painted a rosy future, laid down their goals and never stood on ceremony, conversed lucidly to speak of things that Jason wished his father and brother had done. He had the workers in stupefaction and when he concluded his debriefing, he leaned against a particular cutter and Jason knew he was thinking that this is where it all started, this is where it really began in 1942, a time when Turner watched his sister Molly bleed to death in the arms of his mother. Jason's feeling of contempt for Tom Turner transmuted so quickly that he surprised himself. Not because Turner had accomplished a successful veneer to cover his past but because he had the strength to climb those mountains and achieve a single goal; the rescue of his mother's land. Jason now understood it was not treachery but by necessity to keep his true identity a secret. When the workers set to, going about their daily routines, Jason slipped away unnoticed and followed Turner who walked a lone path by the river with his collar turned up. He watched him fill his lungs with cold, crisp air that seemed to induce the thrill of settling a score, to celebrate the end of embittered memories. Jason's sole intention was to speak to Turner, to gain his confidence so he could forage for information about Luze. Then suddenly, he lost his nerve when Turner halted and regarded the Manor as though he had finally come to the end of his rainbow. It was nestled among extravagant white plantings, slipped into silence, nothing moved or happened.

'Every brick shall be pulverised,' Turner voiced loud. 'Every piece of wood shall be burnt, every pane of glass shall be shattered into fragments and all shall see those things wiped from my mother's land and all shall see a new beginning.'

At this very moment, Mrs Tooley was making her way towards Turner. Jason shot behind a bush and watched her short ankle-fur-trimmed boots brush through the snow at the kick of her uneven strides.

'Oh my,' she wheezed, holding her hand to her chest. 'I never realised how long this garden wus, enough snow here to build an igloo. I expect yew could do with a nice cup of tea.'

'I shall not be stopping, Mrs Tooley.' Turner proffered his hand. 'It is Mrs Tooley?'

'Yew can call me Tools.' She curtsied. 'Everyone does around these parts. Where is your lovely Maria?'

'Maria is at home.'

'Pity, we wus looking forward to seeing her.'

'I shall not need your services in that house. I am returning to Australia.'

'Jason said he negotiated for me to stay on.'

'He is correct. Your wages will be covered. When the factory is built on this site, I would like you to be in charge of catering. Would that suit?'

'Oh my, that would be lovely. I hear yew got places all over the world. Yew must love jigsaw puzzles to hev so many factories.'

'I do not have many factories, just two in Australia and now this one.'

'Jason tried to make his brother see sense. But yew can't make a man see sense when he has a bit of his father's ways.'

'They both have their father's ways.'

Jason winced upon hearing this.

Turner walked on, his sentence garbled. Jason caught the words *Katherine Black* and some of Mrs Tooley's reply *left a poor legacy*. Blast, Jason thought, a man could easily blend if he wore white. Then, by some miracle, he was just about to leave for the Pig and Whistle, when Turner's voice had clarity as though he had changed direction.

'....feel it necessary to put flowers on my sister's grave?'

'Oh he felt ever so bad when he learnt the truth,' Mrs Tooley said. 'He gave her the best room in the house, overlooking this garden.'

'So my daughter stayed here?'

'It wus all proper,' she said quickly. 'Tony's wife wus here though I did all the cooking apart from breakfast. Hark at me, once I get going, I can't stop.'

'What does Jason do?'

'He's ever so clever. He studied chemistry at school, always liked to mix things in bottles and blow things up but his dad never had much time for him so he left to work fer some institution in Boston. He made a discovery.

Don't ask me wat it wus 'cause I haven't a clue but he showed me his medal only the other day. He wus ever so proud of it. Given to him by the president himself, can yew imagine that?'

'Do you mean the President of the United States?'

'He shook his hand an all but look at him now...given it all up to help that daft brother. Yew know where I am if yew need me.'

Jason stuck fast behind the bush, believed he was out of sight when Mrs Tooley headed in his direction, making her way to Strident Cutter. 'I put in a good word for yew,' she said and carried on.

He smiled and took another peek between the gaps of white sticks and leaves, and watched a proud figure diminish into the Manor. He then returned to the Pig and Whistle, entered by the side door and skipped up to his room where he now felt accustomed to its size and layout. His single bed had been pushed to the wall under the window, making way for the trappings of chemicals and equipment. By far he was close but not close enough to the formula that would render a picture by acids from the skin rather than by lemon juice and heat.

Jason spent the rest of the day jammed among his bottles and instruments, occasionally taking a break looking out of Franny's back yard. Then on cue, Tony stomped in after a hard day's work and slammed the door.

'That bastard Turner made me look a right frickin prat!'

Head bent over a microscope, Jason murmured. 'I did wonder.'

'Wonder what?'

'Keep your head low, do your job and all will be well.'

'Huh? What kind of answer is that? Keep your head low, do your job and all will be well? Look at me! My balls are about to drop off and that bloody factory is freezing! You were right, it's damn humiliating. They're all talking behind my back and he never helped, going on about a new era of prosperity as though it's my fault the factory went to pot.' Tony surveyed the room, his voice a little more tempered. 'You're a bit cramped in here, Squirt. Are you still managing to keep Franny out or does she still chase you with her tennis racket?'

Jason looked up. 'You are correct. You look humiliated.'

Tony shook his head and slumped on the bed in a pair of inky overalls. 'You should have been there, Squirt. I felt like a bloody squashed pea on a plate. How's the puzzle coming along? No, don't tell me, you're nearly there but nowhere.'

Reminding his brother to keep his crippled emotions in tact, not to do anything untoward to spoil the plan, Jason then said, 'As so often in development, the first step towards true understanding rather than fanciful speculation is the collection of data, which in this case means identifying the chemicals that react positively in the search to achieve our goal. Unlike the blank jigsaw puzzle that had the element of unknown forces, I am trying to establish the element of known forces. Patience has never been one of your strong suits.'

'Have you ever wondered who made that mystery puzzle?'

Time had evaporated the countless conundrums running through Jason's mind about that puzzle and wondered if, by some measure of a complex universe Molly's soul had never laid to rest. 'One cannot dismiss the possibility it was Molly Turner. She had the strongest motive, had seen it all and died before she had a chance to live.' He stretched his back then stood awhile stroking the hairs on his upper lip. 'We should wet our whistles.' He saw Tony flinch. 'You must face your demons as I faced mine.'

'You got drunk.'

'And so shall you but with my guidance.'

'I suppose it cannot be any worse in the pub than in the factory.' Tony looked at himself. 'Christ, I have lost my identity.' He shuffled out of overalls and closed the door behind them. 'I'm never going to last the term, you know that, don't you? I can't bloody iron my shirts let alone cook. I nearly gassed myself this morning. I wonder what Franny's got on the menu tonight.'

'Are you in a position to pay?'

'Err, thought you might treat me.'

Habit was difficult to shed

CLACKETY-CLACK

True to his word, Turner demolished the three-storey Manor built central on Elizabeth's land. Every piece was either crushed or burnt or splintered into fragments. And even though Mrs Tooley prepared the locals for such an event, from hearsay to fact the short duration caught everyone unawares.

Thereafter, a vast throng of craftsmen swooped on site to create a home for a revolutionary cutter. Day by day, week by week as the weather grew warm, locals caught glimpses of intricate pattern work that threw this edifice into the realms of grandeur. By August the shell had summarised its full contours, and with the same enthusiasm an army of tradesmen walked in to busily work on first and second fixtures under the heat of a mid-day sun. It was on the regional TV news and in the papers, eager journalists ready to expose this esteemed building with potted histories of Turner's career and the Black's olden times, hastily pulled together to show this little empire could offer countless designs and challenges, a good entertainment for a small price.

Meanwhile, the corrugated structure standing ugly by the river where Edward once looked out upon the still and glittering waters was about to have no future at all. During all this time it maintained a degree of stability to keep the factory workers employed. This made it very difficult for Jason because men were working virtually round the clock to clear the decks, ready for the move. However, in the latter part of September, factory workers were straying into sleepy wonderment, shuffling their feet from one building to the next, sometimes engaging into freakish labour.

As with most weekends, Jason crossed the road bright and early from the Pig and Whistle, anxious to get an update from Tony. The cottage was still and silent, Tony was asleep so Jason began his usual ritual and cooked breakfast.

'Smells good.' Tony emerged in his pyjamas, squeezed himself into a chair stuck fast against the wall and mentioned the one thing that really disturbed

Jason. 'Did you know Turner booked a room for himself at the Pig & Whistle?'

Jason kept his eyes peeled to the frying pan, his heart rapping against the walls of his ribs. 'Not just Turner,' he replied, 'but also for his wife.'

'You're kidding! Why the hell would she want to stay at the Pig & Whistle? What does Franny make of it?'

'She is unconcerned. Having Turner and his wife stay at the Pig and Whistle promotes her business.'

'Did she say how long they were staying?'

'Just tonight,' Jason replied as the toaster popped up. 'I wonder why they are here or is the manager failing in his duties?'

'Jerry? Hell no, he's bloody good at his job. He's been teaching me a thing or two, I can tell you. They've probably come to see the new factory.' Tony stretched across the table for the teapot. 'Can you believe how fast that building has gone up?'

Jason pulled out a chair and picked up his utensils. 'We cannot proceed any further.'

'Look, I worked it all out. When the new cutter goes in, the old cutters are going to auction but one is being held back, which means there will be a lull before they start pulling down the old factory. This will give us an opportunity to work at night. And don't forget, nights are drawing in fast.'

'We need the silk screening process. When is that being transferred?'

'Yeah, okay we can't use it. That's being transferred on Monday. I telephoned Allen Smith, you know, the one in Norwich which concentrates on maps. He's agreed you can use his silk-screen to run off the prints. I told him you were trying out new inks and that you'd clear the wells of his printer after you're done but it's got to be when his men leave off.'

'Why is Turner keeping one of the old cutters?'

'It's the one that killed his sister.' Tony pointed his knife. 'Do you remember when Luze sorted out the valuation on the silk screen and one cutter? Well, that was why. And it just so happens to be the cutter that frosted up, remember?'

'How did Luze know that was the cutter?'

'She didn't. How could she? Turner told Jerry to look for the one with the bent arm. It was him that was supposed to come down.'

'Did you have a word with Misery?' Jason asked.

'I can do it. He's been training me on the cutters. I can recalibrate. The workers show too much loyalty to the Turners. That last pay deal did it.'

'It looks as though your time has not been wasted.'

'Hell, Squirt, I've been an utter prick. I have to admire Turner. He's certainly got a handle on things but he's got no idea of what we've got in store for him.'

Jason refused to go there. 'Do you think Jerry is aware of what went on between me and Luze?'

'He keeps tight lipped about his private affairs. Why so concerned?'

'I am not concerned. We can negotiate with any jigsaw manufacturer.'

'No!' Tony muffled hard with a mouthful. 'I have my pride. This is my home, I was born here and I don't want my name to be mud on the lips of these people. I need to get respect and show I'm not a tosser. I want my business back and the name Black put on the boxes.'

'And what if Turner refuses to negotiate?'

'He has to or his empire will go down the pan.'

A critical eye was aimed at Tony. 'The Black name can be put on the box whichever way you view it. You do not have to own any part of the business, you can seek other manufacturers.'

'I do, because people will know Turner hasn't won. I don't care if I just get forty percent. Hell, I will even settle for twenty but the Black name goes back on those deeds and on the boxes. It was Granddad that started the business so why should he have it all?'

In grim repose, Jason fondled his beard with an almost certainty it would need more than time and tide to change Tony's mind, to convince him if they continued on this path, they would be creating conditions that might threaten their long term survival. 'Do you wish to join me tonight at St. George's?'

Tony shook his head. 'I thought we could watch football this afternoon and go to the Pig and Whistle so you can get a handle on Turner.'

'I have a handle on Turner.'

'Since when?' Tony asked, wriggling his way from the table.

'I was there at the meeting when he first appeared at the factory.'

'You never said. Why didn't you say?'

'Must I inform you of my every move?'

Tony grabbed the dish cloth. 'You seem worried, Squirt? Is it the puzzle or Turner's wife?'

If truth be told, Jason would say he was worried, full stop. It was not just the puzzle or the efforts to make Tony see sense but the plan, the sneaking into the old factory. That had the hall marks of deceit, an action which could well be attributable to his father's ways, and he never forgot Turner's words said to Mrs Tooley among sleepy plants laden with snow. Now he posed the very same question to himself, the one he posed about Turner. Treachery or by necessity?

So while Tony followed his pattern of lazy slouching, watching football and shouting until he was hoarse, Jason spent time absorbing the rich diversity of news in his scientific journals. They boasted miraculous cures and doomed forecasts for a world on the brink of an ice-age and when quiet was restored in the cottage, he fell asleep in the chair stuck fast in dreams.

Into the night, Jason woke at the kick of his heels, blinked the sleep from his eyes, stretched and yawned then looked at his watch.

'I'm going to the Pig and Whistle, Squirt. Are you coming?'

Would it be folly? 'Give me a moment to get ready.'

While relieving himself in the toilet bowl, he swayed a little to the left and caught a glimpse of himself in the mirror. This was the face which had no heart. Every time he looked at his reflection, a shop window, a car mirror or any other reflective surface, it reminded him he was not that man who fell in love with his sister. He was another, numbing stranger, one that had his arms, his legs, his eyes, a sleepless, restless stranger who kept walking, kept eating, kept living.

From number 18, the cottages, they walked the dirt track in the semi-gloom towards the Pig and Whistle. Ahead, a Rolls Royce was parked beside the road, shiny and blue with the chrome trimmings buffed to a high degree.

'That's the Turners,' said Tony with a hint of jealousy. 'They hired a bloody Roller just to rub salt in the wounds. You'd think what with Luze being our sister and all that they might have been a little generous in their actions.'

'Turner is not a man to feel generous towards his enemies.'

Once inside the main saloon, Jason sent his eyes to its cluttered lines and jolly faces, most of whom he knew. Then his attention was drawn to Franny with freckles burning on her cheeks, beckoning him over. He filtered through the standing drinkers and spotted Misery gulping down the last of his pint, propping up the bar.

'Here,' Franny said to Jason. 'Ask Misery. He remembers her.'

Misery brought out his tobacco tin. 'She's still handsome.' His head veered towards the snug. 'Yew can see who Miss Luze takes after.'

Jason crooked his head round the wood and opaque glass partition. Her hair was black, formed into a tight plait curled to the nape of her neck and her mature face spoke remnants of Luze. He swallowed hard and looked back at Misery. 'Did it cross your mind when you saw Luze?'

Misery held up an empty pint mug. 'It's thirsty work remembering.'

'Fran, treble whisky for me, single for Tony and a pint for Misery.'

'Hell, Squirt, carry on at that rate and you'll be pissed by nine.' Tony chortled and spotted his old secretary. He nudged Jason, sending a furtive glance. 'That's Claire, the limp celery stick Susan was on about. Come on, I'll introduce you.'

'You go and straighten her up.'

'The moment I saw Miss Luze,' Misery told Jason. 'Her face clicked. I couldn't remember where, not until that trouble started at the factory. I told Franny, she wus the one to stir up the past.'

Franny spoke. 'You told me the trouble started when she arrived.'

'Clean out your ears, woman. I told yew no such thing.' Misery leaned into Jason. 'I knew yew had difficulty in placing her but that's between yew and me.' Misery took his original position. 'When are yew going back to America, boy?'

'I am still on a sabbatical.'

'That's a holiday,' Franny told Misery.

'I know what it means,' Misery irritated. 'So how long are yew staying on this sabbatical or yew hoping to see Miss Luze?'

'That's a point,' Franny said. 'Why isn't she here? She's your sister, so why hasn't she come to see you and Tony?'

'I think we can safely say that my Father's indiscretion has not exactly endeared us towards the Turners.'

Jason preferred to amble along with the conversation until he became conscious of movement from the snug. He felt a tap on his shoulder then swung his head round with a kind of animal desperation to meet Turner's striking blue eyes.

'If you wish to return to America, I give assurances your brother will be treated fair. I too understand the loyalty of family. But in truth, you need to follow your own dreams.'

Jason ignored him and glanced down at Maria. Upon closer inspection he could see a woman in her mid forties, laughter lines at the corner of her mouth, but it was her eyes that drew him in, those beautiful green eyes and now all he could think about was Luze. 'How is my sister?' he asked and immediately felt himself pulled to one side.

Turner kept his voice trimmed. 'Listen to me well, young Black. Do not stir the pond of history. You have your father's ways, so too your brother, black by birth and black by nature. Do I make myself clear?'

'Transparency only occurs when there is something to see on both sides.'

'From where I stand, I see through you not at you.'

'From where I stand, I see nothing at all.'

A smile grew slowly on Turner's face. Decimation was his aim. 'You may think you have my measure. But I gained yours when you hid your black self behind white.'

Jason flushed from the neck up and watched Turner walk off with his wife. He had misjudged the most obvious and now realised with embarrassment, Turner knew he was there that day when the snow lay crisp and white against the Manor. The scene had been manipulated as surely as the scene had been manipulated this night. Those frank, intelligent blue eyes and that proud forehead, the salt and pepper well-barbed hair combined with his well-tanned complexion suggested to Jason this was a man that could destroy him.

'What the hell was that all about?' Tony asked.

Jason was disinclined to say. 'Where is your limp celery stick?'

'I stiffened her up.' Tony guffawed and Misery spluttered his drink. 'Hey, where's your sense of humour, Squirt? That was a good joke. Look, even Misery smiled.' Jokingly, he grabbed Misery round the neck. 'Did you enjoy that you miserable bastard?'

'Arr, it wus good.'

The joviality continued, drawing others into their small circle. After a third round of drinks, Jason loosened his tongue and was now in a place to the little left of the twentieth century. And Tony was not far behind. So it was of no surprise that when the twins spilled out of the pub, they explored their thoughts through whisky breaths under melting stars.

'Do you think he knows, Squirty?' Tony asked.

'He knows nothing and everything, my prick of a brother. But I have his measure as he seems to have mine.'

'Did he have a bigger tape measure?'

Jason smiled to the night that was his, away from a man who certainly had the ability to make him feel small. He drew out a packet of cigarettes and offered one to Tony. Before moving on, he let the smoke curl round his beard, ambushed by the brim of his hat. Now he was ready to portray his feelings, unsure what his brother may make of them. 'He set me up and I feel, felt, fell into his trap but can I blame him...after all said and done his whole family was impaled by ours. He must know how I feel about Luze, he must.'

'So what,' Tony said with his arm hooked loosely round Jason's shoulders. 'He was warning you off, no big deal.'

'Luze was more real, more everything I have ever known and I just want to hold her and make my nightmares disappear.'

'But you can't have her.'

'She doesn't look like the old man.'

'Neither do you.' Tony gestured to the river. 'Let's walk, get our heads clear.' Fat chance of that as they swayed a little in their amble, stumbled partly without an upward glance before Tony continued. 'Now look, Squirty dirty, I know it brought back memories seeing Maria and all that but you've got to get over her...you can't make something out of nothing...remember you saying how we fought like squabbling siblings, yeah? Right away I gelled with Luze and it wasn't sexual. Now usually when I meet something tasty, I look into their eyes and see spanners tightening my nuts...it wasn't like that with her.'

'Why was it so different for me?'

'Ah, that's because you were dribbling with sleepy love over a dream. Whoever gave you that dream, hic....messed with your head. You got all wrapped up in a supernatural event. I tried to tell you, didn't I? I tried to tell you she was dangerous but you wouldn't listen.'

Jason was nodding when suddenly he heard the boom of the bittern and stopped to let its haunting melody fill this intoxicating moment. 'She cast a spell and I don't know how to break it.'

'It's going to be alright, Squirty. I know how to break it....what you need is a woman that can stir your dick not your head...get it out of your system. Claire's got a friend and if she's anything like her then you're on a winner...so how about we make up a foursome?'

Jason shifted his gaze, was plainly summoning his thoughts.

'Since Susan and that girl behind the bicycle shed, how many have you actually screwed?' Three fingers came slowly into view. 'There's no shame in being bashful, Squirty.'

But Jason was far from bashful. On the contrary, if he had a mind, he would pursue the course of emotional entanglement but there was neither the glue of sex nor mutual interests to hold him to any woman he had encountered, except for Luze.

'And how many have you had?'

Tony placed his hands in the air then looked down at his shoes. 'What the hell, to be honest I've lost count. I certainly wasn't going to remain a monk when Susan closed her legs.'

'Did the old man know what you were up to?'

'Whatever you thought went on between him and me....hic....you've got it all wrong. All I wanted was the business...you and me together. Okay, so I made a cock up of things when you brought Susan home. Look, to be honest I would've dumped her and paid for the kid....but she went to Dad and whatever she said, he took her side.' Tony took a breather to get his hiccups under control. 'Perhaps she was blackmailing him then, who knows but it was either marry her and have the business or be out on my arse.'

'Why did you feel it necessary to run Strident Cutter?'

'Because underneath this suit is bugger all, Squirt...mere veneer...anything outside this village, I'm lost.'

'Are you still lost?'

'You found me, didn't you?' Tony paused, feeling a bit dysfunctional himself. 'I want this to work out for us, Squirty. We make a good team, don't we? Do you really want to go back to America?'

Jason shook his head and let his emotions flow beyond that element necessary. 'My heart is here but not my work but my work can centre on new products. I am enjoying the challenge of this new puzzle. It did cross my mind that I could produce an animated one.'

'There you go! You can invent a walking jigsaw...pity the old house was demolished but we can build another on the old factory site. Hey, by the way, I meant to say. I saw the drawings of the new factory and can you believe it, if you were a bird, you could fly high and look down onto a jigsaw piece. The void is in the front, central to the building and the nub is on the left hand side, some sort of round glass tower or whatever.'

'Turner doesn't strike me as a whimsical man.'

'I wonder what happened to Mum's money.'

'Logic dictates it went to him.'

'What, all of it?'

'Can you think of another explanation?'

'Not really,' Tony replied woefully. 'You'd think Mum would have saved a little for us, say put it in trust or something. Makes you wonder if she really loved us.'

'She must have had a good reason. I spoke to Henshaw and she never died intestate, nor did she die broke, so I asked about her Will. Henshaw said she made one but wouldn't say who the beneficiary was.'

'Dad would surely have kicked up a stink. You know, taken it to the courts.'

'No, because if you remember what Tools said about Graves making sure his daughter's money was protected.'

'What do you think about my suggestion? Make up a foursome, get you practiced in the art of making whoopee?' A single nod offered little enthusiasm. 'Come on, Squirty. All you have to do is close your eyes and think of your tripod.'

There seemed to be a grinding predictability to it all. Every time Tony came up with a suggestion, Jason would think about Luze. But Jason did not want to think about Luze because thinking about Luze was too painful.

Now Jason was intoxicated with love, returning to his room at the Pig and Whistle with his stomach tied in knots. It was a physical ache in the pit of his stomach for the want of a woman he could never have and he felt he was being condemned unfairly. What did he do to deserve such agony? However he approached it, the trail would lead off into mysterious surrounds and when he closed his eyes he prayed for a blank dream, prayed he would not dream about the anguish of forbidden love. It took him a long time to get to sleep that night.

Shortly after that little episode, the next few days melted the unbearable pain into a bearable one while his mind tried to concentrate on the matter at hand. Tony gave the all clear. Now the cutter could be used. They had a seven night window of opportunity, failing which they would have to find an alternative venue with an alternative cutter. A set back Tony was ill-prepared to accept but one Jason preferred.

So on the first night, Jason went to the city, used his formula on Alan Smith's silk-screen printer then returned before midnight and parked the Jag at the Pig and Whistle. He kept to the river path secretively winding his way to the rear entrance of the corrugated structure. Tony came out of the shadows and turned on the lone cutter. Under dimly lit torches, and as fast as they could, Jason fed the sheets and Tony collected the puzzles from the trough. In all, the noise of the cutter was sustained for eight minutes and they viewed eight minutes of clackety-clack worth the risk. They covered their tracks and went to the cottage, spent time to interlock some pieces in order for Jason to gauge the depths of his success. It was not very impressive. The formula required some tweaking.

For other nights, it had no prescribed duration and it was always tantalizingly close but on the seventh trial before the poignant cutter found a special place in history, though what that special place might be they never knew it rained as if Little Smeet had been transported to the tropics. Water fell in torrents, bouncing off the corrugated roof like marbles thrown on a dustbin lid. It was touching minds, affecting reason.

Above the deafening noise, Tony revolved his finger in the air, a sign for Jason to feed in the sixth sheet. Perhaps Jason's mind was on something else, perhaps he was feeling a little careworn but he fed it haphazardly. By reflex, Tony rectified its entry under the thin strips of metal with sharpened edges then felt the bite of steel, a second later the bite of realization. Three fingers had been jaggedly sliced off. Blood spurts splattered the immediate area and shouts carried panic. New imperatives crowded in. Tony went into convulsive shock, shaking violently with excruciating pain while Jason worked fast to bind the open wounds with an oil rag. At best it would stem the bleeding. At worst it would cause infection and throw further hazard to the injury.

From the corrugated structure Jason sprinted towards the Pig and Whistle car park, the rain cleansed his face and smattered the front of his clothes flecked with blood and ink. Throwing himself into the driver's seat, he steered the motor towards the corrugated structure, burst out, leaving the car door open. There was Tony, half crippled and on his knees, nursing his hand, trembling and could barely offer recognition. Telling him to hold on, Jason banged his fist on the blood-slick covered surface of the button to close down the cutter and hauled Tony to his feet.

It took moments to distance the Jag from Little Smeet, advancing on slippery country roads towards the hospital that was on the fringe of Norwich City centre. Feeling an all too encompassing hopelessness, Jason offered comfort, a monotony of desperate words as the sleek lines of a meaty engine left huge swells in its wake. A foot never eased off the accelerator until the desired goal was in sight. The motor swung hard round, clipped a free-standing notice *Emergency Patients* and skidded outside the hospital entrance. From there, the situation was taken out of his hands, his attention drawn to an assigned seating area, forbidden to follow. It did not make it easier to be left behind.

SUCCESSFUL INVENTION

Minute after unmarked minute, Jason glanced at his watch waiting for Tony to open his eyes. There was a pattern of bruising beneath the skin of the lids, the breathing was gentle and the bandaged hand was held in a stirrup. An English rose, far too pretty to be a nurse, walked in to check Tony's pulse but Jason said nothing, unwilling to trust his voice.

'He's doing just fine,' she said and with that, Tony opened his eyes, smacking dry lips. 'Would you like a cup of tea, Anthony?'

'Am I in heaven?'

'I take that to mean, yes.' She smiled at Jason. 'Would you like one too?'

Jason refused, watching her plump up Tony's pillows, giving the personal attention only paying occupants for a private room may enjoy. It was the least Jason could do for his brother.

'Did it work?' Tony asked.

Jason moved closer, cleared his throat and said softly, 'I had to rush back during your op to clear up the evidence. I told the duty nurse I slammed the hood on your fingers, they disappeared down the storm drain. Try to remember that.' The next piece of news never helped either to alter Tony's long face. 'Your fingers were in bits, stuck between the metal strips and pieces of cardboard.'

'That bloody cutter is cursed.'

'I was careless.'

'So it's not cursed?'

'I just said I was careless.'

'I'm on drugs. How can I be expected to think straight?'

Jason smiled, his brother was truly awake.

The conversation ceased when the nurse brought in the tea, reignited by Tony when she left. 'Makes you wonder though. Turner must have similar thoughts for why else would he want to keep it?'

'Why else indeed.' Jason went to the wardrobe. 'Your clothes must be destroyed. I shall bring you clean ones tonight. If Turner gets wind, we may have a problem.'

'Why?'

'Your earlier statement was correct. You are on drugs.'

'Have you seen yourself? You need to get back and clean yourself up.'

'I shall return about five. Do you require anything?'

'Can you bring my car magazines and some chocolate? Not bloody grapes or flowers.'

Jason ruffled his hair. 'Enjoy your tea and get some sleep.'

Elsewhere, across the city, the day was beginning with a rush and a shout, the fast whine of cars and heavy vehicles, the hurried clocking off of the early shifters. Jason dumped the clothes in the car park bin and returned to the Jag. With the poorly pale vision of his brother's face, he lit up a cigarette and wondered if the ills of that puzzle had been remedied. There had been a number of false attempts, countless times tweaking the chemicals, entirely dissatisfied with the outcome and considered that perhaps his ambition exceeded his expertise. Moments later he let his cigarette fall, watched it drop, the way it fell, the way it glowed brightly as it accelerated towards the ground and then he swung inside the motor thinking career endings could be so precipitous.

Turning into the Pig and Whistle car park, he halted sharply, switched off the engine and gripped the steering wheel harder, his knuckles turning white. 'Stupid, stupid, fucking stupid,' he said aloud. 'What the hell is wrong with me? Why was I so fucking careless?' He took in a deep breath and slowly let it out. 'Please, let this work... Oh God, please let this work.'

Then a whispered voice seemed to echo his sentiments. *Please let this work.* In a split second of unbridled fear and bewilderment, he turned his head quickly round and looked in the back seat. Nobody was there. He wiped his face with an open hand in a state of mental overload and wondered how he was going to survive the day.

He left the jag and crossed the road, working his way to number 18, the cottages. Here he gathered some clothes and car magazines then neatly packed them in a travel case. Three minutes later he was back at the motor, placed the case on the front seat and grabbed five boxes from the boot.

Once inside his room at the Pig and Whistle, he threw four boxes on the bed and placed the fifth on a sheet of hardboard brought out from the underside of his bed, such a laborious exercise but a necessary one. It began in its usual way, searching for a corner, any corner would do. Occasionally he pinched his nose or adjusted his position on the floor, straining in his attempts to seek out the right nubs into the right voids. But the signs were never wrong, not to a student of new chemistry. Patches of colour spawned brightly across the assembled pieces, the clarity was such it amazed even him. Before, in his earlier experiments the picture was barely distinguishable but now it was one to celebrate, and a crazed joyfulness came over him that conclusion was finally within his grasp. A promise duly kept.

He looked at his watch then at himself, ink, grease and blood, the latter hardly distinguishable among the rest of the stains. Tearing off his clothes, he popped under a shower and later flopped on the bed. Sleep came almost instantaneously.

And if he dreamed, he certainly never remembered when he woke nine hours later. It was dark, the glow and flicker emanating from the single light that lit up the backyard outlined his room. Grateful for that, he shifted off the bed and went directly into the bathroom, grateful for that too. He picked out a pair of jeans and a light-weight V-neck jumper then raked his fingers through his angry hair. Buoyed by an energy and optimism attributable to the success of his invention, he picked his way to the bar before going to the hospital.

'Single whisky please, Fran.'

'You never said anything about your brother,' she said stiffly. 'What on earth happened?'

'It was an accident. I slammed the hood on Tony's fingers.'

'Did they sew them back on?'

'They fell down the storm drain.' Another lie?

One after the other, it was becoming contagious. From the moment he arrived in Little Smeet to save his brother's miserable hide, his integrity had been sorely tested, slowly evaporating under the pretext of necessity, the prerequisite of a lie.

It was only slowly that he became aware of Jeremy Hubbard's presence, and that others had taken up position beside him. He squinted back towards the hubbub, blinking periodically, unlikely to be seen by any but the most dedicated fan.

'I'm sure it wusn't your fault.' Mrs Tooley broke into his thoughts. 'How's he doing?'

'Bearing up, you know Tony. How did you find out so quickly?'

'The Stockton woman works at the hospital but then your mind hasn't been the same since Luze, has it, Jason?'

He held the glass to his lips. 'I wonder if it ever will, Tools.'

She fondly patted his arm, her words heartfelt. 'Pity she turned out to be your sister. Yew made a lovely couple. Wat with her being so bubbly and yew wanting to take on your brother's troubles. Still, yew can't change that.'

It was a mystery how he managed to separate his feelings and pressed the argument home to put himself at ease. 'No, you make a good point, it cannot be changed. I see Jeremy Hubbard is gaining popularity.'

'He's asking a lot of questions, too many for my liking.'

'Did you know Luze was going to marry him?'

'Well I never. He's old enough to be her father.'

Jason looked away from Mrs Tooley, his attention drawn back to a gradual dispersal. Hubbard caught his eye and began his approach.

'See yew later,' Mrs Tooley said.

'Tools, before you go. Are you able to fit in a couple of hours for Tony?'

'Oh I can't Jason. I'm working in the new cafeteria and wat with doing Father Michael, I shan't hev time. Why don't yew move in with Tony? It makes no sense to stay here and waste your money.'

'The same question I would ask,' Hubbard said, the Australian accent noted. Illuminated by his bleach-blond hair, he looked like a life guard stained with suns and heroic rescues. 'I thought it was about time we were introduced. I'm Tom Turner's right hand man, Jerry Hubbard and you're Jason Black, Tony's brother. I understand he had a nasty accident.'

'I doubt if he will be able to operate machinery, not for the foreseeable future.'

They talked idly for a while and even allowing for some exaggeration on Hubbard's part, he had the capacity to make an impact and Jason was beginning to understand why Turner thought him to be good husband material for Luze.

'Are you going back when the factory is up and running?'

'That depends on my boss. Did Luze tell you about me?'

'She did mention you two are getting married.'

'Were.' Hubbard emphasised his loss. 'Had you thought about settling down?'

'I am settled down.'

'So you're not returning to Boston?'

'Nope, this is my home, sharing my fortune with Tony.'

'And Luze was part of your fortune?' It sounded like a statement but Jason knew it was a question and he wondered where this was going. 'A fascinating dilemma,' Hubbard continued. 'One which had me mystified until a little birdie told me she was ambushed by a rapist.'

A fist, full in the face propelled Jeremy Hubbard into flight. He landed hard with a bloody nose while a collective frown creased the features of nearby drinkers.

For Jason, temptation was there to justify his position, to shout his innocence but any defence was likely to be grim, so he walked away leaving Hubbard to work it all out. Outside, his mood was as dark as the sky as he sat silently in the motor awhile, realising the worst possible scenario had happened. He went through moments of depression, despair and anger, spent time agonizing over what seemed to be his dramatically foreshortened prospects in Little Smeet, and reflected on another escape route. Yes, he thought, he would return to America, hope his job might still be open or at worst, get another. But it was more a symptom of the crisis he faced, never a real alternative. He switched on the ignition, swung the motor round and headed for the hospital.

Having thus quietened most of his worst fears, Jason had a future of some sort and with resolution he entered the hospital with his mind characteristically made up. Not for him a life in America. His real family was here, the confined world of Little Smeet, gossip about his family infinitely more real with the prospect of turning his life around with a revolutionary new jigsaw puzzle.

'Hey there, Squirt, thought you'd abandoned me? Did the puzzle work out?'

'Better than anything imaginable.' Jason tried to sound happy. 'Bringing the temperature down two degrees altered the matrix of the tripositive ions. I knew William Crookes was on to something when he said the lanthanides had possibilities. Now they are flourishing with the Cobalt.'

'Squirt, what's that on your hand? Is it blood? Have you cut yourself?'

Rubbing it down his jeans, it all came flooding back. He sunk down on the bed, cupping his hands over his face then sweeping them through his hair. 'I sent one to Hubbard. He thinks I raped Luze.'

'Christ! Where was this?'

'In the Pig and Whistle. If I never knew better, he was deliberately goading me. Did he ever enquire about Luze?'

'No, Squirt. Jerry never said a thing. This is bad, very bad. If Turner thinks you raped his daughter, he's not likely to do business, is he?'

Conversation fell away because Jason was in turmoil, hardly believing Luze would tell Hubbard that. Or maybe she was cornered and did not know how to respond. Looking back, he realised he should have contacted her.

'I must speak to Luze.'

'You'll make things worse,' Tony said, rummaging in the suitcase. 'She's going to mess with your head when you should be focusing on Turner. Ask that nurse you saw this morning. She fancies you, she said as much.'

Jason grimaced, dismayed at the idea. She was nothing like Luze, his beautiful Luze with emerald green eyes and a face meant to smile. It would be one of many sorrows.

'So what do you think?'

'Perhaps,' he said, keeping Tony happy.

'They want to keep me here for a couple of days but I'm already bored out of my mind. Hey, never guess what. Mrs Stockton popped in to see me. Did you know she worked here as a nurse?'

'Tools mentioned it earlier.' He frowned with new thoughts. 'It must be Susan, stirring the shit.'

'That's more than likely.'

'Do you know where she lives?'

'Squirt, don't go there. Remember what she said? She said you would go begging. This is how she works. She probably hyped up Jerry, and Jerry told Turner. I bet Turner is trying to find out the truth. That's probably why Jerry goaded you.'

'He goaded me because Luze dumped him, or was it something else. So maybe Turner does want to know and why not, after all she is, in most respects his daughter.' Jason pinched the bridge of his nose. 'Damn, I have a thumping headache.'

'Take a couple of these.' Tony reached for two tablets on the bedside cabinet. 'They make you feel good. Take them before you climb into bed.'

'If they make you feel good, why are you giving them to me?'

'Hell, I pop these like Smarties, no problem in getting more. Where is the chocolate?'

'I forgot,' Jason replied sorrowfully. 'What is wrong with me, Tony? I am normally on top of everything. If I had just paid attention and fed the board correctly your accident would never have happened.'

'Okay, you fed it on the slant but I straightened it like many other times before. That cutter is cursed. It has a history of being cursed.'

'Then it suggests Molly's spirit is still lingering but why? Why now? Turner has achieved his ambition.'

'It can't be Molly. It has to be Dad. He gives you a crazy dream, shows you the way to save Strident Cutter. You could have covered my debts, developed the puzzle. We would have been quid's in.'

'No, I cannot buy that. The phantom desisted the moment we completed that puzzle, suggesting the correct route was taken. Perhaps the real problem is me. Take Hubbard, why did I rise to his bait?'

'What you need is to take that nurse out.'

And right on cue, *that nurse* walked in, her uniform taut across her breasts. 'Time for your medicine, Anthony.'

This was definitely Jason's cue to leave.

A sadder, more tragic person could not be found. Jason was in turmoil, swallowing tablets that would ordinarily be obtained on prescription. He placed his tumbler on the bookshelf, squirmed out of his clothes and slipped between crumpled sheets wondering if there was the remotest possibility of dropping into a black hole.

The tablets worked. Out like a light, he slept without nightmares or dreams and woke to a sense of well-being. Then thoughts of last night flooded in. Yet somehow it did not seem so painful or confusing and used the morning at his pleasure. First, he cleaned the Jag then took a leisurely stroll along the river that flirted with a couple of sailing boats edging south. What he loved most about this area was skin deep. It laughed easily, refused to follow fashions and gave people a respect of the past where they required a cavalier attitude towards time and distance. Still drifting aimlessly, he later caught glimpses of the corrugated structure being dismantled. That was a good thing, no longer a blot on the landscape. He skipped across the road and processed the path winding its way round the cemetery with a coming breeze to his face in that moment now where the whole village stood still. Here in the graveyard he liked to mull things over, to join the folds of the dead where he felt dead too.

'We need to talk.'

Jason corkscrewed round. The greeting was not one of friendship, the encounter probably not one of coincidence. 'I have nothing to say.'

'But I do,' Hubbard said. 'Sorry for last night. It was out of order.' He crouched low and studied Molly's headstone. 'I wonder how her life might have been if Captain Turner hadn't played a foolhardy game with Edward Black. Would she have found someone to love?'

'What do you know about her?'

'Only what Tom told me. Their father was not a particularly sensible man. Yes, he did do his bit in the war but he had similar faults to your grandfather. Elizabeth took on her maiden name to protect Tom and Maria.' Hubbard stood, about to explain his reasoning. 'Tom had me over the coals when I let Luze take my place. I asked her to be quick, in and out, strictly business. No problem, she said. She was itching to visit this part of England. None of us knew why she felt so drawn to such an insignificant spot on the map. When she returned, Tom took the view she should be told but she never said a word about meeting you or staying in the house. I told her to stay in a hotel at Norwich. Yes, she said, I promise.' He walked on, slowly, feeding his hands through his tailored trouser pockets. 'From what Luze told me, I gathered your brother's wife was a little feisty. She came to see me but my duty is towards Tom, so I told him what she said. The problem was, there were two stories being banded about and I couldn't make sense of it. As a consequence Tom and Maria came here, hoping to get a handle on it.'

'And did he?' Jason asked.

'Don't under estimate Tom. I say that as a favour. Luze has been upset for months, saying nothing to anyone, not even me. A woman doesn't cry for weeks on end just about her parent's past. I don't know exactly what went on between you two and I prefer not to know but I told Tom he only had himself to blame. He should have told Luze, instead he kept putting it off and the longer he put it off the worse it got.'

'Thank you for being frank.'

'No, I'm Jerry.' And he smiled. 'So how's Tony?'

'Bearing up. Mrs Tooley went to see him first thing this morning. I thought I would stroll around to get my head in order and see him later. How is Luze now?'

'More settled, getting back into her routine.'

'What does she do exactly?'

'What doesn't she do is more to the point. She studied architecture but left before obtaining her degrees, found jigsaw puzzles more interesting.'

'I expect she designed the new factory.'

'That's nothing to what she designed in Melbourne.'

'I understand he has two factories.'

'Apart from this one here, he has one in Melbourne and one in Sydney. Tom has a good recipe. He ships the products direct to the distributors and any orders he can't meet he contracts with another manufacture. Doing it that way, he's not financially tied if there's a slump in the markets.'

'Would Turner consider selling this one if he was made a good offer?'

Hubbard drew breath, expelling the word 'never' then went on to say, 'He would never sell his mother's land. The only reason he stayed out of England was because he knew one day he would have this one, by hook or crook.'

'By crook from my understanding.'

'Tom is a business man, Jason. He just bided his time. Your brother is not exactly the entrepreneur of the year. It was amazing how he lasted this long. Tom thought he would go under a couple of years back but somehow, he found a way to hang on.'

And Jason had to reply with a hint of amusement, 'He had an understanding bank manager.' Perhaps the social issues were important but something else was at work here. 'You still want to marry Luze. Am I right?'

It seemed Hubbard was almost afraid to say yes. 'I would have been good for Luze. It may still happen if she heard from you.'

Jason stopped in mid-stream. 'And what would you wish me to say?'

'What you should have said the moment you discovered she was your sister. Let her go, Jason. She has it in her head to live like a nun for the rest of her life. Do you want that on your conscience?'

'There is nothing I can tell her to make any difference.'

'Sure you can. You can tell her it was a mistake, that you found someone else, anything to cut the thread between you.'

'I will not lie to Luze. All her life the people closest to her have been economical with the truth. You tell me, Jerry. Why do you treat her like your pet Labrador? Are you doing Turner a favour or yourself a favour?' Jason watched the face, the hand loosen the tie. It was merely another revelation following another supposition. 'Has Turner promised you a partnership if you marry Luze?'

Their parting was prompt. Hubbard move off, shaking his head. Jason carried on towards the vestibule where he could see the silhouette of Father Michael, head bent over his desk. He tapped on the half-glazed door and walked in.

A face looked up and threw a pen to one side.

'Jason, you are just in time for a little tipple.' Father Michael pulled out a drawer and revealed a bottle of communion wine explaining, 'It looks as though Mrs Tooley has drunk the other half.'

'She likes her new job, I understand.'

'I was sad to hear of Tony's accident.' Father Michael worked between the bookshelves stacked with religious and serious tomes. 'You mustn't blame yourself, these things happen, though I was a little surprised to hear of your carelessness. Were your thoughts elsewhere?'

'My thoughts are all over the place.'

'Tell me your woes, cry on my shoulder.'

'I think there was something more to my dream. Okay, so Tony found the puzzle and it brought us together but now I have invented the very thing I dreamt about. I have produced a blank jigsaw puzzle that when the pieces interlock a picture comes into view.'

'Indeed, a challenging undertaking.'

'It was. But at the very moment of our last trials, three of Tony's fingers were chopped off by that cutter, the same cutter that caused the death of Molly Turner. I thought that was the end to everything but the puzzle finally came through, just as though it was meant to be. Now Tony wants his business back but Turner will never agree and I am at a loss what to do.'

Father Michael sat back, a learned head in company with another. 'Four years ago I was in Rome visiting Father Levin. He was suffering from a reoccurring bout of Malaria, caught it when he was in Egypt. Michael, he gasped on the precipice of God's holy doors, I have a confession to make. I saw my own admission into the pearly gates with Sister Anna holding onto my flesh. Days later, the priest was strutting the convent grounds, tripped over a rock and fell into her arms with her hand on his forgotten parts.' He paused shaking his head in amusement. 'I think the point I am making is that we can make of it as you will. Father Levin may indeed have seen his future but on the other hand he may have subconsciously organised events in order for it to happen. Whether by design or accident, you took advantage of a dream, used your talents to bring something new to the table. Remember the riddle, Jason, waiting for revision. Perhaps this is the revision. Offer the prize to Turner and share equally in its success.'

'Tony wants his name returned on those deeds. Now I feel obligated more than ever.'

'Tony wants what Tony wants.' Father Michael gave a stuffy response to what he perceived as emotional blackmail. 'He has his other hand to scratch his arse.' They laughed. 'Centuries ago, the church believed the earth stood still and was the centre of the universe until Nicholas Copernicus proved otherwise. A good priest but a little intimidated by his order. Now our expertise in the church on such matters precedes the unthinkable truth.'

'And what is the unthinkable truth?'

'That miracles happen, they do happen, Jason. Perhaps a lost soul has given you the chance to make amends and Lord knows your brother needs guidance. Do you intend to stay in Little Smeet?'

'I do.'

'Then why live at the Pig and Whistle?'

'I have been busy on the puzzle and now this. Have you heard the latest gossip?'

'Between you and me, I would have done the same, knocked the man down.'

'Have I made things worse, I don't really know, Michael. I should have walked away, turned the other cheek but it all welled up. Then it transpired he was testing me. Turner wanted to know the truth about what went on between me and Luze.'

'Did you speak of the phantom puzzle?

'I would prefer to keep that little episode quiet.'

'Next time you feel inclined to dig up my parishioners try to cover your tracks.' By now the communion wine had been drunk and Father Michael kicked back in his reclining rocker, put his feet on his desk and his hands behind his head. 'Jason, you do not choose the things you believe in, they choose you. We cannot protect our hearts to the point of exclusion. Our experiences make us what we are. You're a good man, very much admired in these parts. Mrs Tooley is a member of your fan club even though she received a very nice suite from your brother. It does me well in my quarters.'

'We should leave the village in her capable hands then nobody would be wanting for anything.'

'By the way, I meant to thank you for your donation. At least we can complete the bell tower and be in competition to that glass folly. I feel it serves as a look out tower rather than provide ornamentation.'

'I rather like it. Tony said if you could see the building from the air it looks like a jigsaw piece.'

'There you have it. A piece of the puzzle has fallen into your lap.'

But Jason was still a confused parishioner. He was stroking his whiskered chin wondering whether to confess his sin. 'Michael, I made love to Luze. It was not-'

'Hush now, Jason. I cannot hear your confession when there is nothing to confess. To be in love with a woman and take her when she is willing is not a sin. We live in a new era where marriage is a secondary consideration. As a man I understand. What you did, you did in all innocence though I fear she has made a strong mark on your heart.'

'I shall never find another Luze.'

'Never is a long time.'

'If a soul can exist beyond the grave, then mine shall exist for Luze. Until then I feel dead.'

'Sometimes a man's mettle is tested and for certain yours has.' Father Michael got to his feet and dragged Jason's to his, holding his shoulders firm. 'God will not let you live with a dead heart. Maybe your destiny is to continue your good works, to follow a single path but know this. God will not allow you to live in misery if you can find a way to help yourself.'

'I am a scientist.'

'And as a scientist you believe in facts...what you see, what you feel and what you can explain, and yet you cannot explain the phantom jigsaw.'

Jason nodded then smiled, adding before walking away, 'I am working on that one.'

In the late afternoon, sitting on his bed, Jason wondered how he got through the day taking everything in. Yes, he did consider telephoning Luze but it would be like using a cigarette lighter to see how full a petrol tank is. Then he wondered what muted spirit could haul him back to earth after a paradise feast of love. Dreams and hopes were fragile and could be easily destroyed by a single word, a single thought or a single action. He lit up a cigarette, waved the smoke from his eyes and considered it was time to shave off his beard.

Much later, he was still feeling like that same man, that numbing stranger, one that had his arms, his legs, his eyes, a restless stranger who kept walking, kept eating, kept living, but was now clean shaven and traversing the creaky stairs to the exit point. He nodded to Franny, swept out of the main door and was surprised by Tony who was polishing a hand mark on the bonnet of his jag, rubbing at the already gleaming metal as though it were an oil lamp.

'Hey, Squirt. Thanks for cleaning my car.' Tony, encumbered by a bandaged hand held in a sling tried to be cheery but he looked very careworn. Dark blotches were under his eyes, a deep furrowed brow, all reminiscent of his worried days over the business.

'What are you doing out of hospital?'

Mrs Stockton's boy stopped sharply in his mini and got out with an afro hairstyle. He was grinning and called out, 'How goes it, Tony, that's more like it.'

'I'm quite the hero around here, Squirt. Franny said I can use her remote control with my nose.' He expressed amusement but Jason knew he was trying to make light of a bad situation. 'I was glad to get out of that hospital.

Claire brought me home. Christ, I thought, this is it, I'm dead but she drives like a trooper.'

'You should have stayed where you can receive good treatment.'

'Okay, truth is, I want to see the puzzle.' Then he looked closer at Jason. 'You've shaved off your beard.'

'What do you think?'

'Not sure. Go and get a box and I'll see you at the cottage.'

And back at the cottage, Jason said, 'What if we just offer the patent to Turner and in return ask for a royalty on each one he sells?'

'Why?'

'Tony, I have your interests at heart but if Turner refuses to give you what you want then we could find ourselves in a war zone. There are other options.'

'Hey, my business was taken from under my nose. Don't forget how he made that happen and look at the lengths he went to. Rubbed my nose in the salt and made you look like a prat. It wasn't my fault what Granddad did so why should we get the blame. And as for the bit over Maria, it was his beef with Dad. Turner should have tackled him when he was alive but no, instead he waited till Dad popped off and then wham, right in for the kill, thinks he can make my life a misery, call that fair, I don't think so.'

Jason shifted from one foot to another, padding his breast pocket for a cigarette. His expression shifted too, from hope to confusion. Here, he thought, his brother could turn the other cheek, a sign to show unity and understanding for the awkward position he found himself in, and because of it he failed to mention what else he had up his sleeve.

'Do you want something to eat?'

Tony rattled a box. 'No, I want you to show me this.'

Already the hinges of his jaws were cramping as he watched Tony struggle with the lid. And that seemed to be the pattern while Jason connected some pieces in the fug of a kitchen that barely had room to manoeuvre. Tony's good fingers drummed like piston rings on the table waiting for something to materialise. Jason tensed and clipped him round the ear but then, when it happened, in a dazzling instant, the world became Tony's oyster. He expressed himself as a man walking on the path of success, living a life style where money spoke volumes, where esteem would be restored in Little Smeet. Now Jason wondered if he had been wrong, perhaps it was conceivable Tony had taken a lot for granted, had assumed too much and maybe, just maybe *old habits* were returning.

As the afternoon drew to a close, Jason slipped outside for a cigarette. Sharing the world has never been humanities defining attribute, he thought, so why should it be any different for Turner? Why would he want to share the enterprise with a family that had a history of cheating, murder and rape? Of course, he could see Turner's point of view but felt from his own that he had been unnecessarily labelled as black by nature, unjustly. It was unfair, only a little unfair.

Tony emerged and a farm-dog barked far across the estuary, fixing the time and distance exactly. Next door, number nineteen, Misery's wife was taking in her washing, and although she was much older than she had been, and although her body was quicker to become weary, she still had the movement of herself beneath her clothes as a good and special thing.

'Why do women always look sexy near a washing line?'

Jason rolled his eyes and heard her say, 'In your dreams, boy.'

'Is Misery inside?' Tony asked.

'Having his tea,' she said walking over. 'Yew poor boy, how do yew feel now?'

'It's a bit sore.'

'Apart from me, if there's anything yew want don't hesitate to ask.'

'I could do with some help with my laundry.'

'Let's be having it then.'

NEGOTIATIONS

A secret only remains a secret if kept from general knowledge or view, a thing which explanation is unknown. The moment Mary Walters walked in to collect Tony's laundry and caught sight of the puzzle on the kitchen table, it reached the ears of Mrs Tooley the very next day, and within three, the whole village was discussing a mysterious jigsaw puzzle invented by Jason Black. It was the highlight of conversation, a toxic mix of heightened curiosity and business politics.

Unfortunately for Jason, Jeremy Hubbard had no alternative but to contact Turner. His unbalanced allegiances tipped in his boss's favour but it weighed heavy against Jason who was exhibiting the signs of an approaching nervous break-down. First, he had given up smoking, and secondly, he was feeling the pressure coming from Tony. But things were about to change, a defining moment to alter the course of his destiny. He hovered close to a bar stall, had just ordered his whisky when Franny picked up the receiver after the telephone rang three times.

'Pig and Whistle,' she announced then looked astonished. 'Well, I never, fancy that...going very well, thank you and you...no, I haven't...oh yes, he's right here.' Franny waved the receiver under his nose. 'It's your sister.'

His heart jumped into his throat. He took the receiver out of Franny's hands and hoarsed down the line, 'Luze?'

'Oh Nuts, I am sooo sorry, sooo very, very sorry I never telephoned before. I wanted to, oh I so wanted to but things got crazy and everything became hopeless, so hopeless. How have you been?'

Not good. 'Things are fine.'

'You don't want to speak to me, do you? Do you want me to hang up?'

'No,' he quickly responded.

'Then what is it? Are people there?'

'No, Luze, only a quarter of the population.' Although the pub was poor and crowded, it had a lively reek of streaming life and no doubt about their sincerity, or their curiosity. He cupped his hand close to the mouthpiece and dropped his voice confidentially. 'Has Jerry put you up to this?'

'Why on earth should you think that?' Her breath bounced against the mouthpiece. 'Has he been a pain in the Derry air?'

Jason smiled and said nothing.

'Nuts, are you still there?'

'Yes.'

'I had no other number. Jerry said you were still in Little Smeet living at the Pig and Whistle. Can you ring me back?'

'And the same circumstance will apply.' Jason stared at his growing audience. Their eyes were enquiring and fanatical then warmed and lightened with the sparkle of good humour when he motioned with his chin. 'Can a man at least have breathing space?' They grumbled but rarely obeyed. 'Luze,' he said turning his back on them. 'Did you hear about Tony's accident?'

'Yes, but I suspect it wasn't the hood, was it, Nuts? Pappy is on his way to see you. He's up in arms about your puzzle. What's it like?'

'The picture quality is better than anything imagined. There is no doubt it will revolutionise the industry.'

'I know how you feel, about gossip and all that but-' She broke off and he waited in the pause until she continued. 'Nuts, this puzzle can be our saviour.'

'How so?'

'Because I want to be with you. Do you want to be with me?'

Forever. But what could he say? Should he kill the conversation stone dead? Heed Jerry's advice and let her go? Running a finger round the rim of his glass, he thought there was no simple answer, probably no answer at all.

'Nuts? Speak to me, anything, just something.'

'Let me think.'

'Oh God, you don't want me, do you? Go on, be honest.'

'Not true, Luze but what you're suggesting is impossible.'

'Nothing is impossible, not if you want something so badly. There is always a way and that way came when I heard what you had done. You, me and Tony as business partners, nothing untoward. I have the money. We can lease an empty factory and I can live in Norwich. We can do this, Nuts. You might as well know that Pappy is going to give Tony the sack so he will probably have to live in a tent.'

Jason rather liked the idea of Tony living in a tent. 'I suppose it was to be expected.'

'So what do you think? Or are you still thinking?'

'You really do not want to know what I think.'

'I see, so it's a no go then.' Her voice sounded so disappointed and he so desperately wanted to put his arms about her, to give her his succour and protection. 'Nuts,' she went on. 'I would far rather live half a life than have no life at all. I just ask to be close to you. I promise not to put any restrictions on your movements. If your love has faded and-'

'No,' he interjected. 'It burns as brightly as the puzzle but you offer a difficult proposition.'

'Can you honestly say you would prefer to let this opportunity pass us by, be without your composite singularity? I certainly need fusion, even if it's just a spark.'

He laughed down the line and suddenly the floodgates opened. It was almost as if his pain and suffering was floating away and in its place was something worth living for. 'What of your father? What of Jerry?'

'I told Jerry to go and put a leash around someone else's neck and take them for a walk. It's my decision, Nuts. Okay, Pappy will be hopping mad and so will Mammy but it's my life. I am doing nothing wrong and the last thing I want is to look back with regret. I cannot cope with this pain anymore, this terrible emptiness and loneliness. I cannot sleep, I cannot eat, I cannot go anywhere without looking at other men thinking one of them is bound to be you but of course that's impossible because you're there and I'm here.'

'I am similarly inclined.'

'Then tell me truthfully, really truthfully, I won't be very upset if you say maybe or whatever, yes in fact I would be upset but that's neither here nor there, well it is-'

'Luze, spit it out.'

'Do you want your composite singularity?'

'I do.'

'Oh, Nuts,' she screeched gleefully down the line. 'That is super, duper. It will work, I promise it will work. I shall come directly to the Pig and Whistle. Can you book a room for me?'

'When do you anticipate arriving?'

'Four days, your time. Goodbye, my fusion.'

Jason stared at the receiver, comprehension dawning as whispered conversation fell behind him. He slowly dropped the receiver onto its cradle and snatched his glass, swallowing his whisky whole. Now he was trembling with excitement and considered there was no love that was not worth the risk. 'Another whisky, please Fran.'

'Come on, boy,' Misery said impatiently. 'Don't keep us in suspense. What did she hev to say about your puzzle?'

He turned into the room trying to suppress his excitement. 'She is coming down to see it.' There was deadpan silence. This was not enough. 'I believe her father is also on his way.' But still this was not enough. 'She has decided to invest in my invention and is coming down to work by my side.'

'Well fancy that!' Franny exclaimed. And the snug came alive.

'She should be here Thursday,' Jason told Franny. 'Can you give her a nice room? She will need to stay here until she can get her accommodation sorted.'

'Show us this mystery puzzle, boy.' Misery asked. 'My Mary said it had the touch of Molly Turner.'

Arr, show us the puzzle.

Their concern seemed as great as his in this shambles where history had routinely summoned the unknown. He shot up to his room and grabbed another puzzle box off his bedside cabinet leaving two unused. And all the while his thoughts were on that moment in the Jag taking her to the airport, positive she knew her way as though born to him. She was his destiny as surely as he was hers. And even though he knew he would live half a life, it was better than no life at all.

In his absence, the snug had thickened so quickly it was impossible to calculate how. He laid the box on one of the long wooden tables and was drowned by their fumes of sweat and giddy suffocation as he started off in one corner, now practiced in the art of this rudimentary game. Soon, there were oo's and aah's as though witnessing magic but that was the point of the exercise, to bring magic into their lives.

Typically, Jason had depicted a garden of remembrance, a subject close to his heart for secretly there had always been a place in his heart for Molly Turner. Those moments were there, always, but they were rarely noticed and they rarely lasted longer than a flicker of thought.

'That's lovely,' Franny said, wiping the corners of her eyes with a tea cloth.

Arr, thass lovely, her sentiments shared.

Jason dismantled the puzzle. 'This is only a sample. It can be any picture.'

'You're a roit ol' softie, boy,' Smelly said, laying a pint in front of him. Smelly lived for his cows, growing them from birth by the heat of belligerence and milking them daily with affection. 'Those wus bad days, bad days. I wus seeing to my Dad's heifers when Misery came rushing up. We wus a few years older than the Turner boy but we remember the look on his face. He wus lost in your grandfather's madness, thass fer sure.'

'Arr, thass fer sure,' Misery confirmed. '1942, we wus too young, Smelly and me to be conscripted into the war but old enough to know what went on in that factory. It wusn't roit to hev young uns working them cutters.'

'How old was Turner when he tackled my Father outside this pub?' Jason asked Misery.

'He would hev been about twenty at the time, I reckon. Smelly wus one of the men who clawed him off your dad, Franny's being one of them and Bill the other...it wus a terrible do. Smelly wus sick to his stomach, wusn't yew, boy? It wusn't enough to keep Tom at bay until the police arrived. Franny's dad and yours had a go at him after he accused Graves as being accomplice to your grandfather's death.'

'That's news to me,' Franny scolded. 'My dad wouldn't do such a thing.'

'Your dad wus thick as thieves with Charles Black, as well yew know it. They kicked into Tom Turner, bruised him until he wus black and blue. But it brought in good harvests that year. Smelly had good milk, didn't yew, boy? And daffodils, well yew never seen so many daffodils, covered the churchyard and all over the fields, even by the old structure. Smelly reckoned he saw Molly there, roit after that fight.'

'He was drunk,' Franny said.

'I wus not drunk, woman. She wus there in the mist calling out fer her brother.'

'What mist?' Jason asked.

'It wus a blanket of fog that night,' Smelly told Jason and the room huddled in fear. 'It came up fast, like a devil from hell after Tom wus arrested. I couldn't see a damn thing in front of me but I heard her voice like a terrible howling, shouting fer justice she wus...brother, where are yew, where are yew. Calling fer him to be freed. Thass what I reckon. Brother, where are yew....a heart rendering cry the likes I've never heard since. It raised the hairs on my neck, thass fer sure.'

Then the pub was held in awe when the snug door opened by some unseen measure. Everyone held their breaths for a moment until shiny bright buttons emerged.

'Hello, Chappy,' Franny said. 'Fancy a pint of your usual?'

'Don't mind if I do.' He removed his helmet, placed it on the bar and undid the top button of his dark blue inform. 'Dora says I'm putting on too much weight.' But still he requested a packet of crisps. PC Chaps was a whiskered lemonade drinker, smelling sweetly of peppermints and obviously suited to the job for he was a large man who had suffered his share of damage arresting felons. 'What's this I hear about a puzzle?'

'You missed it, Chappy.' Jason said and watched the eyes going to the box. 'Okay, I shall drop off a spare puzzle but you have to do it yourself.'

'What's wrong with that one?'

'Once the picture is revealed, it stays.'

'What's the point of that?' Misery asked.

'I am still working on the process. I thought if I developed it to be light sensitive the picture quality would be sacrificed, or at worst no picture at all.'

'Who does a jigsaw in the dark?' Franny asked.

Jason stifled a smile. 'I was referring to the heat of light.'

'You best be pleased to know that Londoner is selling up,' Chappy told Smelly then he licked the wet of his whiskers. 'You buy that and your cows won't get shuffled by outsiders.'

Smelly had an epiphany. 'There's a place fer yew, Jason! Roit up your street.'

'What place?' Jason asked.

'Why it's your grandfather's old place, the one the Turners rented. Thass a lovely old house with a couple of acres, can't think of a better home. It has some old buildings, nothing yew couldn't put roit.'

Jason stood motionless, his mouth half open. Was this fate?

'Don't do any harm to have a look, boy,' Chappy said. 'He might offer you a cup of tea.'

Jason grabbed his jacket and hat, cuffed Chappy on the shoulder and said, 'On my way I shall drop off a box at the station.'

In the evening air, things were rapidly going through his mind, like transferring large sums without making a dent on his current account, something he kept from Tony for reasons obvious. It was so sudden that he felt as though a camera flash had exploded in his face. And all things sang constant, the odd car passing, the whisper-hum of grass swaying majestically in Smelly's fields, and the crackles of tiny stones crushed under his feet. He had never taken notice of this place before, not this house, not in this manner, had never believed it meant anything other than a home just on the periphery of Little Smeet, exactly one mile from the Pig and Whistle in the opposite direction of the factory.

He stopped at a wide wooden gate, the name partly faded, Mile House. It was a late nineteenth century two storey property with relief work round square patterned windows and set well back from the road. To the rear, the river curled softly against its banks, racing fast in the winter and sauntering in the summer. When he began to walk the frontage, a man called out from behind, the outsider as Chappy pointed out, a Londoner who set out most days, trundling over Smelly's fields acting the village idiot with his shotgun.

'Are you selling up?' Jason asked. 'Our local bobby said this place was up for sale.'

The moment turned. The Londoner was an excitable vendor, talked a lot and was always busy with his hands as though he never knew where to put them unless he had his shotgun. Even when they walked to the river, he still chatted on about its location, how it represented an ideal place in an ideal situation. Negotiations were under way.

Of course, the very next morning, Tony obtained the gist of things from Misery before he set off to work. When Jason walked in with the last puzzle box under his arm, he was confronted with a stormy protest.

'What's this I hear about Luze coming into business with us over the puzzle?'

Jason picked up a frying pan, his mood unchanged from the well of happiness he received last night. 'It solves all our problems, Tony. Scrambled or fried?'

'Put the bloody pan down and speak to me! What happened yesterday?'

Jason turned and his twin was standing in the doorway reserving judgement. 'Luze telephoned. In short, she will be investing monies into our business. She will be an advantage and help us to promote a new line.'

'How can she do that when she's in Australia?'

Jason cracked a few eggs in a bowl, avoiding the answer. 'I am doing scrambled.'

'She's coming here, isn't she? Are you two sodding bonkers or what?'

'She is still our sister.'

'And you remember that when you're screwing her!'

Miserably, Jason hung his head. Those few words spoken might yet cost him a lifetime of angst and he was afraid.

'Look at me, Squirt. I see where you're taking this but we agreed to negotiate with Turner, get back some pride and all that.'

'Turner will not negotiate. From what I gathered, he's coming down and your position in the factory is going to be terminated so you will have to move out.'

'Well that's just bloody great! It's Jerry and his big mouth.'

'No.' Jason corrected. 'It's your big mouth telling Mary.'

Tony pulled out a chair, sat down nursing his arm. His mood somewhat softened. 'We shouldn't look at this negatively. Turner's come here to do a deal...yes, of course he has. Why, he's probably foaming at the mouth for your patent. Of course he's pissed, why wouldn't he be?'

The morning had set its pattern for the day. For elsewhere other things had taken place and were about to encroach upon number 18 while breakfast was currently being served.

Jeremy Hubbard banged his fist on the door and Tony answered. 'Ah! Just the man we need to see. Jason has just made breakfast, do you want some?'

'This is not a social call.' Hubbard looked beyond at Jason. 'Turner wants to see you.'

'We'll be along in twenty minutes. I need to get dressed.'

'No, he wants to see Jason and right now would be a good time.'

'I take it he's not in a good mood?'

'How's your hand coming along?'

The heavy bandages were off, replaced by a light gauze covered by a cotton hand glove. Jason had seen the healing effect of Tony's wound each day, wincing at its ugly raw state and the disfigurement for the rest of his brother's life. 'It itches,' Tony said. 'Odd, because I feel it itches on the parts I haven't got. The doctor said that was normal. I am going to have physiotherapy to get accustomed to the parts I haven't got.'

'Bottom line,' Jason asked Hubbard. 'What's going on?'

'You better tread carefully. He never deals unless he has an ace up his sleeve.'

Jason knew he was past the time of no return, the games of make believe were at an end. He went into the living room, rushed his hands through his mop then placed his Homburg on his head. A glance in the mirror gave him the measure of reassurance to assert his authority then he picked up the last box and walked out to a chill in the air deciding he had no authority at all. He felt utterly confused as though he might be on the brink of being quite out of his depth with also an element of sheer disappointment.

Instead of taking the river path, they padded the dirt track towards the Pig and Whistle, turned right along the high street then right again on the very driveway that once led to the formidable home of the Black generation. Advancing in a straight line, Jason could now appreciate the cleverness of this building in the guise of a jigsaw piece. Dead centre, the brickwork created a hollow bowl where it presented two entrances. On the left, a pair of oak panelled doors, which offered access to the factory and on the right, Jason followed Hubbard through to the main foyer. Beyond this, a spiralling staircase leading to a glass-tower folly, a huge area of copious luxury bathed under natural light. And there, nestled ahead of settees and coffee tables, a bent head of salt and pepper hair over a desk.

Turner looked up above brooding eyes and slowly peeled off his reading glasses as Jason came forward. There was a silence that seemed to stretch to infinity before Turner spoke. 'Present your case and present it wisely.' His manner was wrapped in enmity, his scholarly voice nurtured with purpose.

Jason placed the box on the desk. It was nothing special, just a cast off, frayed at the edges and torn on one corner. Hardly a befitting vessel to show Tom Turner but it triggered a memory for Jason, a vision in an evergreen kitchen picking up a blank piece of a jigsaw puzzle under the scrutiny of his brother's brown eyes. He then went on to explain the process and applied a piece of noteworthy information.

'I have no doubt in my mind this will revolutionise the industry and put you ahead of the game by miles.'

Turner leaned forward and shuffled the lid from its tatty base. 'Your presentation leaves much to be desired.'

'We were saving on costs.' A lame excuse.

Unimpressed, Turner touched upon a piece. Of a single fact he had become certain, it was blank. 'What duration the picture and quality?'

'The picture stays and the quality is significantly higher than any sold on today's market.'

'A remarkable claim,' Turner said, easing back in his chair. 'And what is your proposition?'

'You have the pattern rights, free and simple. In return, the Black name is recognised on the new product line and a stake for my brother in this business, nowhere else, just here.'

'You believe that dolt of a brother can run this business?'

'If things had worked out, my Father and you would have shared this business so why not share it on a good platform.'

'Edward Black and his son rose to their name, black by birth and black by nature.' The veteran Tom Turner smiled, his face wrinkled in admiration. 'You have brains, Jason Black. Pity they live in a fool's paradise.'

'I am no fool.'

'From where I sit, I am looking at a fool who thinks he can solve his family's poverty.' Turner rotated in his chair ninety degrees. 'I have no desire to the deal. A Black will never be part of this business, nor will it ever be printed on any product this factory manufactures, or any other factory owned by me.'

'You are stubborn man, Tom Turner. If you suppress this from your products you will fall behind when others will rush for the selling rights.'

Defiant Turner swivelled back and threw an envelope at Jason. 'I said the name Black will never appear on any of my products. Your invention would not have been so readily possible without my equipment, on my own land and by an employee who falsely claims sympathy for his injury. We shall meet in court then we shall see who the beneficiary of such an invention is.'

They observed each other as if afflicted by the same malady then Jason picked up the envelope from the floor and walked away with another option rolling in his brain. Would Tony thank him for that?

Tony was outstretched on the sofa, ankles crossed, shoes kicked off with a drink in his hand. He looked up when Jason walked in. His own expression had changed. 'Went bad, didn't it?'

'What else did you expect?'

'I expected him to see sense.'

Jason reached inside his jacket pocket and placed the envelope on his chest. 'He served an injunction. Bottom line, we shall not be able to do anything with this patent until the case has been heard in court.'

'So where does this leave us?'

'It leaves the three of us working a new business.'

Tony swung his legs off the sofa. 'Make believe businesses won't solve your problem with Luze. Turner knows damn well he can't claim full ownership of that patent. Without you it would never have been possible.'

'Tony,' Jason sighed. 'We have other options.'

But was Tony really listening? 'Sod him, we'll negotiate with another competitor and watch his empire go down the drain. We'll humiliate him like he humiliated me.'

'Has there ever been a moment in your life when you have considered my needs?'

'You can't have Luze! She's messed with your head, Squirt. Do you think you can play happy families, I don't think so. Now hear me out. You did something good for me, now I'm going to do something good for you and one day you're going to thank me. As soon as she gets here, I am going to send her packing and...Squirt, where are you going?'

Jason never looked back.

STRAINED AND STIRRED

For three days Jason had lived as he wished, knowing he had done what he could, content to be alone. And through all that time he had clung to one fantasy. Now he was ready to face Luze.

He had seen her enter the Pig and Whistle with two suitcases and waited for her to come out. She then crossed the road in a hurry, spilt down the track and made a rat-a-tat-tat on number 18. Every breathless word she said, he heard, every breathless movement she made, he saw.

'Tony, is Jason with you? Franny said she hasn't seen him in days.'

There was something in the way Tony hung on the handle which suggested a hint of concealed pain. 'I thought he buggered off with you.'

'How could he do that when I only just arrived?'

'Last time he did something like this, he went to America. That's where he's at, gone back to his old job. Do you want a cup of tea?'

Luze shook her head. 'It was my fault.'

'No it was mine, ham fisted dopey plonker.'

From his vantage, Jason watched his twin coax Luze into the house as she pulled from her shoulder bag a tissue. He stayed in the cool shadows of the night feeling a return of the familiar, protective love that he had always had for his brother. A cigarette later, he went in hearing one proud voice emanating from the kitchen.

'....you should have been here, Luze. It started off blank, clean as a whistle but as soon as the pieces interlocked the colour came to the foreground and it made you want to carry on all the more. Jason took a photograph of Molly's headstone and got Allen Smith to touch it up then he ran it off on the silk screen printer.'

'I wonder what Pappy will make of it.'

'My thoughts entirely,' said Jason.

He met and answered her arms where they held each other in silence. He had smelt her from the moment he walked over the threshold, had felt his own happiness rise and had seen how she looked, wasted and pale with her hair scruffily tied back in a simple kerchief.

Tony allowed his eyes to drift along to his twin. So much history, so much argument, so much cajoling and it had come to this. His eyes misted with recollection and regret. This last year, his most frequent companions had become doubt and near-despair.

'We must face what must be faced together, Tony.' Jason embraced him. 'Are you prepared to put your animosity aside toward Tom Turner?'

'Yes,' the voice croaked.

'And you, Luze, are you prepared for the road ahead?'

He watched the vigorous nod and kept his expression inscrutable. 'Then we are truly married to a poor situation.' His laughter broke the moment of solemnity. Jason had never felt so happy and while they talked over each other he saw how Luze had instantly found her natural self, convinced this was a new beginning in unchartered territory.

'I will respect you and you will respect me,' he told her. 'And if you feel there comes a day when you hunger for marriage and children, I must be told.' From the corner of his eye he watched Tony move away. 'Tony, there should be no secrets between any of us, not any more.' Now there were things to be said. It required no padding and he provided none. 'Luze, before you came on the scene, I filed a provisional patent for my invention. I lied when you asked me what business I had in mind for Tony. Further, it was my suggestion for Tony to sell the business to your father, get the debts cleared and underhandedly use the factory's resources. I make no excuses save one. I believed what I did was out of necessity but my conscience bothered me and I realise now I could have handled the situation in other ways. I could have curbed Tony's impatience and sought for outside equipment. In truth, I was torn between anger and misery and I never want to be placed in that position again. Remember how adamant you were about your father never selling his mother's land? I knew then I had to cover all eventualities so I split the patent. In effect I have two, one covers jigsaws, the other paper publications. Your father is filing against the jigsaw patent. I do believe his counsel has misinformed him.'

'Did you know?' Luze asked Tony. 'Did you know about the other patent?'

'Tony did not know,' Jason answered for him. 'I am more to blame in the mess we find ourselves in. Now we must come to an agreement. Since we shall begin a new business under one patent for publications, what do we do with the other?'

'I know I am hardly in a position to ask favours,' Luze said, finding a chair. 'But I would like Pappy to be offered it. He's a fair man and will arrive at a fair price. Apparently, Granny Beth, Elizabeth Turner was given some money by your mother so she could make a new life in Australia with Pappy and Mammy. Shortly after I was born, Mammy fell pregnant again and then someone spotted Pappy. He was sent back to England to finish his sentence, a seven year term in a horrible place. Granny Beth and Mammy worked the business so Pappy could have something to come back to.'

Jason thought if he had bad memories then Turner could replicate the smarting sorrow three times over and more. Turner had lost his sister, had witnessed his mother's grief then later Maria's, and had paid a heavy price in the form of British justice. 'Tony, what do you think?'

'I've been an utter prick, that's what I think,' he replied holding a glass of water to his lips. He swallowed his tablets and continued, 'I watched you walk out of that door and honestly believed you would come back after you cooled off but when you never turned up, I thought you and Luze had skipped the country. It was then I really woke up and stopped feeling sorry for myself. I've always wanted you to stay here, work alongside you because I'm such a tosser in business. But working in that factory has taught me a few things, not least how the cutters work and how people should be treated. Okay, so Luze is here and I can see where you're taking this now, so count me in. Anything you want is fine by me.'

'Then we are agreed. The patent should be offered to your father.' Jason dug inside his back pocket and brought out some house details. 'This is where we shall live and work. Chappy told me it was up for sale. It was our Grandfather's old house, where the Turners rented.' Again there was stupefaction as they drawled over their new prospects. 'I made a deal with the owner. With Henshaw's help I moved in pretty quick.'

'I knew this existed but never realised it belonged to Granddad. Look, I don't want to put a damp squib on your choice of accommodation, Squirt but if Luze lives there this village is going to be a hive of gossip.'

'By us keeping together, living and working here in Little Smeet we are effectively saying exactly what we should be saying, that there is nothing immoral in the position we take. To face the opposition with a good heart is far better than to face the opposition with a frightened one.' Jason went to the front door. 'Come on, let's all go home.'

From the cottage, they crossed the road and Jason told them to wait in the Jag. He then disappeared into the Pig and Whistle and emerged ten minutes later with two suitcases, dumping them in the boot.

'I have informed Fran.' Jason shuffled into the driver's seat. 'She will, no doubt, inform everyone else. Tony, we can come back for your things tomorrow.'

'Did you know Pappy calls you a pirate?'

Tony crooked his head round. 'It must have been his beard.'

'A beard? Crikey, what with his hat he must have been frightening.' Luze giggled.

'Arrghh, me hearties where be me treasure,' Jason responded.

'Here,' Luze said so simply.

Jason smiled. The idea of Luze being his untouched treasure appealed to him. 'A pirate needs a parrot. Are you up for it, Tony?'

'Since my feathers were ruffled the most, why not.'

The humour continued until they reached Mile House. Here, Luze questioned the era of the build and took interest in the construction, whereupon Jason explained, thick walls, divisions of rooms and a separate kitchen was common place in a country that never had year round warmer climes.

'Why do men lack foresight,' she said dropping into his study. 'I mean, we say this house is built in the nineteenth century and yet it was built in the 1800's. Why not say, eighteenth century because a century is a hundred?'

Jason stood awhile to consider her reasoning. 'Someone had to start the annuals so the first one hundred years had to be a zero century and so on.'

'Nooo,' she disagreed. 'Surely that man, and it had to be a man because women were recognised as chattel, should have said, right chaps, we are progressing in our first one hundred years so therefore we shall call it the first century. Instead, like always, he has to complicate things. I don't think it was Eve tempting Adam with an apple from the tree of knowledge, I think she was ramming it in his mouth because Eve already had brains.'

'And you think you have brains?'

'I must have brains or why else are we here?' She smiled and sent him dizzy. 'Why do you have a bed in your study?'

'Yes, Squirt. I thought this was a 3 bed property.'

There was method in his madness. 'In here,' he said opening a door 'is my ensuite so I am perfectly self-contained. Now let me show your bedrooms and all will become clear.' Grabbing her suitcases, he led the way upstairs to a wide landing, opened the first door on the right and said to Tony, 'This room is over my study. You can have this bedroom or the one across the hall. It's up to you. Either way you get a view of Smelly's fields.'

'These are not bad sized rooms, Squirt. In fact it's quiet deceiving from the front. Not sure about the wallpaper. Did you say the bloke was a Londoner?'

Jason walked on. 'He lived on his own for the past three years. His wife died of cancer. He wanted to return to London to live near his children. He left a fair bit of furniture so I could settle in right away.' Jason halted at a door to the far end of the landing. He wondered if all his hard work would pay off. 'Luze, I thought you would like this room with a river view.'

'Oh!' She voiced stepping into pink flocked wallpaper and a four poster bed. 'It's loverly, just loverly.' She skipped to the window, veiled by the night. 'Will I be able to see the sun rise to a beautiful but nevertheless minor planet in an insignificant galaxy in what may prove to be an insignificant universe?' She had remembered his words. 'Oh, Nuts it's beautiful. It has remnants of your mother's room. Did you do this for me?'

'It was the best in the house but in the worst taste. Through there is your bathroom so you have no need to go wandering at night.'

'I see,' but did she really see, and moved slowly toward him. 'I might want a cup of tea.'

'Then I shall get you a kettle.'

'Am I going to be held in confinement?'

'There are going to be rules in this house,' Jason warned, and lowered his voice so there was no misunderstanding. 'From this day forward, Tony will lock our doors at night, thus curbing temptation.'

'What happens if I spend a night away?' Tony asked.

'Simple. I will cut across Smelly's fields and shack up with his cows. One of the things I would like to do is open up the fireplace.' Downstairs, he swung into the lounge. 'Luze, this would be a good place to make your mark. As well as unblocking the fireplace, do you think we could have interconnecting doors to the kitchen?'

'Do you know if this is a load bearing wall?'

'You are the architect.'

'Before I do a survey, can I have a cup of tea?'

Jason hit his head with the ball of his hand. 'I forgot. You must be exhausted.'

'Not really,' she said following him into the kitchen. 'I am so excited not even sleeping gas could put me out. Have you given any thought about our new business?'

'For a start we shall be equal shareholders,' he replied switching on the kettle.

'I want to work for my shares.' Tony grabbed a chair. 'You keep my third until I have the money to buy them off you. Luze, can I have a loan?'

There were some things that would never change about Tony, and there were some things that would never change about Luze. She was now in a world of artistic temperament, all of nature and all of art with her head stuck in the fridge.

'We shall start with maps,' she said bringing ham to the table. 'Buried treasure and dragons...a simple but unique game for children then we can expand into books...Tony, cheese or ham?'

'Ham please. Squirt, what do we do about her father? Offering the patent isn't going to soften his mood, not now Luze is here, living with us under one roof. How did you leave it with your father, Luze?'

'I never told him because he already left for England. I told Mammy but prefer to leave out her expletives. Nuts, ham or cheese?'

He shook his head. 'Luze, your father has a very bad opinion of us. I hate to say this but the man is stubborn. He has spent the best part of his life geared to take back his mother's land and during all that while has never laid his ghosts to rest.'

'Let's face it. Your father and grandfather did make a meal of his life. And you have to remember, every time he looked at me, he was looking at what your father did to the woman he loved.'

'I am not vilifying his actions. Far from it so let this gesture be one of goodwill to show him we are not bad people. I am inclined to give him the patent, free and simple. Tony, are you in agreement with me?'

'Absolutely, Squirt. Let's hope he doesn't take it the wrong way.'

'So no court case then.' Luze assumed.

'Make no mistake there will be a court case. This is not about winning or losing.' Jason was aware how the answer had affected her, for she controlled the reflex stiffening of her body and simply nodded her head as she cut through doorstep sandwiches. 'Luze, Tony is right. If we offer the patent now, your father will think we are trying to buy our way out. In court, it gives me and Tony an opportunity to speak the truth.'

She licked the butter off her fingers, one by one and the adrenalin of lust was flowing through his blood. 'I wish Granny Beth was here to see this. She would adore you, Nuts. She was just as crazy and generous as you. Sometimes, she would tickle me with her knitting needle if I had a long face.'

Jason remained where he was, his near dark eyes intelligent and appraising, and his expression as open as that of any who served the same fate. 'Did she refer to her knitting as a scarf of memories?'

'Why yes!' Luze voiced in surprise. 'How did you know that?'

His experience on the plane was repeated several times while he drank cups of tea by the dozen until it never seemed that strange to have a conversation with a ghost who smelt of perfumed witchery. Even so, he was haunted by the mysterious connection, once something vague and intimate, half-forgotten, who knows what?

'We missed her terribly. Mammy nearly went to pieces. It was so unexpected but she had angina and hid it very well.'

'Why didn't she say, Squirt? You know, come out with it, who she was on the plane.'

'I have no answer,' Jason replied.

'Why would Granny Beth make you dream of me?' Luze asked.

'Again, I have no answer.' Jason realised the idea of Granny Beth, like love or the theatre, stayed with Luze. 'To cause upheaval for me is one thing and understandable but to cause upheaval for Luze is another. It makes no sense. Perhaps she was unable to control my dream to that extent. Perhaps I placed my own connotations on Luze yet can we assume she manipulated events so that Luze should come down and not Jeremy Hubbard? Luze, why did you feel the need to come to Norfolk?'

Luze shrugged. 'I really don't know. Certainly my parents or Granny Beth never mentioned Norfolk. I just had this thing in my head, had done ever since-' She cut her sentence short, and sent her eyes away as though pulling back a curtain to a memory. 'How odd,' she finally said. 'It was shortly after Granny Beth died. Yes, I remember now because that was the same week I first mentioned it to Pappy and he said it was the arsehole of England, excuse my language. We were eating pickled sandwiches on the porch. Mammy made them in recognition of Granny Beth because she liked to make pickled sandwiches for tea but it made Pappy burp a lot.' She rose. 'I have something to show you. Come to my room.'

My room. It rolled off her tongue so easily that Jason believed she had been in this house forever. He watched her with total fascination as she swooped down on a case and spilled out her things carelessly on the floor, noting the silky panties and gulped.

'Look,' she said holding up a roll of knitting still attached to its needles and scrambled to her feet with an envelope. 'Granny Beth left this for me to read after her death.' She opened it up and read. 'My sweet, Merluza, always knit the bad as well as the good. Every memory counts, even nightmares. Without our nightmares we have no strength to overcome the hurdles we face in life.'

'When did you start this?' Jason asked.

'When I had my first bad experience, then I stopped for a while and started again when Granny Beth died. See here, this is when we met. I had to knit it in black because that was your name even though it was a happy time. And this is where I was unhappy. I knitted that in red because I was angry.'

'It's nearly half the length.'

'Well what do you expect? I was angry for a very long time.'

Her green eyes were fixed upon his, as nearly all the time they were fixed upon his. He was conscious of momentary affection that went straight to his heart. This happened several times and Jason felt he was not rewarded in a direct sense but here was the underpinning of his dream to be with Luze and to make his home in Little Smeet.

From the moment she telephoned, things had started to fall into place, Mile House, the element in the scene, capable of managing the confused and uncertain situation. He had self-belief and, having laid the logistical groundwork for an effective business run by a threesome, inspiring the community, he saw how he could live half a life with Luze. The other half was a manageable fire burning hot coals in his loins. But he felt it was a small price to pay, a trade-off for everything else. In this he was not simply putting himself in the clear but was bearing his responsibility as the man on the spot, taking it upon himself to manage the sexual politics of the situation.

And as the weeks progressed with relative calm, orbiting the village, Luze, Jason and Tony stabilised their positions as business partners. The outbuildings came to life with a printer that hummed across the river sending a wake-up call to those possessed of curious minds. At first the information that filtered back was of the crudest kind but nothing substantial. Such fragmentary information caused Luze on occasions to push Jason out to enjoy the city with Tony who submerged his anxieties by taking Father Michael into his confidence.

Then word of an impending court battle spread. This was a testing moment for Jason, his first experience of matching his wits against the formidable and unpredictable Turner who had pursued his legalities to the point of excess. A day after he handed the injunction to Jason, Turner returned to Australia leaving his legal eagles to progress with Henshaw, who, under advisement felt sandwiched between two enemies. From Henshaw's point of view he felt Turner was taking things too far, demanding detail and making successive attempts to find out what was happening between Jason and Luze. But regarding his client, Henshaw believed Jason should be represented by a barrister, an adversary equal to Turner's, which in no way diminished Jason's mad courage in wanting to take on the pompous opposition. Thus, Henshaw's optimism was not raised to the point of great expectation.

Despite all this, the weather grew so very cold and a court date finally propelled Jason towards Christmas. Now it was the clash of the Titans.

The morning just before the event, Jason set an impeccable example, and demanded the same which he communicated unambiguously to Tony who was aided by Luze in the bedroom.

'There,' she said standing back. 'You look dandy.'

Tony adjusted his shirt collar in front of the mirror, claiming Luze made a good Windsor knot then studied his hand. The skin rarely peeled, and the colour was gradually returning. The scarring was hard and shiny and new-looking, swirling across his knuckles. He turned them over, his ruined fingers, holding each side of them under the light as though admiring a silver fork.

Luze wrapped herself round him. 'Any woman worth her salt would still love you no matter what.'

'Luze, don't take this the wrong way but I think the world of you.'

'I know,' she said pinching his nose. 'Now see what your brother is up to.'

Jason was waiting downstairs in grey flannel trousers and a navy blazer very much reflecting, as indeed they were, a commitment to make this go right.

As much as he had tried to give up, he pulled a cigarette from a packet lying on the mantelpiece and placed it between his lips, patting his pockets for a lighter. A flame came to his face.

'Your New Year's resolution still stands, Squirt.'

Jason smiled and blew the smoke from the side of his mouth. 'Where's Luze?'

'Upstairs. She looks bloody terrific. How you've managed to keep your hands off her is anyone's guess.'

'I ask the same of myself.'

Just then Luze walked in. 'Are we ready, gentlemen?'

Jason threw his cigarette in the fire place and sidestepped behind her, pulling her coat over her suited-shoulders. 'Luze, are you sure you want to do this?'

'Absolutely sure,' she replied. 'Besides, Pappy hasn't really given me much choice.'

'Let's go. Tony you're driving.'

People were slipping into the city like children getting lost in a crowd, leaving nothing but temporary addresses. And the snow blew into their faces and into their eyes, navigating the cobbled streets for Christmas shopping. But in the heart of this thoroughfare there was a collection of old fashioned assises that adjudicated over troubled affairs and this is where the Jag was heading. Crossing, at last, the rampart to the car park, the three made a dash from the motor and rubbed shoulders with John Henshaw under a monolithic arch.

'Judge Crow is sitting,' he said walking on. 'And he doesn't take too kindly to self representation, so remember to title him correctly. Tony, keep to the facts and nothing more. To delve too much into the past will not impress him.'

'It doesn't impress me either,' he quipped.

'John,' Jason said. 'Keep an eye on Luze.'

'All in hand.'

'Well look at yew.' Mrs Tooley broke into their circle. It surprised them. 'Now don't start fretting. Thought I would come and give moral support.' She peeped between their shoulders. 'I see Luze is with her father.'

'She is witness for the prosecution.' Jason said.

'Who's that bloke on top of her?'

'Turner's barrister,' Henshaw informed.

'Poor man, he has to wear a wig to keep his head warm.'

Jason chuckled. 'Tools, you are the eighth wonder of the world. You will not be able to enter court because we have a closed sitting.' He saw her confusion. 'Unlike open cases where strangers and the press can attend, in our circumstance it's closed off to the public.'

'Never mind. Yew can tell me all about it when yew get home. How's the house? Keeping yew all warm? I heard yew had trouble with the fireplace.'

'It was sealed over by the past owners. Squirt pulled it apart and Luze rebuilt it.'

'Oh my, that girl seems to tackle anything.'

Their conversation was interrupted when the Clerk to the Court called Turner verses Black. Jason adjusted himself. His hair was partly obedient and behind those troubled dark eyes he was nervous. 'Remember, Tony, keep to the facts, nothing more, nothing less.'

'I won't let you down, Squirt.'

'And don't call me Squirt.'

Jason went forward, towards courtroom 3. He passed Turner and Luze, her smile a little weaker. She looked up and he looked down, a fleeting second, a thousand words. Moving on through a pair of swing doors, age and significance created an intimidating scene, the harsh trimmings of a courtroom orchestrated players to do battle for truth and justice. Before him, the elevated bench, to his left prosecuting council, to his right he sat alone. But where was Turner?

One, two, three, four minutes later, still no Turner. Jason looked behind and at that moment a door swung open. Turner walked in, his face looking worse than a wet weekend. He glanced at Jason and narrowed his eyes. The psychological challenge was there.

Now wrapped in their morning stupor, the Clerk to the Court announced, 'Please rise and be upstanding in court for the Right Honourable Judge Crow.'

A red gown and a discoloured grey wig entered from chambers. Above his half-mooned glasses, Crow took one look at Jason and asked, 'Where is your representation?'

'If it pleases, your honour, I shall represent myself in this matter.'

'Do you have experience in law?'

'I can read.'

'As do I,' Crow stated, unconvinced. 'I prefer you had legal council.'

'With all due respect, I do not intend to indulge upon the court's time. My defence is a simple one.'

'Very well then,' said Crow turning to prosecuting council. 'Mr Farraday, you may proceed.'

Farraday stood in his wig and black gown, a most pompous and daunting figure. 'Thank you, your honour. As the defence pointed out, this is a simple matter in that my client will show Jason Black, aided by his brother, Anthony Black did unlawfully enter upon my client's premises for the sole purpose of using my client's machinery to manufacture a blank jigsaw puzzle.'

'What is the purpose of a blank jigsaw puzzle?'

'Your honour, if you will permit, a sample is at hand, Exhibit A.'

The Clerk to the Court passed Exhibit A to the judge who then lifted the lid and picked out one piece. Of a single fact he had become certain, it was blank. 'Mr Farraday, I trust you are not wasting court time. I say again, what is the purpose?'

'When the pieces interlock a picture will form.'

'A remarkable claim,' Crow said. 'Do you expect me to piece it together?'

'If need be, there can be a short demonstration to show effect.'

'I shall take your word. Carry on.'

Farraday with his wonderfully pretentious stance, his hands clutching the lapels of his black robe continued with forced sweetness. 'But for the fact of Jason Black using my client's facilities the said concept would go unaccomplished. Further, we shall demonstrate Anthony Black whilst still in the employ of my client aided his brother to gain entry into my client's premises, which subsequently resulted in the loss of three fingers to his right hand. Simply put, your honour, the patent to this remarkable achievement is challenged by my client.'

Judge Crow regarded Jason. 'Mr Black, I have very little defence papers, can you briefly summarise before we move on?'

Jason stood. 'Your honour, I intend to show the circumstance of how, when and where the puzzle was made by calling upon one witness.'

Crow nodded. 'I will first listen to prosecuting council then to your defence. Continue Mr Farraday.'

'Thank you, your honour. I would like you to look at Exhibit B. It is a report by Professor Mildrew at Cambridge University who examined scrapings taken from a die cut machine owned by my client. It is blood type AB negative, the same rare blood group as Anthony Black. It is alleged in the course of using the said cutter Anthony Black did suffer an accident in the early hours of the 29th September, this year. Professor Mildrew was unable to attend for cross examination but I understand from the defendant there is no dispute.'

'Mr Black do you have a copy of this report?'

Jason stood. 'I do, your honour, and it goes unchallenged.'

'Carry on, Mr Farraday.'

'If it pleases, your honour, I would like to call our first witness. Mr Capelli, the surgeon who attended Anthony Black in the early hours on the 29th September.'

Yes, Turner had his guns armed with powerful ammunition. Nevertheless, as Capelli continued to explain he was at odds with the excuse given by Tony that a car hood slammed down on his fingers, Judge Crow was hunched down in his chair, supporting his chin on his clenched fist, absolutely engrossed in piecing the puzzle. It made Jason wonder if he was paying attention.

'Your honour, I am finished with this witness.'

Crow peered over his glasses. 'Mr Black do you wish to cross examine?'

Jason stood. 'No, your honour.'

'You may continue, Mr Farraday.'

'I would like to call Miss Merluza Claggart to the stand.'

The Judge waved him on. There was a pause. The Clerk to the Court then called out her name. Dressed in a green trouser suit with her hair swept back in a plait, she looked ahead, deliberately avoiding eye contact. After being sworn in, Jason could see she found it embarrassing even to hear any words connected with the whole sorry business and tried to avoid looking at him, keeping her head low while answering questions, questions to Jason's appearance that night when she first met him, questions about their conversations and what really happened behind closed doors.

'So you do not deny entering the defendant's bedroom?' Farraday asked her.

'It was where we conducted business,' she replied.

'Surely your business was with Anthony Black or are we speaking of another type of business?'

Jason stood. 'I object! His remarks are suggestive and have no bearing on the case.'

'I am merely pointing out a man's bedroom is hardly the place to conduct business.'

'Like hell you were!'

Crow asserted his authority and raised his voice. 'I will have order in my courtroom. Mr Farraday, where is this leading?'

'I am trying to establish whether Miss Claggart was aware of the defendant's intention to use my client's facilities.'

'Then ask your witness, instead of pussy footing around.'

Jason knew she was finding it difficult to balance her loyalties, obvious Turner was trying to delve deep, to discover if she had been compromised. She forced herself to break eye contact with her father and instead looked towards the doors. It was an idle glance but then suddenly her eyes flicked ahead, drawn irresistibly by the intensity of a glowering gaze that was fastened upon her. For she had stared once again into Jason's eyes as they had been when she first met him, almost black, fierce and bright, with dark brows arched over them, unforgettable, unforgotten.

Judge Crow looked at Jason and said, 'You may cross examine the witness.'

Jason stood. 'I have one question, your honour.'

'Then ask it and speak up.'

'Luze, when we first encountered each other, did I ever speak to you about developing a new concept for a jigsaw puzzle?'

Prosecuting council sprang angrily to his feet. 'Your honour, this witness must be treated as hostile since she has openly admitted being in partnership with the Blacks, not to mention she apparently resides with them under one roof.'

'Mr Farraday, she is your witness. I would have thought further enquiries might have established this fact. If I remember correctly, this was the very question you required clarity.' He turned to Luze. 'You may answer the question.'

'The first I heard of a new concept was when my Father had been informed by Jeremy Hubbard that Tony had an accident. Then my immediate reaction was to return to Little Smeet to offer my support.'

'I have no further questions.' Jason sat down.

Crow turned to Luze. 'Miss Claggart, what exactly is your relationship with the Blacks?' It would seem Crow had been paying attention after all.

'I am their half sister.'

'Can you explain to me why you do not carry your father's name?'

Farraday jumped up but Crow waved him down.

'Well, unbeknown to me, Pappy changed his name for the sake of the business. He took his mother's maiden name, Claggart so when I was born, my birth certificate showed Claggart but even if it had shown Turner, I would still be the odd one out because I never really knew my true father. And then I met Jason and we discovered my true father was his father.'

'And you are certain of this?'

'Mammy told me and even though she was very upset about keeping it a secret, her motives were sincere. I would prefer not to go into detail.'

'Very well, you may step down.' Judge Crow shook his head still in the throws of fitting pieces. 'I am not entirely convinced you know what you are doing, Mr Black.' Above his half-mooned glasses he looked at Farraday. 'Proceed.'

Farraday stood. 'That is the case for the prosecution, your honour.'

Judge Crow turned to Jason. 'You may proceed with your defence.'

Jason stood. 'If it pleases, your honour, I would like to call my brother, Anthony Black.'

When Tony walked in, hair slicked back with his damaged hand hidden in his suit pocket, he took a deep breath, swore on the bible and then glanced at his twin. It would require him an enormous effort of will to concentrate on the facts without adding superfluities.

'Tony, please, in your own words can you tell the court the circumstance of the puzzle?'

He cleared his throat. 'Well,' he began, 'Strident Cutter was on the brink of receivership and I called Jason in Boston for financial assistance. This time he refused to write out another cheque and volunteered to come home and sort things out. When he arrived, he said my only recourse was to sell Strident Cutter to Claggart but of course we didn't know Claggart was Tom Turner. I was against selling because it would mean I would have to work for a change but Jason said if I allowed the deal to go through the workers would be able to keep their jobs and that if I was prepared to make sacrifices, he would develop a puzzle to revolutionise the industry.'

Crow interrupted. 'Did your brother tell you what sort of puzzle?'

'Yes. The same one you have in front of you.'

'What made him think he could achieve this?'

'Jason is a chemist. He had this vision on the plane.'

'Vision?'

'Yes, you know, a sort of eureka moment, rather like the apple falling on Newton's head.'

Crow smiled. 'Carry on.'

'Jason knew that apart from making up the formula, he would need to use a silk screen printer and a cutter for trials and suggested we could use the ones in the factory. I then contacted my solicitor, John Henshaw, who in turn contacted Claggart's solicitor to inform them I was on for the deal by which time Jason had made a provisional patent. Next, Luze came on the scene to do the valuation for her father and stayed at the Manor instead of a hotel. And that was probably a big mistake because my marriage was in crisis and my wife, Susan, didn't want to sell and that made it very difficult for Luze. So Luze, Jason and me spent time in Jason's room discussing business because the factory was too cold. When Luze went back to Australia, Jason and I learnt that Claggart was Tom Turner and that Luze was our half sister so we never felt bad about using the equipment. When we were finally ready for the trials, Jason went to my mate, used his printer and then we slipped in the old factory round about midnight and used one of the old cutters before the factory was demolished. We had a seven day window and things were not going very well but on the final night we were doing a run with a revised formula and that's when I had the accident. Jason rushed me to the hospital and told the duty nurse he had slammed the car hood on my fingers and I confirmed this with the surgeon. Anyway, that run proved successful and of course, the game was up but I wanted Jason to offer the patent to Turner in exchange for all or part of my business back. Jason said Turner would never go for it and the next thing we knew, Turner slapped an injunction on Jason to stop him from selling it on.'

This astounding testament kept prosecution council stunned until Judge Crow said, 'Mr Black, do I understand correctly that this witness is your defence?'

'In my world truth rises and sets with the sun, lies are a dishonest visitor.'

'Why has this case been brought to my court?'

Farraday stood. 'Your honour, this information was never offered in support of our case.'

'If it pleases the court,' Jason interrupted. 'May I put forward a resolution for settlement?'

'Have you finished with this witness?'

'Yes, your honour.'

Crow turned to Tony. 'You may sit at the back if you wish. Proceed with your thoughts, Mr Black.'

'I propose the patent should be put in Tom Turner's name without conditions.'

'Am I to understand you are giving up all rights to this invention?'

'Not all, your honour. At the time when Miss Claggart arrived to negotiate on her father's behalf for Strident Cutter, she indicated to my brother that he would never sell. Without her or my brother's knowledge, and to safeguard my interests, I made a second provision at the Patent Office, thus allowing one application for jigsaw puzzles, the other for paper publications, which will not conflict with his business.'

'As I understand it, Mr Black, the invention is on the formula. How is it possible to split the patent?'

'Yes, your honour, I understand. But the formula required to manufacture jigsaw puzzles is not identical to the formula for paper publications due to other chemicals interwoven in the backing material for jigsaw puzzles.'

Crow looked at prosecuting council. 'Mr Farraday, I would suggest you advise your client that this proposal seems unquantifiably generous. Do you wish to proceed or shall we take a break so you may consult with your client?'

Farraday bent to Turner's ear. Conferring and decision took time. 'Your honour, my client wishes to accept the proposal.'

'Then that concludes the matter. Each party will bear their own litigation costs.'

'All rise,' the Clerk to the Court announced.

'Mr Black,' Judge Crow said to Jason, 'would you come to my chambers.'

This was an unexpected turn of events.

'I knew your father,' said Crow removing his gown.

'Then you probably knew his background.'

'Indeed, he was a sorry affair. I am rather concerned you never stipulated a condition that Mr Turner must not claim rights to your other patent. One naturally follows the other, if you understand my meaning.'

'Tom Turner would be a very stupid man to pursue further interests.'

'Under the circumstance I shall not reprimand you for taking up the court's time.'

'I needed Turner to see that we have no quarrel with him. The past is the past and we wish him success with the concept.'

'Farraday is a pompous ass, never liked the man.' Crow sat down and indicated for Jason to do the same. 'Far be it from me to exacerbate your problems or indeed the past but I rather gather Miss Claggart wishes to remain in your company. Would you care to enlighten me?'

'Tony and I have a soft spot for Luze. Her father never told her that she was our sister until he discovered she had come to Little Smeet.'

Crow clasped his hands and leaned forward. 'If I was in your shoes, I would be asking myself why Miss Claggart bears no resemblance to your father.'

'Apparently she takes after her mother.'

'And I see your father in your face.'

Jason blinked. 'Is there something I should know?'

'Let us hope so, Jason Black for a man cannot be in love with his sister.' Crow waved him on. 'I have a sitting in one hour.'

Outside, Jason said to Tony, 'Where is Luze?'

'She went off with her father. What did Crow have to say?'

Jason lit up against the white driven snow and began to walk to the motor. 'You drive.'

When Tony climbed in, he repeated, 'What did Crow have to say?'

'That Luze doesn't look like our father.'

'That's because she takes after her mother.'

'And I see our father in your face.'

'Squirt, what the hell are you on about?'

'I had the distinct impression Crow was trying to tell me something, if so, why not come out with it?'

'Well, what else did he have to say?'

'That a man cannot be in love with his sister.'

Tony switched on the ignition. 'You're clutching at straws, Squirt. He could read your face every time you looked at Luze. It's a dead give away. He's just trying to give you some sensible advice. Do you want to go home or stop off at the Pig and Whistle?'

'Where is Tools?'

'She carried on with her Christmas shopping, which reminds me, we haven't done a thing about Luze. Do we buy her a present from both of us or should it be one from each of us?'

'It has to be the latter else wise I would be getting a present from you and Luze and you would be getting a present from me and Luze.'

'Run that by me again?'

'Tony, why do you make things so complicated. Buy Luze a pair of slippers.'

'I don't know her shoe size.'

'She takes a size six.'

'And what are you going to buy her?'

'Nothing extravagant,' Jason replied. 'I bought her a nice little Mini.'

'I thought you said nothing extravagant.'

'She needs a car. Have you not noticed how she walks up the lane? She dislikes the Jag...it's too big for her to drive.'

'She hasn't got a licence, that's why.'

'Then you better teach her to drive. How did she look?'

'Not very happy,' Tony said swinging the wheel hard round into the country lane. 'Henshaw spoke to Turner, never said what about but he never looked happy either.'

'I expect it came like a bolt from the blue when he learnt I had another patent.'

'That's his fault. I meant to ask. Did you get in contact with Roberts?'

'Yes,' Jason confirmed. 'He said he would take three hundred on the proviso we exclude Trimble.'

'We need Trimble. He has more outlets.'

'But Roberts is prepared to pay top whack.'

'This is really going to take off, isn't it, Squirt? We need to extend the main outbuilding before we get another printer, and we should be looking to employ. I thought Luze came up with a good idea about that. By the way, did you notice how I behaved in court? I never once called you Squirt.'

'You did well. Get this car home before my balls freeze up.'

'I told you to wear a vest. Didn't I tell you? And Luze told you. I wear a vest.'

'That's because she warms yours by the fire,' Jason spoke jealously. 'She does your ironing too.'

'I haven't got to grips with my right hand.'

'She mothers you as well.'

Tony grinned. 'I know. Isn't it great? It turned out better than I thought.'

At Mile House, a place that was more than a home, Jason was dropped off since Tony wanted to go to the Pig and Whistle. Here, he walked into a warm living room, poured himself a whisky and sank heavy into a leather armchair, warming his shins by the fire. Now he was feeling the relief of it all, a closed chapter to a vexing situation though it did not exclude any future irritation he might face from Turner about Luze. Yet he was prepared for that. He felt he could hold his head up high and honestly say he treated Luze with respect. Often there were fragile moments of near intimacy and it was extremely hard but he was linked, after all, by love. However, they worked well and Luze had brought so much into the business, her enthusiasm and energy seemed to giddy Tony along who nurtured a brotherly love for Luze.

At some point, Jason closed his eyes. His head rolled to the side and his near empty glass slipped from his hand and quarrelled with the carpet. He was dreaming peacefully about Luze and Tony, how they fought and ratted, built a private structure and lived off each other's brains. Then the scene changed and he saw himself holding Luze by the arm as she struggled to get away but she was happy, not sad. There were shapes around him, the rocks of his life, relics of birthdays and dead relations, wrecks of furniture and cast iron cutters, all resurrected in rainbow nightmares and then a lone voice, *it will happen soon, soon it will happen.*

With a sudden spasm, Jason woke to banging cupboards and clashing pots, quickly assessing Luze was in her own miserable torment. He picked his way from the living room and sheepishly entered through the new interconnecting doors. 'Luze, are you alright?'

She turned in a flourish. 'Oh Nuts, my Father is intolerable. What do you want to eat?'

'What happened?'

'What do you think happened,' she said with a sorrowful face. 'He was angry you had another patent, angry you had pulled a fast one and then after all that he admitted he was sorry for saying that and tried to get me on a plane to Australia. We had this huge argument because he refused to believe we lived liked a pair of chastened humans and said if I got out of the car he would forget he had a daughter.'

He approached and took her into his arms. Wet sobs soaked part of his shirt and moistened his skin. 'Luze, it's going to be alright. He will come round, I promise you. Give him time to come round.' Now, placing his hands to her face, he wiped her coursing tears with his thumbs. 'It will happen soon, soon it will happen. Your father will come round.' He puzzled. 'Odd I should say that. I had a dream about something happening soon.'

'Did you? Was I in it?'

'As a matter of fact you were. Perhaps I felt this would happen. Is it not natural for a father to worry about his daughter?'

'I suppose so,' she sniffled. 'Do you have a handkerchief?'

He brought one from his pocket but said nothing.

'What do you fancy to eat, fish steaks or me?'

For a moment they looked at each other with the veil stripped aside, their eyes and their love naked for the world to see. Holding her he could believe in the illusion of magic. But it was becoming more difficult, day by day, realising how absurd their situation and he wondered whatever made him think such an arrangement could last.

Then the night took on its own pattern until his eyes grew weary and he sought for solace in bed. Sleep had not come easily and when he finally drifted into a dreamless patch he was pulled back by the weight of a mysterious hand on his waist. Electrical impulses flustered across the cells of his brain, back and forth like runners until they converged into a single thought.

'Luze, how did you get in?'

'I stole the key off Tony.'

Switching on the bedside lamp, he grabbed the alarm clock and squinted at the dials. 'It's two o'clock in the morning. You shouldn't be here. Go back to your room. Don't make this any harder than it is.'

'How about I just stay here for awhile with the pillow in between so I can vent my anxieties about Pappy.'

Jason was hardly in the mood for conversation when she wore so little. He watched her caress her own arm, a slow lingering stroke from her wrist to her bare shoulder, the way her fingers travelled, her bosom changing shape, squashing the cleavage and his loins swelled.

'Have I ever told you how much I love your boobies?'

She laughed softly, a throaty little sound, and through the laughter she took his hand and placed it on one breast. 'Is it sufficient?'

'Perfect,' he whispered.

'Now, what are you going to do with your other hand?'

'And what are you going to do with yours?'

He bent to her will, kissing the tight curve of her throat. She was his lover, his mother, his home, there as the glue, that silly sticky stuff which bound them together. He placed soft kisses on her face, playful kisses, long, lingering kisses, sleepy little kisses returned in the middle of the night. They were on the tip of an iceberg, the beginning of cultivating their illicit love, the sensuality of touch and taste with wistful passion that threw everything else into chaos. His feet overlapped the foot of the bed by two inches and the headboard crashed timpani against the wall until they corkscrewed and reversed roles to keep the noise level down. Now he lay beneath her, held her hips as she moved above him then he rose to greet and caress her breasts, her lips, her being. If this were sinful, there was no better wrong, no more pleasing way to enter perdition.

ASSEMBLING A CUTTER

The door opened to Chappy who wore a mantle of tragic doom for Christmas Eve. He rubbed his hands together, blew into them while he stamped his feet hard on the mat before removing his helmet.

'This is not a social call, Jason. I need you to come with me.'

'Can you tell me why?'

'I think you know why.'

Jason considered the uniform, could sense the truth in his message and wondered how his indiscretion with Luze had reached his ears. 'Can you give me a moment?'

'I shan't be going anywhere.'

Jason popped his head round the living room door. Two pairs of enquiring eyes looked up from the fireside. 'I have to go with Chappy. Tony, look after Luze.'

'What's it all about, Squirt?'

He did not answer, felt his own decay and grabbed his coat leaving his Homburg behind.

Outside, Chappy made no apologies for turning up on his bike. 'Now don't you be giving me any trouble, lad. You can run alongside me.'

Against a blackened sky, Jason steadily worked the mile fighting against the snow driven winds. He wondered if this was the start of his punishment, to suck icicles through his teeth and feel his nose go dead. The last stretch to reach the station was perhaps the most difficult until he saw the station house. It gave him the impetus to rush inside before Chappy stored his bike in the shed.

The station coupled up for a home as well as locking away the unruly for a night or two until greater forces intervened. And these doors were very different, the colour, the shape, the way they all spilled along a corridor with numbers chalked on the panels. Open this one and it might be his entry into hell.

'Now lad,' Chappy voiced sternly, 'what have you got to say for yourself?' He paused for an answer, the delay too long. 'I never had you pegged for a wrong un but doing that is a nasty piece of work and it's no good you trying to wheedle out of it.' Growing very dissatisfied with Jason's silence, he continued. 'This is how it works, lad. Come clean and Turner promises he'll show leniency for your state of mind.'

'I want his word no harm will come to Luze or Tony. It was my fault entirely.'

The door opened to the weight of a man. 'You have my word,' Turner said.

Jason puffed out his cheeks and sat forward with his head ashamedly down. This was the worst possible scenario and he had let it happen. 'It's been so hard,' he forlornly spoke, 'so hard these past weeks...I thought I could contain it but it all welled up. I am the greater fool to think I could restrain my emotions.'

Turner grabbed a chair and swung it round to face him, the easier to talk and gain information. 'Did you take my daughter by force?'

'No! I would never harm a hair on her head. We promised each other half a life was better than no life at all. She was upset and I tried to give her strength, instead my own strength diminished.'

The room went quiet as though Turner was thinking things through then ultimately, he asked, 'Why did you feel it necessary to spite me?'

'Spite you? I bear no malevolence towards you.'

'Your lies won't wash with me, Jason Black. A murderous shadow lies hard across your soul.' Turner's eyes were suffused with suspicion. 'You offered the patent without condition in order for me to take the bait and cause ruin to my business. But you shall never have my business. I shall close that factory down and allow the walls to crumble before a Black sets foot on my land.'

Half-crippled with guilt, Jason had this indiscernible feeling it was not his indiscretion with Luze that brought Turner from out of the woodwork. 'This is not about Luze, is it?'

'You did something to your formula,' Chappy said.

'When did you try my formula?' Jason asked Turner.

'The same day we reached an accord.'

'I question how that was possible.'

'I am not to be questioned what is my right!' Turner growled.

'The Patent Office would not have passed over my formula and I did not pass it on until that day. So how were you able to process my formula without knowing what chemicals to use?'

'Your formula was left in the box.' Turner informed.

It took a moment to sink in, to stretch the mind. 'I did not leave my formula in the box.' Jason pointed to his forehead. 'This is where it resides. Has the cutter been affected?'

'Like Jack Frost,' Chappy said.

It's happening all over again. His eyes were fixed to the floor, trying to make sense of Elizabeth's ghost, why she would cause such mayhem for her son. 'I must see for myself.'

Turner nodded to Chappy. 'I can take it from here.'

Stuck close together they trudged and crunched snow beneath their shoes, and everywhere had a faint winter crackle of silence. They walked past the Pig and Whistle, onwards towards the new factory where the turmoil was unfolding.

'Has the boiler been affected?'

'As well you know.'

'I know only what is told or seen.' Jason looked around for a small container and spotted Misery's tobacco tin. It was then he remembered the last time he took a sample from the old cutter but never made a study of it. Blowing out the bits of hand rolling tobacco, he grabbed a cutter's knife and made scrapings from a white frosted substance layered thick on a brand new cutter which dominated the floor. 'We need to talk. Is there anywhere warm in this place?'

Turner swivelled on his heels. 'In my office.'

Gradually the bitter cold drew distance where warmth erupted in the glass tower folly. With an upward glance Jason felt the intimacy of snow. It peeled down in starlets, amassing its habits on the glass roof and he wondered if Luze had calculated for its weight. He brought out a packet of cigarettes then instantly sacrificed his need and put them away, feeling the piercing eyes of Tom Turner upon him.

'What I am about to tell you may seem unbelievable. Sometimes I have difficulty in believing it myself. Luckily, I have Luze to back me up, and also Father Michael.'

Turner sat back and folded his arms. Jason knew he exhibited all the signs of determination in a world of commercial intrigue. After a lapse of about ten seconds Turner said, 'I am listening.'

So Jason said things softly, nervously scratching the back of his hand for even he was unable to comprehend the unearthly topic that sprung from a dream. It was the substance of legend, the nature of tragedy. And soon they were at the stage of standing side by side, looking at a new dawn growing upon the still and settled near icy waters, examining the contours of the river winding through the white flatlands of Norfolk.

Turner spoke of the world and its width and richness, lectured for the waste of lives and the youths for their dumb contentment. 'What do we know about the universe, and how do we know it? We are still in the early stages of a cosmos that is beyond our comprehension. Even the most eminent scientists forage in the dark.'

'Someday these answers may seem as obvious to us as the earth orbiting the sun but for now, we are dealing with something that is beyond understanding.'

'My senses told me there was more than met the eye during my daughter's visit.'

'She was about to tell you but you interceded.'

'I cannot, in all good conscience run her life yet what bodes ill for you bodes ill for Merluza.'

His sleep-starved mind barely registered the inference. 'What would you wish me to do? Turn her away and be resigned to my loss?'

'Yes, be resigned to your loss. True love is sacrifice. Not placing your needs above hers. She is young and fickle, her body will hunger for children and you take without forethought. You may not have taken as your father took but you follow the same path.' Turner paused and looked into Jason's dark eyes drowned in misery. 'I will give you this land and all the assets for my daughter's future. Make the pact with me now and let me take her home.'

Jason stared at the hand that was offered but decided against it. 'Luze cannot be bargained with assets. We should set our differences aside and overcome this problem.'

'The problem is clear. This manifestation intercedes to show the error of your ways.'

'It cannot be that simple.'

'You refuse to accept what is currently unacceptable.'

'I refuse to accept this is about my arrangement with Luze.'

Within seconds Turner responded to the decision of the besieged factory. 'What chemical can be used to make good the cutter?'

'Since we are dealing with supernatural forces, one must consider a different approach, though what that approach should be, I have no idea. I do know this, for some unknown reason I have been placed centre stage by Elizabeth.' Jason sighed and looked at his watch. 'At present I am tired and hungry. It's Christmas Day. Come home with me and spend it with us. Luze would be over the moon to see you. She was very upset when she last saw you.' The hesitation was there. 'See for yourself the home you once lived in and perhaps we can bring our heads together, the four of us, for the sake of the workers.'

And so, by necessity and in the comfort of a Rolls Royce, Turner drove the mile distance along a snow-driven road and swept through the wooden gate, parking next to the Jag wrapped in this magic substance.

There came the wispily greetings and grinnings. Luze clung to her responsive father and Jason was grateful for that. Soon the kitchen and living room walls shuddered and shifted with life and they all fell in talks with one another while a turkey was roasting in the oven. Luze had characteristically donned an apron around Tony, insisting he should peel the potatoes while Jason kept the glasses topped with mulled wine. Of course alcohol on an empty stomach helped to soften the atmosphere.

By mid day the heat was trapped within the sheer walls of the kitchen when they gathered at the table, laid with shiny utensils and vegetable dishes. Luze made a special effort to smooth the mounting tension between Jason and her father by placing a little mistletoe round a tall china candle-stick that once made up a pair owned by Katherine Black. Then she folded the plain cotton napkins and placed each one by the side of their plates.

'I suggest we approach this from a logical angle,' she said watching her father carve the turkey and began to tick off the facts on her fingers. 'One, we know Jason had the dream. Two, we know Granny Beth met Jason on the plane. Three, we know Tony found the puzzle. Four, we know the riddles never deviated from the truth. Five, we know the missing pieces were in the prosthetic leg. Now, let us ask what would have happened if Jerry came down instead of me. I would not have met Nuts, ergo would Pappy have told me about my past? Pappy, would you?'

'Perhaps not...pass me your plate, Jason Black.'

Ignoring her father's rather frosty approach towards the man she loved, Luze continued. 'Thus, we must assume Granny Beth wanted me to know the truth.'

'Luze,' Jason said taking his plate from Turner. 'Where are you taking this?'

'Err, hum....just thought it was a point for discussion,' as if she wanted her father's approval. 'Consider this. If I was not destined to know the truth then it was providence that made it so, providence I should meet Nuts.' She looked at Jason. 'And where would you be if providence never smiled on my journey?'

'Here, eating Christmas dinner.'

'Ah, but would you? I understand my telephone call gave you the impetus to start a new business and buy Mile House.'

'Luze, I had already made two patents knowing your father would not agree to Tony's proposal and in that regard, I would have eventually come across this house, or any house in Little Smeet urging Tony to join me in a new venture.'

'Would you, Squirt?'

'How else are you to survive. No, I think we have to place our romantic notions aside. Perhaps we should ask the question, why was I given the dream?'

'That's simple, Squirt. You were given the dream so you could make that puzzle to give to her father because you're the only one capable of doing it.'

'Okay, fair enough. So the next question, why would Elizabeth create havoc in her son's factory? It makes no sense.' His eyes went to Turner who seemed perfectly content to eat and listen.

'Pappy, what do you think?' Luze asked.

'I like the way you mixed apple sauce with the cranberry.' Turner carried on eating.

'Pappy does that sometimes,' she said smiling with excuses. 'He takes everything on board until he's ready to communicate. Rest assured there's no blank spot in his mind.'

Jason threw down his utensils. What an idiot, he thought. 'There has to be a fourth riddle for why else were those pieces left blank? The revision has not been made. This must be it. We have been guided to this point.' He set his eyes on Turner. 'We are one member missing in our equation.'

Turner looked up. 'If you are referring to my wife then she stays in Australia.'

'But surely we should-'

'The past has been revealed, the truth spoken. She has suffered enough, and suffers further for the want of her daughter to leave your side.'

The table went quiet for a few seconds then Jason scraped back his chair and got to his feet. 'I must find the old tobacco tin. I am sure I put it somewhere.'

'Nuts, you haven't finished your dinner.' Luze stirred uneasily, sending an accusing fork to Turner. 'Pappy, please try to be more civilised. Making innuendoes is not solving your problem.'

'Why do you call him Nuts?'

'Oh that was so silly. He opened up a statement like, I am nuts but I think we have met before, or something to that effect. And since he acted a little bit nutty, I thought it suited him.'

'And you,' Turner said to Tony. 'Why do you call him Squirt?'

'He had the biggest water pistol.'

Luze intercepted. 'He's referring to a toy pistol, Pappy.'

'We never had water pistols,' Tony muffled, picking his teeth. 'We were messing about by the river and caught Dad in the bushes with our third nanny, or was it the second? Anyway, we thought it would be fun to climb the tree and rain on his parade. Jason hit the target and then all hell broke loose. I inched further up the tree and Jason got the blame. When Dad finally caught up with him, he was thrown through the patio doors. Dad walked off and left Jason in a right mess. Brenda, that's Mrs Tooley's mother rushed him to the doctor's surgery and after that he stayed in his bedroom for days, wouldn't come out until Dad lambasted him, telling him he should start acting like a man....see, the thing is, Jason doesn't like to talk about his past. He partly blames himself for what Dad did to him but he forgets he was only a kid. He was definitely the brightest out of us two so Dad saw him running Strident Cutter, spent a lot on his education but Jason wanted to be a chemist.'

'So your father never wanted you to run Strident Cutter?'

'Hell no. I couldn't blame him because my head was full of military history. I had quite a collection of miniature war heroes and armaments by the time I was seventeen then my mind started to veer on skirts and my future. I saw Strident Cutter as my meal ticket. I wanted Jason to stay but I sort of mucked things up when he brought Susan home and the rest you know.'

'And you continue where you left off,' the unforgiving Turner said.

'Look!' Tony bit back. 'It wasn't until Luze returned, did I realise what a prat I'd been and since then things have been good between me and Jason. It's like we found ourselves and whatever he wants goes in my book.'

'That's true, Pappy. Tony has been wonderful and so very supportive. Wait till you see our product line, it's a children's game. It's ready to hit the market place in the New Year and Tony's been working on a military theme using the same principle for the adult market.'

'Just as I thought,' Jason emerged. 'Nothing untoward, just like the new cutter.'

'Run that by me, Squirt?'

Jason sat down, pulled in his chair and picked up his utensils. 'The substance formed on the old cutter was a mixture of grease and water. Thus we can deduce the matter is not unearthly but rather the elements are being manipulated.'

'So if we brought heaters into the factory, we could melt it away?' Luze asked.

'Correct, but it would be a temporary measure. Your grandmother's soul will continue until we find the fourth riddle.'

'We speak of the soul's endurance, so when then does it mean to die?' Turner asked.

'We are not looking to kill it, just placate it,' Jason said. 'What happened to the old cutter?'

'It has been dismantled and stored in the packing room.'

'Excellent. Then we shall produce the original puzzle, use the old cutter and see what transpires.'

'I hate to put a damper on your theory, Squirt but the last time we used that cutter my fingers got chopped off.'

'It's a chance we must take,' Jason muffled.

'You overlook what you refuse to accept,' Turner said, pouring more wine. 'My mother turns in her grave because of your actions.'

'It was she who manipulated my actions so that cannot hold weight.'

'Pappy, I know you find it hard to accept my uncertain future and I'm sorry if I've shamed you but I love Nuts with all my heart. We had one slip up and it was me who encouraged him. It was me who broke the law and slipped into his bed while he was asleep. Can you not find it in your heart to forgive?'

'I would not forgive,' Jason said, placing his utensils aside. He wiped his mouth and folded his arms glaring direct at Tom Turner. 'Your father is correct. We run a fine line on a weak thread and expect others to support our path. Disregarding my feelings for Luze, Elizabeth entered my dream, was there when I woke and has been manipulating events ever since. She was there when we pieced the puzzle together. It was her who caused the verses to manifest and it was her who had us chasing around for missing pieces but it was her who decided not to reveal the fourth riddle. Why? The answer is obvious, because we must be armed with the truth. We have all been manipulated to this point for a reason.' He held up his hand to refrain Turner from speaking. 'I did not contact Luze. She contacted me and yes, her proposal was inviting but not immoral. It was as Luze said, my invention, through a dream, offered the ideal opportunity for us to be together and no, I do not believe Elizabeth would deliberately push us together to cause her grandchild heart ache. I was convinced at the time there should be a fourth riddle. I am convinced even more that we are being guided to replicate that puzzle. It will show how we can make a revision. All needles point in this direction.'

'What revision, Nuts?' Luze asked. 'How can we possibly turn back the clock?'

'If we do nothing we shall never know. I was chosen to forge reality from a puzzle conjured up by unknown forces. Logically, it suggests it has a reason to pull us in. There is one cutter left on Elizabeth's land, has somehow survived and is waiting to be used again. Do we have to assume the worst? Why not assume the best? Tony and I were careless on our last run. We were anxious, tired and I fed the sheet in at right angles. Tony tried to correct it. If we assume there was intention to harm one of us then I would be the target if Elizabeth felt aggrieved by my relationship with Luze. Everyone around this table has felt the effects of that puzzle in one way or another and it's due in no uncertain terms to the knowledge of our past. We have been brought together for a reason.'

'What about Franny?' Tony asked. 'She felt the affects of that puzzle.'

'True, and to that end I can only assume her wall was a confirmation of what happened in her yard all those years ago. The riddle did not elaborate where the incident took place.'

Turner nodded. 'I am reluctant to say this Jason Black but you make sense.' He pulled back his chair and brought out a cigar from his inside jacket pocket then bit off the end and spat it out onto an ashtray as though making his mark of disgust. Next, he cupped his hands around the flare of the match and sucked the cigar smoke down deeply into his lungs. 'It will not be easy to assemble the cutter. We shall take Jerry on board.'

'How long will it take to assemble?' Tony asked.

'A day if we work through the night, perhaps more. I would like my daughter to give me a tour of your house and workshops.'

It was a little while later that Luze shoved a tea cloth in Jason's hand before showing her father round. 'Tony washes, you wipe. We can have our pudding later.'

Waiting a second or two, Tony said to Jason, 'he's miffed about you and Luze.'

'You would be miffed too.'

'What the hell happened, Squirt?'

'She was upset and came into my bedroom. She wanted to talk but somehow the talking stopped.'

Turning on the hot tap, soap bubbles rising, Tony said, 'You're never going to last the distance, are you? He's out to get you two separated.'

'I conveyed my indiscretion to Chappy believing he was hauling me over the coals but it was about the cutter...soon the village will be gossiping again.'

'Chappy won't say anything.' Tony passed over a plate.

'But he will look upon us with different eyes and the community is astute.'

Tony sighed and Jason could see he was conjuring up the desolation and misery, the fearful hardships and loneliness. 'I don't know what to say to you, Squirt. You've rather cooked your goose setting up business here. You should have let her take up a flat in the city or you could've taken her to Boston. I would offer to run the business but I can't guarantee to run it correctly.'

The smile from Jason was weaker. His worries had been initiated and preferred the peace of their surrounds while they fulfilled their duties. Afterwards, they relaxed among soft furnishings by the fireside, watching the flames rage incandescence up the chimney.

'Squirt, do you ever feel tempted to ask about Turner's past?'

'I doubt he would reveal much.'

Luze walked in. 'Pappy is in your study reading the puzzle.' With one eye shut tight, the other looking down the neck of a wine bottle, she said, 'Tony, can we have a cup of tea?

'I just washed up.'

'We need a little privacy.'

Jason regarded the cosy cluttered lines of the furnishings, the silver balls glittering on the Christmas tree in a room that smelt of Luze, his sticky stuff that held him together. He was so sad, hunched in the fireside chair wanting her to throw her arms around him and to pull his head to her and hold him hard, to tell him she would never be ashamed of him. Then he felt one hand on the nape of his neck, the stroking of his densely curled hair.

'It will work out, Nuts. Wait and see. Things happen for a reason. We just have to ride out the storm.'

With his eyes closed and his face uplifted, he said, 'Weakness is tiring, strength is exhausting. You make everything sound so simple.'

She knelt in front of him, placing a hand on each of his knees. 'That's because things are simple, my love. Granny Beth would never knowingly cause pain to her loved ones. She was a wonderful person and I felt so close to her when she was alive.'

'Chappy knows.'

'Do you honestly believe this village is without a clue?'

'Luze, what is going to happen when Tony meets someone he loves? Even now, my resistance is low so what shall it be like when he moves away? I feel such a fool. A day dreamer lost in a place of our making.'

'No cause is lost if there is one fool left to fight for it. Don't let my father cast shadows and doubts. I have never been so happy and neither have you but today your face is a picture of gloom. I have no regrets about the other night. It was wonderful you were there for me and-'

'Luze,' he interjected. 'I will always be there for you but we cannot let this happen again.'

Luze guilty jumped to her feet, adjusting herself when Turner walked in. 'Did you read the puzzle, Pappy?'

Turner searched. 'Where is your brother?'

'Making tea,' they voiced.

'I shall sleep here tonight.' As Turner settled comfortably in the opposite chair by the fireside, he stretched out his long legs. 'I am impressed with your new line...a pirate's map, indeed. How were you able to bring the picture to the forefront without connecting the parts?'

'It's the same principle as the jigsaw puzzle,' Jason replied. 'The acids from the skin provoke the chemicals to react.'

'And you say you were overseen by my Mother as you pieced that blank jigsaw puzzle?'

'I have examined the puzzle. It is what it appears to be, just an ordinary blank jigsaw puzzle, no more, no less.' He watched Turner lift his eyes when Tony entered the room with a tray. 'I never really gave it much thought at the time. Indeed, I had considered it was Susan and then of course we were concerned to get it completed. Of course, we now know this mystery phantom is Elizabeth and again has compromised a cutter. When are your workers returning?'

'In the New Year. It was a fortunate decision to give them leave the day I tried out your formula.'

'It depends how you see it, since Elizabeth pleases herself. But most certainly she sent a message when you tried it out, which, once again proves my point that we have been manipulated to this stage.'

'I don't understand why she doesn't make the fourth riddle appear and be done with it,' Tony said passing a cup to Turner. 'Then we can get on with our lives.'

'I am tired.' Jason stood. 'I have been without sleep these past twenty four hours. Tomorrow will be a long day. Luze, you will stay here. It is far too cold in that factory but we would appreciate a supply of refreshments.'

'We have a cafeteria in the factory.' Controlling Turner stood also. 'The gas cooker is unaffected but yes, my daughter can make us refreshments. I too need sleep.'

'Tony,' Jason said leaning on the door handle. 'You know what to do.'

Turner puzzled and glanced back at Tony. 'What is his meaning?'

'I lock his door every night just in case he goes sleep walking. I do the same for Luze in case she goes sleeping walking too.'

'You see, Pappy. Not all is what it seems. I stole the key from Tony.'

If Turner felt such emotions, his heart and mind were well armoured to contain them. He did not let them surface.

Jason stared through the window, the darkness beyond, feeling perplexed and utterly miserable. It was not as if he expected anything earth-shattering from the conversation he had with Turner but he did expect some leeway. He turned into the room and drew his hands over his face coming to the conclusion his troubled heart will undergo a lifetime of purgatory. Luze seemed to think she could have it all and he was unable to make her see such a foolhardy concept would lead them down a slippery slope of incest.

In the morning Jason gauged Turner's build and height. 'Tony, bring my two skiing jackets. They're in my wardrobe. Do you still have yours?

'Yes.'

'Then I suggest you wear it.' His words were insistent, hung seductive in the gloomy abyss. Within a second, he had reached the front door. Luze stood to attention. 'Can I have ham in my sandwich?'

'No problem,' she said and looked at her father. 'Pappy, do you want turkey, ham or cheese?'

'Turkey with some of that apple and cranberry sauce.' He kissed her forehead. 'Give your mother a ring but try to avoid embellishments. I do not wish her to be worried.'

Tony came trundling down the stairs where he too kissed Luze on the forehead. 'Don't worry, I'll look after them.' His affection was returned whereupon he walked to the Rolls and passed on that affection to Jason. 'That's from Luze.'

Turner shook his head and settled in the driver's seat. It was something entirely beyond his comprehension. But it became increasingly easy to understand their regulations and ignore their extreme humours for it ruled their games and ordered their lives.

At the factory, and starting before dawn, they threw themselves into the job, making space in the packing room until Hubbard emerged. Jason stared ahead, watched Turner greet his man, a moment of confiding.

'What's with those two?' Tony asked.

Jason deferred his thoughts when the two approached.

'Take your brother's side,' Turner said. 'Jerry, take up position with me. We need to bring the frame into the centre.'

Men in place, meaty hands gripped the edge of a wrought iron framework, and then with a damning heave they lifted it up in a flurry of shifting feet, veins protruding, the weighty skeleton destined to centre stage the packing room. From thereon they worked under the leadership of Tom Turner who knew more about the cutter and its foibles than anyone else. And it was blindingly cold, colder than ever thought possible and condemned every part and parcel in the packing room. It made for hard work.

By mid-day and at a hand gesture, Turner led the way to his office and there, Luze had presented doorstop sandwiches and a pot of tea.

'Poppet.' Turner took a sandwich, his voice much calmer. 'How is a man to get his teeth into this?'

'You try cutting thin slices from freshly baked bread. The trick is to squash it so it can accommodate your mouth but you should have no problem since yours is big enough.'

Jason realised Turner had accepted her cheeky ways long, long ago. It was part of her make up and never meant to be derogatory, on the contrary Turner appeared to like it and gave as good as he got.

'Then I shall follow your lead and see if I can match the size of yours.'

'You two are quiet.' Luze said pouring out the tea.

Jason and Tony shook their heads. They sensed the shortages of everything that made life easier at this point in time.

One hour later they were back to the grind stone, the cutter taking shape until an insignificant nut was missing. It later transpired a number of small parts had gone astray until Tony found a greasy box placed in the corner of an adjacent room. And all through the afternoon they were becoming weary and filthy. Each man bore the marks of rust stains and grease to such a degree, from a distance no-one was indistinguishable unless they stood their heights. Turner, marginally taller than the twins still had the makings of strength in his body but against Hubbard he seemed a giant of a man and Jason wondered how he coped in prison, wondered what his thoughts may have been and wondered again how those thoughts may have eaten him alive knowing he was distanced from the woman he loved.

Feeling a little easier, the twins began to drop their reserve, making small talk at first then speaking as though Turner and Hubbard never existed at all.

'Look, Squirt, they can't have it both ways. If they want equality then so should the men. I should get time off too. Pass me the wrench.'

'But inequality arrives because they serve a term of nine months.'

'Exactly my thoughts,' Tony agreed. 'Men don't have babies, women do. That's the nature of the beast. Men are hunter gatherers, women are nest builders. Luze sees my side of the argument.'

'Only because she knows how useless you are.'

'Women are resourceful creatures,' Turner said on his back under a near completed cutter. 'My Mother and Maria were establishing a business whilst caring for two small children.'

Jason used this opportunity to say, 'What happened after the trial?'

There was a pause for a number of seconds before Turner obliged. 'I was taken to Norwich prison but the guards were lax in their duties. I escaped and found passage on a boat to Australia for the three of us. Maria was carrying at the time. For a while I thought I was safe but fate very unkindly brought a visitor to my shores. As a consequence I was extradited and sent to a much harder place.'

A piece of the mystery fell into Jason's lap. 'It was Robert Graves, my Grandfather.'

'Indeed, it was Robert Graves and his obnoxious wife, an embittered woman who blamed Maria for your father's indiscretion.' There was another short pause before he said, 'Ask me, Jason Black. My mood has somewhat softened to your inquisitive nature.'

Jason crouched. 'Did my Mother leave her estate to you?'

'She gave a tidy sum to pay for her husband's wickedness. I have no knowledge of further sums upon her death.'

Just then Luze walked in wrapped up in a fur coat. 'Can I help?'

Hubbard looked at his watch. It said 8.30pm. 'Did you bring something to eat?'

'I made a hot pot. It's being reheated in the cafeteria.'

Jason flicked the snow off her hair. 'Did you walk down?'

'Yes.'

'Why not use the car I bought you?'

'It's against the law for a learner to drive without supervision.'

He felt her hands and they were freezing, her nose was bright against the whites of her cheeks. 'Go upstairs in the warm.'

'There,' Turner said, bringing himself into full view, 'the plate can be fitted.' On his feet, he put his arm about her shoulder. 'Poppet, return home and keep warm.'

She listened to her father, Jason thought, and realised his influence was far reaching, which must have made it almost impossible to follow her own dreams. To Turner, she was that little girl skipping in the wind, and only he would keep her on course. His course.

When she left, the men hoisted up the steel plate and clamped it into position before the thin strips of metal were attached above. Then they stepped back satisfied with that, paying silent tribute to their efforts.

'Good work, lads,' Turner said.

The twins looked at each other, the impact of the telling and receiving translated into silence. Was Turner softening to the Blacks?

Upstairs in the glass tower folly, Tony and Jason had re-acquainted their relationship with Hubbard and there it came to light he had shared a cell with Tom Turner.

'The only real practical justification for joining the merchant navy was to get out of serving two years in the army,' Hubbard said. 'I never fancied parading up and down to the tune of a trumpet. So there I was, hauling rope round the Bay of Biscay when the skipper comes up and tells me to get a hair cut. I said, you get one, so he put me on watch and refused shore leave. That was a bit inconvenient because I was running contraband to the French. I was already inside when Tom appeared.'

'How old were you?' Tony asked.

'Young and stupid that's why I received a shorter sentence...Tom said if I could make my way to Australia there would be a job for me. So I worked my way on a passenger liner waiting tables but it docked in New Zealand. Playing the high and mighty lad out there gets you nowhere. I roamed from place to place then out of the blue I bumped into Tom. He was on holiday with Maria and the two kids. Boss, remember that time we went fishing?' Hubbard gestured with his hands. 'I caught a baby shark, no bigger than a piglet. Tom comes from the galley and freaks out, tells me to shove it back. Next thing, the hull gets rammed. I stumbled back and Tom ditches the shark. After a bit, Tom is looking out to sea with a worried expression then shouted hold fast! Wham! The mother rams us again then we started to sink. Tom grabs the anchor, spots her circling, dropped it clean on her nose.'

'What happened after that?' Jason asked.

'We had to swim back, what else?' Turner said.

'No option when the boat went under,' Hubbard enlightened. 'What was it, Boss, a twenty-five-footer? It was sucked under quicker than a thirsty man's throat. We swam so fast we overtook the turtles.'

Hubbard and Turner dropped their diffidence and spoke of near-death scrapes, whisky battles and scorching kettles boiling over in the mid-day sun. Both appreciated that death could come swiftly in the Australian outback, sensing their chance with danger as an overture to their experiences in prison. Yet their settled faces suggested men of worldly wisdom, credibility and authority, the sort of men who represented father figures. The casual observer would have thought no different, would have been none the wiser.

A telephone ring interrupted their ruminations. Turner processed the office and picked it up. He mumbled a few words then cupped his hand over the receiver. 'Jerry, take the lads down and carry on.'

Jason descended the steps, now accustomed to the sudden coolness, the sound of his boots on steel and concrete. His vacant eyes stared ahead, glazed at the sight of a frosty cutter in the factory. Everything was as it should be. Yet someone had visited. He wrenched Tony back by the shoulder and put his finger to his lips then motioned with his chin. Ahead, a faint blur of light, a wisp of white smoke insinuating itself like a chill into the enveloping quiet. Fear, imagination could exaggerate the encounter but for Jason, it was engraved upon his soul. He moved slowly under the smells of perfumed witchery, reached out but his movement betrayed his presence and it dispersed into the ether.

'What the hell was that?' Tony said in confused panic.

'Do you smell that?' Jason asked. 'That was Elizabeth, the same perfume. Tony, was this the sort of thing you saw in your factory that day?'

'No, Squirt, well maybe, sort of though it never smelt.' He sniffed again. 'I can smell apple sauce.'

Hubbard walked on. 'And I can smell fear.'

'Hey, I wasn't afraid just cautious.' Tony modulated his voice. 'I bet they had a rubber dingy on board.'

Jason smiled. 'You wish.'

In the packing room, Turner joined them five minutes later and was told about their experience. He seemed unperturbed, determined to complete the cutter. And when it was done, he threw down his oily rag and patted Hubbard on the back. Then without a word they all retreated, their expressions fixed in assumed indifference, their gait disguising lost strength. Beyond and up, they caught stolen hours on couches for the want of sleep.

'What do you think?' Tony whispered to his nearest neighbour. 'Was it a ghost or just ice defrosting?'

'Ask the chemist.' Hubbard said.

'Squirt, are you asleep?'

'Do you wish me to gas you?' Turner quipped.

CARDS ON THE TABLE

Pinched of life, Jason squinted to the morning light streaming through glass then swung his legs round, sat up and drew his hands over his face. A tap on his shoulder and he looked sideways at a cup of tea. Such encounters were welcomed.

'What time is it?'

'Eight,' Luze said.

'Where are the others?'

'Downstairs waiting for you.'

He held the cup to his lips. 'You cannot do without me.'

Now he took notice as she padded to her father's desk wearing an off-the-shoulder pink cashmere sweater, trimmed to the waist, extenuating the curves of her hips that somehow wriggled their way into a pair of tight jeans. Her wind-blown hair roamed wild like a tumble weed on a desert plain.

'We tried out the cutter and it's running smoothly,' she said with her head bent to a drawer, 'but I can't find the formula.' She looked up. 'Do you have it in your head by any chance?'

'Luze, please keep away from that cutter, promise me.'

On her way back she picked up a plate from a coffee table, placed it on his lap and knelt before him. 'Sorry it's turkey but I ran out of everything else. Tony told me about the ghost. Since he has a tendency to exaggerate, what is your version?'

'It was some kind of vapour.'

'So you think it was Elizabeth's spirit?'

'That was the impression I gained.'

'Did she say anything?'

He shook his head, his mouth full. Hunger had no limitations. Then his eyes shifted from her face to her cleavage.

'Have you noticed it has stopped snowing,' she said. 'I walked down and the fields were melting and glistening against the red berry hedges. We should plant climbing cotoneasters on the front wall of our house, train them over the door so in winter we'll have a mass of red berries and the birds will come swooping down for their breakfast.'

And still he had his eyes on that cleavage, remembering the time when he cupped her breast and sucked a young nipple before he probed and went deeper into her flesh.

'Nuts, are you alright?'

'Uh?'

'You seem a little taken with my jumper. Do you like it? I bought it especially for Christmas.'

In that moment his bloodstream was infused with an orgy of sex, his concentration sucked in her anvil of creation and his mouth twitched with the thought of it. When he took her lips, it was fiercely, almost roughly, as though he was angry with his own inability to resist, angry with her for leading him into this dangerous wilderness.

He broke away and sprang to his feet, stood over her momentarily before descending the spiral staircase with such anxiety he nearly tripped on his own footing. Going directly into the men's washroom, he relieved himself with difficulty then splashed cold water on his face and took a long hard look in the mirror with little to show that he lived at all. Impelled by old habits, he brought out his comb and quarrelled with his hair at the same time feeling totally out of his depth. A while longer he went outside into natural light and began to stare at the nibbling squirrels and to wonder what would become of his relationship with Luze. She was in that forbidden zone, a treasure house of erotica that tipped him on the edge of insanity every time she came close.

A presence brought calm into his mind. 'Hey, Squirt we wondered where you'd got to.'

'Is Luze still here?'

'Her father sent her home. Boy does he like giving orders.' Then he added with meaningful intensity. 'What's the matter, Squirt? Come on, talk to me. Is this thing getting you down?'

'What was I thinking, Tony? What made me think it could work? She makes me come alive when I am dead. Now I feel positively sickened. I can no more control my urges than the natural pangs of hunger.'

'I dreaded this would happen. It was a funny arrangement, I thought. I mean how can a man live with the woman he loves and not touch? I couldn't do it but you seemed to have it under control. See, it was that trial which kept you focused but as soon as that was over your animal instincts came to foreground and now you can't pack them away.'

'She said the whole village talks about us, whispers and wonders the same. Why is love so bloody painful? Why did she have to be the one?'

'You're going to land up like Dad, if you're not careful. You got on with your life after the shock, remember? Sure, you were down but it was getting better, or was it?'

Jason nodded, slowly. 'It was hardly bearable.'

'Do you think Elizabeth messed with your head? You know, altered your chemical composition in some way?'

'I cannot deny this possibility. I just love her and want to be with her yet now when I am with her, I want what every man wants. I want marriage, children, a secure and loving relation with a family of my own. It seems not to bother Luze. She never speaks of those things, never raises any such thoughts, not even when we were close that night.'

'Look, for what it's worth,' Tony said. 'I'll stick by you whatever you decide. Why not tell her how you feel. Talk it out, be honest with each other. She has to be going through the same thing.'

'She makes everything seem so simple, and stores nothing in gossip.'

'But that's Luze. It's her personality. She sees everything through rose tinted glasses. If you want to put it in perspective, just ask yourself if you're prepared to lock yourself away in that house and play happy eunuchs for the rest of your life?'

Those gentle words wounded him as deeply as any he had ever heard. There was a finality to them he found unbearable and he dropped his head to smother the cry of despair for he knew Tony had spoken the truth.

'We three need to talk,' Turner said.

Jason should have known he had not missed that brief exchange. Luze was right, he thought, Turner saw everything.

The mighty tall Turner encouraged them to stroll, his hands tucked in his trouser pockets exhibiting all the signs of genuine concern. It was seldom discussed, and never with strangers, the facts which Turner took pains to conceal, out of shame and pride, and for the sake of those affected. Now Turner would share them with the Blacks.

'In a cell, a man experiences many things and the one thing that kept me alive was the thought of my freedom, to escape beyond the confines of filth and stench, to breathe fresh air into my lungs...seven long years, seven long years of preparation. Each night I would read my letters and each night I would shed tears until there were none to shed. I grew strong in body and mind, kept focused and built up immunity. The day my freedom came, the first in my arms was Merluza, rushing from the docks onto the gangway, her eyes as bright as buttons and the first thing she said was, pappy, tickle me with your beard. Lies never used to be my currency, Jason but I had to keep my family safe. I was no longer Tom Turner but the return of Sam Claggart, the man who served on a naval vessel protecting the seas to our British colonies. My mother had found a near match to wear a naval uniform and she paid him to visit the factory to keep my memory alive in the community. Here, my mettle was tested. I had achieved a point of where I believed in my own lies. Yet it wore heavy when Merluza returned from Norfolk. I too felt the taste of disgust for keeping things from her. Now your mettle is being tested and a greater one to come. You will read the memories of my daughter each night on your pillow and you will shed your tears until they are shed no more. You will grow strong in body and mind and build up immunity to your losses. But unlike me, you will be free of lies and deceit and you will look into the eyes of your brother and the people around you without the weight of guilt, and there is no greater freedom than that.'

Jason sighed in resignation. 'I shall speak to her.'

'I shall speak to her. Your strength has diminished. I know my daughter.'

'Look, you two,' Tony offered. 'I should do it. Luze will listen to me as the objective party.'

'And what will you say against her tears?' Turner asked.

'For a start, the truth which hasn't been much in her life, has it?' He smoothed his hair straight back with his left hand. 'Now you two concentrate on the puzzle and I'll sort out Luze.'

When Tony was out of sight, Turner said, 'Jerry was right to lay blame at my feet for this problem. I should have told her the truth when she was old enough to understand.'

'And I was cherishing a misty memory believing I could make it come true.'

Turner placed a comforting arm round Jason's shoulders, gave them a squeeze. 'Your intentions were good. I can see that now. It took a long while to understand and if you need to call upon me, I shall not turn you away.' He walked on. 'You may call me Tom.'

A smile grew on Jason's lips as he followed the man to the Clean Room. The cold still persisted, had not worsened, nor the stuff on the new cutter, and overall it seemed things were stable. At a glance Jason identified Hubbard checking the type-set and went to his side.

'Almost word perfect but this line should read *yet to the rescue came a man to fight on one condition*...was it a good fight, Tom?'

'It was a good fight, Jason.'

'What was it like for you, you know, in prison?' Jason asked Hubbard.

'Ever gone to the zoo to see the lions? You can always tell the wild cats, those who miss the thrill of the chase but after a while the soul is lost in their eyes. That's what it's like in a cell without a window and only a bucket to piss in.'

What else was there to ask?

Thereafter Jason concocted his formula overseen by Turner who quickly sprang up to supply one ingredient, Cobalt, an economic element of commercial importance. Once used as an element of surprise, Cobalt was popular for making so-called *sympathetic ink*, which later became better known as invisible ink. This remains unseen until it is warmed and was the basis of Jason's exploration before he took it one stage further.

With everything in place, the room hummed to a silk screen printer that drew a heavy cartridge over white paper, snatching but smoothly efficient. At first, they could see the writing, several times over but within moments the print disappeared. It was then stuck to cardboard and laid out to dry. There was no more to do but wait like a new born with a sense of bewilderment and terror. From that uneasy smell, chaos and cold they ventured upstairs to shake warmth in their bodies, had cups of tea and went endlessly voyaging in that long primeval light.

'Tom,' Jason said. 'It must get very hot in here during the summer unless this glass is refracted.'

'It is and double glazed.'

'That must have been expensive to install.'

'My daughter has no concept of budgets.'

'What made her incorporate this folly?'

'It was a last minute addition. After I divulged my background, she felt it appropriate to afford me a view upon my visits. What did you invent to warrant a medal from the President of the United States?'

Jason dredged up memories of nights half-asleep in the laboratory. 'It was a bio-chemical capsule that dissolves in the stomach's lining releasing the medicine into the blood stream at predetermined intervals. Rather than a quick fix for a short duration, one has quick fixes every three hours over a twelve hour duration. But for the fact of the pharmaceutical company having a finger in the space programme, I doubt a shiny medal would have been pinned on my lapel.'

'The best inventors are English,' Hubbard said. 'Pity the Americans cornered the market on your invention. Just think how rich you would be if you owned the patent.'

Jason smiled. Behind that gesture told a different story.

When the cardboard had dried sufficiently, Turner hit the button on the cutter and it came to life. Its clackety-clack sound reverberated in the packing room, travelled into the ether through the wide open door, no mistaking its aggressive noise that blocked all other sound. Jason fed in the cardboard sheet. The side rollers drew it straight under the thin strips of metal that clamped down and rose in an instant. It then travelled to a collecting trough where it automatically separated the pieces of the puzzle. Was this going to produce what Jason hoped? There was only one way to find out.

Gathering their wits they clambered up the spiral staircase, destined. For whatever way they viewed it, they had no alternative. It began with the contents spilling out onto a cleared desk, thereafter they were gripped in a madness of Jason's making. It was logical to work from left to right but three pairs of hands entwined and clashed, causing confusion, and never had something been so stressful or so frustrating.

'I keep telling you, Boss, that nub doesn't fit in there.' Hubbard pulled it out.

'It does, Jerry.' Turner slotted it back in.

'It doesn't because nothing is happening.'

Jason snatched it out Hubbard's hand and quipped, 'your turn to make tea, Jerry.'

'I shall make it.' Turner arched his back and threw his rimless spectacles on his desk. 'My eyes could do with a rest.'

'Boss, bring up the chocolate biscuits. They're behind the soup tins.'

'Why are they there?' Turner asked.

'Mrs Tooley likes them.'

The mysteries of Mrs Tooley.

'You did the right thing,' Hubbard said to Jason when Turner left the folly. 'Good guys don't mess with their sister.'

Jason never responded nor flinched. Acceptance was now part of his creed. He remembered being temporarily unhinged, disorientated and irrational after the shock of learning Luze was his sister, then the accumulated stress, the risk he had taken when she came on board, and the most apocalyptic example of lust in his study bedroom. And this morning, he had demonstrated once again his head long desire to take her. For the moment, he felt without personal account for his actions, more inclined to feel sorry for himself and going beyond that element necessary to get her out of his mind. But it was still early days and the reality had not really sunk in.

Turner emerged, a tray in both hands. 'Mrs Tooley also hides the ginger nuts.'

'Why?' Hubbard asked as if he never knew.

'Because they are mine and she drinks my sherry.' His voice conveyed disparity as he placed the tray on the desk beside the puzzle. 'I see more talk and less action increased the puzzle by one.'

'It's a difficult puzzle, Boss.'

'Tom, what did my Grandfather say,' Jason asked. 'Did he speak to you about his intention to change his Will?'

'Edward had altered his disputation, no longer had the streak of madness for the business when his youngest son died. My Mother and Edward grew fond on each other in a strange way and found comfort in sharing their losses. He took me to one side and explained it was not for discussion, that I must look after my Mother and aid in the business as a fifty percent shareholder with your father. When your father returned from Lincoln, he was displeased. I asked Edward if it was possible to be remunerated in other ways and allow your father sole ownership of Strident Cutter for that seemed to be the answer to solve the current dissent. Edward refused to consider the proposition and decided his Will should state all assets on this land to be shared equally. Your father would have the house and the strip of land it stood upon and I would have the cottages. The business split between two, worked between two.'

'What made you suspicious about his death?'

'Edward was a strong man, both in mind and body. It was claimed he died of a heart attack but I knew differently. What I speak of now must not be mentioned beyond these walls. Only Jerry and my Mother were ever taken into confidence. Do I have your word?'

Jason nodded.

'Shortly after his burial I exhumed his body. There had been no post mortem as claimed by Robert Graves and further there was blue on his tongue to suggest he had been poisoned by arsenic. I went to see the district coroner who refused to entertain my suspicions. My Mother later discovered he had been paid a handsome sum by your father...enough to set him up in a fine house. It was obvious the rivers of deceit ran deep. Who to trust, there was our dilemma. My Mother advised we should keep our heads down, work our passage towards other ventures, save hard...then it changed when Maria came on the scene.'

'At your trial, did you mention this?' Jason asked.

'Did I not say the rivers of deceit ran deep? My trial was a farce. Your father had the judge in his pocket, like he had Robert Graves and the coroner. Money spoke volumes in those days, Jason. It controlled the wheels of commerce and encouraged dishonesty. Sometimes I found it hard-pressed not to follow the same route and have, in minor ways, deviated in order to meet my objective yet Strident Cutter would not have been gained but for the incompetence of your sibling.'

'True,' Jason agreed. 'I cannot blame you for that.'

'Explain to me why you split the patents.' Turner asked.

'It's like the black swan scenario. You think it's never going to happen but you should always look ahead just in case it does. After I discussed the concept with Tony, he was mind-set on getting back Strident Cutter and I was unable to change his mind. Then, of course when Luze came on the scene, she made it clear you would never sell.'

'How ironic,' Turner said. 'Had you stayed to run Strident Cutter my opposition would have been a formidable one. Perhaps my campaign was equally unjustified but it stemmed from what your father did to Maria.'

'I would have shot him.'

'A fool hardy action, you would have suffered the death penalty.' Turner took in a deep breath, recalling the worst of his memories. 'The knife that shone in my face was your father's choice, not mine. I sang joyful praises when it pierced his muscle. I felt the squelch of damage. Had I been allowed one more minute, a second strike would have seen us both dead, he by my hand and me by the gallows. I look back now, grateful for that, grateful for intervention.'

'Do you feel inclined to tell me what happened?'

'You read the verse, use your imagination.' Turner replied unwilling to relent to details. He carried on with the puzzle for a while then said, 'Maria paid a heavy price, know that and also know your father and the inn keeper were given carte blanche when I accused Graves as accomplice in the murder of Edward.' They beat and kicked him for the sake of themselves, as he lay there face down, groaning. He never stirred again until the police arrived.

'What had you done to make John Whistle so obtuse?'

Turner met his brows. 'Nothing, I did no harm.'

Jason had something else to think about. 'Would you know why my Grandfather stipulated in the deeds that only a Black had the final say in selling his land?'

'Edward did what many men did in those days...set a clause so no bastard child was able to claim ownership of his estate.'

'Has there been anything to feel proud about my family,' he said as if to himself.

'Your mother, Katherine was a good woman. She played no part in Edward's death. When she heard what had happened to Maria, she offered a tidy sum to give us a new beginning in Australia.' Turner leaned back against his chair, the puzzle seemingly less important now it was approaching near end. 'She too understood the loss my Mother felt when Molly died.'

'What was Molly like?'

Turner delved into his back pocket and brought out a black and white picture from his wallet. It was faded and spent. 'I used to brush her hair by the fireside after she washed it. This is all I have left of her.'

Jason remembered the magazine photograph showing Luze as a little girl and something he once considered before but immediately disregarded was now back in his mind. He stayed motionless, looking at the picture and then at Turner. There was likeness there, remote, but still there was a hint of family resemblance. So why was there no hint of family resemblance between Charles and Luze, or between him and Luze? The judge had asked the same question and now Jason was asking himself, again, that same question.

'Luze takes after her mother, thank goodness.' Jason was probing. 'If she had taken after my father, it would be a poor reminder over the years.'

'I would love her no less.'

'I understand your father died serving his country. You must be very proud of him.'

Turner took back the photograph and gave a short snort. 'Proud of a father who gambled his wife's land on a whim of a card, changed his family's future forever...no, lad, I have nothing but contempt for the man.'

Jason shifted his gaze to the puzzle. No fourth-riddle had been exposed and he mentally queried why. He got to his feet and swept down the spiral staircase, the temperature unchanged and he knew before looking that the cutter was still affected. Behind him, he felt Turner's presence.

'Did you not say my Mother was manipulating the elements? Was she not here? Why is there no fourth riddle?'

'I am at a loss,' was all Jason could say.

Turner glanced at his watch then at Hubbard. 'Jerry, I suggest you return to your accommodation in Norwich. I shall call if you are needed.'

'OK Boss. See you later, Jason.'

'Thanks, Jerry.' Jason then asked Turner, 'Are you coming back to Mile House?'

'I would prefer my room at the hotel. Let us meet here in the morning with a possible view to get blow heaters into this factory to melt the ice off that cutter.'

'Since the factory's boiler refuses to work, there is every indication the heaters will pack up too. I cannot understand why Elizabeth wants to keep this factory out of production. Have you got any ideas?

'None whatsoever.'

Jason could see a worried man, a confused man. 'Tom, I promise I will get to the bottom of this. I shall do some calculations...see if I can find an element to counteract the stuff on that cutter...at least I can give it a try, even if the measure is only temporary.'

'Good man. If my daughter is still-'

'Tom, I know what I have to do.'

'Do you wish me to give you a lift?'

'No, I prefer the walk to clear my head.'

Their parting was a gradual process and a merciful one in Jason's mind. He so desperately wanted his own company, to let the cool wind claw at his face and work out the missing link. He looked back once and noticed Turner walking across the road toward the church and wondered if he had something to confess. At first, Jason was scared of raising his hopes but now he felt near certainty Luze was not his father's child. And that begged the question, why would Turner deny this? Perhaps Turner did not know himself, and if so, it begged another question. Why would Turner's wife, Maria O'Grady keep this information from him? 'It's all supposition,' Jason muttered to himself. 'I was wrong about the fourth riddle, so am I wrong about Luze?' His pace quickened when he realised there was only one way to find out and that he should have done this way before now.

Years ago there was paternity testing by blood types but it was unreliable. But of course things advanced when a team of geneticist in 1953 unravelled the three-dimensional structure of the blueprint of life and this changed his understanding of how genetic information was passed from one generation to the next.

That night was no stranger to assumptions or queries or even the malady of confusion. While Jason walked the mile distance, elsewhere, Turner walked into the Catholic Church. That time when Luze returned to Australia from Little Smeet, he remembered his anger welling inside, the spiralling argument which incurred his wrath. But once it had started it had seemed so difficult to stop. He identified such acts, and encouraged the right mood, fostered the appropriate response, and braced himself for her incoming. She never said anything at first as they walked the office corridors, his back straight as ever, his breathing a little loud but his face still impassive. But it was only when he thought about her now, probably still at Mile House he knew she was no longer his little girl skipping in the wind but a woman in love with the wrong man. And although he had been genuinely impressed by Jason, had recognised his tenacity, his expertise, his willingness to remedy the ills of the past, and no greater love for his daughter, it was still a sad state of affairs. His heart was strained in similar measure.

Aware of a presence, Father Michael swung round and smiled from the altar with an outstretched hand. 'At last we meet. Tom Turner, yes?'

'Father Michael.' Turner acknowledged and sent his eyes to the candle, his nose to the heavy incense. 'I can return later if this is a bad time.'

Father Michael showed the way. 'Let us proceed to my sanctuary.' His private surrounds were littered by meaningful things as he had spent his spare time stuffing the crannies of his life with a ballast of wayward objects, a collector of tin soldiers and model planes that strung along shelves from ceiling to floor. 'This must have something to do with Jason and Luze.' He took Montgomery out of Turner's hand. 'I am still painting him. A drink, I think.' He rummaged in the coal bucket. 'My new hiding place,' he said. 'At last I have confused Mrs Tooley.'

'She also eats my ginger nuts.'

'We all have our crosses to bear.'

Grief or madness was not so private now. Removing catalogues off seats, popping the stopper, blowing dust from the glasses and pouring sherry, Father Michael heard Turner's story told in dramatic pyramids, seeking ravenous conclusion, and he could hardly keep still. He prowled slowly around Father Michael's treasures, opening boxes, picking up figures and placing them back elsewhere.

'One is always under the misapprehension a soul is equal to another when in truth each soul carries its own value and contribution,' said Father Michael.

'And the sins of the father shall carry to the sixth generation.'

'Come now, Jesus forgave Mary Magdalena. I should imagine Jason's shoulders are heavily burdened and lost at this point in time. Give him a little latitude.' The easily forgiving Father Michael leaned forward, could sense the agitation and see the shallow rise and fall of the chest. 'Tom, what is really troubling you?'

'At this very moment I feel my daughter is still at Mile House and what Jason shall make of it, is left to conjecture. How much endurance can a man take before she possesses him again? And what will happen if a birth occurs?'

'Tom, you must have more faith in them. They fell in love, a deep love and it survived its trials, even up to a point when your daughter returned to join Jason in a business venture, even up to the point of your court case. One slip does not make them sinful, just human. Perhaps their relationship is rocky at present but I am almost certain Jason will restore the balance given half the chance. Surely you know from your own experiences how hard it is to cope with the loss of loved ones.'

'Perhaps Molly blames me for not saving her. It was my duty to care for both but my manner was lax and wasteful that night.'

'You were a lad.'

'I was a man. Fourteen years old, yes but still head of the house. Must I be punished for my youth or my absence by her grave?'

'I understood it was Elizabeth haunting the factory.'

'So Jason believes. Yet why would my Mother cause anxiety? True, Merluza is not my daughter but I have always loved her as my child. I never treated her differently from my son.'

'Tom, what is your wife's opinion?'

'Maria knows nothing of these past events. She sits thousands of miles distant and scorns my absence from the family on Christmas day. She took the news of our daughter's decision to work alongside the Blacks very badly, and I cannot blame her for that. The trial was upsetting. My counsel advised against putting Merluza on the stand but I had to know what went on.'

Harsh times, bitter thoughts, and it required a level of new thinking. 'Did you ever see the puzzle Jason made of Molly's garden of remembrance?' Father Michael got to his feet and rummaged through his cluttered shelves until finally he brought out a tray. 'Chappy and I put the pieces of this together. We spent a good two nights burning the midnight oil.'

A tear came to the eye, long enough to reach inside and liberate the angst from his mind. 'Why did the lad do this?'

'You might say he did it to benefit his brother's cause but in truth he felt distressed about the whole sorry business. It was his way of apologising and to ask you to put the past away and look on him and Tony in a new light.'

'Had my Mother not interfered, Merluza would be home where she belongs and my factory secure. What my Mother has done is evil.'

Father Michael did not attempt to deny it, did not offer false comfort. He reached over and picked up Hitler. 'If ever a soul was possessed by demons, then here is your example. You must ask the question, why do those last pieces refuse to show a fourth riddle, and the answer becomes obvious. There is something else to learn.'

'How can we learn when it does not appear?'

'Since your mother works through Jason, then I fear it is for him to find out. When you stayed at Mile House, did it not bring happy memories?'

'Happy memories drowned by darker ones. I watched them that day, standing around Molly's grave, legs apart, head slightly bowed and expensive shoes pressing into freshly dug earth. The coffin was hoisted into position by the bearers and held there for a moment and in that moment, I watched them look at each other, Edward Black and Robert Graves, poised for the outside world. One day, Mother said, we will have a home of our own and I said one day is far away. I do not want these memories they are too painful.'

'Ah, so now we come full circle. We all have our mischievous sprite dancing on our shoulders. Tomorrow is a new day. Get some sleep, brush off your sprite and join forces with Jason. Two minds are greater than one.'

At the door Turner said, 'You have a fine collection.'

'It was once Tony's collection. He enjoyed military history. I studied physics before entering the church, encouraged Jason to do the same. He chose chemistry, so our conversations were very much in tune, sometimes argumentative in our subjects. Jason can be most expressive when he wants to be. A number of days after his brush with death, there he was, standing in front of me just after mass. Jason, my son, I said in astonishment, what have you done to yourself. He replied, next time I shall piss a little higher and move a lot faster.'

TURNING THE TIDE

Mile House was empty of warm bodies, something Jason did not expect and aimed frantically for her bedroom, breathing the last of her. There he sat on her bed, leaning forward, hands curled around his stomach as though around a warm cup of tea and looked ahead at pretty flock wallpaper, then at all the empty spaces which lacked her bits and pieces. The wardrobe door was hinged open, inside, that too was empty. His sticky stuff, the glue which held him together was apparently gone so easily as though Tony had found a miraculous solvent to melt her away from his arms.

In the bathroom sink the water sat undrained, cooling. And from the bath, he watched a trickle of water weave its way down the hanging towel, falling away from broken blue handprints, falling softly to the floor. He closed his eyes for a moment, a small hard crack of a smile. It had been a long, long journey taken in fragile footsteps so intense she had possessed him completely. And somehow, he felt that whatever else, Luze was still his destiny and that no solvent would dissolve her from him.

The slam of a door and Tony called out, 'Are you about?'

'In here,' Jason shouted.

Tony walked in, flushed from his endeavours. 'I'm bloody starving. Come to think of it, the last time I ate was this morning. Want something to eat?'

But Jason was in that place far beyond reaching. Tony's mental conflict about food was irrelevant. 'How did you persuade Luze to go?'

Tony shrugged. 'Ask her yourself. She's in the kitchen ready to give you a pasting.'

Jason grinned, heaving himself out of the bath. 'What happened?'

'Arguing with Luze is like re-arranging deck chairs on the Titanic. But she does make a good point. Yesterday, you said so yourself. All of us were brought together for a reason and since you two have the deepest connection you have to ask why? She went crazy and moved into the spare bedroom to make you suffer.'

Jason brushed by and left behind a puddle of water and a wet crumpled towel. He went into his study bedroom, threw on some clothes then all at once she was upon him. In her eyes the lustre of defiance.

'Shame on you, a man who presumes to speak of departure when it's my departure you request. This is my home and my business as much as yours.' With her hands on hips, Jason could see it was all she could do to withhold a smile. 'Well, what do you have to say for yourself, whimpering dog?'

An eyebrow rose. 'You threw a bone and I licked it.'

'Oh damn it, Nuts! When are you going to realise we are not pitiful heathens but intelligent people brought together by something – who knows what? Some ancestral toughness perhaps. I'm inclined to believe it was Granny Beth that put us together and it's in our best interests to work through this, together, all of us. Isn't that so, Tony?'

'Absolutely, couldn't agree more. What's for tea?'

'Turkey!' They harmonised.

In the brief silence that followed, Jason held Luze by the shoulders. 'My mind is all over the place, Luze. I went through a bad patch and your father was very persuasive. He said I could call him Tom.' As if that mattered.

Luze appeared unimpressed. 'Perhaps he should be a permanent fixture in this house. So, alright, you got frisky. I get frisky but it was only a kiss for heaven's sake. I mean, it's not as if we were about to have a roll in the hay. I shall now make us something to eat and leave you to your stupid meanderings.' On her way out she said, 'By the way you need a shave.'

Jason motioned to Tony and went into the bathroom. 'No fourth riddle appeared.'

'So where that does leave the factory?'

'Cold,' Jason mumbled, lathering up. 'I saw Tom walk towards the church. Now I ask myself, does he have something to confess, seeking redemption or is he a worried man? Tony, we do not look like Luze. She has no family resemblance whatsoever.'

Tony settled on the toilet seat and crossed his legs. 'And you think she's not our sister.'

'All I need is a sample of her blood.'

'But why would Tom hold back that information?'

'Okay, it's conjecture at present, but if she is not related to us, it's possible he doesn't know. He thinks the world of Luze. Why he even offered to give back his mother's land if I would just let her go.'

'Then if you're right, Maria O'Grady is the only one left who knows the truth. Who do you think she may have shacked up with?'

'Perhaps Tom is her real father.'

'No, can't see that, Squirt. Why would she not tell him? Are you going to say anything to Luze about this?'

'No,' he replied, straining his vocal cords as the wet blade passed down his throat. He then leaned on the sink and looked sideways at Tony. 'I could be wrong. I hope to God I am not but if I am it will cause unnecessary grief for Luze. How can we get a sample of her blood without her becoming suspicious?'

'That's the least of our worries. If what you say turns out to be true, how are we going to get the truth from Maria? Whatever she's holding back must be mighty important.'

'You make a good point,' Jason muffled in a towel.

He makes a good point.

Jason shot round. 'Did you say that?'

'Say what?'

'I heard someone agree with your assumption.'

'Oh Squirt. You're definitely losing it.'

Jason threw down the towel. 'I heard another voice. In fact, I heard a voice in the car after I took you to the hospital.' He needed this to be an important conversation but it was not. One glance at Tony shaking his head, he was now buoyed up and opened the bathroom cabinet with gusto, brought out a clean blade. 'It matters not how you do it but get me a sample of her blood.'

'Eh? How do you expect me to do that?' He followed Jason into the room. 'Come on Squirt, this is ridiculous. Tell her or are you just clutching at straws?'

'If she is told, can you imagine her next step? She will contact her mother and we shall lose the advantage of surprise. Maria has kept this information from Tom for a reason. I cannot confirm one way or the other who her father is but it is within my capabilities to find out if she is related to us.' Jason had found what he was looking for and put a receptacle in Tony's hand.

'What do I do with this?'

'Put her blood in there.'

'Well that's just great. Not only do I have-'

Suddenly a yelping cry! The unexplained was unfolding as it did before. They tore into the kitchen and there was Luze holding her hand under the tap, diluted blood swirling down the drain.

'I cut my thumb on the steak knife,' she said visibly shaken. 'I don't know what happened. One minute I was cutting off the fat, next it sliced into my thumb.'

These were seconds Jason fortuitously used and withdrew her hand from running water, caught precious drops of blood into the receptacle and then stuck her thumb in his mouth.

Half amused, she looked at the receptacle, at him, and back at the receptacle, not such a fool as to mistake her blood was his keepsake. 'Why did you do that?'

'Thmetmighthvbninfeted,' he garbled.

'I never understood a word you said.' She pulled out her thumb from his mouth and stuck it in hers.

'Luze, I cannot emphasise enough the measures I would take to ensure your safety. I must go and check your infection. Call me when tea is ready.'

Leaving Tony in his search for a sticky plaster, Jason drifted on those times Luze was sad, happy or ill and it would go almost unmentioned as though nothing out of the ordinary had happened. He remembered trying to hold his breath while she asked him how the new printer worked, her voice sounding strange. Have you got a cold, he asked and she would reply, no, I'm allergic to wasp stings. And it never worried him, because she always seemed to be better the next day, saying oh it was one of those things.

In his study, Jason cut swiftly into his thumb and smeared his blood onto a slide. It was no simple matter to test DNA, a subject of recent discovery. But there were few better men and luckily Jason was one of them.

'Phew!' Tony walked in and closed the door. 'That was a near miss. Luze grew very suspicious until I told her Smelly nearly lost his arm after he came in contact with cow's blood.'

'Smelly milks his cows,' Jason said with his eyes in a book.

'Look, I had to think of something. I could have told her aliens were landing, instead I improvised and told a whacking great lie.' Tony brought out his slim-line silver cigarette case and pulled one out, tapping the filter on the casing. 'Let's say there is no fourth riddle. Why? Maybe because we learnt all there is to learn about our side of the family.'

'Not a bad assumption,' Jason said turning over a page. 'Why do you think Elizabeth hid those pieces in the old man's leg?'

'I think Luze was right when she said it was a form of acknowledgement. We learnt our past and that was it...full stop. You kept asking, why Elizabeth would push Luze towards you, why would she allow Luze to suffer? If your test proves right, then Elizabeth must have known Maria was not carrying Dad's child. Now it would make sense. She sees you as a good suitor for Luze, the fourth riddle would no doubt appear but I reckon it would not appear on the puzzle you made but on the original puzzle we found.'

Jason looked up. Tony had made a valid point. He walked across the room to a side table and glanced down at that puzzle, still in its entirety on the tray. 'At which point would the fourth riddle come into view?' He glanced back at Tony. 'Perhaps when we learn the truth?'

'My accident was no accident, Squirt, you do realise that.'

Jason went to his glass cabinet and brought down a blue bottle from the shelf. 'It would seem a harsh thing to do when all said and done, the invention would come to light the moment we offered it to Turner.'

'So you think Luze cutting her thumb was a coincidental accident? I don't think so. My accident forced Tom to come here, not forgetting Luze coming here too. No, it seems to me there's a pattern in all this. What do you think it might be, you know, the secret Maria is keeping close to her chest? I mean, if she screwed someone else there must be a very good reason why she keeps quiet.'

'I would have thought that obvious.'

'No, not obvious, Squirt. She loves Luze, I presume, so why not come clean? Why allow her daughter to suffer?'

Jason glanced up, not sure whether to respond to that or carry on working. He decided against it and buried his eyes in the microscope leaving Tony to leaf through a number of theories, all of which were bizarre.

However, there soon came a point when Jason slid her details under the scope. His thoughts now went to the illicit grandeurs of his forebears, and wondered what he would do, wondered if he would be ready, and wondered if he would be as lucky as the man on the news who fell from a tree but never broke any bones. He looked through the lens, adjusted accordingly, examined, looked up and rubbed his eyes and looked through the lens again just to be sure, just to be absolutely certain. And when he was absolutely certain, he looked away biting his bottom lip, listening to the increasing rhythm of his heart beats, suspended in a plateau of shooting stars.

Tony clicked his fingers. 'Are you with me, Squirt?'

'I can marry Luze.'

Even with the earlier preparation of such a possibility, even hearing these words, Tony still needed confirmation. 'Are you sure?'

'Yes,' he said nodding vigorously. 'One hundred percent certain, she is not our sister. '

'Hell, so you were right.' The twins embraced. 'Good for you, Squirt. All we have to do now is fly half way round the world, tap Maria up for her secret, fly back and stir the pot with Tom.'

'Yes, a difficult venture.'

Tony cocked his ear as if he was the only one to hear Luze. 'Tea is ready. Now take that grin off your face or she'll suspect something.'

'I am a very happy man, Tony.'

'I know you are, Squirt. I'm happy for you but no smooching or going mad. Okay? You lead and I'll pick up the gist.'

Exhilarated, though somewhat mischievous, Jason walked into the kitchen, drew out a chair alongside Luze, sat down, and picked up his knife and fork. 'This looks good,' he said to Luze knowing full well she was waiting for his verdict. He cut into his steak, popped a piece of medium rare into his mouth and allowed the juices to flow.

'Tony,' Luze said with a tinge of sarcasm. 'Did you by any chance catch my disease?'

'Can a man finish eating before extrapolating on your infection?' Jason teased.

Luze dug her fork into his meat and placed it on her plate. 'There,' she said. 'You're finished.'

With a deadpan face, he said, 'I was overly cautious, that's all. What with Tony's accident and the experiment failing, one cannot be too sure where this is taking us.'

She smiled, returning the meat to his plate. 'So no fourth riddle then?'

'Unfortunately not,' Jason replied. 'Tell me about your mother. You never speak much about her. Or are you still upset she refuses to take your calls.'

'No, we are on speaking terms. I called her the same night Chappy took you away. I wanted to wish her Happy Christmas. She seems resigned to my decision but of course she wished I was there. She's a patron for the UM. When Granny Beth died, she decided to help unmarried mothers who were incapable of looking after their children. Unlike England where unmarried mothers are given accommodation, in Australia there is no support other than charitable works.'

'So your mother is held in high esteem among certain circles?'

'Yes, so you can imagine how she feels about my actions but I said, I am here Mammy and you are there.'

'These high society circles, do they know your father's past?' Tony asked.

'Why should they? Little Smeet is hardly a place to attract their attention. Besides, Pappy is Sam Claggart there and Tom Turner here.'

Jason felt a surge of heat rushing to his head. 'What made your father sail so close to the wind? Has he ever considered selling up and retiring?'

'You mustn't under estimate Pappy. He always has all eventualities covered. If it ever got out, he would turn it around and become the hero. The Australians are very down to earth people. They love the thought of a man's struggle against the odds.'

'Well,' Jason said, ready for an opening gambit. 'I am convinced a fourth riddle never appeared because Elizabeth wanted your mother here. Since your father refuses to involve her, the best I can do is try to find a chemical that might clear the cutter but it will only be temporary, if at all possible.'

'Then we must try to clear up this mess. Temporary arrangements will only prolong Pappy's misery. I shall speak to Mammy, reason with her and see if I can get her to come over.'

'Not a good idea,' Tony said. 'I think Elizabeth took a secret to her grave and your mother might possibly know what it is.'

'But Mammy would have told Pappy.'

'Not necessarily,' Tony argued. 'What if, and this is only a long shot, what if Elizabeth and Maria had something more going on with our Mother. Since she is dead, we can hardly ask her. Maybe the three of them made some sort of pact, after all, lets face it, Mum had a great deal of money so where did it all go?' Tony had hit upon the one argument that might just work.

And Jason followed it up. 'He's right, Luze. We're not saying Elizabeth and Maria never deserved Mother's money. But how do you think your father would feel if he knew. He told me Graves and his wife went to Australia to get back their daughter's money and as a consequence shopped him.'

'Oh dear,' she said slowly dropping her utensils to the plate. 'Pappy is a terribly proud man and if what you say is true it will make him feel awful. Worst, he would be so hurt that Mammy kept this from him. You're right, it's not a good idea for her to come here so I must go there.'

'That's not a good idea either,' said Tony. 'It's possible Elizabeth wants us to know the truth, which need not necessarily involve your father. If Squirt and I go, you would be needed here to cover our tracks, keep your father sweet and all that.' He gave that time to register and then asked, 'What do you think, Luze? Is it a shot worth taking?'

'Anything is worth taking but what do I say to Pappy when he asks where you two have gone?'

'That's simple. Just say Squirt took off when he realised you were still here and that I went after him.'

'Okay,' she said simply. 'I shall give you directions to my place.'

Jason swallowed his last mouthful. 'Why your place?'

'My brother and I share the old home Granny Beth purchased when they first arrived in Melbourne. I use the ground floor and my brother uses the top floor. He's not very happy with Pappy because Pappy decided to stay here. We always spend Christmas together.' She collected the plates and stood. 'Who fancies mince pies and ice cream? Alternatively, there is left over Christmas pudding or Christmas cake.'

Jason got to his feet, sending a signal for Tony's departure. Alone, he wanted to tie things up with Luze and remembered vividly every last detail of those forbidden minutes in his bed and the heat rose in his cheeks. It gave him a funny perverse twinge for she was his sister then.

'Luze, we should get going.'

'I thought you might say that.' She swung round to face him. 'Nuts, I should warn you. Mammy is very anti you so please tread carefully.'

'Am I not the treading careful type?' He placed his hands each side of her face, kissed her softly then brought her into his arms. 'I love you, Luze. I promise not to act the idiot again.'

'Do you know that's the first time you have told me you loved me...not that it matters because I know you do. Just keep fighting for us, Nuts and I promise to keep fighting too.'

AUSTRALIA

In Australia's second great metropolitan city which sprawls around the head of Port Phillip Bay at the outlet of the muddy Yarra River, they found themselves walking across St Vincent's Square, weariness dragging at their heels. Here, in South Melbourne, one of the most attractive of all inner city residential areas, fine houses in a variety of styles were laid out around central gardens. One in particular drew their attention.

'What now?' Tony stood in contemplation. 'We could mull around, wait until she comes out or go for it now.'

'Not sure,' Jason admitted, and considered the gleaming green door hiding a cocktail of mischief inside. 'If we wait to tackle her when she comes out it might disadvantage our position. On the other hand, the door might be slammed in our faces.' A dilemma, one in which Jason found hard to decide. He looked up closing his eyes to the sun-baked sky and caught the kisses of heat on his face. To leave it with no decision at all would be a shame. 'Okay. Let's do it now.' Of all the countless times he tried to envisage how this would go, the light at the end of his tunnel had already been reached with Luze, so whatever the outcome, law and love were on his side.

Two loud knocks and the door opened. 'Come,' she said waving them in. 'I have tea on the veranda.'

Jason and Tony looked at each other in bewilderment. The welcome was not only warm but unexpected. They marched through a home smelling cool of fresh sheets and baby oil. There were framed photographs dotted between vases full of flowers, abstract paintings hung on bright walls, bits and bobs settled on shelves and a kettle that had hissed its way to the boil. Further on, past these wonderful fancies, the sun struck through, a golden beam of brilliant light scared off by a portico that shaded and cooled occupants over mid-day meals. Here, they were invited to sit down in wrought iron chairs next to a matching table, a most welcome sight, flowery teapot and cups struck dumb in the silence.

Where should Jason begin, now, later or until he was asked?

'It's a long flight you must be very tired.' Her voice was possessed by an indestructible barrier and she poured tea with an elegance of manner as though her approaches to life were bred and nourished from birth. 'My daughter telephoned and mentioned you would call upon me.' She glanced at Jason. 'Mr. Black, I advised-'

'Please, call me Jason.'

'I would prefer to keep this meeting on a formal basis.' She passed a cup to Tony. 'The only reason I agreed to this meeting was due to the strangeness of my daughter's call whereby she claimed something had happened in my husband's factory. I do hope this is not some kind of elaborate hoax to gain my approval over your liaison with my daughter.'

Tony answered. 'It's no hoax, Mrs Turner. Elizabeth is behind it.'

'Elizabeth? If you are referring to Tom's mother, she passed away some years ago.'

'Ah, that's the point.' Tony leaned over and took a biscuit. 'She's been in contact with Jason.'

'How intriguing, was the conversation as stimulating to the one we are having now?'

Her sarcasm was directed at Jason who was stirring his tea, full of apprehension, truth or part truth, what difference did it make? 'Vision, illusion, fantasy or nightmare, call it what you will but your daughter was planted in my head three days before I met her. And there we were, investigating the past by the aid of unknown forces while Strident Cutter was put out of commission. Now we skip nearly a year to the day of the trial and the moment your husband tried a run on his new cutter with my formula, the same thing was happening all over again but this time far worse.'

'And what do you expect of me?'

'I believe you hold the key to the fourth riddle.'

'Mr Black, I am hardly a poet let alone your answer to solve whatever it is you claim to be haunting our factory. If there are such things as ghosts then it surely resides in your conscious when you purposely set out to inveigle my daughter into your camp.'

'So you hold no credence to our claim?' Jason asked.

'Neither my husband nor my daughter has spoken about such things.'

'Are you not slightly curious as to why?'

'My husband is a busy man, and my daughter has her head filled with nonsense.'

'And you dwell on the past.'

Jason hit a nerve. She bridled at his remark. 'Have you come to stir trouble?'

'Look,' Tony intervened. 'We have flown half way across the world to get to the root cause of the problem. Maybe we can solve it and maybe we can't but just listen to what my brother has to say.'

Her poise seemed to have deserted her. She was sitting like a lost child, gawking at Jason. His eyes were deepening to a startling shade of black, and they distracted her. 'Very well,' she finally said, 'I shall listen.'

And he began slowly at first, bit by bit in stages until the longing for a solution became irresistible, filled his mind to obsession so much so he rambled with little pause, his words sucked down in the crown jewel of this house, a sun kissed garden stocked with an incredible range of plants. In Melbourne's kind climate, shrubbery did not die or fall foul to ice and snow, only in the mountains on the highest slopes but in spite of that, he still lost time. At first, he thought the dim shadows were only in his mind but when he rolled his head and looked into the west, he saw the orange hues of a sunset thinking of Luze and what it would mean if this journey proved fruitless.

Maria had recognised the weary discoloured bruising beneath his eyes from lack of sleep. What had it been now, two days, maybe less? Though her voice was steady and business like, to Jason, she appeared wrought as though she was crumbling in her own ghostly apparitions. She stood, went forward and folded her arms leaning against a wooden pillar looking out to the carroty sky, shivering in the wind like a dying last leaf on a tree.

'I did consider I was chosen because of my expertise in chemistry but there hung the mystery of why Elizabeth brought us together.' And now Jason felt his timing was right. 'I know Luze is not our sister.'

Maria briefly glanced back and gave a strange sharp clear look and uttered not another word, just returned to her outlook. Tony motioned with his chin for Jason to carry on.

'Luze always speaks so highly of you both. She cannot praise your virtues enough, even Tom's. But I cannot help wonder if Tom is also in the dark, for he would not have said the things to me that he did. So the only other person I have left is you. I know you were there with Elizabeth at our home when Mother was alive. Perhaps my Mother concealed something from us and you might know what it is.'

She turned and held his gaze, her eyes watered by the secret she had held for so long. 'I love my husband, Mr Black more than life itself. He has suffered enough.'

'And your daughter, would you let her suffer?' Tony asked.

'She appears happy in her present state.'

Tony was dissatisfied with that and refused to let the matter drop. 'Two people, one you purport to love are going to live in a veil of gossip for the rest of their lives, unable to have a family and you stand there like Miss Congeniality all because of what? Did another man go between your sheets and you lost count?'

She stiffened and wiped her eyes quickly with her fingers. 'What gives you the right to come here and insult me when your whole family impaled ours? I want you to leave. You are not welcome any longer.'

Tony got to his feet. 'We had to face up to our past. Do you think it was easy for my brother, an eminent chemist to hold up his head knowing that everyone had talked behind our backs, held fire-side stories for a winter break? Yes, death, murder and rape. Black by name and black by birth, that's how we've been labelled. Now Jason has incest added to his list, an unnecessary lie to condemn his relationship with the woman he loves. And make no mistake, Luze loves him too. Jason tried to let her go but she refused because she believes in him.'

'Then we are all equally in the hands of God.'

'Rest assured, this meeting never happened, perhaps it never happened when you shacked up with another bloke.' Jason said it bitterly and did not seem to expect an answer, was so immersed in dejection that any question was rhetorical. All she had to do, he thought, was to tell the truth for beyond all her clumsiness, he could sense she was hiding a terrible secret so painful it was eating her alive.

Outside, on the doorstep he brought out a packet of cigarettes purchased at the airport. He was in a mindless numb world because he seemed to be asking too much and everything welled up, his jaw clenched to fight back his drowning emotions.

'Did I push too hard?' Tony asked.

Jason shook his head and said nothing.

'Hey, you're my brother, Jason.'

'Now you remember my name.'

And they were just about to move off when a soft hand clamped on his shoulder. 'Both of you come inside. I have something to say.'

What they did not know in this interval, her distress was equally compelling, bringing up her terror in the bathroom, shame and guilt, heaving and retching until her stomach was empty and the muscles of her chest ached. She looked hot and miserable with the horrible beginnings of tears.

'What I am about to tell you must never go beyond these walls. Can you give me your assurances?'

Jason answered. 'You have our word.'

'No,' Tony objected. 'Surely, we should try to sort out the mess, not keep secrets. This has been the problem, keeping secrets.'

'Tony,' Jason irritated. 'Why are we here?'

'To find out the truth.'

'Exactly. But we shall never find out the truth if you refuse to give your word. So I suggest you find something else to do while I listen to what Mrs Turner has to say.'

'Hey, that will mean I shall never know the truth.' Tony paused to their stubborn silence, bit the side of his lip and finally said, 'Okay, you have my word.'

'Despair drains me,' she began with the sun crushed below the horizon. 'My life will be a sad and sorry affair, a grinding daily struggle to maintain my pride if my family ever find out.' For a second, she seemed to be looking at Jason, and her face, white, with a dark red mouth and hair black, had all the mournful vulnerability of a clown. 'One lie pressed upon another and one thinks it's the end of a matter, like a wee sandwich, eaten and forgotten. When Tom came into my life nothing else mattered. He was so naive and trusting. He believed good things would come from our relationship and that we had a wonderful future. Even his mother, Elizabeth felt there was a turning point.'

There was a long pause with a heavy sigh then she faced Jason. Tiny arrowheads of strain and worry had been chiselled at the corners of her eyes and mouth but they softened when she pulled out a few pins from her hair, the plait fell as though it was a sign she had finally succumbed.

'The night your father first laid eyes on me I knew what was going through his dirty mind, the same thoughts that went through many men's minds. I came from a poorhouse, Jason Black. I used my looks to my advantage, but I did not consent to bed with your father. I despised him for what he did to Tom and Elizabeth. I taunted him and there was my mistake. He caught me unawares, a brief interval to rid his lust and in my anger, I told Tom. During the trial I told Elizabeth I was pregnant but she told me to keep quiet, that we could use my predicament to free Tom and make a good life...and I so wanted to live my life with Tom. I so wanted to see him freed from that terrible, terrible place. He never deserved such treatment and I felt so guilty. The look in his eyes was something I never wish to see again, such terrible torment and pain and the worst is to know he was innocent. It was not his fault. He had done nothing wrong. But Elizabeth had great strength and went to see your mother and told her the child I carried was your father's. Your mother was heart-stricken and desperate to get rid of me. She believed if I stayed with his bastard child she would lose him. But your mother was no fool. It was she who suggested Australia. She said money would be waiting in a Melbourne bank but we had to take Tom. That was her condition and it suited us well. On the proviso of him escaping she would hand over a letter of credit for us to present to the bank when we arrived. She gave us some money so we could pay off a guard to allow Tom to escape.'

She paused for a heavy intake of breath and expelled it as though a weight was finally lifting from her shoulders. 'And when he showed himself on the doorstep, from there we made our escape to Southampton to take up passage on the first boat to Australia. Tom was so wonderful, so caring. He would place his hand on my swollen stomach and say this would be his child, that he would love as a father should love, and that all the past is behind us.'

Pausing again, she wiped her tears and consolidated her voice. 'We were going to tell Tom, tell him what we had done but Elizabeth backed out. She was worried it may be too soon because he was still so angry about your father. So we allowed him time and forgot who we were. I was Mrs Claggart married to Sam Claggart. Then I fell pregnant again and he was a man in heaven. He was so happy and content, building up a new business on the outskirts of Melbourne and before we could finally tell him the truth, disaster happened as though we were to have no life at all. After your mother's death the Graves turned up. He knew the child was not your father's and he was angry his daughter gave us money, angrier still his daughter had left her estate to us. We never understood. We had none of her estate but he refused to believe this. So Elizabeth tried to scare him off by saying she would implicate him in the duplicity of Edward's death, that she would write to the medical board and for a while it seemed to have worked, which gave Elizabeth time to make plans for us to abscond but it was too late, the police arrived and took Tom away.' She felt the pot. 'Would you like another cup of tea?'

They followed her through to the open plan kitchen and watched her go from fridge to cupboard, from cupboard to fridge expecting any moment for her to continue but it was Jason who prompted her further.

'So what happened then?'

'Elizabeth took it so badly, how she hated the Graves and your father. Graves taunted her, told her it was her lesson for lying to him and Elizabeth just pulled the trigger and that was that. He died instantly and then we were faced with what to do about his horrible sour-faced wife.'

Tony gulped. 'Did she go the same way?'

'I'm afraid so.' She went quiet, opening a packet of dates.

'What happened to the bodies?' Jason asked.

Somehow, she had gained composure and was telling the story like an outsider, as though it never really happened to her. 'They are buried in this back yard. The business grew, and a man was hired to keep Tom's memory alive for the children until he could be released. It was wonderful to see him, to hold him and know we would be safe at last. He was so white and drawn, so lost but so happy. Elizabeth told him her plans for revenge and he loved that idea. It gave him focus, something to sooth his anger for what your father had done. We did talk about telling Tom everything but realistically Elizabeth said it would destroy him and all what we had worked so hard to achieve. And it seemed not to matter for he loved Merluza. Sometimes we wondered if he loved her that little bit extra than his son. We would sit out under the portico and smile. Elizabeth would look at me and I would look at her while Tom played with the children over their graves. There seemed to be some irony to the whole event.'

'Well, glad we got that one sorted,' Tony said. 'So where did Mum's money go?'

Jason was uninterested. 'Tell me more about Elizabeth?'

'She was such a wonderful woman, truly wonderful. And took up knitting, liked to knit memories into a scarf, good or bad, she said all were valuable experiences in life. But after her death, Tom wanted us to move on and I was so frightened about selling this house and I was compounding one lie upon another in order to stay here. I missed her strength. There were times when Tom and I would argue in front of the children about moving, and she would always back me up but after she died it was becoming virtually impossible. Of course money was never an issue. Tom got his way. He bought a yard and had a home built. Then a miracle happened when Merluza and Adrian came up with the idea of taking on this house. Jason, I know how it is to love. I feel deeply for you and my daughter, but there is nothing I can do. Over these past months I have been concerned for her and want for her happiness but do I put her happiness above my son, my husband, our business, our marriage?'

'There has to be a way round this.'

'There is,' she replied. 'Let her go.'

Let her go? It rolled off her tongue so easily. One minute Luze was his betrothed, next she was his sister now she was neither and whichever way he viewed it, his love was forbidden. Now he toyed with a platter of dates to summon the courage to speak those words that were jangling in his head.

'Was it John Whistle?' he asked and saw that look in her eyes believing he had guessed correctly, feeling her shame and her compounding of that shame. 'He offered you a room, money, a chance to get on with your life. I now understand why John Whistle held Tom down when that fight occurred. It was obvious he was also anxious to get rid of Tom so he could keep you working at the bar, and whatever else was on his mind. But was my Father aware John Whistle and you had a relationship?'

'John Whistle,' she said in contempt. 'A most horrid man who winkled out of his duty was my puppet on a string. While I kept him dangling, my job was secure so I could stay near Tom. Jason, you never lived in those times. Money never flowed freely in order to give us choices. I had a fair notion I was pregnant that night when your father came upon me but I was uncertain. I told Elizabeth and what she proposed sounded wonderful.'

'I suppose you never bargained for me coming onto the scene,' Jason said tugging at his ear lobe, slightly apprehensive but desperate to grasp at any opportunity. 'Would it not be possible to tell Tom part of the story? Tell him who her real father is and then I can marry Luze.'

'And he would say, why. Why withhold this? And I would have to give in and confess all. He has spent years of making something of himself, focused on achieving his mother's dreams and yes, he prides himself on trying to be a decent man. This would kill him. It would destroy everything he ever believed in. I cannot let him suffer anymore than he has.'

'But you do that to Luze,' Tony stated simply, and she looked uncomfortable. 'What must have been going through your mind when you discovered Luze had fallen in love with my brother?'

'You think me a whore, don't you? That look in your eye will be the same look in Tom's if ever he found out.'

'Hey, I'm looking at a genuine sorrowful set of circumstance. If you want a comparison to a whore, you should meet my wife. She had everything mapped from the day she clapped eyes on Jason and when that didn't work, she made a beeline for me and when she finally netted her catch, she dropped me in a holding tank and blackmailed my Father. We all do things to survive, even me. I married her because I never had the balls to follow my brother's lead. No, you're not a whore but a survivor placed in a damn sticky situation. Tom said women can be resourceful creatures. You and

Elizabeth gave Tom something to live for in that hell hole and even though Luze has been some sort of conjecture, she turned out to be a great person. I think the world of her. She mothers me more than she mothers Jason and quite frankly if I ever get a chance to meet someone like Luze, I would put my hands together and say thank you. It's just so bloody unfair that Jason and Luze are condemned for the rest of their lives. They're perfect for each other and for the first time in my life I feel I have a decent family. Hell, I even admire Tom. I just wish we could find a way for us all to put the past behind us and be happy. Don't you think so, Squirt?'

'I share Tony's sentiments. I do not consider you anything less than a female lion fighting for her cubs cornered by her enemies. Perhaps Elizabeth is trying to find a way forward, maybe this is the revision. She wants to stop your suffering and bring our families together. The past lay in grief and pain, waiting for revision.'

'You are a romantic, Jason. You cannot alter the past. If you could, the revision must stem from the date when your grandfather cheated at cards. If, as you say, Elizabeth's spirit is alive, why would she want the horrible truth to come out knowing it could ruin us?' She took hold of Tony's damaged hand. 'Look at this, you poor man. If you had just stayed away from the cutter this would never have happened.'

'It's not so bad. A small price to pay...Elizabeth or chance, who knows, but it dealt with me the same way as it dealt with my brother. Mine is visual, his is hidden.'

'Mrs Turner,' Jason said. 'Maria, we cannot help circumstance, and we try to survive on this circumstance the best way we know how. But surely you cannot believe Tom and Luze would think any the less of you.'

'So I tell them. Where does that put you, Jason? Where does that put the likes of Tony's wife who profits from other people's misery? Do you think it will all be cuddles and kisses? Questions will be asked if you marry my daughter. The papers will rake up the past. I never supported Tom in his vendetta to recapture his mother's land. At the time I believed it was just in the moment, that soon it would peter out but it grew to a frenzy after Elizabeth died.'

The reaction on her face was self evident. Without uttering a sound, she picked up a photograph in a wooden frame, showing it to Jason with pride.

'This is Tom and Adrian,' she said, 'when they went camping. Although my son looks like me, he has his father's proud forehead, very stubborn.' Then she picked up another. 'We were in Sydney when this was taken. Merluza had spent two years at University and then dropped out. I was annoyed but Tom secretly wanted her back so he could keep an eye on her whimsical nature and work in the business. I just wanted the best for her. Can you imagine how I felt when she took Jerry's place and went to Norfolk? Since then I have hardly slept. I am torn to pieces. I heard her crying, night after night. I knew there was something more, something she was not telling me.'

Jason could see the strong likeness between Adrian and his mother, an obvious genetic preference, he thought. 'Children are not born as a corrupting influence. It's the parents that nurture their characters. Only forty percent of genetic characteristics are passed on, did you know that?'

'They both have my eyes and dark hair but Merluza tries to emulate Tom, full of courage and enthusiasm, such a zest for life and such nonsense in her head.' She cleared her throat, returning the photograph to its designated spot. 'I sacrifice my daughter in return for everything else, for Tom, for my son and for the business.' Maria began to work her fingers to her hair, forming a thick plait and deftly twirled it to the back of her head. 'I can understand what my daughter sees in you. I shall never forget the day I first met you. I must have known you were going to find out my secrets.'

'When I first saw you, I wondered whether I dreamt of the right woman.'

'You are a flatterer, Jason Black. A woman of my age takes all the compliments she can get.'

'Luze said she believed she took after you.'

'She is rather funny, isn't she? I used to do silly things. When you grow older you grow wiser and I had Elizabeth to lean on. My daughter is like a little girl at times, skipping in the wind with her eyes closed.'

'I can assure you her modesty belies her talent. She is clever, resourceful, and full of courage. She sees things in a very cut and dry manner. She's been a little girl skipping in the wind because she loves Tom. She wants him to be proud of her. One of the reasons I might add for her accepting Tom's choice of future husband material.' Jason looked at Tony stuffing his face with biscuits. 'We can eat at the airport.'

'You are welcome to stay.' Maria offered.

'No, we should be going.' Now Jason was unsure how to say goodbye. Even though placed in an awkward position, he was aware how difficult it had been for her to take them into her confidence. 'Thank you,' he said and softly pecked her cheek.

'Take good care of my daughter, Jason.'

'I will,' he replied.

'Have I made things worse or better for you?'

'Certainly not worse, certainly not better but at least my mind is a lot clearer.'

She glanced up at Tony. 'Is your mind a lot clearer?'

'My mind is never clear.' Tony felt obliged to do the same. 'Thanks for the tea and biscuits. By the way, I think I've eaten all your dates.'

Now the night was theirs.

Jason walked on, stopped for a second to light up a cigarette, and then continued with weariness dragging at his heels. There was not much to say, he thought, not much at all. He glanced at Tony deep in thought. There was not much to say there either.

On the plane, by far a long way to go, it was here Jason felt more in the mood to talk rather than sleep. 'Elizabeth wants the secrets to come out but what good will it do? Realistically, it would create greater damage.' He shrugged, believing he was taking a jaundiced view of virtually everything he had done to make his life easier with Luze. 'I suppose I could legitimately illicitly sleep with her now.'

'You have to break your promise to Maria, Squirt. Tell Luze. You can trust her.'

'It's not a question of trust. It's a question of integrity. We both gave our promise not to disclose the information.'

'Honesty is not always synonymous with the truth. You can bend a bit to suit your needs and your need is to have Luze as your wife not your sister.'

For a few moments Jason leafed through his thoughts, regarded Tony had imprudently adopted a rather high and mighty tone. 'Luze pointed out arrogance was rarely supplanted with decency. And you are arrogant.'

Tony laid back and closed his eyes. 'I suggest you think about that one. You forget the puzzle is still in your study.'

'And?'

Tony opened one eye. 'And no doubt the fourth riddle will be revealed.'

Jason gulped. 'I better telephone Luze when we land.'

Like a fresh baptism, Jason tried to disguise the brutal anonymity of what they had done and after a while he relaxed back in his seat. Each time his breath softened he sounded more comfortable, his face got more relaxed. And then he was almost closing his eyes, listening to two men talking in the seats behind him.

'This has to go smooth. Take your time on this one.'

'You know me, I always take my time. Thorough Don, that's my motto.'

'That bastard thinks he can get away with it.'

'Did you get the scrubber, the same one I had before?'

'All set up, no problem. When you've finished with her, give her to Mike and he'll put her on ice.'

'I need to stretch my legs. Fancy a drink at the bar?'

'I'm getting some shut eye.'

Jason had not expected to be so absorbed by this brief conversation, but his interest grew more intense as the seconds went on. Not even the melodious drum in the cabin could settle his curiosity. He looked askance at Tony whose mouth was open catching some dreams, and slipped out of his seat to process the aisle towards the lounge, strictly catering for first class passengers. After surveying the layout, his eyes cobbled together two men at the bar. One stood legs apart, his back straight as though he had some form of military bearing. Near also was a bloated grotesque. Now Jason wondered which one?

'Whisky and soda, no ice,' Jason asked the hostess and drew out a packet of cigarettes.

'Can't you sleep either?'

Jason recognised the voice and propped his elbow on the bar facing a man with a white goatee beard. 'I hate the long hauls. Are you travelling on business?'

'Most certainly am. And you?'

'Going home. What's your line of work?'

'Talk to the dead.' He smiled with a mouthful of teeth. 'Court pathologist.'

'Ah.' It now became clear. 'That sounds like an interesting occupation.'

'Usually when I tell people my job, they ask if I interrogate the cadavers.'

'An intriguing thought if that were possible.'

'I had a cadaver on a slab, just about to slice him up when his jaw dropped open.'

'Did he say anything?'

'Not possible, he had no tongue.' He laughed and held out his hand. 'Don Cutter.'

'Is this another joke?'

'That's my name, Don Cutter.'

'Jason, Jason Black.'

Don lifted up his glass. 'Another round, please twinkle.' He looked back at Jason. 'I chance my luck and say you're some sort of inventor on the brink of a discovery.'

'Not bad, not bad at all. How did you arrive at that?'

'Your fingers have dark stains, reminds me of a chap in the print trade but you have money or else you wouldn't be travelling first class. Your face looks as if it's been in the way of an experiment.'

Jason nodded. 'It was no experiment but close enough. I am a chemist by trade.'

'Give me more time on your body and I should be able to tell you what you've been doing with your life.'

'But then I would have to be dead.'

'That won't be far off if you carry on smoking.'

Jason stubbed it out. 'I hope to give up in the New Year. So tell me, I am intrigued, how do you go about weighing up cadavers?'

'I haven't got time. My job is to find out how they died.'

'I challenge you to guess my profession.' A high-pitched voice and air of effeminacy sat at odds with the short and corpulent body. 'Gerald Parker. I was listening to your conversation. Where would you pigeon hole me?'

'You are easy, my friend. You like your food so you are either a cordon bleu chef or you own a chain of restaurants.'

'No, I suspect not,' Jason told Don. 'He felt very confident in challenging your expertise which may suggest he does something unusual. Am I right?' But Gerald was giving nothing away.

Stroking his white goatee beard, Don looked Gerald over more than twice, stared at his patent shoes, walked to the back of him and then said, 'by the size of you, you're a sumo wrestler.'

They burst out laughing.

THE REVISION

The brakes screeched!

Jerked out of sleep, Jason said, 'How long has it been like this?'

'It hasn't,' Tony replied, reversing the motor a few yards. 'See. No fog. The only time I remember it this bad is when we went to the Samson and Hercules.' Tony smiled with the engine ticking over. 'Hey, that was the first time we went searching for girls, and you gave that bloke one in the eye.'

Jason sagged back and rubbed the sleepiness from his closed eyelids. 'I remember it was you who stirred his brains. Put the wipers on and keep to the curb.'

Into first gear, Tony proceeded at a snail's pace worried about oncoming traffic. 'This is weird,' he kept repeating until he reached a brighter mist and halted to the lights thrown from the Pig and Whistle. 'What do you think? Should we go in? Start of the New Year and all that...have a quick one before going home. Luze maybe there, that's probably why she never answered the 'phone.'

It suggested to Jason a different atmosphere to one of celebration. 'Stay here. I shall go in and see if I can spot her.'

The mist moved thickly around him as he snaked between ominous shadows before stepping inside to a lobby with astonishment. Through the half glazed door that led directly to the snug he saw square-rumped farmers and housewives, workers and old gardeners, they nodded and prodded and pointed at each other and some faces seemed familiar but unfamiliar. Active sounds came drifting in garbled messages and journeyed beyond his understanding. Everything appeared strange and comic, like a magic construction joined together in a perpetual embrace of the past. Then a figure inched forward to the bar, signalling at another man. Jason recognised those faces to be the younger version of his father and John Whistle. He squeezed his eyes tight shut and opened them again just to confirm it was no manifestation then spotted a young girl picking up glasses from the tables. It was Maria O'Grady. She had a softening in her eyes, a wide smile aimed at a face Jason could not make out. Wildly struggling with his feelings, he was almost certain this was the night.

Swinging his legs into the passenger's seat, he sat stoic and silent with his tongue exploring his upper lip, running it over five day's growth. Tony waited quietly, this time he seemed to give no direction to Jason, no matter how subtle. But Jason hesitated, uncertain whether to speak his thoughts and finally said, 'Follow me.'

The fog began to lift at an alarming rate, rising stealthily from the ground to uncover Little Smeet. And there, in front of them, the Manor grew more perilous by the minute.

Tony blinked rapidly with comical astonishment. 'Is this a joke?'

'We have walked into the past, Tony. I saw Maria and the old man.' Jason knew his brother could not really grasp it, but sensed the enormity of what he had told him and saw it in his eyes. 'This is it, Tony, a chance to make that revision. It has to be April Fool's Day, 1950.'

'Waugh, now just hang on a minute!'

'Look,' Jason said pointing to the manor. 'There is the proof. We have stepped into the past. This must be the night.'

'I may not be a scientist but interfering with the rape of Maria O'Grady won't guarantee Dad doesn't try it later.'

If Jason was sure about one thing, he knew Tony made sense. 'Okay, we need to get the car off the road and work it out.'

To the rear of the church was meadow land, and beyond that an untamed orchard where even in the future seventies no-one ever knew its owner.

'What is the objective,' Jason asked a rhetorical question. 'If the events must play themselves out, why are we here? The last line on each of those riddles said, the past lay deep in grief and pain, waiting for revision. So why have we been sent to 1950 when we could have been sent to 1942 to save Molly, or earlier when Elizabeth's husband played a foolhardy game of cards with Grandfather?'

'Maybe we have to learn something else, Squirt. Something Elizabeth took to the grave. Or maybe this has something to do with Mum. Hey, we could pay her visit.'

Jason smiled at that tempting thought. 'The one person who deserves to die is the old man.'

'What! Have you lost your marbles?'

'Think about it. We save Mother from her own mental suicide. She will put Tom in charge of Strident Cutter and he will stay in Little Smeet, marry Maria and I will marry Luze.'

'What makes you think it will pan out that way? No, I can't see it, Squirt. There has to be a Claggart, there has to be Luze and her brother in Australia, there has to be dead bodies in their back yard or else we return to utter mayhem. You're not thinking straight. You should be, because you're the bloody scientist. Go back to the question, why would Elizabeth bring us here? We must be here to see something.'

Now suddenly, for Jason the gulf between the absurd and the rational had closed. 'I feel so damn stupid. It was pointed out many times, how can a revision be made? A simple question which required a simple answer, we cannot change what has been done. We are here to see Elizabeth because she can see a greater catastrophe to come. Reputations take a lifetime to build, seconds to destroy.'

'I don't understand. Are you suggesting we should visit Elizabeth?'

'It was Elizabeth at the helm. Maria was young and in love through turbulent times and her sheet anchor was Elizabeth who was fighting for her son's life, and she still fights for him. Look how they thought they could escape England, make a new life in Australia and along comes Graves. There is always some bastard like Susan who wants to make easy money, feeding off other people's misery. We cannot make the revision, not in our time because the wheels are already in motion. Tom bought Strident Cutter, built a new factory which incurred publicity. His face was in the newspapers. Elizabeth can see a greater catastrophe.' Jason turned in his seat and stared into Tony's face intently. 'We must see Elizabeth, in the flesh, to tell her the future. This is what her soul requires.'

'Luze was right. You're nutty as a fruit cake. By telling Elizabeth the future, it's going to give her ideas. It might be us coming on the scene that's created the problem in the first place. Christ, I'm so bloody confused not even I can work that one out.'

'Tony, what is done cannot be undone. This is the night and Elizabeth cannot alter her son's prescribed course, of this I am certain. But when Tom escapes, that is another matter. She must tell him the truth. He will know what to do.'

'Like what?'

'Get rid of the evidence. Burn those bodies and make sure the trail leading to our Grandparents is clean, without any come back. Tony, I need you with me on this. I cannot do it without your help. Elizabeth might regard me as some mad man but if you show your face, she will recognise the old man's features.'

'Hell, how far back do we go? Are you saying it was providence Dad pushed you through the patio doors?'

'Why not, Tony? Why not consider each person has a prescribed course?'

'I just hope we get back to the time we're supposed to be in.'

'I cannot guarantee that.'

'Well, when do you think we get back?'

'Logically, and of course depending upon Elizabeth's actions it could be earlier, say round about the time I was on that plane from Boston then I would have no memories of what went on the following year, alternatively, since the factory was unaffected, it could be after the trial, there again-'

'In other words you don't know.'

Jason sent his eyes to the dim shadows playing with the apple trees and considered why it had to be so difficult. 'No, Tony. I don't know. When we were on our return flight from Australia, Gerald Parker said something most poignant. There is an irreconcilable gulf between those who are motivated to take great challenges, and those who fear them. I fear my life without Luze, yet I have a greater fear of what I can offer her if this situation goes unresolved. She will be torn apart to see her mother and Tom destroyed, and I will be comforting her arms knowing if I had the courage, I could have made a difference.'

'Do you think your destiny is to meet Luze?'

'I would like to hope so yet I cannot dismiss the fact Luze was also part of Elizabeth's plan. After all, she planted her in my head, manipulated events to reach to this point. Whatever the cost, I have been chosen by Elizabeth to do this.'

'Remember when the three of us got together in the kitchen at number 18? I said whatever you want, is fine by me. Susan bent my mind for seven years and the only good thing that happened was us working together on a new business. That was my dream, and I love Luze too. Sure, not in the same way but I felt I belonged to a decent family for a change. It still goes, Squirt. Whatever you want is fine by me. Do we know what cottage Elizabeth and Tom occupied?'

'Yes, number 18. See how everything falls into place? Come on, let's survey the Manor first and see if Mother is home, have a little peep.'

There was a nervous laughter at this and it brought no miracles of relief when it soon transpired the Manor stood ordered and occupied. Light was escaping from the gaps in drawn curtains and a tree where Susan's Mercedes once stood basked under stars, its branches stuck out like stiffened arms.

They continued a slow circuit to the rear of the manor, talking in whispers against a place of comforting and familiar horrors. Jason went down on his stomach and belly-crawled towards the glass patio doors that shed light from the kitchen where a woman was kneading dough. Beautiful were the motions of her hands, their movements so long rehearsed. The result was a structure of tight perfection, a ball of pastry that was placed in the bread tin and set above a warm stove. Next, she sat relaxed and put on her steel-rimmed glasses to read a newspaper in wait of the yeast rising. Her hair was coiled and pinned, the colour of straw with fly-away strands caressing a blood drained face. Jason thought about their world of behaviour in her arms and crawling about on the kitchen floor through forests of chair legs, how they went hand in hand through the rain, towards the river bank and mother came scrambling down, uttering cries that were not singing. He never expected to see another day.

'Just had a thought,' Tony whispered. 'We're probably upstairs in our beds.'

His face screwed in alarm. 'I wonder what would happen if we met ourselves?' He watched Tony clamp a hand over his mouth trying to hold back his laughter and asked, 'What's so funny?'

'Just imagine you in charge of yourself growing up. Now there's a paradox.'

Jason smiled and glanced back to look at his mother. 'I wish I could hold her, tell her how much I loved her. Do you think in light of what we tell Elizabeth that it held some significance why Mother never left us her money?'

'Perhaps she told Mum part of the story...you know, how successful you became and me being a prat. I did think it odd at the time Mum leaving us out. Do we know what time we should speak to Elizabeth?'

Jason automatically looked at his watch. 'If this is correct, we have a couple of hours. We know Tom will be in the Pig and Whistle when Maria told him. The fight took place outside round about ten. We must assume Elizabeth will be alone in her cottage.'

'Did you see Tom?'

'No. But that's not to say he's with his mother.'

Jason got to his feet and motioned with his hand. They took long strides towards the river then turned right on the water's path until they reached the end cottage, turned right again into the dirt track between two rows of workers cottages. At number 18 they halted, took a deep breath and Jason rapped his knuckles lightly on the door.

It took a moment before the door swung open and there she stood, mysteriously detached, graceful in face and figure. 'Can I help you, gentlemen?'

Tony spoke first. 'This may sound odd. We desperately need your help.'

She came forward. 'Do I know you? You look very familiar, you remind me so very much of someone I knew.'

Now Tony was going to play a wild card. 'Perhaps Edward Black?'

Her hands flew to her face. 'Oh! Are you his lost son?'

'We really need to talk and there's not much time,' Tony insisted.

She remembered with a twinge of nostalgia how she had slept beside a man with whom she blamed for the loss of her daughter. Now there were regular stages at each memory, the servants living permanently in the attic to service the rest of the Manor, providing hot meals and hot baths and a log fire in the hearth on those crisp frosty nights. The traffic on the road was heavy with the regular convoy of soldiers carrying fuel and stores.

Added to all this she was hearing something virtually beyond comprehension, the very heavens seemed to quiver with fire but Tony did it so skilfully that she sat elegantly with her hands clasped in the folds of her apron without a hint of scepticism. But there was a limit to how far he could go without a shrewd question thrown in his face before she allowed him to continue.

And all this while Jason sat patient and quiet under these difficult circumstances and often, he would catch her stealing a glance in his direction as though infinity was growing between them. Then finally she smiled at him and he smiled back. Was that the moment which confirmed he had made the right decision?

'So what do you think?' Tony asked Elizabeth, having exhausted the well of his throat.

'Tell me about the riddles.' She asked Jason.

'Ah, now if I tell you the riddles that would mean I was the one that made them up.' He smiled but the smile disappeared quickly into realization. 'It was us to give the verses to you!' His statement was true and complete. 'Tony, we have come full circle. Indeed a greater paradox, for one must consider the pattern of the universe.'

Tony shook his head as though trying to get his mind into gear. 'Are you saying we're going to go round in circles doing this for the rest of our lives?'

'No, I am pointing out a continuum in spatial matter. Imagine matter in looped circles interlocking events where time as we know it doesn't exist and then add-'

'Squirt, we are not here to solve the universe.'

'I suspect you think me quite mad?'

Elizabeth smiled, tapping her knees. 'A cup of tea is in order, I think.'

'Have we managed to convince you?' Jason was eager to find resolve and looked at his watch. 'It will happen tonight and we have so little time. When it does, will you at least remember what my brother has told you? Try to understand that this is real?'

'Do not make the same mistake so many men make.' She lifted the kettle warming on the stove. 'Our bodies serve a different purpose but our brains work no less efficiently. So far, I have heard a fascinating tale. I know my son. He would not compromise Maria, nor would he allow her to be compromised. Is this some ploy by Charles Black to create division, if so, he shall not succeed.'

'Elizabeth,' Jason said softly. 'Tom exhumed my Grandfather's body and discovered he had a blue tongue to suggest arsenic poisoning.' She did not move but her hand was shaking, the china cup chattering against the saucer. 'We fight the same enemy for the same cause, Elizabeth. Time is short. Too little of it to explain the ins and outs of a world we know very little about. But you must try to believe we are real, we are here, and you have to let the events play out, but you have the chance to tell Tom the truth. Tell him what you did when the Graves turned up. That is your entry point to avert a greater catastrophe. And when Merluza is old enough, she should be told who her real father is.'

She sat down, her hands clutching at her skirted knees, her face and knuckles white. 'And you think I can do this? Watch my son go to prison for something your father did?'

Jason crouched on the cold floor and placed his hands on top of hers. 'You have no choice, Elizabeth. The event will happen and he will be charged. Anything beyond that, I cannot stress enough the repercussions if you try to alter his prescribed course. Your soul came to me, you sat by me on the plane as an older woman to speak about visiting your family while you knitted memories in your scarf. I did not know it then but I know it now. Your soul stayed by my side, manipulated events so it would lead to this point. You wanted me to tell you everything, in this time, now, your time. In my time, Tom purchased Strident Cutter, tore down the Manor and built a new factory but his face and past gained publicity. I am certain if he had knowledge of the truth, he would have done things differently.'

'How did my son fare?'

'You would be so proud of him, Elizabeth. He is a prominent figure among high circles yet he wears his manner without conceit or greed. Yes, sometimes he is a little stubborn but he is also very clever and astute. Merluza is very beautiful and looks like her mother, Maria and your son loves her very much. He offered me your land and everything that stood on it if I would let Merluza go. He is in great pain, Elizabeth and I fear a greater pain to come if you fail to tell him the truth.'

Her hand came upon his face. 'You love her very much.'

'I do, Elizabeth. I wanted to marry Luze but it would result in dire consequences. Now I am pleading for resolve. We have all suffered equally by your mischievous sprite, but out of it there has come a great deal of understanding. Luze once said to me, no cause is lost if there is one fool left to fight for it. Be that fool, Elizabeth and believe us.'

'If, what you say comes to pass, I can alter-'

'No, Elizabeth. You will find it hard to alter your prescribed course. Even if you tried to save your son from his fate this night, I feel certain providence will intervene.'

'So I am to barter with your Mother and seek passage to Australia?'

'It will come naturally for you. I promise you this. My Mother will give you financial help so you can build a new life for Tom and his family. I know it will be hard to see him being dragged away twice to serve out his time but when he returns you must allow Maria to tell Tom the truth about Luze and you must tell him about the two people you vanquished to hell. It is for him to protect you, not for you to protect him. There, the misery ends, the past will not lay deep in grief and pain. The revision truly made.' Jason turned to Tony who was scribbling things down on the back of an envelope lying on the table. 'What are you doing?'

'Giving her the riddles, what else.'

Her mouth opened to speak when a hard knocking turned her attention to the door.

'Beth!' A desperate voice shouted. 'Beth! Oh dear Jesus, Beth, help me! It's Tom.'

'And so it has begun,' Elizabeth said. Against the continual hammering on the door she grabbed her shawl and hurried towards it, looking back once. 'Leave when you can and do not be seen.'

'That was Maria,' Tony told Jason. 'Do you want to have a gander?'

'As tempting as it may seem we cannot afford to be seen.'

'So what do you think? Will she abide by the rules?'

'I think we should make our way back and get to the car.'

Tony drowned his throat with tea, placed the cup on the draining board and caught up with Jason who was scouting the area from the threshold. Jason could hardly see down the dirt track since the mist had returned and he was worried. Under the grizzled light and echoing shouts, they picked their way towards the river and turned left on its path with a closer understanding and respect for Elizabeth. The little things, insignificant at the time but now full of meaning came crowding back.

'On the plane she said if all goes well, she will return to knit in those happy memories and retire in warmer climes.'

'You can say that again, Squirt. I don't know whether we have cracked this or not. I don't know whether I'm going to find myself as a history teacher or married with a bunch of kids. I don't even know if I'm going to keep any memories of what's happened to us but most of all, I haven't got a clue where we are. This mist is getting heavy and my sodding hand is giving me jip.'

Jason had this imperceptible feeling it was too late to get to the Jag. As they cut through the Manor grounds, the mist had overtaken them and once again, Tony yelled, 'I can't see a damn thing!'

The influx of fog swelled and Jason said, 'Here, take hold of me.' But there was nothing to take. 'Brother, where are you? Tony?' With a stuttering heart and the beginning of panic, Jason kept calling out, foraging like a blind man, unable to see his own hand let alone see anything of Tony. The fog worked against him like a protective wall, the atmosphere awash with menace, the ground awash with obstacles. He tripped and fell headlong into soft grass, could smell the scent of crushed leaves, could imagine his unpredictable future taking him towards a time of who knows when? *My brother,* he wailed like a banshee pinned in a tight corner. It was the quiet prelude to change. With dogged fatalism, he crawled on all fours and did not give up, the choreography of last resort. It was merely a few steps to a brick wall, part of the Manor which he finally touched. He now followed its lines, felt its curvature, hopeless measures taken by a desperate man. *Get to the car, get to the car at all costs or be left in 1950.* He worked it out he would be fifty-three in 1974, the year he met Luze, a middle-aged man, twice her age.

Perhaps he had been wrong. It was conceivable Elizabeth wanted it this way, had gained what she needed to know and he was the obstacle as well as the instrument for change. Then at last a turning point as the fog slowly dissipated, outlines came into view, the rear lights of a motor turning out of the Manor's drive. He took two steps forward, tripped over a suitcase, went headlong and landed prostrate on the ground, his Homburg rolling two feet away in the rain.

'Hey, Squirt. What are you doing on your arse?'

Jason sat up, shaking his head. 'I was lost.'

Tony picked up his suitcase. 'How can you be lost? You are here, aren't you?'

It had simplicity about it, a single and defining end.

Jason scrambled to his feet, grabbed his hat off the drive, brushed it clean against his trousers and followed Tony into the Manor.

Tony dropped the suitcase in the hall and went straight to the drinks cabinet in the drawing room. 'How was your trip? I take it you want a whisky?'

'Make it a single,' he said wondering if Tony's memory was in tact. It would require delicate handling should this be the case. He had established by process of elimination and deduction that he was in the winter year 1974, the day he arrived to sort out Tony's problems. 'Is Susan about?'

Tony passed over his drink, his face void of expression. 'Who the hell wants to see that cow?' He chinked glasses. 'Drink up, Squirt. I need to get you pissed before I can tap you up for money.'

Jason stood there gauging his brother until Tony's face creased with amusement. 'You sod,' Jason said, lightly punching his arm. 'You nearly had me fooled.'

'Look, Squirt!' Tony raised his right hand. 'My fingers are back. Good old Elizabeth, she knew, didn't she. She took with one hand and gave with another.'

'Where did you get to?'

'My hand was bloody thumping. I tripped over something, probably the threshold, found myself in the kitchen facing Susan. She was in her dressing gown and the first thing she said was, my darling, are you alright? I thought, Christ, that's unusual, a decent woman, kisses for tea and all that. I asked her without thinking, do we have a decent business and she cracked my nuts, vilifying my incompetence. But Squirt, I got some information. This is the night you arrived from Boston and guess what…she never battered an eyelid when I mentioned the name Claggart. It was almost as if she never heard of it.'

They stood awhile staring at each other. 'Did she react to the name Turner?'

'I never asked,' Tony replied, lighting up two cigarettes. He passed one over to Jason who hesitated. 'Your promise to give up starts New Year 1976.'

'Thank God for that.'

'Squirt, why are our memories in tact? In theory, we shouldn't have memories of the future.'

'One would ask if it is possible to change the future if you knew the future. However, our set of circumstance is now dictated by what Elizabeth has done. So the future might not be the future we think. Already we have learnt that Susan has never heard of a company called Claggart. Where is she now?'

'Upstairs, I suppose. She did her usual, walked off complaining about her nails and I went into the drawing room when headlights of a car flashed through the window. By the time I got to the front door, I saw you tripping over your suitcase.'

Movement betrayed Susan's presence. Tony put his finger to his lips and tip-toed to the door, grabbed the handle and swung it open to a rigid lamppost. 'Come to give your husband a goodnight kiss?'

She found her composure and brushed past him. The twins burst out laughing. They were absolutely at this moment in the absurdity, to see her there without a clue, parading in her satin dressing gown, her sense of self-importance ballooning. She asked to be served with a Martini and sat on the sofa, crossing her legs.

'Susan, has Tools made my bed?' Jason asked.

'That's what she's here for.' Now her tone moderated. 'Jason, all we need is enough to get through this hump.'

'And what hump is that?'

She looked up at Tony as he passed over her drink. 'Have you not told him?'

'No sweetheart.'

'The bank is refusing to extend our credit. They're threatening to put us into liquidation.'

'What about selling to a competitor?' Jason asked.

'Do wake up, Jason. Who in their right mind would want to buy that crumbling old factory?'

Tony sat beside her. 'You look rather dishy tonight, pity about your hair.'

She flustered and her fingers went to the nape of her neck. 'What is wrong with my hair?'

'I just thought you could let it grow, sweetheart…you know, be that sexy lady I met seven years ago…all full of excitement about having our child.' And he clicked his fingers. 'Sorry, sweetheart, I forgot. It was Jason's child.' Then he clicked his fingers again. 'What the hell am I saying? Forgive me, sweetheart, it wasn't anyone's child.'

Her eyes narrowed in contempt. 'Grow up. It happened. You messed around with other women, including that limp celery stick of a secretary. Why are you here, Jason, to cover old ground or to help us out?'

Jason looked down at her glass as she held it up for a refill. 'Would you like soda with your arsenic?'

Her face was impassive, the only signs of her anger that he knew so well were the soft flush of blood that strained at her throat and the steady rhythmic tap of her foot on the floor. 'I never forced you to leave,' she said. 'You were the one to walk out on me. Everything would have worked out if you had just stayed, but no, you had to act the wounded lover, betrayed by your brother, betrayed by your father and never once did you ever ask how I felt.'

'I remember telling you how I felt,' Jason said. 'For seven years you allowed Tony to believe he had conceived a child which you so conveniently lost through a lie after he placed a wedding ring on your finger. Now it may not appear much to you yet by my reckoning I think it constitutes a strong case for divorce.'

She sent an abstract laugh. 'Where is your proof?'

'Hey,' Tony said. 'I'm still divorcing you and you can move in with what's his name.'

'Stop being ridiculous,' she retorted. 'There has been nobody else since your father.'

Tony jumped to his feet. 'How long were you screwing him?'

'My dear, since you refused to screw me, I thought we could keep it in the family.'

And then the argument started.

Jason shook his head and walked through the interconnecting doors where he had flash backs of Luze moving among shining saucepans and breathless pot-plants whose cool green leaves scattered the ledges and caressed the caddies. It was almost as if she belonged to this house, like she belonged to the house a mile up the road.

'Sorry about that, Squirt.' Tony walked in with the whisky bottle but Jason refused a top up. 'Christ, she gets under my skin. It's like little ants eating away at my flesh and I can't get rid of them.'

Jason looked at his brother, the thorny subject of Susan returned. 'There was a time when I thought she was quite attractive. Indeed, I will go so far as to say she had me in a spin but beneath that exterior dwells an unsavoury character which needs to learn some common decency.'

'What do you suggest? I can't physically throw her out.'

'Will you leave me to deal with the matter?'

'Why should you take on my baggage?'

'It was I who first brought her here and it would give me the greatest of pleasure to be the last to get her out of here.' Jason now focused more on the room, in his own tangled memories. 'I love this house. Mother lived here and she baked bread. I intend to hold on to that memory.'

'Me too.' Tony advocated similar thoughts. 'Squirt, we need to get a handle on things quickly.'

'It is obvious Elizabeth was unable to stop the confrontation and Tom's incarceration. Whatever Elizabeth may have done, it appears so far, not to have changed our position. What is astonishing is that our memories of the future are still in tact.'

'What if it happens all over again? You know, finding the puzzle and all that.'

'Tomorrow, we must make enquiries. Let us hope no major deviations have occurred then we can go to plan B.'

'Huh? Did I miss something? What was plan A?'

KATHERINE'S LEGACY

Jason slowly opened his eyes to the sound of a vacuum cleaner and smiled. Mrs Tooley was keeping the home fires burning.

Propped up on his elbows, he called out 'Tools!' His door flew open and there she stood, about to open her mouth when he said, 'Have you missed me?'

'Well,' she said, marching into the room, her familiar face warmed his heart. 'Of course I missed yew. I won't say I'm sorry to hear about your father. After yew left, he wus virtually confined to this house.'

'I see nothing has changed.'

'Won't be fer long, will it, Jason?' She tapped his legs and he pulled them over to create room enough for her to sit. 'I hear there's trouble brewing with the bank or hev yew come down to bail him out again?'

Relaxing against the headboard, he made relevant enquiries until she had unveiled the complete story of his ancestors as though this was a tale that had mysteriously escaped his attention. However, it was in the latter part of her account, Mrs Tooley had finally come circumspectly to the issue that interested him the most.

'...your dad got hold of a magazine and saw Tom and the O'Grady girl, married with two little mites. He kept that to himself until Susan found it. She worked it all out and told your dad the little girl in the picture wus his. Well, he blew his top. He wus that angry he virtually smashed every plate he could get hold of. But she's a wily slut if ever I come across one. She preened his feathers, told him want he wanted to hear just so she could get half of Strident Cutter. And she got it by doing him some favours, if yew get my meaning. Tony had his faults but he never deserved that bitch.'

'Where is she now?'

Mrs Tooley rolled her eyes. 'Where else but getting her hair done.'

'There are going to be some radical changes around here, Tools. One of them is getting rid of Susan. The first on the agenda is to lock all the downstairs windows, bolt the front and back doors and make me a coffee. Are you up for the challenge?'

This was war without declaration. She stood to attention and said, 'Not before time,' then marched out like a militant figure.

Jason sprang from the bed, popped in the bathroom for a quick wash and shave then pulled out an old pair of jeans and jumper from his wardrobe. His next port of call was his brother's bedroom. He removed the top drawer of a dresser, forage at the back and brought out his mother's jewellery box. As suspected, the diamond necklace and earrings were gone but there, glowering green among the more salubrious items was that modest emerald ring. He wondered if it would ever be placed on her finger again.

'I expect yew want wat that bitch wus given by your dad.' Mrs Tooley startled him. 'Your dear mum,' she said passing over his coffee, 'would hev wanted her jewellery given to good girls for her sons. Yew made a good choice, Jason. Your mum loved that ring. I wus told she was given that by Elizabeth Turner, who wus given it by your grandfather, Edward. This is only gossip, so don't hold me to it but it wus said them two found a little patch of happiness. Wat Elizabeth felt when he wus taken before his time, is anyone's guess. It must hev meant something special for her to give it to your mum.'

Jason swallowed, hard. 'I never knew.'

'Do yew hev a lady friend, Jason?'

'Do you believe in providence, Tools?' He answered with a question, reasserting his belief about Luze. 'There is someone with eyes the colour of this stone and she is destined to share my life.'

'Yew can't be too picky, Jason. She might hev blue eyes and love yew just as much.'

'No, she has green eyes,' he replied adamantly, closing the jewellery box lid. 'She is my composite singularity as surely as I am her fusion.'

'Sounds to me like a match made in heaven. Do yew hev Susan's key?'

After informing Mrs Tooley he had not, he strode out Tony's bedroom, down the long and wide hall, eyed up the situation and with one hefty kick, Susan's bedroom door flew open with an almighty splintered crack. Here, it left them speechless. It was bedecked in satins, silks and pure gold trimmings, priceless porcelain figures displayed on priceless antique furniture. Now Jason was on the hunt. He ransacked every drawer, felt every pillow, foraged every nook and cranny, while Mrs Tooley raped the wardrobes and stuffed Susan's clothes in plastic bags, shoving them out of the window where they fell squarely on the drive. Some time later, and by a fortunate mishap with a hung painting, Jason discovered a built-in wall safe, combination unknown.

In the hall he picked up the telephone and dialled the factory. Tony answered and Jason asked, 'Do you know the combination to Susan's safe?'

'I never knew she had one?'

'Okay. I shall be over soon. If you see Susan, keep her busy.' Jason set the receiver down softly as if afraid it would break and said to Mrs Tooley, 'I must go to the factory. Will you be alright on your own for a couple of hours?'

'Don't yew worry about me, Jason. I can handle Susan.'

He had no doubt about that.

Picking his way across the wet drive, without his jacket or Homburg he vaulted the lowest part of the laurel hedge and strode into Strident Cutter. Bright smiling faces looked up. The factory was warm and he wondered why until he caught sight of blow heaters vigorously fanning into the atmosphere.

Walking into the office with gusto, Tony looked up, threw his pen to one side and smiled. 'Nothing has changed, Squirt. I'm still a tosser and the bank is about to foreclose.'

Jason laughed and sat on the edge of the desk, looking down at his brother's scribbles. 'What's this?'

'My speech to the men. I pinched some of Tom's words, thought it would carry weight. Anyway, I made a few enquiries. Good news. Tom calls his business Turner instead of Claggart. He still has two factories in Australia, none anywhere else. Luze still works for him, so does her brother. I can't find a damn thing about any offer coming forward to buy Strident Cutter so I telephoned Henshaw and he said I was talking out of my arse. Anyway, he did confirm Susan owns fifty percent of the business but I have the last say on selling the assets. What did you find out?'

'Tools confirmed everything, apart from one minor variation. The old man went berserk and smashed the crockery when Susan informed him Luze was his child. The Manor is shut down tight. Tools bagged up Susan's clothes and threw them out the window. Her room blinded me. I have never seen anything like it. She has been storing up priceless antiques, has a safe I cannot open but I suspect the rest of Mother's jewellery is in there including some cash.'

'Bitch!'

Jason picked up the receiver. 'I need to call my attorney in Boston.'

'Give me a break,' said a voice down the line. 'I heard you already.'

'I hear it's still hunky-dory down there?' Jason said.

'Jason! I thought that was Mike. I keep telling him, divorce is a difficult business, and never more so than when you're filthy rich. So what's this call for, not that I need two guesses, you're going to bail him out, aren't you?'

'I am staying, Nick. This is what I want.'

'Now why did I have this feeling you were going to say that. Only yesterday, I said to Bill, Jason's not coming home. We're going to lose our best poker player.'

'Do I play poker?'

'Not really, that's why we like having you around.'

Jason could tell from Nick's strangled tone that he had the handset wedged between his chin and chest and was no doubt engaged in some form of paper exercise. 'Nick, I need you tie things up for me. The apartment can be sold with the furniture. I need my private papers sent by courier.'

'And your beach house?'

'No, I want to keep that. I shall send you a list of the things you can transfer from the apartment to there. The rest I can handle from here.'

'Where are you, at the Manor or the factory?'

'Presently at the factory.' Jason was now in two minds because there was the matter of Luze. 'Nick, do you have a contact in Australia? I need someone to check out a woman.'

'Sure, no problem. Give me the details.'

'Her name is Merluza Turner. Her father runs a jigsaw manufacturing business. I think she works from his Melbourne office and lives in St Vincent's Square, South Melbourne. I need to know if she still lives there, and if she's married or not.'

'Will do. Is that dopey brother of yours still bending your mind?'

Jason let the comment pass by. 'Thanks, Nick. I owe you one.'

'Did you ever play poker?' Tony asked when Jason replaced the receiver.

'After I returned from the ice caps, I filled in for Larry.'

'So things haven't changed for you?'

'No,' said Jason. 'I found my medal in the suitcase last night so I was fairly certain I trod the same path.'

Tony pushed back his chair and got to his feet. 'Look, Squirt,' he said concernedly, walking round the desk to give Jason a level stare. 'What are you going to do if you find out Luze is married? Don't get me wrong. I go along with your plan for Turner but it rather puts you in the middle of things if he takes up our offer.'

This is not what Jason wanted to hear, the thought appalled him. 'I prefer to believe we are destined for each other. If she is married then she married Jeremy Hubbard and if that's the case I will do my utmost to make her see sense and divorce him.'

'Okay, so is it likely she still has her memories?'

'That telephone would be ringing hot if she had her memories.'

'So why haven't you rung her?'

'Because she would know I wouldn't do that.'

Although it was easy for Tony to empathise with Jason's by now overwhelming urge to meet up with Luze *again*, he had come to the point of recognising desperate times called for desperate measures. 'Last night, I got to thinking about things. Why don't you write about it? You know, put pen to paper. And, if it turns out Luze is still the same, not married and all that, you have something to show her. After all, you're not that good in the romantic stakes, are you?'

'But how can I be certain what I write is what she's been told?'

'We've been down this road before, Squirt. Now by my reckoning, we have our memories in tact. Elizabeth asked for the truth to come out and here's your chance to write the truth down. Elizabeth would be a fool to withhold the truth because she must have known we would keep our memories or am I talking rubbish?'

Jason rubbed his chin between thumb and forefinger and looked beyond the glass partition, contemplating how Luze had encouraged him to be that fool fighting for their cause. Everything appeared to be so simple in her eyes, no complications to a complicated world. 'No, Tony. You make sense. Whether by design or accident, our memories of a time lived are still in tact so why not take advantage.'

'But don't be too clever like writing it in invisible ink. She won't take it seriously. Hey, had a thought, can you still make up the formula?'

Jason grinned and said nothing.

'I don't know why I ask such bloody silly questions.' It was a brief response against what he felt. As he too looked beyond the glass partition, Jason knew he was contemplating a *real* future, a future without placing his interests first. 'The men out there deserve better days, Squirt. I gave Misery the go ahead to start dismantling that cutter. It's going for scrap metal.'

'And we will renovate the cottages, Tony.'

From the *old* moment of arriving in Little Smeet to the *unfathomable* moment of starting all over again their relationship had been storm and sunny weather alternating so rapidly that even they themselves were not always certain as to how matters stood between them at any given time.

'So,' Tony said, rubbing his hands together. 'Are we ready to tell the men?'

Jason picked up Tony's scribbled notes and screwed the paper in a tight fist. 'You do not need Turner's words. Use your own and be the man you have become.' He watched his brother's face and stance take on new meaning. If he had to remember anything, Jason thought, it would be this proud moment where he felt a thud of gratitude for Elizabeth's intervention.

The machinery came to a standstill. Tony stood aloft on a wooden crate and drew the workers in. Not a man moved, coughed, or created sound.

'For seven years,' Tony began, 'I have neglected my duties at Strident Cutter but not any more. As you know, this company was built by my Grandfather. He took advantage of his market and labour force but he learnt a hard lesson after the death of his youngest son. It was your misfortune when my Father inherited Strident Cutter and mine to see Jason leave Little Smeet. Now my brother has returned, together we are going to give Strident Cutter a new future. Starting tomorrow, we are going to give you pay rises, work out a bonus structure and show you our plans for this building. The corrugated sheets will be replaced by a new shell and the cutters will go, one by one until our present orders are completed to make room for a brand new business.' He paused to their mumblings. 'Yes, a revolutionary new concept is going to be manufactured here, at Little Smeet. And I think it appropriate my brother, since he's the inventor, should offer an explanation.' Tony stood down and joined in with the applause.

Jason did not expect this. He gave Tony a squinted glance then shook his head. Rather than stand on ceremony, he walked among them. 'Cast your minds back to the days of short trousers, the cut and thrust of a pirate's blade defending your floating raft on the waters of this river.' He paused for a vocal change. 'Arrghh me hearties, hand over ye treasures,' and he made them laugh just like Luze had made him laugh. 'Imagine,' he said, holding up a finger. 'Tracing a clean parchment concealing hurdles and risks...or tracing blank pages of a book, reading a fairy tale as it appears. This gentlemen, is going to be our new product line. From here, we shall use new inks that will hide print from view.'

The workers stood in stupefaction for a moment before they questioned detail, demanded answers to what seemed to them something out of this world. Each had made their intentions clear. They were committed to build a new future for Strident Cutter.

At the close of day, Jason was on his way out when a hand clamped firm on his arm. 'I enjoyed your speech, boy.' It was Misery emerging behind in the gloom of the corridor. 'We wus wondering what caused the change in your brother.' He patted Jason on the arm and fell into step as he resumed his walk. 'He doesn't seem the same man, knows more about those cutters than me.'

'Let us just say he found his senses. Are you happy with the arrangement?'

'Oh yes, boy, very happy. Are we to see Mrs Black prancing about in her high heels?'

'Mrs Black will soon be Mrs Gone. Quite simply, we have a clean sheet and your duties will include laughing at our jokes.'

'Thass no problem.' Misery halted with a small smile playing on his lips, his tour of duty done. 'I shall be in the Pig and Whistle tonight. Come over with Tony and hev a drink on me.'

That was a first. Jason nodded and continued alone, his thoughts travelling to different matters, his steady pace carrying him on toward the Manor. Ahead was a silver Mercedes. Susan jumped out of the driver's seat. Her garish colours insulted his eye.

'Jason!' She met him, wagging her finger. 'I shall call the police and have you arrested!'

'Looking at you proves evolution had a sense of humour. Now get off my land.'

'It's not your land! Your father left you nothing! Half of this is mine!'

'Is that so,' he said, bringing out a piece of paper and stuffed it down her blouse. 'I think you will find I own everything. You are welcome to have the cutters.'

Jason was in a place where the struggles of life could not reach him, where guilt did not course in rivulets on his face, where grief did not empty his guts. He had surmounted his difficulties, brought transition to the table, liberated his brother from purgatory and contented himself with a random speculation that Luze would know her way as though born to him.

And what happened in the following weeks only enhanced his commitment leaving the community of Little Smeet in astonishment for they could neither have predicted such a change in Tony's attitude, Jason's decision to stay, Susan's immediate absence nor Strident Cutter on the cusp of an exciting new venture.

There had been a fluster of activity with Henshaw. Papers and telephone calls flew back and forth until they were in his office *again* as though by some such circumstance providence designed it that way. In his salubrious leather and oak room with everything laid out, spread in separate piles on his desk, the fastidious Henshaw appeared like a mutinous child trying to comprehend Tony's new leaf frame of mind.

Jason was reading a document in one of Tony's Bond Street suits, remembering the last time he was here, almost the same date, virtually the same weather. 'John, there is no provision for secure tenancy.'

'Why would there be? Workers only have secure tenancy while they do their job, and do it properly. You would be very stupid to do otherwise.'

'Not on.' Tony broke in. 'Some must have secure tenancy based on length of service. They've earned the right.'

'Are you in agreement with this, Jason?'

'You heard what my brother said.'

Henshaw's deep set eyes glinted with bemusement then he pushed back his chair and stood up, flaying the survey map on his desk. 'I need you both to confirm the boundaries.'

They glanced over the land with road and river frontage. There would be no missed opportunities this time, no impending gloom. Henshaw brought out his pen, unscrewed the gold top and handed it to Jason. It was simply a matter of brotherly love and tying up loose ends. Jason wanted Tony to own half, held in trust until his divorce was made final.

Henshaw had prepared for this momentous occasion and brought a bottle of champagne with three glasses to the desk. It was a pleasant ritual, toasting to a new era. 'To you both, gentlemen,' he said. 'Let it prosper for Strident Cutter.'

Tony held his glass up to Jason. 'To you, Squirt. The best brother a man can have.'

'Hear! Hear!' Henshaw echoed those sentiments and asked Tony, 'Why the sudden transformation?'

'This see,' Tony replied showing his right hand. 'I got my knuckles wrapped,' and they laughed but it held special meaning to the twins.

'Seriously, I know what you are thinking, John. I'm not going to let Squirt down, not ever again. I want to earn my way. Squirt is going to get every penny back I ever borrowed off him, even if it takes me a lifetime.'

'John, there is something else we need you to do.' Jason bent down and brought up his brief case to rest on Henshaw's desk. 'We want you to contact Turner and make sure he receives this jigsaw puzzle.' He produced a shiny black box with the Turner's name printed in white.

Henshaw prised the lid open and looked inside. Of a single fact he had become certain, the pieces were blank. 'Is this a joke?'

'Black magic,' Tony said in order to get a reaction. And the reaction was one of astonishment. It suited him well. 'When the pieces interlock a picture will form.'

'A remarkable claim or are you pulling my leg?'

'No, John. It's all above board. Jason filed the concept at the Patent Office in London. I brought in another for you to try, but that one must go to Turner. We want you to advise him that he can have sole rights on this patent without any catches. You must also make him aware of the other patent to cover publishing. We decided to sell our cutters and go into printing.'

'Why?' Henshaw asked.

'Well, for a start the factory is too small to house the up-to-date cutter. So what we're going to do is build brick walls around it then we'll remove the corrugated sheeting. This will be less disrupting. We already have the silk screen printer and once those cutters are gone we can modify inside. So what do you think?'

'I am speechless and sceptical. How was this made possible and why this sudden turn around?'

'You know, John,' Jason said. 'I would have expected you to say, why Turner, which rather indicates you know the Black's history.'

'Are you trying to avoid my question?'

'I came home with an idea, had a long talk with Tony and we decided to give the concept a try. It worked. Then we discussed who should benefit. Now, we all know Turner's family got a raw deal and we also know Turner has the outlets so it made sense to give this to him. Lay to rest the misery, show good faith. It's what Grandfather wanted for Tom, to share in his success before the old man intervened. But we cannot make it happen without you. If we get involved, it would look suspect but coming from you, it will add validity.'

Henshaw produced a cigarette, lit it then slipped his gold lighter into his trouser pocket, his face a mask of resignation and stern resolve. After a few moments with the smoke whirling about his head, he said, 'Sit down, gentlemen. There is a matter I must draw to your attention.'

As the twins settled themselves down, Henshaw returned to his leather recliner and drew in, leaning both arms on his desk, his cigarette held between his thumb and forefinger as though it was important to avoid the tell-tale stains of nicotine.

'My father,' Henshaw began, 'was given explicit instructions by your mother and upon his death that duty transferred to me. I never believed the time would come when I would see you two offering a gesture of good will to Tom Turner. Allow me to explain. Your grandfather, Dr Robert Graves made certain provisions for his daughter, Katherine before she entered into marriage with your father. She was given a sizeable sum where her father was trustee to ensure your father could not get his hands on her money. Shortly after you two were born, Dr Robert Graves transferred his trusteeship to my father. He gave no explanation other than to say his relationship with his daughter had become strained.'

'I know why,' Jason interjected. 'Mother discovered she had been a pawn in the conspiracy of my Grandfather's death.'

Henshaw continued, making no further comment about that. 'At the same time, your mother made new provisions. She wanted you two to inherit her estate. It was agreed that on your twenty-first birthdays, whatever was left would pass equally. In the event of her death prior to your twenty-first birthdays, the term was to be extended until you reached thirty where she felt you would have reached the age of wisdom.'

'So Mum did think of us?' Tony said.

'Very much so,' Henshaw spoke sadly. 'From what I gathered, you two were her life, but bear with me, for the circumstance changed when she gained certain information to your father's infidelity in 1950. My Father supported her wishes to draw monies from her estate, a certain sum to aid the Turners.

At the same time, as trustee, my Father agreed to relinquish the rest of her estate.' Henshaw pulled out a drawer and produced two white envelopes. They had been there for almost eternity and every time he saw those tantalizingly unopened envelopes, he would consider how they were aging without prospects. 'There were only two people who knew their contents, my Father and your mother. My instructions were to give you this one if it can be shown you made a gesture of goodwill to Tom Turner, failing which the other envelope is opened upon your demise. I consider you have fulfilled the requirements.' And with that he brought out his lighter and torched the other envelope, saying 'as per my instructions.'

While the smoke rose in silence, the paper curling into crispy ashes, the twins just stared at the one on Henshaw's desk, the one which had the words written *to my beloved sons.*

'You open it, Squirt.'

Jason shook his head and felt the weight of it. 'You open it.'

Henshaw stood and offered his hand. 'Go home and read it together. Our meeting is concluded, gentlemen. I shall contact Turner as per instructions.'

Tucking the letter in his suit jacket pocket, Jason led the way to the streets below feeling the touch of white crystals upon his face. He remained mute until reaching the Jag. Throwing his butt end in the gutter, he opened the driver's door and waited for Tony to settle before offering his opinion. 'Now it makes sense,' he said turning in his seat to face Tony, his hand on the steering wheel. 'Her original instructions would have carried forward had it not been for the old man lusting after Maria O'Grady.'

'Last time, we never knew what happened to Mum's money and that's because we hadn't reached the age of wisdom. Are you wise at thirty? Anyway, I think us going back to 1950, speaking to Elizabeth caused a change in Mum's wishes and there's only one way to find out. Read her letter.'

The snow drifted aimlessly over the bonnet, sparkling in a million directions and it seemed Jason was in a different world entirely. 'My dearest sons,' his voice low, 'if by some miracle you are reading this, it confirms you are with knowledge of the past and I am with knowledge of your visit to Elizabeth Turner. You have shown decency and rectitude in casting no aspersions upon Elizabeth and her actions, and because she is by nature a protective mother

I shall follow by example. Where Syringa weeps follow her tears and pluck out her heart. I do not know if my life will extend beyond this year and Elizabeth did not say nor would she say. But know this. My body is not as strong as I would wish, having suffered countless of ailments these past few years. Do not grieve but rejoice. I watched you that night, approaching the Manor and thought no more, just two young men swallowed in a mist until Elizabeth told me of your visit and gave me a mental picture of you both. It is ingrained on my mind, to take with me always. I am so proud my heart overflows with joy. Whatever journeys you undertook, I can only imagine. You may lament the inevitable checks and misfortunes, but the glorious certitude of having acted with virtuous intensions will forever support you whatever adverse circumstance may arise. I look at you now, two young hopefuls tugging at my skirt, asking for one more biscuit before bed time. Tonight and future nights will be special. I shall kiss you to sleep, pamper your every whim and wake beside you until my time is done. The Lord is a very good friend. Everything is so clear it is impossible to misunderstand him. Hold my memory to your hearts always. Mother.'

Here there was purpose and preparation, Jason thought as he folded the letter in quiet contemplation. His eyes clouded, as were Tony's and nothing more was said until they reached home. And somehow *home* was all the more important, the talking floorboards with their mother's secrets, hot and cold areas, the standing lamps throwing shadows in rooms and a fire burning brightly in the hearth. It was a tranquil, bitter-pleasant moment.

Jason tossed the car keys to Tony and padded upstairs. Assuming Mrs Tooley to have prepared them dinner, and assuming she was in the kitchen he threw open Tony's bedroom door and brought out his mother's jewellery box. He picked out a pearl necklace and sighed when he caught sight of that ring. *One day it will be on her finger.*

'I made you a nice steak and kidney pie,' said Mrs Tooley to Tony.

'Give us a hug.'

'Oooh,' she exclaimed as her feet left ground. 'Wat's this all about?

'We saw Henshaw. It's official,' Tony said.

'I'm glad fer yew both.' She took off her apron and began folding it in her customary ritual. 'I best be off and see to my George. Misery popped in and said the builder had a look round.'

Jason emerged and slipped the row of pearls over her head. 'We want you to have these,' he said, fastening the clasp then kissed the tight crease of her neck. 'They match the earrings your mother had.'

She was surprised, Jason could see that. A gleam came to her hazy eyes and a special stance to her body, clutching them to her throat. 'I don't know what to say.'

'Well that's a first,' said Tony.

'Look at yew both, so handsome and decent. Your mum would be so proud of yew two.' She waved her hand like a paper fan in front of her face, defying herself not to cry. 'Hark at me,' she went on, more definitely now. 'I best go or the kitchen will flood.'

When she was gone, Tony asked, 'Who is Syringa?'

'Syringa is the Latin name for willow.'

'What willow? The only willow I know is the one we climbed up as a kid and pissed on Dad's parade.'

'Do you want to go on a treasure hunt?'

They slipped out into the dusk of snow. Everywhere was quiet, had the feint crackling silence of winter. Huddled together they traipsed towards the river where the familiar Syringa wept her lifeless branches over the water's edge.

'Do you know, Squirt, I never realised how big this tree had grown.'

Jason caressed the bark, contemplating his surrounds. 'What did Mother say exactly in her letter?' He pulled it out from his back pocket and reading it to himself, he said, 'This is her clue. Where Syringa weeps follow her tears and pluck out her heart.'

They took a few paces forward to the edge of the bank and looked down into the glistening waters, the sagging branches gently weeping into an ice cold river. It was freezing yet not for a moment did they feel the cold, working their fingers under the weeping branches, up to their arms in this watery element. Suddenly, the rough edge of metal and they gave the chain a hard yank, plucking at the heart of this mystery, hauling up a metal box three times the size of a biscuit tin.

As though released from a spell, they each took a handle and broke into a run for the Manor and never stopped until they were inside the kitchen. Impatient, at last, to discover the extent of their bounty, they pulled back the bolt and flew open the lid. Mrs Tooley was not the only one left speechless that late afternoon.

Euphoric insanity took over hunger as they tipped the contents onto the hearth rug and started to count their fortune from a massive pile of South African Krugerrands. All sights twice brilliant and smells twice-sharp. They had all night, and the whole of the moon.

Never in a million years, Jason thought, could he have imagined this happening. And somehow all his grief and pain during his childhood years seemed irrelevant, holding no significance at all. He wanted to keep his mother's memory alive as though she had been the instrument for his nurture and not the father he so despised.

'How could she be certain we would return to our time? How could she be certain that the future would be the same for us? It only needed one deviation from Elizabeth and who knows, our lives may have altered substantially. So where would that leave this fortune? A chance she was ill-prepared to take in case the old man found a way of obtaining it. I reckon Elizabeth must have told her just about everything, even about the puzzle I invented. That would make sense. And based on that assumption it would be logical to withdraw all her funds, buy gold, bury it and as a precautionary measure she insisted we only receive it if we make a goodwill gesture to Turner.'

'Because she knew we did that in the first place,' added Tony.

'Precisely, and gold is a durable element. It never corrodes, it always remains the same so in the unlikely event of it never being found in our time, the second envelope must come into play, to give some other poor soul a chance in life. So what are we going to do with it?'

'Not so long ago I would be looking at a Roller, ordering myself a yacht and scratching my arse wondering what castle to buy in Scotland. But you know...I don't feel inclined to do any of those things. Okay, I might want a little flutter later but for now I'm paying you back, every penny. Do you understand what I'm trying to say, Squirt or am I speaking a load of crap?'

'I feel exactly the same. You do speak a load of crap.'

Jason rolled about hysterically by the heat of mellowness, red-faced and powerless should Tony have the presence of mind to enquire the date and nature of his death.

'You should be a bloody comedian. That pile is yours.'

Jason corrected him. 'That pile is ours. I wonder if Mother gained the foresight to visualise what the old man might have got up to under that tree.'

'Here's a question. How can we be certain we never dreamt it? The whole lot might have been a dream. That could explain why we have our memories.'

'Without doubt we were there. Smelly believed he saw Molly that night in the mist calling out for her brother, shortly after Tom was arrested. Well that was me, calling out for you.'

'Ah but that might have been in the dream.'

'No,' he corrected Tony again. 'I spoke to Smelly. He did confirm he heard a voice calling out in the mist.' His gaze briefly snagged on Tony's right hand. 'Do you believe it was a dream about your accident?'

'Oh, Squirt,' Tony replied, flexing his fingers. 'I never felt pain like it. I wanted to be knocked out.'

'I would have accommodated your wishes if I had known.'

'What?'

Jason smiled and lazed back against the seat of the armchair, folding his arms, his interest in counting gold pieces gone from his mind. Now he was thinking of Luze, how he wrote things down in a note book, but he never turned the pages back to look again at what he had written. They were public, yet as private as dreams. He did not speak of this, not to Mrs Tooley, not even to Henshaw.

'Melbourne is ten hours in front,' he said to Tony. 'Theoretically, Luze will be opening her package in a few hours.'

'I think you sent it too soon. You should have waited for Henshaw to contact Turner.'

'And risk him coming here before she had time to read it? Knowing Luze as I do, she will make sure she comes with her father.'

'That's on the basis he wants to come here.'

Jason yawned, his arms up, his fists knuckling childishly on each side of his head. He smiled at his brother, his softest, most beguiling smile. 'All this excitement has made me feel quite weary. Do you feel tired?'

'Drinking on an empty stomach doesn't help. There's a pie in the oven.'

Jason got up easily and tapped his twin fondly on the head. 'You eat it. I'm going to have a shave and an early night. See you in the morning.'

In the bathroom, Jason opened the mirrored cabinet and foraged between tubs and cans and packets, knocking over the shampoo. He looked at the after-shave, unscrewed the lid and smelt it. It was a good smell, a tingling smell, and he remembered that awestruck afternoon, splashing this aftershave on, how he drew close to his mirrored face and adjusted his tie before taking that ring out of his mother's jewellery box. Despite his affluence and influence, he was modest and unpretentious, and apparently determined to stay that way regardless. He was a man that had everything, and nothing.

Now in the bedroom, sat on the bed and absorbed with the memories of Luze that he was totally unaware of being observed. Though already, he could smell that perfumed witchery and it did not alarm him, nor would it. For there she was, Elizabeth Turner, small and forlorn, settled in his chair by the desk knitting in new memories no doubt.

'Have you come for my memories?'

'I know you wish to keep them, dear, but if you know your future, you have no future.'

Jason felt disappointed and scared. 'Conjecture,' he argued. 'I have the freedom to take action where needed.'

'It would leave your position exposed. You were a little naughty sending my Granddaughter your story. Though it was to be expected, I suppose.'

'Will you let her read it?'

'At this very moment it is advancing to her desk.'

He wondered how long he had left to remember, wondered how the exchange would take place and wondered again if he had to surmount further obstacles to gain her affection. But did it matter if he had no memories? 'You will be taking away my experiences. Remember what you told me on the plane? Without good and bad memories we never grow wise.'

'Now why would you want future memories of bad experiences?'

'Because they were good,' and he grinned.

She smiled and placed her knitting aside. 'You cannot live in a future that hasn't happened, dear. What you need is a change. A person needs a change, to find new experiences, without change something sleeps inside us.'

'I don't want a change. I want my composite singularity.'

'Oh, I wouldn't worry, dear. It will all come out in the wash. Things usually do. You have a good night's sleep and make the most of your memories.'

Now she seemed to exude a sort of salty sharpness as her presence slowly evaporated, her cool misty witchery tapering eerily away so there was no more to be seen of her, no more perfume to smell.

He removed his shirt and heard himself whispering, *I'm going to be lucky, I must be lucky. But it's true, I am lucky* and he closed his eyes in sweet anticipation of hearing from Luze, he knows he can take that much for granted. With his eyes still closed, he rolled on the bed and drifted into a lazy spell, remembering that mile long road, the future working its way behind, slowly by the hour slipping into another dimension.

LEVITY BROWN

ALSO BY LEVITY BROWN

GALLOWS HUMOUR

IT'S A MATTER OF LIFE AND DEATH

Solomon Monday is ready to jump off the media rungs and accept his bizarre legacy, a converted mid-18th-century courthouse tucked in the folds of Norfolk...and so begins an extraordinary mystery which has its roots in the eccentric staff, six poor souls innocently hanged at the gallows. It takes the appearance of Izabo Tuesday to force Monday to confront his demons and find their ancestor's book, Week's Work, the element to clear Gallows Humour of its hauntings.

In a place where love and membership comes at a very high price, Gallows Humour is simply irrsistible.

BOOK OF HORTUS

A TIME FOR HEROES

Sat naked in a puddle of mud, all that he knows of himself is his name - Quercus Coccinea. Befriended by Nina, a librarian, this legendary hero will never yield - one hundred years does not make a man forgive or forget. In a world of breathtaking beauty, Quercus gathers his thousand-strong army to defeat an unbeatable enemy, gain immortality and find the lost halves of the Book of Hortus.

**Suspenseful and endlessly exciting,
this mystery is sure to thrill anyone who enjoys action,
mysticism and nature on an epic scale.**

GIDDY MIDNIGHT

THE GRAND EXIT

Warrior Queen Boudicca called upon the Goddess Andate for victory in battle against the Roman army. But what transpired gave rise to a curse inflicted upon two opposing bloodlines.

Lukas Giddy, disadvantaged by the curse, is determined to lift it.

Marcus Metellus, advantaged by the curse, is determined to stop him.

**For one woman caught between the two,
her love for Giddy and his furry companion is an act of courage.**

COMEBACK

THE LADY IN GREY

The Chief Executive

Godfrey Shilling of Fair Life Assurance is limiting the liabilities against his company. Shortly issuing a million pound life policy, the client drops dead of natural causes. Coincidence? With no proof, he calls upon the woman in Grey.

The woman in Grey

Enigmatic, expensive to hire, Miss Grey walks into a Norfolk Town as Godfrey Shilling's Trojan horse. With a 100% success rate as a ruthless private investigator, she is about to turn a carpenter's world upside down.

The Carpenter

Ruben Stone, hiding more than a secret or two, lives above a shop selling beautiful dollhouses and related items. No profit, no loss, no gain, no shame.

The Black Panther writes again in this stylish mystery murder is on the menu for those who want to die and live again.